"Thrillingly tight."
—The New York Times

"[Gibson] weaves an unnerving tapestry of
technology, violence, and anxiety."
—The Daily Telegraph

"Fascinating."
—The Seattle Times

"Uncanny."
—San Antonio Express-News

"Brilliant, entertaining, and bittersweet."
—io9

Hollis Henry worked for the global marketing magnate Hubertus Bigend once before. She never meant to repeat the experience. But she's broke, and Bigend never feels it's beneath him to use whatever power comes his way—in this case, the power of money to bring Hollis onto his team again. Not that she knows what the "team" is up to, not at first.

Milgrim is even more thoroughly owned by Bigend. He's worth owning for his useful gift of seeming to disappear in almost any setting, and his Russian is perfectly idiomatic—so much so that he spoke Russian with his therapist, in the secret Swiss clinic where Bigend paid for him to be cured of the addiction that would have killed him.

Garreth has a passion for extreme sports. Most recently he jumped off the highest building in the world, opening his chute at the last moment, and he has a new thighbone made of rattan baked into bone, entirely experimental, to show for it. Garreth isn't owned by Bigend at all. Garreth has friends from whom he can call in the kinds of favors that a man like Bigend will find he needs, when things go unexpectedly sideways, in a world a man like Bigend is accustomed to controlling.

As when a Department of Defense contract for combat wear turns out to be the gateway drug for arms dealers so shadowy that even Bigend, whose subtlety and power in the private sector would be hard to overstate, finds himself outmaneuvered and adrift in a seriously dangerous world.

"*Zero History* is another smartly scouted roadmap of alternate routes through today's global culture, as powered by what a friend of mine used to call the military-industrial-greeting-card complex. It's a world where cool is king, but also the key to power—and the future. . . . But what makes *Zero History* work is that Gibson's radar is deftly tuned to the changes in the culture that many of us are missing."

—*Milwaukee Journal Sentinel*

continued . . .

"The science-fiction luminary's third straight novel set in something like the present day is just as uncanny as his futuristic classics, which is a neat trick. The books have the feel and pace of thrillers, but with different concerns: trend-hunting, viral video, brand awareness, the link between the military and cutting-edge fashion. Gibson writes like he's spent years embedded in a shadow world that touches everyone though very few know it exists." —*San Antonio Express-News*

"*Zero History* offer[s] up a modern-day Rome whose denizens are shopping online while the global financial crisis burns away at its center. . . . For those who glory in the circuitous patois of Gibsonian dialogue, the electrical noir of the book's locales and the Machiavellian menace of Hubertus Bigend, this world's worrying puppet master, the plunge down the rabbit hole is just as dizzying. . . . Bigend makes for a marvelous mouthpiece, allowing Gibson to deliver his cutting observations about the modern world with the most offhand laissez-faire. . . . Gibson touches on so many contemporary phenomena that it's often easy to feel lost among the semiotics alchemy and Möbius-strip storytelling that riddles the novel, despite its mischievous humor." —*The Denver Post*

"Gibson loves to immerse his readers in the details and specialized language of everything from fashion and high-end promotional stunts to armored cars and UAVs. And always, Gibson introduces us to everyday technologies as if they came from the future or an alternate world. . . . *Zero History* is a brilliant, entertaining, and bittersweet conclusion to Gibson's only trilogy about the present day. . . . In this series, Gibson has managed to capture the weirdness of present-day corporate life, as well as the ephemeral moments of artistic and economic rebellion that can thwart even the spookiest of government plots." —io9.com

"The singular and compelling achievement of the novel, its emotional and phenomenological centre, is Milgrim himself, around whom the rest of the book sometimes seems to rain like so many foam packaging pellets tipped out of a box. Newly awakened from a decade of drug-haze, Milgrim stares at the world as though it is fresh-minted, prompting most of Gibson's best writing in the mode of naggingly tangential observation and some subtle, humane comedy." —*The Guardian* (UK)

TITLES BY WILLIAM GIBSON

WILLIAM GIBSON

zero history

BERKLEY BOOKS, NEW YORK

A BERKLEY BOOK
Published by the Penguin Group
Penguin Group (USA) Inc.
375 Hudson Street, New York, New York 10014, USA
Penguin Group (Canada), 90 Eglinton Avenue East, Suite 700, Toronto, Ontario M4P 2Y3, Canada
(a division of Pearson Penguin Canada Inc.)
Penguin Books Ltd., 80 Strand, London WC2R 0RL, England
Penguin Group Ireland, 25 St. Stephen's Green, Dublin 2, Ireland (a division of Penguin Books Ltd.)
Penguin Group (Australia), 250 Camberwell Road, Camberwell, Victoria 3124, Australia
(a division of Pearson Australia Group Pty. Ltd.)
Penguin Books India Pvt. Ltd., 11 Community Centre, Panchsheel Park, New Delhi—110 017, India
Penguin Group (NZ), 67 Apollo Drive, Rosedale, Auckland 0632, New Zealand
(a division of Pearson New Zealand Ltd.)
Penguin Books (South Africa) (Pty.) Ltd., 24 Sturdee Avenue, Rosebank, Johannesburg 2196,
South Africa

Penguin Books Ltd., Registered Offices: 80 Strand, London WC2R 0RL, England

PRINTING HISTORY
G. P. Putnam's Sons hardcover edition / September 2010
Berkley trade paperback edition / August 2011

Berkley trade paperback ISBN: 978-0-425-24077-9

The Library of Congress has cataloged the G. P. Putnam's Sons hardcover edition as follows:

Gibson, William, date.
Zero history / William Gibson.
p.   cm.
ISBN 978-0-399-15682-3
I. Title.
PS3557.I2264Z47   2010   2010016974
813'.54—dc22

PRINTED IN THE UNITED STATES OF AMERICA

10   9   8   7   6   5   4   3   2   1

To Susan Allison,
my editor

1. CABINET

Inchmale hailed a cab for her, the kind that had always been black, when she'd first known this city.

Pearlescent silver, this one. Glyphed in Prussian blue, advertising something German, banking services or business software; a smoother simulacrum of its black ancestors, its faux-leather upholstery a shade of orthopedic fawn.

"Their money's heavy," he said, dropping a loose warm mass of pound coins into her hand. "Buys many whores." The coins still retained the body heat of the fruit machine from which he'd deftly wrung them, almost in passing, on their way out of the King's Something.

"Whose money?"

"My countrymen's. Freely given."

"I don't need this." Trying to hand it back.

"For the cab." Giving the driver the address in Portman Square.

"Oh Reg," she said, "it wasn't that bad. I had it in money markets, most of it."

"Bad as anything else. Call him."

"No."

"Call him," he repeated, wrapped in Japanese herringbone Gore-Tex, multiply flapped and counterintuitively buckled.

He closed the cab's door.

She watched him through the rear window as the cab pulled away. Stout and bearded, he turned now in Greek Street, a few minutes past midnight, to rejoin his stubborn protégé, Clammy of the Bollards. Back to the studio, to take up their lucrative creative struggle.

She sat back, noticing nothing at all until they passed Selfridges, the driver taking a right.

The club, only a few years old, was on the north side of Portman Square. Getting out, she paid and generously tipped the driver, anxious to be rid of Inchmale's winnings.

Cabinet, so called; of Curiosities, unspoken. Inchmale had become a member shortly after they, the three surviving members of the Curfew, had licensed the rights to "Hard to Be One" to a Chinese automobile manufacturer. Having already produced one Bollards album in Los Angeles, and with Clammy wanting to record the next in London, Inchmale had argued that joining Cabinet would ultimately prove cheaper than a hotel. And it had, she supposed, but only if you were talking about a very expensive hotel.

She was staying there now as a paying guest. Given the state of money markets, whatever those were, and the conversations she'd been having with her accountant in New York, she knew that she should be looking for more modestly priced accommodations.

A peculiarly narrow place, however expensive, Cabinet occupied half the vertical mass of an eighteenth-century townhouse, one whose façade reminded her of the face of someone starting to fall asleep on the subway. It shared a richly but soberly paneled foyer with whatever occupied the other, westernmost, half of the building, and she'd formed a vague conviction that this must be a foundation of some kind, perhaps philanthropic in nature, or dedicated to the advancement of peace in the Middle East, however eventual. Something hushed, in any case, as it appeared to have no visitors at all.

There was nothing, on façade or door, to indicate what that might be, no more than there was anything to indicate that Cabinet was Cabinet.

She'd seen those famously identical, silver-pelted Icelandic twins in the lounge, the first time she'd gone there, both of them drinking red wine from pint glasses, something Inchmale dubbed an Irish affection. They weren't members, he'd made a point of noting. Cabinet's members, in the performing arts, were somewhat less than stellar, and she assumed that that suited Inchmale just about as well as it suited her.

It was the decor that had sold Inchmale, he said, and very likely it had been. Both he and it were arguably mad.

Pushing open the door, through which one might have ridden a horse without having to duck to clear the lintel, she was greeted by Robert, a large and comfortingly chalk-striped young man whose primary task was to mind the entrance without particularly seeming to.

"Good evening, Miss Henry."

"Good evening, Robert."

The decorators had kept it down, here, which was to say that they hadn't really gone publicly, ragingly, batshit insane. There was a huge, ornately carved desk, with something vaguely pornographic going on amid mahogany vines and grape clusters, at which sat one or another of the club's employees, young men for the most part, often wearing tortoiseshell spectacles of the sort she suspected of having been carved from actual turtles.

Beyond the desk's agreeably archaic mulch of paperwork twined a symmetrically opposed pair of marble stairways, leading to the floor above; that floor being bisected, as was everything above this foyer, into twin realms of presumed philanthropic mystery and Cabinet. From the Cabinet side, now, down the stairs with the widdershins twist, cascaded the sound of earnest communal drinking, laughter and loud conversation bouncing sharply off unevenly translucent stone, marbled in shades of aged honey, petroleum jelly, and nicotine. The damaged edges of individual steps had been repaired with tidy rectangular inserts of less inspired stuff, pallid and mundane, which she was careful never to step on.

A tortoise-framed young man, seated at the desk, passed her the room key without being asked.

"Thank you."

"You're welcome, Miss Henry."

Beyond the archway separating the stairways, the floor plan gave evidence of hesitation. Indicating, she guessed, some awkwardness inherent in the halving of the building's original purpose. She pressed a worn but regularly polished brass button, to call down the oldest elevator she'd ever seen, even in London. The size of a small, shallow closet, wider than it was deep, it took its time, descending its elongated cage of black-enameled steel.

To her right, in shadow, illuminated from within by an Edwardian museum fixture, stood a vitrine displaying taxidermy. Game birds, mostly; a pheasant, several quail, others she couldn't put a name to, all mounted as though caught in motion, crossing a sward of faded billiard-felt. All somewhat the worse for wear, though no more than might be expected for their probable age. Behind them, anthropomorphically upright, forelimbs outstretched in the manner of a cartoon somnambulist, came a moth-eaten ferret. Its teeth, which struck her as unrealistically large, she suspected of being wooden, and painted. Certainly its lips were painted, if not actually rouged, lending it a sinisterly festive air, like someone you'd dread running into at a Christmas party. Inchmale, on first pointing it out to her, had suggested she adopt it as a totem, her spirit beast. He claimed that he already had, subsequently discovering he could magically herniate the disks of unsuspecting music executives at will, causing them to suffer excruciating pain and a profound sense of helplessness.

The lift arrived. She'd been a guest here long enough to have mastered the intricacies of the articulated steel gate. Resisting an urge to nod to the ferret, she entered and ascended, slowly, to the third floor.

Here the narrow hallways, walls painted a very dark green, twisted confusingly. The route to her room involved opening several of what she assumed were fire doors, as they were very thick, heavy, and self-closing. The short sections of corridor, between, were hung with small watercolors, landscapes, unpeopled, each one featuring a distant folly. The very *same* distant folly, she'd noticed, regardless of the scene or region depicted. She refused to give Inchmale the satisfaction he'd derive from her asking about these, so hadn't. Something too thoroughly liminal about them. Best not addressed. Life sufficiently complicated as it was.

The key, attached to a weighty brass ferrule sprouting thick soft tassels of braided maroon silk, turned smoothly in the lock's brick-sized mass. Admitting her to Number Four, and the concentrated impact of Cabinet's designers' peculiarity, theatrically revealed when she prodded the mother-of-pearl dot set into an otherwise homely gutta-percha button.

Too tall, somehow, though she imagined that to be the result of a larger room having been divided, however cunningly. The bathroom, she suspected, might actually be larger than the bedroom, if that weren't some illusion.

They'd run with that tallness, employing a white, custom-printed wallpaper, decorated with ornate cartouches in glossy black. These were comprised, if you looked more closely, of enlarged bits of anatomical drawings of bugs. Scimitar mandibles, spiky elongated limbs, the delicate wings (she imagined) of mayflies. The two largest pieces of furniture in the room were the bed, its massive frame covered entirely in slabs of scrimshawed walrus ivory, with the enormous, staunchly ecclesiastic-looking lower jawbone of a right whale, fastened to the wall at its head, and a birdcage, so large she might have crouched in it herself, suspended from the ceiling. The cage was stacked with books, and fitted, inside, with minimalist Swiss halogen fixtures, each tiny bulb focused on one or another of Number Four's resident artifacts. And not just prop books, Inchmale had proudly pointed out. Fiction or non-, they all seemed to be about England, and so far she'd read parts of Dame Edith Sitwell's *English Eccentrics* and most of Geoffrey Household's *Rogue Male*.

She took off her coat, putting it on a stuffed, satin-covered hanger in the wardrobe, and sat on the edge of the bed to untie her shoes. The Piblokto Madness bed, Inchmale called it. "Intense hysteria," she recited now, from memory, "depression, coprophagia, insensitivity to cold, echolalia." She kicked her shoes in the direction of the wardrobe's open door. "Hold the coprophagia," she added. Cabin fever, this culture-bound, arctic condition. Possibly dietary in origin. Linked to vitamin A toxicity. Inchmale was full of this sort of information, never more so than when he was in the studio. Give Clammy a whole hod of vitamin A, she'd suggested, he looks like he could use it.

Her gaze fell on three unopened brown cartons, stacked to the left of the wardrobe. These contained shrink-wrapped copies of the British edition of a book she'd written in hotel rooms, though none as peculiarly memorable as this one. She'd begun just after the Chinese car commercial money had come in. She'd gone to Staples, West Hollywood, and bought three flimsy Chinese-made folding tables, to lay the manuscript and its many illustrations out on, in her corner suite at the Marmont. That seemed a long time ago, and she didn't know what she'd do with these copies. The cartons of her copies of the American edition, she now remembered, were still in the luggage room of the Tribeca Grand.

"Echolalia," she said, and stood, removing her sweater, which she folded and put in a chest-high drawer in the wardrobe, beside a small silk land mine of potpourri. If she didn't touch it, she knew, she wouldn't have to smell it. Putting on an off-white Cabinet robe, more velour than terry but somehow just missing whatever it was that made her so unfond of velour bathrobes. Men, particularly, looked fundamentally untrustworthy in them.

The room phone began to ring. It was a collage, its massive nautical-looking handset of rubber-coated bronze resting in a leather-padded cradle atop a cubical box of brass-cornered rosewood. Its ring was mechanical, tiny, as though you were hearing an old-fashioned bicycle bell far off down a quiet street. She stared hard, willing it to silence.

"Intense hysteria," she said.

It continued to ring.

Three steps and her hand was on it.

It was as absurdly heavy as ever.

"Coprophagia." Briskly, as if announcing a busy department in a large hospital.

"Hollis," he said, "hello."

She looked down at the handset, heavy as an old hammer and nearly as battered. Its thick cord, luxuriously cased in woven burgundy silk, resting against her bare forearm.

"Hollis?"

"Hello, Hubertus."

She pictured herself driving the handset through brittle antique rosewood, crushing the aged electro-mechanical cricket within. Too late now. It had already fallen silent.

"I saw Reg," he said.

"I know."

"I told him to ask you to call."

"I didn't," she said.

"Good to hear your voice," he said.

"It's late."

"A good night's sleep, then," heartily. "I'll be by in the morning, for breakfast. We're driving back tonight. Pamela and I."

"Where are you?"

"Manchester."

She saw herself taking an early cab to Paddington, the street in front of Cabinet deserted. Catching the Heathrow Express. Flying somewhere. Another phone ringing, in another room. His voice.

"Manchester?"

"Norwegian black metal," he said, flatly. She pictured Scandinavian folk jewelry, then self-corrected: the musical genre. "Reg said I might find it interesting."

Good for him, she thought, Inchmale's subclinical sadism sometimes finding a deserving target.

"I was planning on sleeping in," she said, if only to be difficult. She knew now that it was going to be impossible to avoid him.

"Eleven, then," he said. "Looking forward to it."

"Good night. Hubertus."

"Good night." He hung up.

She put the handset down. Careful of the hidden cricket. Not its fault.

Nor hers.

Nor even his, probably. Whatever he was.

2. EDGE CITY

Milgrim considered the dog-headed angels in Gay Dolphin Gift Cove.

Their heads, rendered slightly less than three-quarter scale, appeared to have been cast from the sort of plaster once used to produce worryingly detailed wall-decorations: pirates, Mexicans, turbaned Arabs. There would almost certainly be examples of those here as well, he thought, in the most thoroughgoing trove of roadside American souvenir kitsch he'd ever seen.

Their bodies, apparently humanoid under white satin and sequins, were long, Modigliani-slender, perilously upright, paws crossed piously in the manner of medieval effigies. Their wings were the wings of Christmas ornaments, writ larger than would suit the average tree.

They were intended, he decided, with half a dozen of assorted breed facing him now, from behind glass, to sentimentally honor deceased pets.

Hands in trouser pockets, he quickly swung his gaze to a broader but generally no less peculiar visual complexity, noting as he did a great many items featuring Confederate-flag motifs. Mugs, magnets, ashtrays, statuettes. He considered a knee-high jockey boy, proffering a small round tray rather than the traditional ring. Its head and hands were a startling Martian green (so as not to give the traditional offense, he assumed). There were also energetically artificial orchids, coconuts carved to suggest the features of some generically indigenous race, and prepackaged collections of rocks and minerals. It was like being on the bottom of a Coney Island grab-it game, one in which the eclectically ungrabbed had been accumulating for decades. He looked up, imagining a giant, three-pronged claw, agent of stark removal, but there was only a large and heavily varnished shark, suspended overhead like the fuselage of a small plane.

How old did a place like this have to be, in America, to have "gay" in its name? Some percentage of the stock here, he judged, had been manufactured in Occupied Japan.

Half an hour earlier, across North Ocean Boulevard, he'd watched harshly tonsured child-soldiers, clad in skateboarding outfits still showing factory creases, ogling Chinese-made orc-killing blades, spiked and serrated like the jaws of extinct predators. The seller's stand had been hung with Mardi Gras beads, Confederate-flag beach towels, unauthorized Harley-Davidson memorabilia. He'd wondered how many young men had enjoyed an afternoon in Myrtle Beach as a final treat, before heading ultimately for whatever theater of war, wind whipping sand along the Grand Strand and the boardwalk.

In the amusement arcades, he judged, some of the machines were older than he was. And some of his own angels, not the better ones, spoke of an ancient and deeply impacted drug culture, ground down into the carnival grime of the place, interstitial and immortal; sun-damaged skin, tattoos unreadable, eyes that peered from faces suggestive of gas-station taxidermy.

He was meeting someone here.

They were supposed to be alone. He himself wasn't, really. Somewhere nearby, Oliver Sleight would be watching a Milgrim-cursor on a website, on the screen of his Neo phone, identical to Milgrim's own. He'd given Milgrim the Neo on that first flight from Basel to Heathrow, stressing the necessity of keeping it with him at all times, and turned on, except when aboard commercial flights.

He moved, now, away from the dog-headed angels, the shadow of the shark. Past articles of an ostensibly more natural history: starfish, sand dollars, sea horses, conchs. He climbed a short flight of broad stairs, from the boardwalk level, toward North Ocean Boulevard. Until he found himself, eye-to-navel, with the stomach of a young, very pregnant woman, her elastic-paneled jeans chemically distressed in ways that suggested baroquely improbable patterns of wear. The taut pink T-shirt revealed her protruding navel in a way he found alarmingly suggestive of a single giant breast.

"You'd better be him," she said, then bit her lower lip. Blond, a face he'd forget as soon as he looked away. Large dark eyes.

"I'm meeting someone," he said, careful to maintain eye contact, uncomfortably aware that he was actually addressing the navel, or nipple, directly in front of his mouth.

Her eyes grew larger. "You aren't foreign, are you?"

"New York," Milgrim admitted, assuming that might all too easily qualify.

"I don't want him getting in any trouble," she said, at once softly and fiercely.

"None of us does," he instantly assured her. "No need. At all." His attempted smile felt like something forced from a flexible squeeze-toy. "And you are . . . ?

"Seven or eight months," she said, in awe at her own gravidity. "He's not here. He didn't like this, here."

"None of us does," he said, then wondered if that was the right thing to say.

"You got GPS?"

"Yes," said Milgrim. Actually, according to Sleight, their Neos had two kinds, American and Russian, the American being notoriously political, and prone to unreliability in the vicinity of sensitive sites.

"He'll be there in an hour," she said, passing Milgrim a faintly damp slip of folded paper. "You better get started. And you better be alone."

Milgrim took a deep breath. "I'm sorry," he said, "but if it means driving, I won't be able to go alone. I don't have a license. My friend will have to drive me. It's a white Ford Taurus X."

She stared at him. Blinked. "Didn't they just fuck Ford up, when they went to giving them f-names?"

He swallowed.

"My mother had a Freestyle. Transmission's a total piece of shit. Get that computer wet, car won't move at all. Gotta disconnect it first. Brakes wore out about two weeks off the lot. They always made that squealing noise anyway." But she seemed comforted, in this, as if by the recollection of something maternal, familiar.

"Right as rain," he said, surprising himself with an expression he might never have used before. He pocketed the slip of paper without looking at it. "Could you do something for me, please?" he asked her belly. "Could you call him, now, and let him know my friend will be driving?"

Lower lip worked its way back under her front teeth.

"My friend has the money," Milgrim said. "No trouble."

>>>

"And she called him?" asked Sleight, behind the wheel of the Taurus X, from the center of a goatee he occasionally trimmed with the aid of a size-adjustable guide, held between his teeth.

"She indicated she would," Milgrim said.

"Indicated."

They were headed inland, toward the town of Conway, through a landscape that reminded Milgrim of driving somewhere near Los Angeles, to a destination you wouldn't be particularly anxious to reach. This abundantly laned highway, lapped by the lots of outlet malls, a Home Depot the size of a cruise ship, theme restaurants. Though interstitial detritus still spoke stubbornly of maritime activity and the farming of tobacco. Fables from before the Anaheiming. Milgrim concentrated on these leftovers, finding them centering. A lot offering garden mulch. A four-store strip mall with two pawnshops. A fireworks emporium with its own batting cage. Loans on your auto title. Serried ranks of unpainted concrete garden statuary.

"Was that a twelve-step program you were in, in Basel?" asked Sleight

"I don't think so," said Milgrim, assuming Sleight was referring to the number of times his blood had been changed.

>>>

"How close will those numbers put us to where he wants us?" Milgrim asked. Sleight, back in Myrtle Beach, had tapped coordinates from the pregnant girl's note into his phone, which now rested on his lap.

"Close enough," Sleight said. "Looks like that's it now, off to the right."

They were well through Conway, or in any case through the malled-over fringes of whatever Conway was. Buildings were thinning out, the landscape revealing more of the lineaments of an extinct agriculture.

Sleight slowed, swung right, onto spread gravel, a crushed limestone, pale gray. "Money's under your seat," he said. They were rolling, with a smooth, even crunch of tires in gravel, toward a long, one-story, white-painted clapboard structure, overhung with a roof that lacked a porch beneath it. Rural roadside architecture of some previous day, plain but sturdy. Four smallish rectangular front windows had been modernized with plate glass.

Milgrim had the cardboard tube for the tracing paper upright between his thighs, two sticks of graphite wrapped in a Kleenex in the right side pocket of his chinos. There was half of a fresh five-foot sheet of foam-core illustration board in the back seat, in case he needed a flat surface to work on. Holding the bright red tube with his knees, he bent forward, fishing under the seat, and found a metallic-blue vinyl envelope with a molded integral zipper and three binder-holes. It contained enough bundled hundreds to give it the heft of a good-sized paperback dictionary.

Gravel-crunch ceased as they halted, not quite in front of the building. Milgrim saw a primitive rectangular sign on two weather-grayed uprights, rain-stained and faded, unreadable except for *FAMILY*, in pale blue italic serif caps. There were no other vehicles in the irregularly shaped gravel lot.

He opened the door, got out, stood, the red tube in his left hand. He considered, then uncapped it, drawing out the furled tracing paper. He propped the red tube against the passenger seat, picked up the money, and closed the door. A scroll of semitranslucent white paper was less threatening.

Cars passed on the highway. He walked the fifteen feet to the sign, his shoes crunching loudly on the gravel. Above the blue italic *FAMILY*, he made out *EDGE CITY* in what little remained of a peeling red; below it, *RESTAURANT*. At the bottom, to the left, had once been painted, in black, the childlike silhouettes of three houses, though like the red, sun and rain had largely erased them. To the right, in a different blue than *FAMILY*, was painted what he took to be a semi-abstract representation of hills, possibly of lakes. He guessed that this place was on or near the town's official outskirts, hence the name.

Someone, within the silent, apparently closed building, rapped sharply, once, on plate glass, perhaps with a ring.

Milgrim went obediently to the front door, the tracing paper upheld in one hand like a modest scepter, the vinyl envelope held against his side with the other.

The door opened inward, revealing a football player with an Eighties porn haircut. Or someone built like one. A tall, long-legged young man with exceptionally powerful-looking shoulders. He stepped back, gesturing for Milgrim to enter.

"Hello," said Milgrim, stepping into warm unmoving air, mixed scents of industrial-strength disinfectant and years of cooking. "I have your money." Indicating the plastic envelope. A place unused, though ready to be used. Mothballed, Edge City, like a B-52 in the desert. He saw the empty glass head of a gum machine, on its stand of wrinkle-finished brown pipe.

"Put it on the counter," the young man said. He wore pale blue jeans and a black T-shirt, both of which looked as though they might contain a percentage of Spandex, and heavy-looking black athletic shoes. Milgrim noted a narrow, rectangular, unusually positioned pocket, quite far down on the right side-seam. A stainless steel clip held some large folding knife firmly there.

Milgrim did as he was told, noting the chrome and the turquoise leatherette of the row of floor-mounted stools in front of the counter, which was topped with worn turquoise Formica. He partially unfurled the paper. "I'll need to make tracings," he explained. "It's the best way to capture the detail. I'll take photographs first."

"Who's in the car?"

"My friend."

"Why can't you drive?"

"DUI," said Milgrim, and it was true, at least in some philosophical sense.

Silently, the young man rounded an empty glass display-case that would once have contained cigarettes and candy. When he was opposite Milgrim, he reached beneath the counter and drew out something in a crumpled white plastic bag. He dropped this on the counter and swept the plastic envelope toward the far end, giving the impression that his body, highly trained, was doing these things of its own accord, while he himself continued to survey from some interior distance.

Milgrim opened the bag and took out a pair of folded, unpressed trousers. They were the coppery beige shade he knew as coyote brown. Unfolding them, he lay them out flat along the Formica, took the camera from his jacket pocket, and began to photograph them, using the flash. He took six shots of the front, then turned them over and took six of the back. He took one photograph each of the four cargo pockets. He put the camera down, turned the pants inside out, and photographed them again. Pocketing the camera, he arranged them, still inside out, more neatly on the counter, spread the first of the four sheets of paper over them, and began, with one of the graphite sticks, to make his rubbing.

He liked doing this. There was something inherently satisfying about it. He'd been sent to Hackney, to a tailor who did alterations, to spend an afternoon learning how to do it properly, and it pleased him, somehow, that this was a time-honored means of stealing information. It was like making a rubbing of a tombstone, or a bronze in a cathedral. The medium-hard graphite, if correctly applied, captured every detail of seam and stitching, all a sample-maker would need to reproduce the garment, as well as providing for reconstruction of the pattern.

While he worked, the young man opened the envelope, unpacked the bundled hundreds, and silently counted them. "Needs a gusset," he said as he finished.

"Pardon?" Milgrim paused, the fingers of his right hand covered with graphite dust.

"Gusset," the young man said, reloading the blue envelope. "Inner thighs. They bind, if you're rappelling."

"Thanks," Milgrim said, showing graphite-smudged fingers. "Would you mind turning them over for me? I don't want to get this on them."

>>>

"Delta to Atlanta," Sleight said, handing Milgrim a ticket envelope. He was back in the very annoying suit he'd forgone for Myrtle Beach, the one with the freakishly short trousers.

"Business?"

"Coach," said Sleight, his satisfaction entirely evident. He passed Milgrim a second envelope. "British Midland to Heathrow."

"Coach?"

Sleight frowned. "Business."

Milgrim smiled.

"He'll want you in a meeting, straight off the plane."

Milgrim nodded. "Bye," he said. He tucked the red tube beneath his arm and headed for check-in, his bag in his other hand, walking directly beneath a very large South Carolina state flag, oddly Islamic with its palm tree and crescent moon.

3. SLUT'S WOOL

She woke to gray light around multiple layers of curtains and drapes. Lay staring up at a dim anamorphic view of the repeated insectoid cartouche, smaller and more distorted the closer to the ceiling. Shelves with objects, *Wunderkammer* stuff. Variously sized heads of marble, ivory, ormolu. The blank round bottom of the caged library.

She checked her watch. Shortly after nine.

She got out of bed, in her XXL Bollards T-shirt, put on the not-velour robe, and entered the bathroom, a tall deep cove of off-white tile. Turning on the enormous shower required as much effort as ever. A Victorian monster, its original taps were hulking knots of plated brass. Horizontal four-inch nickel-plate pipes caged you on three sides, handy for warming towels. Within these were slung sheets of inch-thick beveled glass, contemporary replacements. The original showerhead, mounted directly overhead, was thirty inches in diameter. Getting out of the robe and T-shirt, she put on a disposable cap, stepped in, and lathered up with Cabinet's artisanal soap, smelling faintly of cucumber.

She kept a picture of this shower on her iPhone. It reminded her of H. G. Wells's time machine. It had probably been in use when he began the serial that would become his first novel.

Toweling off, applying moisturizer, she listened to BBC through an ornate bronze grate. Nothing of catastrophic import since she'd last listened, though nothing particularly positive either. Early-twenty-first-century quotidian, death-spiral subtexts kept well down in the mix.

She took off the shower cap and shook her head, hair retaining residual stylist's mojo from the salon in Selfridges. She liked to eat lunch in Selfridges' food hall, escaping through its back door before the communal trance of shopping put her under. Though that was all it was likely to do, in a department store. She was more vulnerable to smaller places, and in London that could be very dangerous. The Japanese jeans she was pulling on now, for instance. Fruit of a place around the corner from Inchmale's studio, the week before. Zen emptiness, bowls with shards of pure solidified indigo, like blue-black glass. The handsome, older, Japanese shopkeeper, in her *Waiting for Godot* outfit.

You'll have to watch that now, she advised herself. Money.

Brushing her teeth, she noticed the vinyl Blue Ant figurine on the marble sinktop, amid her lotions and makeup. You let me down, she thought to the jaunty ant, its four arms akimbo. Aside from a few pieces of jewelry, it was one of the few things she owned that she'd had since she'd first known Hubertus Bigend. She'd tried abandoning it, at least once, but somehow it was still with her. She'd thought she'd left it in the penthouse he kept in Vancouver, but it had been in her bag when she'd arrived in New York. She'd come, however vaguely, to imagine it as a sort of inverse charm. A cartoon rendition of the trademark of his agency, she'd let it serve as a secret symbol of her unwillingness to have anything further to do with him.

She'd trusted it to keep him away.

She really hadn't had that much other property to replace, she reminded herself, swishing mouthwash. The dot-com bubble and an ill-advised foray into retailing vinyl records had seen to that, well before he'd found her. She wasn't quite that badly off now, but if she'd understood her accountant correctly she'd lost nearly fifty percent of her net worth when the market had gone down. And this time she hadn't done anything to cause it. No start-up shares, no quixotic record store in Brooklyn.

Everything she owned, currently, was here in this room. Aside from devalued money market shares, and some boxes of American author's copies, back in the Tribeca Grand. She spat mouthwash into the marble sink.

Inchmale didn't mind Bigend, not the way she did, but Inchmale, as formidably bright as she knew him to be, was also gifted with a useful crudeness of mind, an inbuilt psychic callus. He found Bigend interesting. Possibly he found him creepy, too, though for Inchmale, interesting and creepy were broadly overlapping categories. He didn't, she guessed, find Bigend that utter an anomaly. An overly wealthy, dangerously curious fiddler with the world's hidden architectures.

There was no way, she knew, to tell an entity like Bigend that you wanted nothing to do with him. That would simply bring you more firmly to his attention. She'd had her time in Bigend's employ; while brief, it had been entirely too eventful. She'd put it behind her, and gone on with her book project, which had grown quite naturally out of what she'd been doing (or had thought she'd been doing) for Bigend.

Although, she reminded herself, fastening her bra and pulling on a T-shirt, the money she'd seen reduced by almost half had come to her via Blue Ant. There was that. She pulled a sheer black mohair sweater over the T-shirt, smoothed it over her hips, and pushed up the sleeves. She sat on the edge of the bed, to put on her shoes. Then back into the bathroom for makeup.

Purse, iPhone, key with its tassel.

Out, then, and past the identical follies in their different landscapes. To press the button and wait for the lift. She put her face close to the iron cage, to see the lift rise toward her, atop it some complex electromechanical Tesla-node no designer had even had to fake up, the real deal, whatever function it might serve. And decked, she always noted with a certain satisfaction, with a bit of frank slut's wool, the only actual dust she'd yet seen in Cabinet. Even a few errant cigarette butts, the English being beasts that way.

And down, to the floor above the paneled foyer, where the night's boozing and networking had left no evidence, and the serving staff, reassuringly immune to the long room's decor, were about their morning business. She made her way to the rear, taking a seat at a place for two, beneath what might originally have been a gun rack in parquetry, but which now held half a dozen narwhale tusks.

The Italian girl brought her a pot of coffee, unbidden, with a smaller one of steamed milk, and the *Times*.

She was starting her second cup, *Times* unread, when she saw Hubertus Bigend mount the stairhead, down the full length of the long room, wrapped in a wide, putty-colored trench coat.

He was the ultimate in velour-robe types, and might just as well have been wearing one now as he swept toward her through the drawing room, unknotting the coat's belt as he came, pawing back its Crimean lapels, and revealing the only International Klein Blue suit she'd ever seen. He somehow managed always to give her the impression, seeing him again, that he'd grown visibly larger, though without gaining any particular weight. Simply bigger. Perhaps, she thought, as if he grew somehow *closer*.

As he did now, breakfasting Cabineteers cringing as he passed, less in fear of his vast trailing coat and its dangerously swinging belt than out of awareness that he didn't see them.

"Hollis," he said. "You look magnificent." She rose, to be air-kissed. Up close, he always seemed too full of blood, by several extra quarts at least. Rosy as a pig. Warmer than a normal person. Scented with some ancient European barber-splash.

"Hardly," she said. "Look at you. Look at your suit."

"Mr. Fish," he said, shrugging out of the trench coat with a rattle of grenade-loops and lanyard-anchors. His shirt was palest gold, the silk tie knit in an almost matching shade.

"He's very good," she said.

"He's not dead," said Bigend, smiling, settling himself in the armchair opposite.

"Dead?" She took her seat.

"Apparently not. Just impossible to find. I found his cutter," he said. "In Savile Row."

"That's Klein Blue, isn't it?"

"Of course."

"It looks radioactive. In a suit."

"It unsettles people," he said.

"I hope you didn't wear it for me."

"Not at all." He smiled. "I wore it because I enjoy it."

"Coffee?"

"Black."

She signaled to the Italian girl. "How was the black metal?"

"Tremolo picking," he said, perhaps slightly fretfully. "Double-kick drumming. Reg thinks something's there." He tilted his head slightly. "Do you?"

"I don't keep up." Adding milk to her coffee.

The Italian girl returned for their breakfast order. Hollis asked for oatmeal with fruit, Bigend for the full English.

"I loved your book," he said. "I thought the reception was quite gratifying. Particularly the piece in *Vogue*."

"'Old rock singer publishes book of pictures'?"

"No, really. It was very good." He tidied the trench coat, which he'd draped across the arm of his chair. "Working on something else now?"

She sipped her coffee.

"You want to follow that up," he said.

"I hadn't noticed."

"Barring scandal," he said, "society is reluctant to let someone who's become famous for one thing become famous for another."

"I'm not trying to become famous."

"You already are."

"Was. Briefly. And in quite a small way."

"A degree of undeniable celebrity," he said, like a doctor offering a particularly obvious diagnosis.

They sat silently, then, Hollis pretending to glance over the first few pages of the *Times*, until the Italian girl and an equally pretty and dark-haired boy arrived, bearing breakfast on dark wooden trays with brass handles. They arranged these on the low coffee table and retreated, Bigend studying the sway of the girl's hips. "I adore the full English," he said. "The offal. Blood pudding. The beans. The bacon. Were you here before they invented food?" he asked. "You must have been."

"I was," she admitted. "I was very young."

"Even then," he said, "the full English was a thing of genius." He was slicing a sausage that looked like haggis, but boiled in the stomach of a small animal, something on the order of a koala. "There's something you could help us out with," he said, and put a slice of sausage in his mouth.

"Us."

He chewed, nodded, swallowed. "We aren't just an advertising agency. I'm sure you know that. We do brand vision transmission, trend forecasting, vendor management, youth market recon, strategic planning in general."

"Why didn't that commercial ever come out, the one they paid us all the money to use 'Hard to Be One' in?"

He dabbed a torn toast-finger into the runny yellow eye of a fried egg, bit off half of it, chewed, swallowed, wiped his lips with his napkin. "Do you care?"

"That was a lot of money."

"That was China," he said. "The vehicle the ad was for hasn't made it to roll-out. Won't."

"Why not?"

"There were problems with the design. Fundamental ones. Their government decided that that wasn't the vehicle with which China should enter the world market. Particularly not in the light of the various tainted food product scandals. And whatnot."

"Was it that bad?"

"Fully." He forked baked beans adroitly onto toast. "They didn't need your song, in the end," he said, "and, as far we know, the executives in charge of the project are all still very much alive. Quite an optimal outcome for all concerned." He started on his bacon. She ate her oatmeal and fruit, watching him. He ate quickly, methodically topping up whatever metabolism kept him firing on those extra cylinders. She'd never seen him tired, or jet-lagged. He seemed to exist in his own personal time zone.

He finished before she did, wiping the white plate clean with a final half-triangle of golden Cabinet toast.

"Brand vision transmission," he said.

"Yes?" She raised an eyebrow.

"Narrative. Consumers don't buy products, so much as narratives."

"That's old," she said. "It must be, because I've heard it before." She took a sip of cooled coffee.

"To some extent, an idea like that becomes a self-fulfilling prophecy. Designers are taught to invent characters, with narratives, who they then design products for, or around. Standard procedure. There are similar procedures in branding generally, in the invention of new products, new companies, of all kinds."

"So it works?"

"Oh, it works," he said, "but because it does, it's become de facto. Once you have a way in which things are done, the edge migrates. Goes elsewhere."

"Where?"

"That's where you come in," he said.

"I do not."

He smiled. He had, as ever, a great many very white teeth.

"You have bacon in your teeth," she said, though he didn't.

Covering his mouth with the white linen napkin, he tried to find the nonexistent bacon shard. Lowering it, he grimaced widely.

She pretended to peer. "I *think* you got it," she said, doubtfully. "And I'm not interested in your proposition."

"You're a bohemian," he said, folding the napkin and putting it on the tray, beside his plate.

"What does that mean?"

"You've scarcely ever held a salaried position. You're freelance. Have always been freelance. You've accumulated no real property."

"Not entirely through want of trying."

"No," he said, "but when you do try, your heart's scarcely in it. I'm a bohemian myself."

"Hubertus, you're easily the richest person I've ever met." This was, she knew as she said it, not literally true, but anyone she'd met who might have been wealthier than Bigend had tended to be comparatively dull. He was easily the most problematic rich person she'd yet encountered.

"It's a by-product," he said, carefully. "And one of the things it's a by-product *of* is my fundamental disinterest in wealth."

And, really, she knew that she believed him, at least about that. It was true, and it did things to his capacity for risk-taking. It was what made him, she knew from experience, so peculiarly dangerous to be around.

"My mother was a bohemian," he said.

"Phaedra," she remembered, somehow.

"I made her old age as comfortable as possible. That isn't always the case, with bohemians."

"That was good of you."

"Reg is quite the model of the successful bohemian, isn't he?"

"I suppose he is."

"He's always working on something, Reg. Always. Always something new." He looked at her, across the heavy silver pots. "Are you?"

And he had her, then, she knew. Looking somehow straight into her. "No," she said, there being nothing else really to say.

"You should be," he said. "The secret, of course, is that it doesn't really matter what it is. Whatever you do, because you are an artist, will bring you to the next thing of your own. That's what happened the last time, isn't it? You wrote your book."

"But you were lying to me," she said. "You pretended you had a magazine, and that I was writing for it."

"I did, potentially, have a magazine. I had staff."

"One person!"

"Two," he said, "counting you."

"I can't work that way," she told him. "I won't."

"It won't be that way. This is entirely less . . . speculative."

"Wasn't the NSA or someone tapping your phone, reading your e-mail?"

"But now we know that they were doing that to everyone." He loosened his pale golden tie. "We didn't, then."

"You did," she said. "You'd guessed. Or found out."

"Someone," he said, "is developing what may prove to be a somewhat new way to transmit brand vision."

"You sound guarded in your appreciation."

"A certain genuinely provocative use of negative space," he said, sounding still less pleased.

"Who?"

"I don't know," he said. "I haven't been able to find out. I feel that someone has read and understood my playbook. And may possibly be extending it."

"Then send Pamela," she said. "She understands all that. Or someone else. You have a small army of people who understand all that. You must."

"But that's exactly it. Because they 'understand all that,' they won't find the edge. They won't find the new. And worse, they'll trample on it, inadvertently crush it, beneath a certain mediocrity inherent in professional competence." He dabbed his lips with the folded napkin, though they didn't seem to need it. "I need a wild card. I need you."

He sat back, then, and regarded her in exactly the way he'd regarded the tidy and receding ass of the Italian girl, though in this case, she knew, it had nothing at all to do with sex.

"Dear God," she said, entirely without expecting to, and simultaneously wishing she were very small. Small enough to curl up in the slut's wool that crowned the steampunk lift, between those few cork-colored filter tips.

"Does 'The Gabriel Hounds' mean anything to you?" he asked.

"No," she said.

He smiled, obviously pleased.

4. PARADOXICAL ANTAGONIST

With the red cardboard tube tucked carefully in beside him, under the thin British Midlands blanket, Milgrim lay awake in the darkened cabin of his flight to Heathrow.

He'd taken his pills about fifteen minutes earlier, after some calculations on the back cover of the in-flight magazine. Time-zone transitions could be tricky, in terms of dosing schedules, particularly when you weren't allowed to know exactly what it was you were taking. Whatever the doctors in Basel provided, he never saw it in its original factory form, so had no way of figuring out what it might be. This was intentional, they had explained to him, and necessary to his treatment. Everything was repackaged, in variously sized featureless white gelatin capsules, which he was forbidden to open.

He'd pushed the empty white bubble-pack, with its tiny, precisely handwritten notations of date and hour, in purple ink, far down into the seatback pocket. It would remain on the plane, at Heathrow. Nothing to be carried through customs.

His passport lay against his chest, beneath his shirt, in a Faraday pouch protecting the information on its resident RFID tag. RFID snooping was an obsession of Sleight's. Radio-frequency identification tags. They were in lots of things, evidently, and definitely in every recent U.S. passport. Sleight himself was quite fond of RFID snooping, which Milgrim supposed was one reason he worried about it. You could sit in a hotel lobby and remotely collect information from the passports of American businessmen. The Faraday pouch, which blocked all radio signals, made this impossible.

Milgrim's Neo phone was another example of Sleight's obsession with security or, as Milgrim supposed, control. It had an almost unimaginably tiny on-screen keyboard, one that could only be operated with a stylus. Milgrim's hand-eye coordination was quite good, according to the clinic, but he still had to concentrate like a jeweler when he needed to send a message. More annoyingly, Sleight had set it to lock its screen after thirty seconds of idle, requiring Milgrim to enter his password if he stopped to think for longer than twenty-nine seconds. When he'd complained about this, Sleight explained that it gave potential attackers only a thirty-second window to get in and read the phone, and that admin privileges were in any case out of the question.

The Neo, Milgrim gathered, was less a phone than a sort of tabula rasa, one which Sleight could field-update, without Milgrim's knowledge or consent, installing or deleting applications as he saw fit. It was also prone to something Sleight called "kernel panic," which caused it to freeze and need to be restarted, a condition Milgrim himself had been instantly inclined to identify with.

Lately, though, Milgrim didn't panic quite as easily. When he did, he seemed to restart of his own accord. It was, his cognitive therapist at the clinic had explained, a by-product of doing other things, rather than something one could train oneself to do in and of itself. Milgrim preferred to regard that by-product obliquely, in brief sidelong glances, else it somehow stop being produced. The biggest thing he was doing, in terms of the by-product of reduced anxiety, the therapist had explained, was to no longer take benzos on as constant a basis as possible.

He no longer took them at all, apparently, having undergone a very gradual withdrawal at the clinic. He wasn't sure when he'd actually stopped having any, as the unmarked capsules had made it impossible to know. And he'd taken lots of capsules, many of them containing food supplements of various kinds, the clinic having some obscure naturopathic basis which he'd put down to basic Swissness. Though in other ways the treatment had been quite aggressive, involving everything from repeated massive blood transfusions to the use of a substance they called a "paradoxical antagonist." This latter produced exceptionally peculiar dreams, in which Milgrim was stalked by an actual Paradoxical Antagonist, a shadowy figure he somehow associated with the colors in 1950s American advertising illustrations. Perky.

He missed his cognitive therapist. He'd been delighted to be able to speak Russian with such a beautifully educated woman. Somehow he couldn't imagine having transacted all of that in English.

He'd stayed eight months, in the clinic, longer than any of the other clients. All of whom, when opportunity had afforded, had quietly asked the name of his firm. Milgrim had replied variously, at first, though always naming some iconic brand from his youth: Coca-Cola, General Motors, Kodak. Their eyes had widened, hearing this. Toward the end of this stay, he'd switched to Enron. Their eyes had narrowed. This had partly been the result of his therapist's having ordered him to use the internet to familiarize himself with the events of the previous decade. He had, as she'd quite rightly pointed out, missed all of that.

>>>

He dreams this in the tall white room, its floor of limed oak. Tall windows. Beyond them, snow is falling. The world outside is utterly quiet, depthless. The light is without direction.

"Where did you learn your Russian, Mr. Milgrim?"

"Columbia. The university."

Her white face. Black hair matte, center-parted, drawn back tight.

"You described your previous situation as one of literal captivity. This was after Columbia?"

"Yes."

"How do you see your current situation as differing from that?"

"Do I see it as captivity?"

"Yes."

"Not in the same way."

"Do you understand why they would be willing to pay the very considerable fees required to keep you here?"

"No. Do you?"

"Not at all. Do you understand the nature of doctor-patient confidentiality, in my profession?"

"You aren't supposed to tell anyone what I tell you?"

"Exactly. Do you imagine I would?"

"I don't know."

"I would not. When I agreed to come here, to work with you, I made that absolutely clear. I am here for you, Mr. Milgrim. I am not here for them."

"That's good."

"But because I am here for you, Mr. Milgrim, I am also concerned for you. It is as though you are being born. Do you understand?"

"No."

"You were incomplete when they brought you here. You are somewhat less incomplete now, but your recovery is necessarily a complexly organic process. If you are very fortunate, it will continue for the rest of your life. 'Recovery' is perhaps a deceptive word for this. You are recovering some aspects of yourself, certainly, but the more important things are things you've never previously possessed. Primary aspects of development. You have been stunted, in certain ways. Now you have been given an opportunity to grow."

"But that's good, isn't it?"

"Good, yes. Comfortable? Not always."

>>>

At Heathrow there was a tall black man, head immaculately shaven, holding a clipboard against his chest. On it, in medium-nib red Sharpie, someone had written "mILgRIm."

"Milgrim," Milgrim said.

"Urine test," the man said. "This way."

Refusing to submit to random testing would have been a deal-breaker. They'd been very clear about that, from the start. He would have minded it less if they'd managed to collect the samples at less awkward times, but he supposed that was the point.

The man removed Milgrim's red name from his clipboard as he led him into an obviously preselected public restroom, crumpling it and thrusting it into his black overcoat.

"This way," walking briskly down a row of those seriously private British toilet-caves. Not cubicles, or stalls, but actual narrow little closets, with real doors. This was usually the first cultural difference Milgrim noticed here. Englishmen must experience American public toilets as remarkably semicommunal, he guessed. The man gestured him into a vacant toilet-room, glanced back the way they'd come, then quickly stepped in, closing the door behind him, locked it, and handed Milgrim a plastic sandwich bag containing a blue-topped sample bottle. Milgrim propped the red cardboard tube, carefully, in a corner.

They had to watch, Milgrim knew. Otherwise, you might switch containers, palm off someone else's clean urine. Or even use, he'd read in New York tabloids, a special prosthetic penis.

Milgrim removed the bottle from the bag, tore off the paper seal, removed the blue lid, and filled it, the phrase "without further ceremony" coming to mind. He capped it, placed it in the bag, and passed it over, in such a way that the man wouldn't have to experience the warmth of his fresh urine. He'd gotten quite good at this. The man dropped it into a small brown paper bag, which he folded and stuffed into his coat pocket. Milgrim turned and finished urinating, as the man unlocked the door and stepped out.

When Milgrim emerged, the man was washing his hands, fluorescent lights reflecting off the impressive dome of his skull.

"How's the weather?" Milgrim asked, soaping his own hands from a touch-free dispenser, the cardboard tube resting on the water-flecked faux-granite counter.

"Raining," said the man, drying his hands.

When Milgrim had washed and dried his own hands, he used the damp paper towels to wipe the bottom plastic cap of his tube.

"Where are we going?"

"Soho," the man said.

Milgrim followed him out, his overnight bag slung over one shoulder, the tube tucked under the opposite arm.

Then he remembered the Neo.

When he turned it on, it began to ring.

5. THIN ON THE GROUND

And when she'd watched him, from her chair, the collar of his coat popped like a vampire's cape, finally descend the stairs to Cabinet's foyer, dropping further out of sight with each step, she put her head back against slippery brocade and gazed at the spiraled lances of the narwhale tusks, in their ornate rack.

Then she sat up and asked for a white coffee, a cup rather than a pot. The breakfast crowd had mostly gone, leaving only Hollis and a pair of darkly suited Russian men who looked like extras from that Cronenberg film.

She got out her iPhone and Googled "Gabriel Hounds."

By the time her coffee arrived, she'd determined that *The Gabriel Hounds* was the title of a novel by Mary Stewart, had been the title of at least one CD, and had been or was the name of at least one band.

Everything, she knew, had already been the title of a CD, just as everything had already been the name of a band. This was why bands, for the past twenty years or so, had mostly had such unmemorable names, almost as though they'd come to pride themselves on it.

But the original Gabriel Hounds, it appeared, were folklore, legend. Dogs heard coursing, however faintly, high up in the windy night. Cousins it seemed to the Wild Hunt. This was Inchmale territory, definitely, and there were even weirder variants. Some involving hounds with human heads, or hounds with the heads of human infants. This had to do with the belief that the Gabriel Hounds were hunting the souls of children who'd died unbaptized. Christian tacked over pagan, she guessed. And the hounds seemed to have originally been "ratchets," an old word for dogs that hunt by scent. Gabriel Ratchets. Sometimes "gabble ratchets." Inchmaleian totally. He'd name the right band the Gabble Ratchets instantly.

"Left for you, Miss Henry." The Italian girl, holding out a glossy paper carrier bag, yellow, unmarked.

"Thank you." Hollis put the iPhone down and accepted the bag. It had been stapled shut, she saw, and she envisioned the oversized brass stapler atop the pornographic desk, its business end the head of a turbaned Turk. A pair of identical business cards, multiply stapled, held the two handles together. PAMELA MAINWARING, BLUE ANT.

She pulled off the cards and tugged the bag open, staples tearing through the glossy paper.

A very heavy denim shirt. She took it out and spread it across her lap. No, a jacket. The denim darker than the thighs of her Japanese jeans, bordering on black. And it smelled of that indigo, strongly, an earthy jungle scent familiar from the shop where she'd found her jeans. The metal buttons, the rivet kind, were dead black, nonreflective, oddly powdery-looking.

No exterior signage. The label, inside, below the back of the collar, was undyed leather, thick as most belts. On it had been branded not a name but the vague and vaguely disturbing outline of what she took to be a baby-headed dog. The branding iron appeared to have been twisted from a single length of fine wire, then heated, pressed down unevenly into the leather, which was singed in places. Centered directly beneath this, sewn under the bottom edge of the leather patch, was a small folded tab of white woven ribbon, machine-embroidered with three crisp, round black dots, arranged in a triangle. Indicating size?

Her gaze was drawn back to the brand of the hound, with its almost featureless kewpie head.

> > >

"Twenty-ounce," the handsomely graying professor of denim pronounced, the Gabriel Hounds jacket spread before her on a foot-thick slab of polished hardwood, atop what Hollis guessed had been the cast-iron legs of a factory lathe. "Slubby."

"Slubby?"

Running her hand lightly over the jacket's sleeve. "This roughness. In the weave."

"Is this Japanese denim?"

The woman raised her eyebrows. She was dressed, today, in a tweed that looked as if the brambles had been left in, khaki laundered so often as to be of no particular color, oxford cloth so coarse it seemed handloomed, and at least two tattered paisley cravats of peculiar but differing widths. "Americans forget how to make denim like this. Maybe loomed in Japan. Maybe not. Where did you find it?"

"It belongs to a friend."

"You like it?"

"I haven't tried it on."

"No?" The woman moved behind Hollis, helping her remove her coat. She picked up the jacket and helped Hollis into it.

Hollis saw herself in the mirror. Straightened. Smiled. "That's not bad," she said. She turned up the collar. "I haven't worn one of these for at least twenty years."

"Fit is very good," the woman said. She touched Hollis's back with both hands, just below her shoulders. "By-swing shoulders. Inside, elastic ribbons, pull it into shape. This detail is from HD Lee mechanic jacket, early Fifties."

"If the fabric is Japanese, would it have to have been made in Japan?"

"Possible. Build-quality, detailing, are best, but . . . Japan? Tunisia? Even California."

"You don't know where I could find another like it? Or more of this brand?" She didn't, somehow, want to name it.

Their eyes met, in the mirror. "You know 'secret brand'? You understand?"

"I think so," she said, doubtfully.

"This is *very* secret brand," the woman said. "I cannot help you."

"But you have," Hollis said, "thank you," suddenly wanting to be out of the beautifully spare little shop, the musky pong of indigo, "thank you very much." She pulled her coat on, over the Gabriel Hounds jacket. "Thank you. Goodbye."

Outside, in Upper James Street, a boy was hurrying past, a hemisphere of thin black wool pulled down level with his eyes. All black, save for his white, blotchily unshaven face and the pavement-smudged white sole-edges of his black shoes.

"Clammy," she said, reflexively, as he passed her.

"Fucking *hell*," hissed Clammy, in his recently and somewhat oddly acquired West Hollywood American, and shuddered, as if from some sudden massive release of coiled tension. "What are *you* doing here?"

"Looking for denim," she said, then had to point back at the shop, having no idea what it was called, discovering simultaneously that it apparently had no sign. "Gabriel Hounds. They don't have any."

Clammy's eyebrows might have gone up, beneath his black beanic.

"Like this," she said, tugging at the unbuttoned denim jacket beneath her coat.

His eyes narrowed. "Where'd you get that?"

"A friend."

"Next to fucking impossible to find," pronounced Clammy, gravely. As if suddenly taking her, to her amazement and for the first time, seriously.

"Time for a coffee?"

Clammy shivered. "I'm fucking ill," he said, and sniffled noisily. "Had to get out of the studio."

"Herbal tea. And something I have for your immune system."

"Were you Reg's girl, in the band? My mate says you were."

"Never," she said, firmly. "Neither symbolically nor biblically."

Blank.

"They always think the singer must be fucking the guitarist," she clarified.

Clammy smirked, through his cold. "Tabloids said that about me 'n' Arfur."

"Exactly," she said. "A Canadian-made, ginseng-based patent medicine. Herbal tea chaser. Can't hurt."

Clammy, snuffling, nodded his consent.

She hoped he really did have a virus. Otherwise, he was in the early onset of heroin withdrawal. But probably a cold, plus the very considerable stress inherent in working in the studio with Inchmale.

She'd gotten him to swallow five capsules of Cold-FX, taking three herself as a prophylactic measure. It usually didn't seem to do anything, once symptoms were advanced, but the promise of it had gotten him around the corner and into the Starbucks on Golden Square, and she hoped he was prone to the placebo effect. She was herself, according to Inchmale, who was an adamant and outspoken Cold-FX denier. "You have to keep taking them," she said to Clammy, placing the white plastic bottle beside his steaming paper cup of chamomile. "Ignore the instructions. Take three, three times a day."

He shrugged. "Where'd you say you got the Hounds?"

"It belongs to someone I know."

"Where'd they get it, then?"

"I don't know. Someone told me it was a 'secret brand.'"

"Not when you know," he said. "Just very hard to find. Thin on the fucking ground, your Gabriel Hounds."

"Is he starting to talk about rerecording the bed tracks?" She guessed that if she tried to change the subject, he might resist, and she could go along with that, not seem too interested.

Clammy shivered. Nodded.

"Has he talked about doing it in Tucson?"

Clammy frowned, forehead masked behind black cashmere. "Last night." He peered out, through plate glass, at Golden Square, deserted in the rain.

"There's a place there," she said. "One of his secrets. Do it. If he wants to go back later for the overdubs, do it."

"So why's he breaking my balls now, remixing?"

"It's his process," she said.

Clammy rolled his eyes, to heaven or his black cap, then back to her. "You ask your friend where they got the Hounds?"

"Not yet," she said.

He turned on his stool, swung his leg out from beneath the counter. "Hounds," he said. The jeans he wore were black, very narrow. "Twenty-ounce," he said. "Brutal heavy."

"Slubby?"

"You blind?"

"Where did you find them?"

"Melbourne. Girl I met, knew where and when."

"A store?"

"Never in shops," he said. "Except secondhand, and that's not likely."

"I tried Google," she said. "A Mary Stewart book, a band, CD by someone else . . ."

"Go further, on Google, and there's eBay," he said.

"Hounds on eBay?"

"All fake. Almost all. Chinese fakes."

"The Chinese are faking it?"

"Chinese are faking everything," Clammy said. "You get a real Hounds piece on eBay, someone makes an offer high enough to stop it. Never seen an auction for real Hounds run off."

"It's an Australian brand?"

He looked disgusted, which was how he'd looked in whatever few previous brief conversations they'd had. "Fuck no," he said, "it's *Hounds*."

"Tell me about it, Clammy," she said. "I need to know."

6. AFTER THE GYRATORY

The Neo's plastic case reminded Milgrim of one of those electronic stud-finders they sold in hardware stores, its shape simultaneously simple and clumsy, awkward against his ear.

"Gussets?" demanded Rausch, on the Neo.

"He said they needed them. One in each inner thigh."

"What are they?"

"An extra piece of material, between two seams. Usually triangular."

"How do you know that?"

Milgrim considered. "I like details," he said.

"What did he look like?"

"Football player," Milgrim said. "With a sort of mullet."

"A what?"

"I have to go," Milgrim said. "We're at the Hanger Lane Gyratory System."

"Wha—"

Milgrim clicked off.

Pocketing the Neo, he brought himself more upright, feeling the Jankel-armored, four-doored, short-bedded Toyota Hilux's ferocious engine-transplant gather itself for their plunge into England's most famously intimidating roundabout, seven lanes of fiercely determined traffic.

According to Aldous, the Hilux's other driver, this route from Heathrow, decidedly nonoptimal, was part of his job requirement, meant to maintain certain skills one was otherwise unable to practice in London traffic.

Braced for the discomfort of rapid acceleration on run-flat tires, from a standing stop, Milgrim glanced down, to his right, glimpsing the pinstriped thigh of the driver in the adjacent lane, and missed seeing the light change.

Then they were in it, fully gyratory, the driver expertly and repeatedly inserting the Hilux's secretly massive but oddly skittish bulk sideways, it seemed, into absurdly tiny lane-change gaps.

Milgrim had no idea why he'd come to enjoy this so much. Prior to his stay in Basel, he'd have kept his eyes shut for the whole thing; if he'd been expecting it, he'd have upped his medication. But now, grinning, he sat with the red cardboard tube upright between his legs, holding it with the fingertips of both hands, as though it were a joystick.

Then they were out of it. He sighed, deeply if mysteriously satisfied, and felt the driver's glance.

This driver wasn't as talkative as Aldous, but that might have something to do with the urine test. Aldous had never had to administer the urine test, or drive back to London with a vial cooling in his overcoat pocket.

Aldous had told Milgrim all about the Toyota Hilux, about the Jankel armor and the bulletproof glass and the run-flats. "Cartel grade," Aldous had assured him, and unusual for London, at least as far as a silver-gray pickup truck went. Milgrim hadn't asked why these particular features had been deemed necessary, but he suspected that that might be a sensitive area.

Eventually, now, after a much less entertaining stretch of the journey, it became Euston Road, and the beginnings of his idea of actual London.

Like entering a game, a layout, something flat and mazed, arbitrarily but fractally constructed from beautifully detailed but somehow unreal buildings, its order perhaps shuffled since the last time he'd been here. The pixels that comprised it were familiar, but it remained only provisionally mapped, a protean territory, a box of tricks, some possibly even benign.

The run-flats were nasty on mixed pavement, worse on cobbles. He sat back and held on to the red cardboard tube as the driver began taking an endless series of corners, keeping roughly parallel, Milgrim guessed, to Tottenham Court Road. Headed for the heart of town, and Soho.

>>>

Rausch, his translucently short black hair looking like something sprayed from a nozzle, was waiting for them in front of Blue Ant, the driver having phoned ahead as they'd crept along through the traffic on Beak Street. Rausch held a magazine above his head, to ward off the drizzle. He looked characteristically disheveled, but in his own peculiar way. Everything about his personal presentation was intended to convey an effortless concision, but nothing quite did. His tight black suit was wrinkled, bagged at the knees, and in extending his arm above his head to hold the magazine, he'd untucked one side of his white shirt. His glasses, whose frames came equipped with their own squint, would be in need of cleaning.

"Thanks," Milgrim said when the driver pushed a button, unlocking the passenger-side door. The driver said nothing. They were behind a black cab, not quite there yet.

When Milgrim opened the door, it swung out with an alarming, weight-driven velocity, to be stopped by a short pair of heavy nylon straps that prevented it from tearing itself off its hinges. He climbed down, with the red tube and his bag, briefly glimpsing the red tank of fire-extinguishing foam beneath the passenger seat, and tried to bump the door shut with his shoulder. "Ouch," he said. He put the bag down, tucked the tube under his arm, and used the other hand to heave the armored door shut.

Rausch was bending to pick up his bag.

"He's got the pee," Milgrim said, indicating the truck.

Rausch straightened, grimacing fastidiously. "Yes. He takes it to the lab."

Milgrim nodded, looking around at the pedestrian traffic, which tended to interest him in Soho.

"They're waiting," said Rausch.

Milgrim followed him into Blue Ant, Rausch holding a security badge over a metal plate to unlock the door, a single sheet of greenish two-inch-thick glass.

The lobby here suggested some combination of extremely expensive private art school and government defense establishment, though when he thought about it, he'd never been in either. There was a massive central chandelier, constructed from thousands of pairs of discarded prescription eyeglasses, that contributed very handsomely to the art school part, but the Pentagon part (or would it be Whitehall?) was harder to pin down. Half a dozen large plasma screens constantly showed the latest house product, mostly European and Japanese automobile commercials with production budgets dwarfing those of many feature films, while beneath these moved people wearing badges like the one Rausch had used to open the door. These were worn around the neck, on lanyards in various shades, some bearing the repeated logos of various brands or projects. There was a smell of exceptionally good coffee.

Milgrim looked obediently at a large red plus sign, on the wall behind the security counter, while an automated camera moved lazily behind a small square window, like something in a very technical reptile house. He was shortly presented with a large square photograph of himself, very low in resolution, on a hideous chartreuse lanyard minus any branding. As always, he suspected that this was at least partially intended to serve as a high-visibility target, should the need arise. He put it on. "Coffee," he said.

"No," said Rausch, "they're waiting," but Milgrim was already on his way to the lobby's cappuccino station, the source of that fine aroma.

"Piccolo, please," said Milgrim to the blond barista, her hair only slightly longer than Rausch's.

"He's waiting," said Rausch, beside him, tensely stressing the first syllable of "waiting."

"He'll expect me to be able to talk," said Milgrim, watching the girl expertly draw the shot. She foamed milk, then poured an elaborate Valentine's heart into the waiting shot in Milgrim's white cup. "Thank you," he said.

Rausch fumed silently in the elevator to the fourth floor, while Milgrim was mainly concerned with keeping his cup and saucer level and undisturbed.

The doors slid aside, revealing Pamela Mainwaring. Looking, Milgrim thought, like some very tasteful pornographer's idea of "mature," her blond hair magnificently banged.

"Welcome back," she said, ignoring Rausch. "How was South Carolina?"

"Fine," said Milgrim, who held the red cardboard tube in his right hand, the piccolo in his left. He raised the tube slightly. "Got it."

"Very good," she said. "Come in."

Milgrim followed her into a longish room with a long central table. Bigend was seated at the table's far end, a window behind him. He looked like something that had gone wrong on a computer screen, but then Milgrim realized that that was the suit he was wearing, in a weirdly electric cobalt blue.

"If you don't mind," Pamela said, taking the red cardboard tube and handing it on to Milgrim's favorite in Bigend's clothing design team, a French girl, today in a plaid kilt and cashmere pullover. "And the photographs?"

"In my bag," Milgrim said.

While his bag was placed on the table and opened, motorized shades tracked silently shut across the window behind Bigend. Overhead, fixtures came on, illuminating the table, where Milgrim's tracings were being carefully unfurled. He'd remembered to leave his camera atop his clothes, and now it was being passed from hand to hand, up the table.

"Your medication," said Pamela, handing him a fresh bubble-pack.

"Now, then," said Bigend, rising, "be seated."

Milgrim took the chair to the right of Pamela's. They were extremely fine workstation chairs, either Swiss or Italian, and he had to restrain himself from fiddling with the various knobs and levers projecting from beneath the seat.

"I see the Bundeswehr NATO pattern," someone said. "The legs are pure 501."

"But not the box," said the girl in kilt and cashmere. The box, he had learned, was everything, in a pair of jeans, above the top of the leg. "The two small pleats are absent, the rise lower."

"The photographs," said Bigend, from behind her chair. A plasma

screen, above the window he'd been sitting in front of, flared turquoise, around coppery coyote brown, the Formica counter in Edge
City Family Restaurant making itself known in this darkened room
in central London.

"Knee pads," said a young man, American. "Absent. No pockets
for them."

"We hear they have a new pad-retention system," said the French
girl, with a surgeon's seriousness. "But I don't see that here."

They watched, then, silently, while Milgrim's photographs
cycled.

"How tactical are they?" asked Bigend as the first photograph re-
appeared. "Are we looking at a prototype for a Department of Defense
contract?"

A silence. Then: "Streetwear." The French girl, much more confident than the others. "If these are for the military, it isn't the American military."

"He said they needed gussets," said Milgrim.

"What?" asked Bigend, softly.

"He said they were too tight in the thighs. For rappelling."

"Really," said Bigend. "That's good. That's *very* good."

Milgrim allowed himself a first careful sip of his coffee.

7. A HERF GUN
IN FRITH STREET

Bigend was telling a story, over drinks in a crowded Frith Street tapas place Hollis suspected she'd been to before. A story about someone using something called a "herf" gun, high-energy radio frequency, in Moscow, to erase someone else's stored data, in a drive in an adjacent building, on the opposite side of a party wall. So far the best thing about it was that Bigend kept using the British expression "party wall," and she'd always found it mildly if inexplicably comical. The herf gun, he was explaining now, the electromagnetic radiation device, was the size of a backpack, putting out a sixteen-megawatt pulse, and she suddenly found herself afraid, boys being boys, of some punch-line involving accidentally baked internal organs. "Were any animals harmed, Hubertus," she interrupted, "in the making of this anecdote?"

"I like animals," said Milgrim, the American Bigend had introduced at Blue Ant, sounding as though he were more than mildly surprised to discover that he did. He seemed to have only the one name.

After Clammy had decided to go back to the studio, her white plastic bottle of Cold-FX wedged precariously into a back pocket of his Hounds, departing the Golden Square Starbucks during an unexpected burst of weak but thoroughly welcome sunlight, Hollis had gone out to stand for a few moments amid the puddles in Golden Square, before walking (aimlessly, she'd pretended to herself) back up Upper James to Beak Street. Turning right, crossing the first intersection on her side of Beak, she'd found Blue Ant exactly where she remembered it, while simultaneously realizing that she'd been hoping it somehow wouldn't be there.

When she'd pressed the annunciator button, a square pattern of small round holes had said hello. "Hollis Henry, for Hubertus." Was she expected? "Not at all, no."

A handsome, bearded child, in a corduroy sports coat considerably older than he was, had opened the thick glass door almost immediately. "I'm Jacob," he'd said. "We're just trying to find him." He'd offered his hand.

"Hollis," she'd said.

"Come in, please. I'm a huge fan of The Curfew."

"Thank you."

"Would you like coffee, while you wait?" He'd indicated a sort of guardhouse, diagonally striped in artfully battered yellow and black paint, in which a girl with very short blond hair was polishing an espresso maker that looked set to win at Le Mans. "They sent three men from Turin, to install the machine."

"Shouldn't I be being photographed?" she'd asked him. Inchmale hadn't liked Blue Ant's new security measures at all when they'd last come here, to sign contracts. But then the phone in Jacob's right hand had played the opening chords of "Box 1 of 1," one of her least favorite Curfew songs. She'd pretended not to notice. "In the lobby," he'd said to the phone.

"Have you been with Blue Ant long?" she'd asked.

"Two years now. I actually worked on your commercial. We were gutted when it fell through. Do you know Damien?" She didn't. "The director. Gutted, absolutely." But then Bigend had appeared, in his very blue suit, shoulder-draped in the bivouac-tent yardage of the trench coat, and accompanied by Pamela Mainwaring and a nondescript but unshaven man in a thin cotton sportscoat and wrinkled slacks, a black nylon bag slung over his shoulder. "This is Milgrim," Bigend had said, then "Hollis Henry" to the man, who'd said "Hello," but scarcely anything since.

"What kinds of animals?" she asked him now, in a still more naked bid to derail Bigend's narrative.

Milgrim winced. "Dogs," he said, quickly, as though surprised in some guilty pleasure.

"You like dogs?" She was sure that Bigend had been paying whatever lowlife had been wielding that herf gun, though he'd never come right out and tell you that, unless he had some specific reason to.

"I met a very nice dog in Basel," Milgrim said, "at . . ." A microexpression of anxiety. "At a friend's."

"Your friend's dog?"

"Yes," said Milgrim, nodding once, tightly, before taking a sip of his Coke. "You could have used a spark coil generator instead," he said to Bigend, blinking, "made from a VCR tuner. They're smaller."

"Who told you that?" asked Bigend, suddenly differently focused.

"A . . . roommate?" Milgrim extended an index finger, to touch his stack of tiny, elongated white china tapas dishes, as if needing to assure himself that they were there. "He worried about things like that. Out loud. They made him angry." He looked apologetically at Hollis.

"I see," said Bigend, although Hollis certainly didn't.

Now Milgrim took a pharmacist's folded white bubble-pack from an inside jacket pocket, flattened it, and frowned with concentration. All of the pills, Hollis saw, were white as well, white capsules, though of differing sizes. He carefully pushed three of them through the foil backing, put them in his mouth, and washed them down with a swig of Coke.

"You must be exhausted, Milgrim," said Pamela, seated beside Hollis. "You're on east coast time."

"Not too bad," Milgrim said, putting the bubble-pack away. There was a curious lack of definition to his features, Hollis thought, something adolescent, though she guessed he was in his thirties. He struck her as unused to inhabiting his own face, somehow. As amazed to find himself who he was as to find himself here in Frith Street, eating oysters and calamari and dry shaved ham.

"Aldous will take you back to the hotel," Pamela said. Aldous, Hollis guessed, was one of the two black men who'd walked over with them from Blue Ant, carrying long, furled umbrellas with beautifully lacquered cane handles. They were waiting outside now, a few feet apart, silently, keeping an eye on Bigend through the window.

"Where is it?" Milgrim asked.

"Covent Garden," said Pamela.

"I like that one," he said. He folded his napkin, put it beside the white china tower. He looked at Hollis. "Nice meeting you." He nodded, first to Pamela, then to Bigend. "Thanks for dinner." Then he pushed back his chair, bent to pick up his bag, stood up, shouldering the bag, and walked out of the restaurant.

"Where did you find him?" Hollis asked, watching Milgrim, through the window, speak to the one she supposed was Aldous.

"In Vancouver," Bigend said, "a few weeks after you were there."

"What does he do?"

"Translation," Bigend said, "simultaneous and written. Russian. Brilliant with idioms."

"Is he . . . well?" She didn't know how else to put it.

"Convalescing," said Bigend.

"Recovering," said Pamela. "He translates for you?"

"Yes. Though we're beginning to see that he may actually be more useful in other areas."

"Other areas?"

"Good eye for detail," said Bigend. "We have him looking at clothing."

"Doesn't look like a fashion plate."

"That's an advantage, actually," said Bigend.

"Did he notice your suit?"

"He didn't say," said Bigend, glancing down at an International Klein Blue lapel of Early Carnaby proportions. He looked up, pointedly, at her Hounds jacket. "Have you learned anything?" He rolled a piece of the dry, translucent Spanish ham, waiting for her answer. His hand fed the ham to his mouth carefully, as if afraid of being bitten. He chewed.

"It's what the Japanese call a secret brand," Hollis said. "Only more so. This may or may not have been made in Japan. No regular retail outlets, no catalog, no web presence aside from a few cryptic mentions on fashion blogs. And eBay. Chinese pirates have started to fake it, but only badly, the minimal gesture. If a genuine piece turns up on eBay, someone will make an offer that induces the seller to stop the auction." Turning to Pamela. "Where did you get this jacket?"

"We advertised. On fashion fora, mainly. Eventually we found a dealer, in Amsterdam, and met his price. He ordinarily deals in unworn examples of anonymously designed mid-twentieth-century workwear."

"He does?"

"Not unlike rare stamps, apparently, except that you can wear them. A segment of his clientele appreciates Gabriel Hounds, though they're a minority among what we take to be the brand's demographic. We're guessing active global brand-awareness, meaning people who'll go to very considerable trouble to find it, tops out at no more than a few thousand."

"Where did the dealer in Amsterdam get his?"

"He claimed to have bought it as part of a lot of vintage new old stock, from a picker, without having known what it was. Said he'd assumed they were otaku-grade Japanese reproductions of vintage, and that he could probably resell them easily enough."

"A picker?"

"Someone who looks for things to sell to dealers. He said that the picker was German, and a stranger. A cash transaction. Claimed not to recall a name."

"It can't be that big a secret," Hollis said. "I've found two people since breakfast who knew at least as much about it as I've told you."

"And they are?" Bigend leaned forward.

"The Japanese woman at a very pricey specialist shop not far from Blue Ant."

"Ah," he said, his disappointment obvious. "And?"

"A young man, who bought a pair of jeans in Melbourne."

"Really," said Bigend, brightening. "And did he tell you who he bought them from?"

Hollis picked up a slice of the glassine ham, rolled it, dipped it in olive oil. "No. But I think he will."

8. CURETTAGE

Milgrim, cleaning his teeth in the brightly but flatteringly lit bathroom of his small but determinedly upscale hotel room, thought about Hollis Henry, the woman Bigend had brought along to the restaurant. She hadn't seemed to be part of Blue Ant, and she'd also seemed somehow familiar. Milgrim's memory of the past decade or so was porous, unreliable as to sequence, but he didn't think they'd met before. But still, somehow familiar. He switched tips on the mini-brush he was using between his upper rear molars, opting for a conical configuration. He would let Hollis Henry settle down into the mix. In the morning he might find he knew who she was. If not, there was the lobby's complimentary MacBook, in every way preferable to trying to Google on the Neo. Pleasant enough, Hollis Henry, at least if you weren't Bigend. She wasn't entirely pleased with Bigend. He'd gotten that much on the walk to Frith Street.

He switched to a different tool, one that held taut, half-inch lengths of floss between disposable U-shaped bits of plastic. They'd fixed his teeth, in Basel, and had sent him several times to a periodontal specialist. Curettage. Nasty, but now he felt like he had a new mouth, if a very high-maintenance one. The best thing about having had all that done, aside from getting a new mouth, was that he'd gotten to see a little bit of Basel, going out for the treatments. Otherwise, he'd stayed in the clinic, per his agreement.

Finishing with the floss, he brushed his teeth with the battery-powered brush, then rinsed with water from a bottle whose deep-blue glass reminded him of Bigend's suit. Pantone 286, he'd told Milgrim, but not quite. The thing Bigend most seemed to enjoy about the shade, other than the fact that it annoyed people, was that it couldn't quite be re-created on most computer monitors.

He was out of his mouthwash, which contained something they used in tap water on airplanes. You were only allowed to take a little bit of liquid with you on the plane, and he didn't check luggage. He'd been rationing the last of that mouthwash, in Myrtle Beach. He'd ask someone at Blue Ant. They had people who seemed able to find anything, who had doing that as a job description.

He put out the bathroom lights, and stood beside the bed, undressing. The room had slightly too much furniture, including a dressmaker's dummy that had been re-covered with the same brown and tan material as the armchair. He considered putting his pants in the trouser press, but decided against it. He'd shop tomorrow. A chain called Hackett. Like an upscale Banana Republic but with pretensions he knew he didn't understand. He was turning down the bed when the Neo rang, emulating the mechanical bell on an old telephone. That would be Sleight.

"Leave the phone in your room tomorrow," Sleight said. "Turned on, on the charger." He sounded annoyed.

"How are you, Oliver?"

"The company that makes these things has gone out of business," Sleight said. "So we need to do some reprogramming tomorrow." He hung up.

"Good night," Milgrim said, looking at the Neo in his hand. He put it on the bedside table, climbed into bed in his underwear, and pulled the covers to his chin. He turned out the light. Lay there running his tongue over the backs of his teeth. The room was slightly too warm, and he was aware, somehow, of the dressmaker's dummy.

And listened to, or at any rate sensed, the background frequency that was London. A different white noise.

9. FUCKSTICK

When she opened Cabinet's front door, pinstriped Robert was not there to help her with it.

Due, she saw immediately, to the jackbooted advent of Heidi Hyde, once the Curfew's drummer, in whose assorted luggage Robert was now draped, clearly terrified, back in the lift-grotto, next to the vitrine housing Inchmale's magic ferret. Heidi, beside him, was fully as tall and possibly as broad at the shoulders. Unmistakably hers, that direly magnificent raptorial profile, and just as unmistakably furious.

"Was she expected?" Hollis quietly asked whichever tortoise-framed boy was on the desk.

"No," he said, just as quietly, passing her the key to her room. "Mr. Inchmale phoned, minutes ago, to alert us." Eyes wide behind the brown frames. He had something of the affect, beneath his hotel-man's game-face, of a tornado survivor.

"It'll be okay," Hollis assured him.

"What's wrong with this fucking thing?" Heidi demanded, loudly.

"It gets confused," Hollis said, walking up to them, with a nod and reassuring smile for Robert.

"Miss Henry." Robert looked pale.

"You mustn't press it more than once," Hollis said to Heidi. "Takes it longer to make up its mind."

"Fuck," said Heidi, from some bottomless pit of frustration, causing Robert to wince. Her hair was dyed goth black, signaling the warpath, and Hollis guessed she'd done it herself.

"I didn't know you were coming," Hollis said.

"Neither did I," said Heidi, grimly. Then: "It's fuckstick."

At which Hollis understood that Heidi's unlikely sub-Hollywood marriage was over. Heidi's exes lost their names, at termination, to be known henceforth only by this blanket designation.

"Sorry to hear that," Hollis said.

"Running a pyramid scheme," Heidi said as the lift arrived. "What the fuck is *this*?"

"The elevator." Hollis opened the articulated gate, gesturing Heidi in.

"Please, go ahead," Robert said. "I'll bring your bags."

"Get in the fucking elevator," commanded Heidi. "Get. In." She backed him into the lift with sheer enraged presence. Hollis nipped in after him, raising the brass-hinged mahogany bench against the back wall for more room.

Heidi, up close, smelled of sweat, airport rage, and musty leather. She was wearing a jacket that Hollis remembered from their touring days. Once black, its seams were worn the color of dirty parchment.

Robert managed to push a button. They started up, the lift complaining audibly at the weight.

"Fucking thing's going to kill us all," said Heidi, as if finding the idea not entirely unattractive.

"What room is Heidi in?" Hollis asked him.

"Next to yours."

"Good," said Hollis, with more enthusiasm than she felt. That would be the one with the yellow silk chaise longue. She'd never understood the theme. Not that she understood the theme of her own, but she sensed it had one. The room with the yellow chaise longue seemed to be about spies, sad ones, in some very British sense, and seedy political scandal. And reflexology.

Hollis opened the gate, when the lift finally reached their floor, then held the various fire doors for Heidi and the heavily burdened Robert. Heidi seethed her way through the windowless green mini-hallways, body language conveying a universal dissatisfaction. Hollis saw that Robert had Heidi's room key tucked for safekeeping between two fingers. She took it from him, its tassels moss green.

"You're right next to me," she said to Heidi, unlocking and opening the door. She shooed Heidi in, thinking of bulls, china shops. "Just put everything down," she said to Robert, quietly. "I'll take care of the rest." She relieved him of two amazingly heavy cardboard cartons, each about the size required to contain a human head. He began immediately to unsling Heidi's various luggage. She slipped him a five-pound note.

"Thank you, Miss Henry."

"Thank you, Robert." She closed the door in his relieved face.

"What," demanded Heidi, "the fuck is this?"

"Your room," said Hollis, who was arranging the luggage along a wall. "It's a private club that Inchmale joined."

"A club for *what*? What's *that*?" Indicating a large framed silkscreen that Hollis herself found one of the least peculiar articles of decor.

"A Warhol. I think." Had Warhol covered the Profumo scandal?

"I should have fucking known Inchmale would come up with something like this. Where is he?"

"Not here," Hollis said. "He rented a house in Hampstead, when Angelina and the baby came from Argentina."

Heidi hefted a wide-based crystal decanter, unstoppered it, sniffed. "Whiskey," she said.

"The clear one's gin," Hollis advised, "not water."

Heidi splashed three fingers of Cabinet Scotch into a highball glass, drank it off at a go, shuddered, set the decanter down and flicked the crystal stopper back into its neck with a dangerously sharp click. She had a spooky gift for aiming things; had never lost a game of darts in her life, but didn't play darts, just threw them.

"Do you want to talk about it?" Hollis asked.

Heidi shrugged out of her leather jacket, tossed it aside, and pulled her black T-shirt off, revealing an olive-drab bra that looked as combat-ready as any bra Hollis had ever seen.

"Nice bra."

"Israeli," said Heidi. She looked around, taking in the contents of the room. "Jesus Christ," she said. "The wallpaper's like Hendrix's pants."

"I think it's satin." Vertically striped, in green, burgundy, ecru, and black.

"What I fucking said," said Heidi, giving her Israeli army bra a tug, and sat down on the yellow silk chaise longue. "Why did we stop smoking?"

"Because it was bad for us."

Heidi sighed, explosively. "He's in jail," she said, "fuckstick. No bond. He was doing something with other people's money."

"I thought that's what producers do."

"Not like that, it isn't."

"Are you in any trouble yourself?"

"Are you kidding? I've got a prenup thicker than fuckstick's long. It's his problem. I just needed to get the fuck out of Dodge."

"I never understood why you married him."

"It was an experiment. What about you? What are you doing here?"

"Working for Hubertus Bigend," Hollis said, noting just how little she enjoyed saying it.

Heidi's eyes widened. "Fuck me. That asshole? You couldn't stand him. Creeped you totally out. Why?"

"I guess I need the money."

"How bad did the crash do you?"

"About half."

Heidi nodded. "Did everybody about half. Unless you had some-body like fuckstick doing your investing for you."

"And you didn't?"

"Are you kidding? Separation of church and fucking state. Always. I never thought he had any sense that way anyway. Other people did, though. Know what?"

"What?"

"The salt of the fucking earth never tells you it's the salt of the fucking earth. People who get scammed, they're all people who don't know that."

"I think I'll have a whiskey."

"Be my guest," said Heidi. Then smiled. "Good to fucking see you." And started to cry.

10. EIGENBLICH

Milgrim woke, took his medication, showered, shaved, brushed his teeth, dressed, and left the Neo charging but turned on. The U.K. plug-adaptor was larger than the phone's charger. Keeping the dressmaker's dummy out of his field of vision, he left the room.

In the silent Japanese elevator, descending three floors, he considered pausing to Google Hollis Henry on the lobby MacBook, but someone was using it when he got there.

He wasn't always entirely comfortable with the lobby here, what there was of it. He felt like he might look as though he were here to steal something, though aside from his wrinkled post-flight clothing he was fairly certain he didn't. And really, he thought, stepping out into Monmouth Street and tentative sunlight, he wouldn't. Had no reason to. Three hundred pounds in a plain manila envelope in the inside pocket of his jacket, and nothing, today, telling him what he needed to do with it. Still a novel situation, to a man of his history.

Addictions, he thought, turning right, toward Seven Dials' namesake obelisk, started out like magical pets, pocket monsters. They did extraordinary tricks, showed you things you hadn't seen, were fun. But came, through some gradual dire alchemy, to make decisions for you. Eventually, they were making your most crucial life-decisions. And they were, his therapist in Basel had said, less intelligent than goldfish.

He went to Caffè Nero, a tastier alternate-reality Starbucks, crowded now. He ordered a latte and a croissant, the latter shipped frozen from France, baked here. He approved of that. Saw a small round table being vacated by a woman in a pinstriped suit and swiftly occupied it, looking out at the Vidal Sassoon, across the little roundabout, where young hairdressers were going in to work.

Eating his croissant, he wondered what Bigend might be up to with designer combat pants. He was a good listener, careful to not let people know it, but Bigend's motives and modus eluded him. They could seem almost aggressively random.

Military contracting was essentially recession-proof, according to Bigend, and particularly so in America. That was a part of it, and perhaps even the core of it. Recession-proofing. And Bigend seemed centered on one area of military contracting, the one in which, Milgrim supposed, Blue Ant's strategic skill set was most applicable. Blue Ant was learning everything it could, and very quickly, about the contracting, design, and manufacture of military clothing. Which seemed, from what Milgrim had seen so far, to be a very lively business.

And Milgrim, for whatever reason or lack of one, was along for the ride. That was what Myrtle Beach had been about.

Volunteer armies, the French girl had said, the one who'd worn the plaid kilt at yesterday's meeting, in an earlier PowerPoint presentation that Milgrim had found quite interesting, required volunteers, the bulk of them young men. Who might otherwise be, for instance, skateboarding, or at least wearing clothing suggestive of skateboarding. And male streetwear generally, over the past fifty years or so, she said, had been more heavily influenced by the design of military clothing than by anything else. The bulk of the underlying design code of the twenty-first-century male street was the code of the previous mid-century's military wear, most of it American. The rest of it was work wear, most of that American as well, whose manufacture had coevolved with the manufacture of military clothing, sharing elements of the same design code, and team sportswear.

But now, according to the French girl, that had reversed itself. The military needed clothing that would appeal to those it needed to recruit. Every American service branch, she said, illustrating each with a PowerPoint slide, had its own distinctive pattern of camouflage. The Marine Corps, she said, had made quite a point of patenting theirs (up close, Milgrim had found it too jazzy).

There was a law in America that prohibited the manufacture of American military clothing abroad.

And that was where Bigend, Milgrim knew, hoped to come in. Things that were manufactured in America didn't necessarily have to be designed there. Outerwear and sporting-goods manufacturers, along with a few specialist uniform manufacturers, competed for contracts to manufacture clothing for the U.S. military, but that clothing had previously been designed *by* the U.S. military. Who now, the French girl had said, somewhat breathlessly, as though she were closing in on a small animal in some forest clearing, clearly lacked the newly requisite design skills to do that. Having invented so much of contemporary masculine cool in the midcentury, they found themselves competing with their own historical product, reiterated as streetwear. They needed help, the French girl had said, her mouse clicks summoning a closing flurry of images, and they knew it.

He sipped his latte, looking out, watching people pass, wondering if he could see the French girl's thesis proven in the garments of this morning's pedestrians. If you thought of it as a kind of pervasive subtext, he decided, you could.

"Excuse me. Would you mind if I shared the table?"

Milgrim looked up at this smiling American, ethnically Chinese, in her black sweatshirt, a small plain gold cross, gold-chained, worn atop it, one white plastic barrette visible, as some unsleeping module of addict street-alertness, hardwired to his very core, crisply announced: cop.

He blinked. "Of course. You're welcome." Feeling muscles in his thighs bunching, tight, readying themselves for the dash out the door. Malfunction, he told the module. Post-acute withdrawal syndrome. Flashback: His limbic brain was grooved for this, like the tracks of the wheels of Conestoga wagons, worn ankle-deep in sandstone.

She put her sacklike white pleather purse on the table, her plastic-lidded pale blue Caffè Nero cup beside it, pulled out the chair opposite him, and sat. Smiled.

Embroidered in white, on the black sweatshirt, were the crescent moon and palm tree of the South Carolina state flag, a bit larger than one of Ralph Lauren's polo ponies. Milgrim's buried module instantly extruded an entire DEW line of arcane cop-sensing apparatus.

Paranoia, his therapist had told him, was too much information. He had that now as the woman dipped into her purse, brought up a matte silver phone, opened it, and furrowed her brow. "Messages," she said.

Milgrim looking straight into the infinitely deep black pupil that was the phone's camera. "Uh-oh," she said, "I see I have to run. Thanks anyway!" And up, purse under her arm, and out into Seven Dials.

Leaving her drink.

Milgrim picked it up. Empty. The white lid smudged with a dark lipstick she hadn't been wearing.

Through the window he saw her pass an overflowing trash canister, from which she'd likely plucked this cup for her prop. Quickly crossing the intersection, toward Sassoon. Vanishing around a corner.

He stood, straightening his jacket, and walked out, not looking around. Back up Monmouth Street, toward his hotel. As he neared it, he crossed Monmouth diagonally, still moving at a calculatedly casual pace, and entered a sort of brick tunnel that led to Neal's Yard, a courtyard gotten up as a kind of New Age mini-Disneyland. He bolted through this so quickly that people looked after him. Out into Shorts Garden, another street.

Purposeful pace now, but nothing to attract attention.

All the while aware of his addiction, awakened by the flood of stress chemicals, urgently advising him that something to take the edge off would be a very good idea indeed. It was, some newer part of him thought, amazed, like having a Nazi tank buried in your back yard. Grown over with grass and dandelions, but then you noticed its engine was still idling.

Not today, he told the Nazis in their buried tank, heading for Covent Garden tube station through an encyclopedic anthology of young people's shoe stores, spring's sneakers tinted like jelly beans.

Not good, another part of him was saying, not good.

As much as he wished to appear relaxed, the usual crew of beggars, floating in solution on the pavement in front of the station, faded at his approach. They saw something. He had again become as they were.

He saw Covent Garden as if from a great height, the crowd in Long Acre drawing back from him like magnetized iron filings.

Take the stairs, advised the autonomic pilot. He did, head down, never looking back, a unit in the spiral human chain.

Next he'd take the first train to Leicester Square, the shortest journey in the entire system. Then back, without exiting, having assured himself he wasn't being followed. He knew how to do that, but then there were all these cameras, in their smoked acrylic spheres, like knockoff Courrèges light fixtures. There were cameras literally everywhere, in London. So far, he'd managed not to think about them. He remembered Bigend saying they were a symptom of auto-immune disease, the state's protective mechanisms 'roiding up into something actively destructive, chronic; watchful eyes, eroding the healthy function of that which they ostensibly protected.

Did anyone protect him now?

He took himself through what one did in order to determine that one wasn't being followed. While he did so, he anticipated his immediate return to this station. Imagined his ascent in the elevator's dead air, where a dead voice would repeatedly advise him to have his ticket or pass ready.

He would be calmer, then.

Then restart the day, as planned. Go to Hackett in King Street, buy pants and a shirt.

Not good, said the other voice, causing his shoulders to narrow, bone and sinew tightening almost audibly.

Not good.

11. UNPACKING

Heidi's room looked like the aftermath of a not-very-successful airplane bombing. Something that blew open every suitcase in the luggage compartment without bringing the plane down. Hollis had seen this many times before, touring with the Curfew, and took it to be a survival mechanism, a means of denying the soulless suction of sequential hotel rooms. She'd never actually seen Heidi distribute her things, nest-build. She guessed it was unconscious, accomplished in the course of an instinctive trance, like a dog walking tight circles in grass before it lay down to sleep. She was impressed now, to see how effectively Heidi had created her own space, pushing back whatever it was that Cabinet's designers had intended the room to express.

"Fuck," said Heidi, ponderously, apparently having slept, or passed out, in her Israeli army bra. Hollis, who had taken the key with her when she'd left, saw that there was barely a finger of whiskey left in the decanter. Heidi didn't drink often, but when she did, she did. She lay now under a wrinkled pile of laundry, including, Hollis saw, several magenta linen table napkins and a cheap Mexican beach towel striped like a serape. Apparently Heidi had dumped the contents of the laundry hopper at Chez Fuckstick into one of her bags, departing, then pulled it out here. It was this she'd slept under, not Cabinet's bedclothes.

"Breakfast?" Hollis began picking up and sorting the things on the bed. There was a large freezer-bag full of small, sharp-looking tools, fine-tipped brushes, tiny tins of paint, bits of white plastic. As if Heidi had adopted a twelve-year-old boy. "What's this?"

"Therapy," Heidi croaked, then made a sound like a vulture about to bring up something too putrid to digest, but Hollis had heard it before. She thought she remembered who Heidi had learned it from, a supernaturally pale German keyboardist with prematurely aged tattoos, their outlines blurred like felt pen on toilet paper. She put the bag and its mysterious contents on the dresser and picked up the phone, French, early twentieth century, but covered entirely in garishly reptilian Moroccan beading, like the business end of a hookah in the Grand Bazaar. "Pot of coffee, black, two cups," she said to the room service voice, "rack of dry toast, large orange juice. Thanks." She removed an ancient Ramones T-shirt from what was then revealed as a foot-tall white china reflexology model, an ear, complexly mapped in red. She put the T-shirt back, arranging it so that the band's logo was optimally displayed.

"What about you?" asked Heidi, from beneath her laundry.

"What about me?"

"Men," said Heidi.

"None," said Hollis.

"What about the performance artist. Jumped off skyscrapers wearing that flying-squirrel suit. He was okay. Hot, too. Darrell?"

"Garreth," said Hollis, probably for the first time in over a year, not wanting to.

"Is that why you're here? He was English."

"No," said Hollis. "I mean yes, he was, but that's not why I'm here."

"You met him in Canada. Bigend introduce you? I didn't meet him till later."

"No," Hollis said, dreading Heidi's skill at this other, more painful unpacking. "They never met."

"You don't do jocks," said Heidi.

"He was different," said Hollis.

"They all are," said Heidi.

"Was fuckstick?"

"No," said Heidi. "Not that way. That was me, trying to be different. He was as undifferent as you can get, but he was somebody else's undifferent. I just had this feeling that I could step into somebody else's shoes. Put all the tour stuff in boxes. Shop at malls. Drive a car

I'd never have thought of driving. Get a fucking break, you know? Time-out."

"You didn't seem very happy with it, when I saw you in L.A."

"He turned out to be a closet creative. I married a tax lawyer. He started trying to produce. Indie stuff. He was starting to mention directing."

"And he's in jail now?"

"No bond. We had the FBI in the office. Wearing those jackets with 'FBI' on the back. They looked really good. Great look for a small production. But he couldn't be on the set."

"But you're okay, legally?"

"I had Inchmale's lawyer, in New York. I won't even lose the share of his legitimate property I'm entitled to as the ex. Should they leave him any, which is unlikely. But seriously, fuck it."

Breakfast arrived, Hollis taking the tray from the Italian girl at the door, with a wink. Tip her later.

Heidi batted her way out of the laundry pile. Sat on the edge of the bed, pulling on an enormous hockey jersey which Hollis, born without the gene for following team sports, recalled as having belonged to someone quite famous. Heidi definitely did jocks, though only if they were sufficiently crazy. Drumming for the Curfew, she'd had a spectacularly bad string of boxers, however good it might have been for publicity. She'd put one of them out cold with a single punch, at a pre-Oscars party. Very frequently now, Hollis was grateful for having had a pre-YouTube career.

"I never got what he did, Garret," said Heidi, pouring herself half a cup of coffee, then topping it up with what remained in the whiskey decanter.

"Garreth. Do you think that's a good idea?"

Heidi shrugged, her shoulders almost lost within the jersey. "You know me. Get this down and I'm good for six months of mineral water. Actually what I need now's a gym. Serious one. What did he do?"

"I'm not sure I could explain that," Hollis said, pouring her own coffee. "But I made a very firm agreement never to try."

"Crook?"

"No," said Hollis, "though some of what he did involved breaking laws. You know Banksy, the graffiti artist?"

"Yeah?"

"He liked Banksy. Identified with him. They're both from Bristol."

"But he wasn't a graffiti artist."

"I think he thought he was. Just not with paint."

"With what?"

"History," said Hollis.

Heidi looked unconvinced.

"He worked with an older man, someone with a lot of resources. The old man decided what should be done, what the gesture would be, then Garreth worked out the best way to do it. And not get caught. Dramaturge to the old man's playwright, sort of, but sometimes actor as well."

"So what was the problem?"

"Scary. Not that I didn't approve of what they were doing. But it was scarier than Bigend's stuff. I need the world to have a surface, the same surface everyone sees. I don't like feeling like I'm always about to fall through, into something else. Look what happened to you."

Heidi picked up a triangle of dry toast, considering it the way a potential suicide might consider a razor. "You said they weren't crooks."

"They broke laws, but they weren't crooks. But by the very nature of what they did, they constantly made enemies. He came to L.A., we hung out. I was starting the book. He went back to Europe. Saw him again when I was over here to sign the car contract."

"I got a proxy." Biting off a corner of toast, chewing it dubiously.

"I wanted to be here." Hollis smiled. "Then he came back with me, to New York. He wasn't working. But then they were gearing up again. It was the run-up to Obama's election. They were getting ready to do something."

"What?"

"I don't know. If I did, and kept my promise, I couldn't tell you anyway. I just got really busy with the book. He wasn't around as much. Then he just wasn't around."

"Miss him?"

Hollis shrugged.

"You're a difficult fit, you know that?"

Hollis nodded.

"Must make it harder." Heidi got up, carried her whiskey and coffee into the bathroom, and splashed it into the sink. She came back and poured herself more coffee. "Feel like you're on hold?"

"Definitely."

"No good," said Heidi. "Call him. See what's up. Work through it."

"No."

"Got a number?"

"For emergencies. Only."

"What kind?"

"Only if having known them ever got me into trouble."

"Use it anyway."

"No."

"Pathetic," said Heidi. "What the fuck is *that*?" She was staring into the bathroom.

"Your shower."

"You're kidding."

"Wait'll you see mine. What's in those two boxes?" Pointing, where she'd put them down after taking them from Robert the night before. Hoping to change the topic. "A pair of concrete blocks?"

"Ashes," Heidi said, "cremains."

"Whose?"

"Jimmy's." The Curfew's bass player. "There was nobody to claim them. He always said he wanted to be buried in Cornwall, remember?"

"No," said Hollis. "Why Cornwall?"

"Fuck if I know. Maybe he'd decided it was the opposite of Kansas."

"That's a lot of ashes."

"My mom's too."

"Your mother's?"

"I never got around to doing anything with them. They were in the basement, with my tour stuff. I couldn't leave 'em there with fuckstick, could I? I'll take 'em both to Cornwall. Jimmy never had a mother anyway."

"Okay," said Hollis, unable to think of anything else to say.

"Where the fuck is Cornwall?"

"I can show you. On a map."

"I need a fucking shower," said Heidi.

12. COMPLIANCE TOOL

Bigend's office, when Milgrim was finally ushered in, was window-less and surprisingly small. Perhaps it wasn't that specifically his office, Milgrim thought. It didn't look like an office anyone actually worked in.

The Swedish boy who'd brought Milgrim in put a gray folder on the teak desk and left silently. There was nothing else on the desk except a shotgun, one that appeared to have been made from solidi-fied Pepto-Bismol.

"What's that?" Milgrim asked.

"The maquette for one of the early takes on a collaboration be-tween Taser and Mossberg, the shotgun manufacturer." Bigend was wearing disposable plastic gloves, the kind that came on a roll, like cheap sandwich bags. "A compliance tool."

"Compliance tool?"

"That's what they call it," said Bigend, picking the thing up with one hand and turning it, so that Milgrim could see it from various angles. It looked weightless. Hollow, some sort of resin. "I have it because I'm trying to decide whether a collaboration like this is the equivalent of Roberto Cavalli designing a trench coat for H&M."

"I've been made," said Milgrim.

"Made?" Bigend looked up.

"A cop took my picture this morning."

"A cop? What kind?"

"A Chinese-American missionary-looking one. Her sweatshirt was embroidered with the South Carolina state flag."

"Sit down," said Bigend.

Milgrim sat, his Hackett shopping bag on his lap.

"How do you know she was a cop?" Bigend removed the glove-baggies, crumpled them.

"I just did. Do. Not necessarily in the sense of a law enforcement officer, but I wouldn't put it past her."

"You've been shopping," said Bigend, looked at the Hackett bag. "What did you buy?"

"Pants," said Milgrim, "a shirt."

"Ralph Lauren shops at Hackett, I'm told," said Bigend. "That's an extremely complex piece of information, conceptually. Whether it's true or not." He smiled. "Do you like to shop there?"

"I don't understand it," Milgrim said, "but I like their pants. Some of their plainer shirts."

"What don't you understand?"

"The English football thing."

"How so?"

"Are they *serious* about that, Hackett?"

"Exactly what I value in you. You go effortlessly to the core."

"But are they?"

"Some would maintain that a double negative amounts to a positive. Where did this person take your picture?"

"Coffee place near the hotel. Seven Dials."

"And you have informed—?"

"You."

"Don't mention this to anyone else. Except Pamela. I'll inform her."

"Not Oliver?"

"No," said Bigend, "definitely not Oliver. Have you spoken with him today?"

"He had me leave my phone in the room, charging and turned on. He said that he needed to reprogram it. I haven't gone back there yet."

Bigend stared at the pink shotgun.

"Why is it that pink?" asked Milgrim.

"Output from a 3-D printer. I don't know why they use pink. Seems to be the default shade. Those phones are an Oliver project.

When you use one, you aren't to consider it secure, whether for voice, text, or e-mail. But since this is England, really, you aren't to consider any phone secure. Understood?"

"You don't trust Oliver?"

"I don't," said Bigend. "What I want you to do, now, is to go about your business, as though you hadn't noticed being photographed. Simply that."

"What *is* my business?" asked Milgrim.

"Did you like Hollis Henry?"

"She seemed . . . familiar?"

"She was a singer. In a band. The Curfew."

Milgrim remembered a large silvery black-and-white photograph. A poster. A younger Hollis Henry with her knee up, her foot on something. A tweed miniskirt, that seemed mostly to have unraveled, drawn taut. Where had he seen that?

"You'll be working with her," said Bigend. "A different project."

"Translating?"

"I doubt it. This one is apparel-based as well."

"Back in Vancouver," Milgrim began, then stopped.

"Yes?"

"I found a woman's purse. There was quite a lot of money in it. A phone. A wallet with cards. Keys. I put the purse and the wallet and the cards and the keys in a mailbox. I kept the money and the phone. You started phoning. I didn't know you. We started talking."

"Yes," said Bigend.

"That's why I'm here today, isn't it?

"It is," said Bigend.

"Whose phone was that?"

"Do you remember that there was something else in that purse? A black plastic unit, roughly twice the size of the phone?"

Milgrim did now. He nodded.

"That was a scrambler. It belonged to me. The person whose purse you found was an employee of mine. I wanted to know who had her phone. That was why I tried the number."

"Why did you keep phoning back?"

"Because I became curious about you. And because you kept answering. Because we began to have a conversation that led eventually to our meeting, and, as you say, to your being here today."

"Did it cost more to have me here today than . . ." Milgrim thought about it. "More than the Toyota Hilux?" He felt as though his therapist were watching him.

Bigend's head tilted slightly. "I'm not certain, but it probably did. Why?"

"That's my question," said Milgrim. "Why?"

"Because I knew about the clinic in Basel. It's highly controversial, very expensive. I was curious as to whether or not it would work, with you."

"Why?" asked Milgrim.

"Because," Bigend said, "I'm a curious person, and can afford to satisfy my curiosity. The doctors who examined you in Vancouver were not optimistic, to put it mildly. I like a challenge. And even in the condition I found you in, in Vancouver, you were an exceptional translator. Later"—and Bigend smiled—"it became evident that you have an interesting eye for a number of things."

"I'd be dead now, wouldn't I?"

"My understanding is that you probably would be, if you'd been withdrawn from the drug too quickly," Bigend said.

"Then what do I owe you?"

Bigend reached for the shotgun, as though he were about to tap it with his finger, then caught himself. "Not your life," he said. "That's a by-product. Of my curiosity."

"All that money?"

"The cost of my curiosity."

Milgrim's eyes stung.

"This is not a situation in which you're required to thank me," Bigend said. "I hope you understand that."

Milgrim swallowed. "Yes," he said.

"I do want you to work with Hollis on this other project," Bigend said. "Then we'll see."

"See what?"

"What we see," said Bigend, reaching across the shotgun for the gray folder. "Go back to the hotel. We'll phone you."

Milgrim stood, lowering the Hackett bag, which had been covering the startled-looking digital portrait of himself he wore around his neck, on its lanyard of chartreuse nylon.

"Why are you wearing that?"

"It's required," said Milgrim. "I don't work here."

"Remind me to fix that," said Bigend, opening the gray folder, which contained a thick sheaf of what appeared to be clippings from Japanese magazines.

Milgrim, who was already closing the door behind him, said nothing.

13. MUSKRAT

They ate muskrat," Heidi said as they walked in gritty sunlight to Selfridges, for her appointment with Hollis's stylist, "but only on Fridays."

"Who?"

"Belgians. Got the church to say it was okay, because muskrats live in the water. Like fish."

"That's ridiculous."

"It's in the *Larousse Gastronomique*," said Heidi. "Look it up. Or just look at your boy. You can see he's had some."

Hollis's iPhone rang as they were nearing Oxford Street. She looked at the screen. Blue Ant.

"Hello?"

"Hubertus."

"You eat muskrat, Fridays?"

"Why do you ask?"

"I'm defending you from a racial slur."

"Where are you?"

"On my way to Selfridges with a friend. She's getting her hair cut." Getting Heidi the last-minute appointment had required epic stylist-suckery, but Hollis was a firm believer in the therapeutic power of the right haircut. And Heidi, for her part, now seemed neither hungover nor jet-lagged.

"What are you doing while she does that?" asked Bigend.

Hollis debated telling Bigend she was getting a cut herself, but it didn't seem worth it. "What do you have in mind?"

"The friend we had tapas with," he said. "I want you two to talk."

The translator, the one who liked dogs. "Why?"

"That will emerge. Talk while your friend has her hair cut. I'll have Aldous run him over now. Where shall he meet you?"

"The food hall, I suppose," said Hollis. "Patisserie."

He hung up.

"Shit," said Hollis.

"Muskrat," said Heidi, pulling Hollis in beside her and taking on the remorseless afternoon pedestrian-flow of Oxford Street like a broad-shouldered icebreaker, homing on Selfridges. "You really are working for him."

"I am that," said Hollis.

> > >

"Hollis?"

She looked up. "Milgrim," she said, remembering his name, which Bigend had been unwilling to use over the phone. He'd shaved, and looked rested. "I'm having a salad. Would you like something?"

"Do they have croissants?"

"I'm sure they do." There was something she found deeply peculiar about his affect, even in this brief an exchange. He seemed genuinely mild, amiable, but also singularly alert, in some skewed way, as if there were something else looking out, around corners, swift and peripheral.

"I think I'll have one," he said, quite seriously, and she watched him walk to the nearby counter. He wore darker trousers today, the same thin cotton sportscoat.

He returned with his white tray. A croissant, a small rectangular slice of some compacted meat product in a pastry shell, and a cup of black coffee.

"You're a Russian translator, Mr. Milgrim?" she asked as he put down the tray and took a seat.

"Just Milgrim," he said. "I'm not Russian."

"But a translator of Russian?"

"Yes," he said.

"Do you do that for Hubertus? For Blue Ant?"

"I'm not a Blue Ant employee. I suppose I'm freelance. I've done some translation for Hubertus. Mostly literary." He looked hungrily at his tray.

"Please," she said, picking up her salad fork. "Go ahead. We can talk afterward."

"I missed lunch," he said. "I have to eat, with my medication."

"Hubertus mentioned you were recovering from something."

"Drugs," he said. "I'm an addict. Recovering." And the peripheral thing was right there, peering around some inner angle, taking her measure.

"Which ones?"

"Prescription tranquillizers. That sounds respectable, doesn't it?"

"I suppose it does," she said, "although I don't imagine it makes it any easier."

"It doesn't," he said, "but I hadn't had a prescription for anything for quite a long time. I was a street addict." He cut a neat slice from one end of his cold meat tart.

"I had a friend who was a heroin addict," she said. "He died."

"I'm sorry," he said. He began to eat.

"It was years ago." She picked at her salad.

"What do you do for Hubertus?" he asked

"I'm freelance as well," she said. "But I'm not sure what I do. Not yet."

"He's like that," he said. Something caught his attention, across the hall. "Foliage green, those pants."

"Whose?"

"He's gone. Do you know coyote brown?"

"Who?"

"It was the fashionable shade in U.S. military equipment. Foliage green is newer, trending. Alpha green was up briefly, but foliage green is on top now."

"U.S. military equipment comes in fashion shades?"

"It certainly does," said Milgrim. "Hubertus doesn't talk with you about that?"

"No."

He was still trying to find the pants he'd glimpsed, in the distance. "It's not a shade you'll see much of this year, commercially. Next year, probably. I don't even know the Pantone number." He brought his attention back to his meat tart. Quickly finished it. "I'm sorry," he said. "I'm not very good with new people. At first."

"I wouldn't say that. You get right down to things, it seems to me."

"That's what he says," said Milgrim, blinking, and she guessed he meant Bigend. "I saw your picture," he said. "A poster of you. I think on St. Mark's Place. A used record store."

"That's a very old picture."

Milgrim nodded, tore his croissant in half, began to butter it.

"Does he talk to you about denim?"

Milgrim looked up, mouth full of croissant, shook his head.

"Gabriel Hounds?"

Milgrim swallowed. "Who?"

"It's a very secretive jeans line. That seems to be what I do, for Hubertus."

"But what do you do?"

"I investigate it. I try to find out where it comes from. Who makes it. Why people like it."

"Why do people like it?"

"Possibly because it's almost impossible to find."

"Is that it?" asked Milgrim, looking at her jacket.

"Yes."

"Well made. But it's not military."

"Not that I know of. Why is he interested in fashion, now?"

"He isn't. In any ordinary sense. That I know of." And the obliquely-looking-out thing was there again, around that interior corner, and she felt its intelligence. "Do you know there's a trade show specifically for manufacturers who hope to produce equipment for the Marine Corps?"

"I didn't. Have you been?"

"No," said Milgrim, "I missed it. It's in South Carolina. I was just there. In South Carolina."

"What is it, exactly, that you do, for Hubertus, around clothing? Are you a designer? A marketer?"

"No," said Milgrim. "I notice things. I'm good with detail. I didn't know that. It was something he pointed out to me, in Vancouver."

"Did you stay with him? In that penthouse?"

Milgrim nodded.

"In the room with the maglev bed?"

"No," Milgrim said, "I had a small room. I needed . . . focus." He finished the last of his croissant, took a sip of coffee. "I was, I think the word is 'institutionalized'? I wasn't comfortable with too much space. Too many options. Then he sent me to Basel."

"Switzerland?"

"To begin my recovery. If you don't mind me asking, why are you working for him now?"

"I ask myself that," she said. "It's not the first time, and after the first time, I certainly didn't want there to be a second time. But it proved weirdly lucrative, that first time, in a very roundabout way, a way that had nothing to do with what I was supposedly doing for him. Then I lost a lot of that money in the crash, hadn't found anything else I wanted to do, and suddenly he was insisting I do this. I'm not entirely comfortable with it."

"I know."

"You do?"

"I can tell," said Milgrim.

"Why are you working for him?"

"I need a job," said Milgrim. "And because . . . he paid for the clinic, in Basel. My recovery."

"He sent you to detox?"

"It was very expensive," he said. "More than an armored truck. Cartel grade." He straightened his knife and fork on the white plate, amid crumbs. "It's confusing," he said. "Now he wants me to work with you." He looked up from the plate, both elements of his oddly fragmented self seeming for the first time to see her simultaneously. "Why don't you sing?"

"Because I don't sing," she said.

"But you were famous. You must have been. There was a poster."

"That's not really what it's about," she said.

"It just seems it might be easier. For you, I mean."

"It wouldn't," she said.

"I'm sorry," he said.

14. YELLOW HELMET

In Shaftsbury Avenue, on the way back to Milgrim's hotel, through light rain, a dispatch rider on a dirty gray motorcycle caught up with the Hilux at a pedestrian crossing. Aldous powered down the window on the passenger side, squeegeeing raindrops from the bulletproof glass, as the helmeted rider took an envelope from his jacket and passed it to Milgrim, his glove like a Kevlar-armored robot hand. The window slid back up as the bike pulled away between the lanes of traffic ahead of them, the rider's yellow helmet dwindling steadily. The back of it was marred, as if mauled by the swipe of some great paw, revealing a white substrate.

He looked down at the envelope. MILGRIM, centered, in a cartoonist's loose caps, PM lower right. Pamela. It felt empty, or almost so, as he opened it. A limp transparent ring-binder sleeve, containing the inkjet image of his cop from Caffè Nero. Though not in Caffè Nero, here. Behind her, nicely in focus, Gay Dolphin Gift Cove's dog-headed angels. And there the sweatshirt had been red, though he could make out the same white moon-and-palm logo. A different colorway. Had Sleight taken this? It appeared to be a candid shot. He imagined her sleeping, back in the coach compartment of his British Midlands flight.

The cab filled with the opening chords of Toots and the Maytals' "Draw Your Brakes." "Aldous," said Aldous, to his iPhone. "Certainly." He passed it to Milgrim.

"You see," said Bigend.

"That's her," said Milgrim. "When I was there?"

Remembering Bigend's advice about telephones, he didn't ask where the image had been found, or how. "More or less," said Bigend, and hung up, Milgrim returning the iPhone to Aldous's large, waiting, beautifully manicured hand.

15. THE DROP

"Fitzroy," Clammy said, on her iPhone. She was staring up at the round bottom of Number Four's birdcage, having left a freshly coiffed Heidi in Selfridges, preparing to test for residual viability in several of fuckstick's credit cards.

"Fitzroy?"

"This neighborhood," Clammy said, "Melbourne. 'Round Brunswick Street. Rose Street, off Brunswick. Rose Street's got this artists' market. Mere took me. Meredith. Ol' George knew her."

That would be "Olduvai" George, the Bollards' brilliant, virtually forehead-free keyboardist, whom Inchmale said had more brains in his little finger than the rest of them put together. An even No. 2 crop that looked like a very tight fur hat. Like one of Clammy's black cashmere beanies, except he couldn't take it off. Massive jaw and cheekbones, permanent glossy black stubble, huge deep-set intelligent eyes.

"First thing I saw was her Hounds, girls' Hounds," Clammy continued.

"Looked good?"

"Hit it in a minute."

Meaning, she thought, that he hadn't, but would've. In theory at least. "And you had Hounds in common?"

"Wanted to," Clammy said, "worst way. I'd seen that pillock Burton in a pair. Fat ass." The transition from "arse" not yet quite bridged. Burton, whose fat ass she thought she'd heard cited before, did something in a band Clammy detested. The intensity of loathing one professional musician could manifest for another had been one of her least favorite things about the business. She'd bypassed it, she supposed, by generally avoiding the company of professional musicians. They weren't all like that, by any means, she knew, but better safe than sorry.

"So you admired her jeans?"

"Made it known," Clammy said, "that I knew what they were."

"And?"

"She asked me if I'd like a pair. Told me she knew of a drop."

"Drop?"

"A shipment."

"Where from?"

"Didn't want to ask," he said, gravely. "Wanted me Hounds. Next day, she said. Said she'd take me."

It was growing dark outside, taking Number Four with it. The bottom of the birdcage hung above her, the shadow of a mothership, discoidal, like solidified dusk. Waiting to radiate some energy, carve her with crop circles perhaps. She became momentarily aware of a susurrus, the sea of London traffic. The fingers of her free hand on the scrimshawed walrus-ivory of the Piblokto Madness bed. "And?"

"The others, they figured we were hooking up. 'Cept George. He knew her."

"Where from?"

"Cordwainers. London College of Fashion. She'd studied shoe design. Had two seasons of her own line. Went back to Melbourne after that, making belts and purses. Serious girl, George said."

"He was at Cordwainers?"

"Fucking Oxford, George. Seeing another Cordwainers girl, friend of hers."

Hollis realized that she was framing all of this, visualizing it, in a Melbourne that had almost nothing to do with any actual city. They'd played Melbourne and Sydney twice each, touring, and each time she'd been so jet-lagged, and so embroiled with band politics, that she'd scarcely registered either place. Her Melbourne was a collage, a mash-up, like a Canadianized Los Angeles, Anglo-Colonial Victorian amid a terraformed sprawl of suburbs. All of the larger trees in Los Angeles, Inchmale had told her, were Australian. She supposed the ones in Melbourne were as well. The city in which she was imagining

Clammy now wasn't real. A stand-in, something patched together from what little she had available. She felt a sudden, intense urge to go there. Not to whatever the real Melbourne might be, but to this sunny and approximate sham. "And she got them for you?" she asked Clammy.

"Came in the morning. Drove me to Brunswick Street. Eggs and bacon in a vegan lesbian café bar."

"Vegan bacon?"

"Open-minded. We talked about Hounds. I got the idea she'd met someone here, London, when she'd been at Cordwainers, who was in on the start of Hounds."

"It started here?"

"Didn't say that. But someone here had known something about it, early stages."

The bottom of the cage was perfectly dark now, the insectoid wallpaper dimly floral. "We have a deal," she reminded him.

"We do," he agreed, "but there may be less to it than you're expecting, now I've had time to think about it."

"Let me be the judge of that."

"So breakfast, and we talk, then we hit the market. I'd thought it would be more like the clothes end of Portobello, or Camden Lock. But it was more artists, craftsy stuff. Japanese prints, paintings, jewelry. Things the sellers had made."

"When was this?"

"Last March. Still hot. People had been lining up, for Hounds, while we ate. Market's not very big. Mere leads me straight to this queue, inside, I'd say twenty people, more after us. Out in a yard. I'm thinking, That's not for us, but she says it is, we have to queue too."

"What were the other people like, waiting?"

"Focused," he said. "No chatting. And they all seemed to be alone. Trying to look casual, like."

"Male? Female?"

"More male."

"Age?"

"Mixed."

She wondered what that meant, to Clammy.

"And they were waiting for . . . ?"

"There was a table, in under this old beach umbrella. We were in the sun, getting hotter. He's sitting under there behind the table."

"He?"

"White. Maybe thirty. American."

She guessed Clammy might be unable to estimate age accurately, over about twenty or so. "How do you know?"

"Spoke with him, didn't I, when I got up there."

"What about?"

"Shrinkage," Clammy said. "Sizing. Hounds are sized to shrink to the label size. Just under, in the waist, then that stretches a little. True sizes, no vanity sizing."

"Anything else?"

"He'd only sell me the one pair. Had three in my size. Showed him the readies. Said he couldn't. One to a customer. Kept things moving. 'Nother twenty, thirty people behind us."

"What was he like?"

"Reddish hair, freckles. A white shirt I wondered about."

"Why?"

"If it might be Hounds. Simple, like, but then not so simple. Like Hounds. He had his cash folded in one hand. No coins. Cash only."

"How much?"

"Two hundred Australian."

"Was he alone?"

"Two Aussie girls. Friends of Mere's. It was actually their pitch he was using. Sell Mere's belts, T's they print, jewelry."

"Names?"

"Nah. Mere'd know."

"She's in Melbourne?"

"Nah. Paris."

She let the darkness of the mothership's hull fill her field of vision. "Paris?"

"What I said."

"Do you know how to reach her?"

"She's at some vintage clothing fair. Two days. Starts tomorrow. Ol' George is there with her. Inchmale's pissed that he left while we're in studio."

"I need to meet her. Tomorrow or the next day. Can you arrange that?"

"Remember our agreement?"

"Absolutely. Get on it now. Call me back."

"'Kay," said Clammy, and was gone, the iPhone suddenly inert, empty.

16. HONOR BAR

She was waiting for Milgrim when he got back to his hotel. On the upholstered bench where they kept their complementary Mac-Book leashed, on the left side of the crossbar of the T-shaped lobby, opposite the desk.

He hadn't seen her there as he asked the Canadian girl for his room key. "Someone's waiting for you, Mr. Milgrim."

"Mr. Milgrim?"

He turned. She was still seated there, just closing the MacBook, in the black sweatshirt. Flanked on the bench by her large white purse and a larger Waterstone's bag. She stood, slinging the purse over her right shoulder and picking up the Waterstone's bag. She must have had the card out, ready, because he saw it in her right hand as she approached him.

"Winnie Whitaker, Mr. Milgrim." Handing him the card. Badge-like emblem in gold foil, upper left corner. WINNIE TUNG WHITAKER. He blinked. SPECIAL AGENT. Looking past that, desperately seeking escape, into the Waterstone's shopping bag, where he saw at least two Paddington Bear fuzzy toys, with their iconic yellow hats. Then back to the card. DEPARTMENT OF DEFENSE. OFFICE OF INSPECTOR GENERAL. DEFENSE CRIMINAL INVESTIGATIVE SERVICE. "DCIS," pronouncing the individual letters of the acronym, then pronouncing it again as "dee sis," stress on the first.

"You took my picture," Milgrim said, sadly.

"Yes, I did. I need to have a talk with you, Mr. Milgrim. Is there somewhere more private?"

"My room's very small," he said. Which was true, though as he said it he realized there was absolutely nothing in his room that he had to keep her from finding. "The honor bar," he said, "just up the stairs here."

"Thank you," she said, and gestured with the Waterstone's bag for him to lead the way.

"Have you been waiting long?" he asked as he started up the stairs, hearing his own voice as though it belonged to a robot.

"Over an hour, but I got to tweet my kids," she said.

Milgrim didn't know what that meant, and had never fully taken the measure of the honor bar, and wasn't sure how many rooms it might actually consist of. The one they entered now was like one of those educational display corners in a Ralph Lauren flagship store, meant to suggest how some semimythical other half had lived, but cranked up, here, into something else entirely, metastasized, spookily hyper-real.

"Wow," she said appreciatively as he looked down at the card, hoping it would have become something else entirely. "Like the Ritz-Carlton on steroids. But in miniature, sort of." She put her bag of Paddingtons carefully down on a leather hassock.

"Can I offer you a drink?" asked Milgrim's robotically level voice. He looked down at the horrible card again, then tucked it into the breast pocket of his jacket.

"Do they have a beer?"

"I'm sure they do." With some difficulty he located a paneled-in refrigerator, its door covered in red mahogany. "What would you like?"

She peered into the cold matte-silver interior. "I don't know any of those."

"A Beck's," suggested his robot. "Not the one they have in America."

"And yourself?"

"I don't drink alcohol," he said, passing her a bottle of Beck's and choosing a canned soft drink at random. She opened it, using something sterling, with a thick haft of deer antler for a handle, and took a swig directly from the bottle.

"Why did you take my picture?" Milgrim asked, unexpectedly bypassing his robot voice and sounding like a completely different person, the one you automatically and immediately arrest.

"I'm obsessive," she said.

Milgrim blinked, shuddered.

"Basically," she said, "I collect things. In accordion files, mostly. Pieces of paper. Photographs. Sometimes I put them on the wall, in my office. I have a booking shot of you, from a narcotics arrest in New York, 1997."

"I wasn't charged," Milgrim said.

"No," she agreed, "you weren't." She took a sip of Beck's. "And I have a copy of your passport photograph, which of course is much more recent. But this morning, following you, I decided I'd be talking to you this afternoon. So I wanted to get a picture of you before I did. In situ, sort of. Actually, though, I really am obsessive about pictures. I'm not sure now whether I decided I'd talk to you this afternoon, first, or whether I just decided to take your picture, which would mean I'd be talking to you this afternoon." She smiled. "Don't you want your drink?"

Milgrim looked down at the small can, popped the top, and poured something yellowish and carbonated into a highball glass.

"Let's sit down," she said, and settled into a leather club chair. Milgrim took the one opposite her.

"What have I done?"

"I'm not psychic," she said.

"Excuse me?"

"Well," she said, "you haven't filed income tax for about a decade. But maybe you haven't been earning enough to need to file."

"I don't think I have," Milgrim said.

"But you're employed now?"

"On a sort of honorarium basis," Milgrim said, apologetically. "Plus expenses."

"Some serious expenses," she said, looking around the honor bar. "By this ad agency, Blue Ant?"

"Not formally, no," said Milgrim, not liking the way that sounded. "I work for the founder and CEO." "CEO," he realized, having said this, had started to sound somehow sleazy.

She nodded, making eye contact again. "You don't seem to have left much of a trail, Mr. Milgrim. Columbia? Slavic languages? Translation? Some government work?"

"Yes."

"Zero history, as far as ChoicePoint is concerned. Means you haven't even had a credit card for ten years. Means no address history. If I had to guess, Mr. Milgrim, I'd say you've had a problem with drugs."

"Well," said Milgrim, "yes."

"You don't look to me like you've got a problem with drugs now," she said.

"I don't?"

"No. You look like you've got a set of reflexes left over from having had a problem with drugs. And like you may have a problem with the company you're keeping. But that's what I'm here to talk with you about."

Milgrim took a sip of whatever was in his glass. Some corrosively bitter Italian lemon soda. His eyes teared.

"Why did you go to Myrtle Beach, Mr. Milgrim? Did you know the man you met with there?"

"His pants."

"His pants?"

"I made tracings," Milgrim said. "I photographed them. He was paid for that."

"Do you know how much?"

"No," said Milgrim. "Thousands." He made a thumb-and-forefinger gesture unconsciously indicating a certain thickness of hundred-dollar bills. "Say ten, tops?"

"And were they Department of Defense property, these pants?" she asked, looking at him very directly.

"I hope not," Milgrim said, out of a deep and sudden misery.

She took a longer swallow of her beer. Continued to look at him that way. Someone chuckled in one of the honor bar's adjoining rooms, from behind drawn French doors of that same red mahogany. The chuckle seemed to match the decor.

"I can tell you they weren't," she said.

Milgrim swallowed, painfully hard. "They weren't?"

"But they'd like to be. That could be a problem. Tell me about the man who let you see them."

"He had a mullet," Milgrim said, "and he was wearing Blackie Collins Toters."

"He was wearing—?"

"Toters," Milgrim said. "I Googled them. They have Cordura Plus pocket linings, for guns and things. And outside pockets for knives or flashlights."

"Oh," she said, smiling briefly, "sure."

"Sleight said he was special . . . something?"

"I'm sure he thinks he is."

"Forces? Had been?"

"Sleight," she said, "Oliver. British national, resident in Canada. Works for Blue Ant."

"Yes," said Milgrim, imagining Sleight's picture on her wall. "Otherwise, he said almost nothing. Said they needed gussets."

"Gussets?"

"The pants." Then, remembering: "Blue Ant's smartest design analyst thinks they aren't military. Thinks they're streetwear. I think she was right."

"Why?"

"Coyote brown." He shrugged. "Last year. Iraq."

"I was in Iraq," she said. "Three months. In the Green Zone. I got tired of that color too."

Milgrim could think of nothing to say. "Was it dangerous?" asked his robot.

"They had a Cinnabon," she said. "I missed my kids." She finished her beer, and put the bottle down on a cut-glass coaster with a frilled sterling lip. "That was his wife you met, in the gift shop. He's been in Iraq too. First in an elite unit, then later as a contractor."

"I was afraid of him," Milgrim said.

"I imagine he's fairly dysfunctional," she said, as though that wasn't something warranting any surprise. "What is it with that Toyota?"

"The Hilux?"

"What local cooperation I have is via the FBI's legal attaché here. The Brits were willing to follow you from the airport, and to let me know where you were staying. But they're curious about the truck."

"It's Bigend's," Milgrim said. "It has armor fitted by a firm named Jankel, special engine, tires that keep going if they're shot up." He didn't say cartel grade.

"Is that really his name?"

"The French pronunciation would be 'Bayh-jhan,' I think. But he seems to favor the other."

"Why would he need a truck like that?"

"He doesn't need to need it. He just needs to be curious about it."

"Must be nice."

"I don't know if I'd describe him that way," Milgrim said. "But he's definitely curious."

"And extremely well connected here. When my Brits ran the registration, I got the feeling, they decided that a tail from the airport and the name of your hotel was about all I'd be getting. Though that might have been all I'd have gotten anyway. But they did ask about the truck."

"There aren't that many genuinely eccentric rich people," Milgrim said. "Evidently. Not even here."

"Couldn't prove it by me."

"No," Milgrim agreed, and took a tiny, careful sip of his bitter lemon pop.

"Why did they want the specs on those pants?"

"They're interested in military contracts," Milgrim said. "Designing. The actual clothing and equipment has to be manufactured in the United States. There's a law."

"No kidding," she said.

"That's what I've been told."

"No," she said, "I mean no kidding that they're looking at contracting?"

"None," said Milgrim. "They are. It's a major current project."

"Fucking hilarious," she said.

Milgrim looked at his lemon pop, confused.

"Do you have a phone number?"

"I do," said Milgrim, fishing the Neo from his jacket and showing it to her. "But it's on this, and Bigend says it's tapped."

"Skip that, then. I arrested a serious shitbird who had one of those."

Milgrim shuddered.

"Not because he had it. Something else. Do you have an e-mail address?"

"A Blue Ant address."

"How about a Twitter account?"

"A what?"

"Sign up for one," she said. "As Gay Dolphin Two, all caps, no spaces. Numeral two. From the laptop in the lobby. As soon as you finish your drink. Make your updates private. I'll ask to follow you. I'll be Gay Dolphin One. Allow me to follow you, refuse anybody else. It'll mostly be porn bots anyway."

"Porn bots? What is it?"

"It's how I talk to my kids. You'll register. That will be how we keep in touch. Let's try to keep you out of trouble."

Milgrim winced.

"You don't want to leave town without letting me know. Or change hotels."

"I have to go where they send me," Milgrim said. "It's what I do."

"Perfect. I'll be in touch." She stood. "Thanks for the beer. Don't forget about that registration. Gay Dolphin Two. Numeral two. All caps. No spaces."

When she was gone, he continued to sit there, in the club chair. He took her card from his pocket. Held it without looking at it. Fingers on its sharp edges.

"No spaces," his robot said.

17. HOMUNCULI

She found Heidi in Cabinet's bar, monochromatically resplendent in a sort of post-holocaust drum majorette jacket, cut from several different shades and textures of almost-black.

"Fuckstick's cards worked?"

"Two did," said Heidi, raising a steaming glass of clear liquid in a highball glass. Her fresh-cut hair had been reblackened, likewise in several shades, and she seemed to have hit the makeup counter as well.

"What's that?" Hollis asked, indicating the glass.

"Water," Heidi said, and sipped.

"Want to go to Paris with me, tomorrow morning?"

"What for?"

"My day job. There's a vintage clothing fair. I may have found someone who knows what Bigend wants me to find out. Part of it, anyway."

"How did you find them?"

"I think she's dating the keyboard player from the Bollards."

"Small world," said Heidi. "And he's the only cute one. Rest are homunculuses."

"Homunculi."

"Little douche bags," Heidi countercorrected. "I'll pass. Throat's bothering me. Fucking planes."

"No, Eurostar."

"I mean the one I came over on. When are you back?"

"Day after tomorrow, if I can find her tomorrow. I guess I'll take Milgrim, then."

"How was he?"

"Profoundly. Fucking. Peculiar." Hollis blew gently on the thin tan island of foam afloat in her half pint of Guinness, to see it move, then drank some. Always a mysterious beverage to her. Unsure why she'd asked for it. She liked the way it looked more than how it tasted. How would it taste, she wondered, if it tasted the way she thought it looked? No idea. "Though maybe not in such a bad way. Not his fault Bigend found him. We know how that is."

"Robert's found me a gym. Old school. East side."

"End. Not side."

"He's cute."

"Don't you dare. 'No civilians,' remember? If you'd stuck with the rule, you wouldn't have to be divorcing fuckstick."

"Look at you. Motherfucker's on YouTube, jumping off skyscrapers in a flying-squirrel suit."

"But it was *your* rule, remember? Not mine. After the boxers, you stuck with musicians."

"Homunculuses," Heidi said, nodding, "douche bags."

"I could've told you that," Hollis said.

"You did."

The bar's level of early-evening drinking-crowd noise tilted, suddenly. Hollis looked up and saw the Icelandic twins, their identical frosty pelts aglitter. Behind them, somehow worryingly avuncular, loomed Bigend.

"Shit," said Hollis.

"I'm out of here," said Heidi, putting down her water and standing, giving her shoulders an irritated shrug within her new jacket.

Hollis rose too, half-pint in hand. "I'll have to speak with him," she said. "About Paris."

"You're the one with the job."

"Hollis," said Bigend. "And Heidi. Delighted."

"Mr. Bellend," said Heidi.

"Allow me to introduce Eydis and Fridrika Brandsdottir. Hollis Henry and Heidi Hyde."

Eydis and Fridrika smiled identically, in eerie unison. "A pleasure," said one. "Yes," said the other.

"I'm leaving," said Heidi, and did, men turning to follow her with their eyes as she strode off through the bar.

"She isn't feeling well," said Hollis. "The flight's affected her throat."

"She is a singer?" asked either Eydis or Fridrika.

"A drummer," said the other.

"May I speak with you for a moment, Hubertus?" Hollis turned to the twins. "Please excuse me. Take these seats."

As they settled in the armchairs that Hollis and Heidi had vacated, Hollis stepped closer to Bigend. He'd forgone the blue suit this evening, and wore one in some peculiarly light-absorbing black fabric that somehow looked as though it didn't have a surface. More like an absence, an opening into something else, antimatter paired with mohair. "I hadn't known Heidi was here," he said.

"We're all surprised. But I wanted to tell you that I'm going to Paris tomorrow, to try to speak with someone who may know something about Hounds. I thought I'd take Milgrim."

"You got along?"

"Well enough, considering."

"I'll have Pamela e-mail you in a few minutes. She can handle any reservations."

"Don't bother. I'll keep track of expenses. But I don't want to give up my room here, so I'll keep it and you can cover that."

"I already am," Bigend said, "plus incidentals. Can you tell me anything about Paris?"

"I may have found someone who was involved with whatever the beginning of Hounds was. 'May.' That's all I know. And it may not be true. I'll call you from there. Anyway, you've got company." Smiling in the direction of Eydis and Fridrika, now coiled like slender silvery arctic mammals in their matching armchairs. "Good night."

18. 140

The Neo rang while he was still trying to grasp Twitter. He was registered, now, as GAYDOLPHIN2. No followers, following no one. Whatever that meant. And his updates, whatever those were, were protected.

The harsh faux mechanical ring tone had attracted the attention of the girl at the desk. He smiled anxiously, apologetically, from his seat on the leather padded laptop-tethering bench, and answered it, the Neo awkward against his ear. "Yes?"

"Milgrim?"

"Speaking."

"Hollis. How are you?"

"Well," said Milgrim, automatically. "How are you?"

"Wondering if you're up for Paris tomorrow. We'd take an early Eurostar."

"What's that?"

"The train," she said. "Chunnel. It's quicker."

"What for?" Sounding, he thought, like a suspicious child.

"I've found someone we need to try to speak with. She's there tomorrow, and the day after. After that, I don't know."

"Will we be gone long?"

"Overnight, if we're lucky. Seven-thirty out of St. Pancras. I'll arrange for someone from Blue Ant to pick you up at the hotel."

"Does Hubertus know?"

"Yes. I just ran into him."

"All right," he said. "Thank you."

"I'll have the car phone your room."

"Thank you."

Milgrim put the Neo away and went back to webmail and Twitter. He'd just heard from Twitter, asking whether he was willing to have GAYDOLPHIN1 follow him. He was. And now he'd have to tell her about Paris. In bursts of a hundred and forty character spaces, apparently.

As he was finishing this, someone called CyndiBrown32 asked whether he was willing to have her follow him.

Remembering Winnie's instructions, he wasn't. He closed Twitter and logged out of webmail. Closed the MacBook.

"Good night, Mr. Milgrim," said the girl at the desk as he went to the elevator.

He felt as though something new and entirely too large was attempting to fit within him. He'd shifted allegiances, or acquired a new one. Or was he simply more afraid of Winnie than he was of Bigend? Or was it that he was afraid of the possibility of the absence of Bigend?

"Institutionalized," he said to the brushed stainless interior of the Hitachi elevator as its door closed.

He'd gone from where he'd been before, somewhere he thought of as being extremely small, and very hard, to this wider space, to his not-quite-job running errands for Bigend, but suddenly that seemed not so wide. This succession of rooms, in hotels he never chose. Simple missions, involving travel. Urine tests. Always another bubble-pack.

Reminded of his medication, he calculated. He had enough for two nights away. Whatever it was.

The door opened on the third-floor hallway.

Take your medicine. Clean your teeth. Pack for Paris.

When had he last been in Paris? It felt as though he never had. Someone else had been, in his early twenties. That mysterious previous iteration his therapist in Basel had been so relentlessly interested in. A younger, hypothetical self. Before things had started to go not so well, then worse, then much worse, though by then he'd arranged to be absent much of the time. As much of the time as possible.

"Quit staring," he said to the dressmaker's dummy as he stepped into his room. "I wish I had a book." It had been quite a while since he'd found anything to read for pleasure. Nothing since the start of his recovery, really. There were a few expensively bound and weirdly neutered bookazines here, rearranged daily by the housekeepers, but he knew from glancing through them that these were bland advertisements for being wealthy, wealthy and deeply, witheringly unimaginative.

He'd look for a book in Paris.

Reading, his therapist had suggested, had likely been his first drug.

19. PRESENCES

Tossing makeup and toiletries into a bag, she noticed that the Blue Ant figurine wasn't there on the counter, her failed employment-avoidance totem. Moved by the housecleaners in yesterday's tidy, she supposed, but unlike them. She zipped the makeup bag. Checked her hair in the mirror. A voice with a BBC register was flowing smoothly, meaninglessly, from the ornate wall-grid.

Out past the steamy glass slabs and nickel-plate bumpers of the H. G. Wells shower, multiply towel-draped now.

Glancing around Number Four in hope of finding something she might have forgotten to pack, she saw the three unopened cartons of the British edition of her book. Remembering Milgrim, when she'd first met him, on their walk to the tapas place, expressing interest. Bigend, of course, had brought it up. Milgrim had seemed taken, for a few seconds, with the idea that she'd written a book.

She should take him one, she decided.

She wrestled a ridiculously heavy carton onto the unmade bed and used the foil-ripper on the room's Victorian corkscrew to slit the transparent plastic tape. Releasing a bookstore smell as she opened the carton, but not a good one. Dry, chemical. And there they were, square and individually shrink-wrapped, *Presences*, by Hollis Henry. She took one off the top, slid it into the side pocket of her roll-aboard.

Then out, through liminal green hallways, lift, and down, to the coffee-smelling foyer, where a tortoise-spectacled young man presented her with a tall white coffee in a crisp white paper cup, lidded with white plastic, and offered her a Cabinet umbrella.

"Is the car here?"

"Yes," he said.

"I won't need an umbrella, thanks."

He carried the roll-aboard out for her and put it in the popped trunk of a black BMW, piloted by the bearded young man who'd admitted her to Blue Ant.

"Jacob," this one said, smiling. He wore a waxed cotton motorcycle jacket. It lent him a sort of post-apocalyptic élan, she thought, this rainy morning. Props should've given him a Sten gun, or some other weapon looking equally like plumbing.

"Of course," she said. "Thank you for picking me up."

"Traffic's not terrible," opening her door for her.

"We're meeting Mr. Milgrim?" As he slid in behind the wheel, she noted his wireless earpiece.

"All sorted. Been picked up. Ready for Paris?"

"I hope so," she said as he pulled away from the curb.

Then Gloucester Place. Had she been walking, she'd have taken Baker Street instead, which she'd dreamed of as a child, and which retained, even at this stage of supposed adulthood, a certain small sharp sense of disappointment. Though perhaps game was afoot in Paris, she thought, and now merely a rather long subway ride from here.

In the traffic of Marylebone Road, stopping and starting, she kept noticing a dispatch rider, armored in samurai plastics, the back of his yellow helmet scarred as if something feline and huge had swatted him and almost missed, his clumsy-looking fiberglass fairing mended with peeling silver tape. He seemed to keep passing them, somehow, rolling forward between lanes. She'd never understood how that worked here.

"I hope I can find Milgrim at the station."

"No fear," said Jacob. "They'll bring him to you."

>>>

Sky-blue steel-girdered vastness. Towering volume of sound. Pigeons looking unconfused, about their pigeon business. Nobody did train stations like the Europeans, and the British, she thought, best of all. Faith in infrastructure, coupled with a necessity-driven gift for retrofitting.

One of Bigend's lanky, elegant drivers, hand to earpiece, hove toward her steadily through the crowd, Milgrim in tow like a Sunday rowboat. Gazing around like a child, Milgrim, his face lit with a boy's delight in the blue-girdered drama, the Dinky Toy grandeur of the great station.

One of the wheels of her roll-aboard began to click as she headed in their direction.

20. AUGMENTED

Milgrim glanced up from the square, glossy pages of *Presences: Locative Art in America*, and saw that Hollis was reading too. Something clothbound, black, no jacket.

They were somewhere under the Channel now, seated in Business Premier, which had wifi and a croissant breakfast. Or not wifi, but something cellular, requiring what she'd called a "dongle," and had plugged into the edge of her MacBook for him. He'd borrowed it earlier, a weirdly thin one called an Air, and gone to Twitter, to see if Winnie had said anything, but she hadn't. "Going through Kent now," he'd written, then erased it. Then he'd tried "Hollis Henry" on Google and found her Wikipedia entry. Which had made for an odd read, as she was seated just opposite him, across the table, though she couldn't see what he was looking at. Though now they were in the tunnel, there was no phone either.

She'd been described, in a retrospective piece written in 2004, as having looked, when she performed, like "a weaponized version of Françoise Hardy." He wasn't sure he could see it, exactly, and he'd also Googled Françoise Hardy to make the direct comparison. Françoise Hardy was more conventionally pretty, he thought, and he wasn't sure what "weaponized" was supposed to mean, in that context. He supposed the writer had been trying to capture something of whatever she'd projected in live performance.

Hollis didn't look like Milgrim's idea of a rock singer, to the extent that he had one. She looked like someone who had a job that allowed you to wear what you wanted to the office. Which she did have, he supposed, with Bigend.

When he was finished with her computer, she'd offered him this copy of the book she'd written. "I'm afraid it's mostly pictures," she'd said, unzipping a side pocket on her black suitcase and pulling out a glossy, shrink-wrapped slab. The cover was a color photograph of tall nude statues of several very slender, small-breasted women, with identical helmet-like haircuts and matching bracelets, rising out of what seemed to be a rather small flower bed. They were made of something like solidified mercury, perfectly mirroring everything around them. The back cover was the same image, but minus the heroically erotic liqui-chrome statuary, which made it possible to read a sign they had concealed: Château Marmont.

"That's a memorial to Helmut Newton," she'd said. "He lived there, part of the time."

"The back is 'before'?" Milgrim had asked.

"No," she'd said, "that's what you see, there, unaugmented. The front's what you see augmented. Construct's tied to the GPS grid. To see it, you have to go there, use augmented reality."

"I've never heard of that," Milgrim had said, looking at the back, then the front.

"When I wrote the book, there was no commercial hardware. People were building their own. Now it's all iPhone apps. Lots of work, back then, trying to render the pieces effectively. We had to take high-rez photographs of the site, from as many angles as you can, then marry them to whatever that exact angle on the construct would look like, then choose from those."

"Did you do that yourself?'

"I chose, but Alberto did the photography and the imaging. That Newton memorial is one of his own pieces, but he rendered all of the others." She pushed a strand of hair back from her eye. "Locative art probably started in London, and there's a lot of it, but I haven't seen much of it there. I decided to stick to American artists. Less to bite off, but also because it all has some peculiarly literal sense of place. I thought I had a marginally better chance of understanding it there."

"You must know a lot about art."

"I don't. I stumbled on this stuff. Well, that's not true. Bigend suggested I look at it. Though at the time I had no idea it was him doing the suggesting."

He'd worked the corner of his thumbnail under the shrink-wrap. "Thank you," he'd said, "it looks very interesting."

Now she closed the black book, saw him looking at her. Smiled.

"What are you reading?" he asked.

"*Rogue Male*. Geoffrey Household. It's about a man who tried to assassinate Hitler, or someone who's exactly like Hitler."

"Is it good?"

"Very good, though it really seems to be about wriggling down into the heart of the British countryside. Third act all seems to take place inside a hedgerow, down a badger hole."

"I like your book. Like people were able to freeze their dreams, leave them places, and you could go there and see them, if you knew how."

"Thank you," she said, putting *Rogue Male* down on the table, without bothering to mark her place.

"Have you seen them all, yourself?"

"Yes, I have."

"What's your favorite?"

"River Phoenix, on the sidewalk. It was the first I saw. I never went back. Never saw it again. It made such a powerful impression. I suppose it was really why I decided to try to do a book, that impression."

Milgrim closed *Presences*. He put it on the table, opposite *Rogue Male*. "Who are we going to see in Paris?"

"Meredith Overton. Studied at Cordwainers, shoe design, leather. She lives in Melbourne. Or did. She's in Paris for the Salon du Vintage, selling something. She's with a keyboard player named George, who's in a band called the Bollards. Do you know them?"

"No," said Milgrim.

"I know another Bollard, plus the man who's currently producing their music."

"She knows about Gabriel Hounds?"

"My other Bollard says she knew someone in London, when she was at Cordwainers, who knew someone involved in Hounds getting started."

"It started in London?"

"I don't know. Clammy met her in Melbourne. She was wearing Hounds, he wanted Hounds. She knew of Hounds locally. Some would be sold at a sort of art fair. He went with her and bought jeans. Says there was an American man there, selling them."

"Why do you think she'll talk to us?"

"I don't," she said. "But we can try."

"Why do people care? Why do you think Bigend does?"

"He thinks someone's copying some of his weirder marketing strategies," she said, "improving on them."

"And you think people want this brand because they can't have it?"

"In part."

"Drugs are valuable because you can't get them without breaking the law," Milgrim said.

"I thought they were valuable because they worked."

"They have to work," said Milgrim, "but the market value is about prohibition. Often they cost next to nothing to make. That's what it all runs on. They work, you need them, they're prohibited."

"How did you get out of that, Milgrim?"

"They changed my blood. Replaced it. And while they were doing that, they were reducing the dose. And there was a paradoxical antagonist."

"What's that?"

"I'm not sure," said Milgrim. "Another drug. And cognitive therapy."

"That sounds terrible," she said.

"I liked the therapy," Milgrim said. He could feel his passport against his chest, tucked safely into its Faraday pouch.

Rainy French countryside leapt on the carriage's windows, hurtling, as if a switch had been thrown.

21. MINUS ONE

Foliage green," she heard Milgrim say, flatly, as she paid the driver with euros she'd gotten from an ATM in the Gare du Nord. She turned. "What?"

He was half out of the cab, clutching his bag. "That department store, Oxford Street," he said. "Foliage green pants. Same man, just walked in. Where we're going." That sharp, nervy thing fully present now, the mildly confused semiconvalescent gone entirely. He looked as though he were sniffing the air.

"Keep the change," she said to the driver, shooing Milgrim out of the way and pulling her roll-aboard after her. She closed the door and the cab pulled away, leaving them on the sidewalk. "Are you sure?"

"Someone's watching us."

"Bigend?"

"Don't know. You go in."

"What will you do?"

"I'll see."

"Are you sure?"

"Let me borrow me your computer."

Hollis bent, unzipped the side of her bag, and pulled out her Mac. He tucked it under his arm, like a clipboard. She saw that vagueness returning, the blinking mildness. He's cloaking himself, she thought, then wondered what that meant.

"You go in now," he said, "please."

"Euros," she said, passing him some bills.

She turned and wheeled her bag across the pavement, into the crowd around the venue's entrance. Was Milgrim imagining things? Possibly, though there was Bigend's penchant for attracting the most unwanted forms of attention, then following whatever followers turned up. Exactly what Milgrim claimed to be about to do. She looked back, expecting to see him, but he was gone.

She paid an entrance fee of five euros to a Japanese girl and was asked to check her bag.

A cobbled courtyard was visible through arches. Young women there were smoking cigarettes, making it look at once natural and profoundly attractive.

The Salon du Vintage itself was being held within the retrofitted seventeenth-century building to which the courtyard belonged, a previous decade's idea of sleek modernity smoothly folded into its fabric.

Every second or third person in her field of vision was Japanese, and many were moving in approximately one direction. She went with them, up a minimalist stairway of pale Scandinavian wood, emerging into the first of two very large bright rooms, chandeliers glittering above carefully arranged racks of clothing, glass-topped display tables and pieces of period furniture.

This year's iteration of the Salon du Vintage was devoted to the Eighties, she knew from having Googled it. She always found it peculiar to encounter a time she had actually lived through rendered as a period. It made her wonder whether she was living through another one, and if so, what it would be called. The first decades of the current century hadn't yet acquired any very solid nomenclature, it seemed to her. Seeing relatively recent period clothing, particularly, gave her an odd feeling. She guessed that she unconsciously revised the fashion of her own past, turning it into something more contemporary. It was never quite as she remembered it. Shoulders tended to be peculiar, hems and waistlines not where she expected them to be.

Not that her own Eighties had been anything like Gaultier, Mugler, Alaïa and Montana, which she was now gathering was the version mainly being presented here.

She checked the handwritten price tag on a mulberry wool Mugler jacket. If Heidi were here, she decided, and were into this sort of thing, which she wasn't, fuckstick's remaining credit cards could probably be flatlined in an hour, with the resulting swag still fitting easily in a single cab.

She looked up, then, and winced at herself, in Anton Corbijn's 1996 portrait, enlarged and dry-mounted, suspended with transparent fishing line above the rack of Mugler. Anachronism, she thought. Not even her era.

Eager to escape the portrait, she declined an offer to try the Mugler on. Turning away, she brought out her iPhone. Bigend seemed to pick up before his phone had had a chance to ring.

"Do you have someone else here, Hubertus?"

"No," he said. "Should I?"

"You didn't have someone watching us, in Selfridges?"

"No."

"Milgrim thinks he's seen someone, someone he saw there."

"Always a possibility, I suppose. Paris office hasn't been told you're there. Would you like some company?"

"No. Just checking."

"Do you have anything for me?"

"Not yet. Just got here. Thanks." She hung up before he could say goodbye. Stood there with her arm cocked, phone at ear-level, suddenly aware of the iconic nature of her unconscious pose. Some very considerable part of the gestural language of public places, that had once belonged to cigarettes, now belonged to phones. Human figures, a block down the street, in postures utterly familiar, were no longer smoking. The woman in Corbijn's portrait had never seen that.

The number Clammy had given her the night before rang several times before it was answered. "Yes?"

"George? It's Hollis Henry. We met at Cabinet, when Reg was still there."

"Yes," he said. "Clammy rang. You're needing to speak with Mere."

"I'd like to, yes."

"And you're here?"

"Yes."

"Afraid it's not possible." George sounded much more like a young barrister than the Bollards' keyboard player.

"She doesn't want to discuss it?"

"Not at all."

"I'm sorry," she said.

"No, really," he said, "not at all. She's closing a deal on the Chanel she brought from Melbourne. Tokyo dealers. Taken her out to lunch. Left me minding the shop."

Hollis held the iPhone away as she sighed with relief, then returned it to her ear. "She wouldn't mind talking with me, then?"

"Not at all. Loves your music. Mother's a great fan. Where are you?"

"Second floor. Not far from the stairs."

"Did you see they've a picture of you there?"

"Yes," she said, "I noticed."

"We're at the very back. I'll look out for you."

"Thanks." She walked on, passing a display of denim work clothing she doubted was Eighties. All of it older than its dealer, she guessed, and she judged him to be in his forties. He watched her sharply as she passed; the Hounds jacket, she thought.

She found Olduvai George beyond an archipelago of transparent inflatable orange furniture which didn't look Eighties to her either. He was smiling, natty and attractively simian, in jeans and a khaki raincoat.

"How are you?"

"Well, thanks," she said, shaking his hand. "How are you?"

"Haven't had a nibble since the Tokyo mob took Mere away. I don't think I have the retail gene."

Oxford, Inchmale had said of George, when she'd pressed him the night before. Balliol, graduated with a starred first PPE. Which she supposed she remembered perfectly now, because she had absolutely no idea what it might mean, other than that George was assumed to be monstrously overeducated for present employment. "And please don't tell anyone," Inchmale had added.

"Good thing you don't need it," she said, considering eight very petite, identically cut Chanel suits, displayed on austere charcoal-gray dress forms, that seemed to be the whole of Meredith Overton's stock. All cut from some thick fabric that resembled a highly magnified houndstooth check, in color combinations on the order of hot orange and mustard. She vaguely remembered oven mitts made of a similar material, similarly thick. She'd actually seen suits like this worn to very good effect once, but only once, and in Cannes. It had all depended, she'd thought at the time, on the way in which the two pieces resolutely refused to conform to the body. Now she saw that each garment had been threaded through with a slender steel cable, coated in transparent plastic. "Are they very valuable?"

"Hoping so. She found them in an estate sale in Sydney. They were made in the early Eighties, for the wife of a very successful property developer. Couture, exclusive fabrics. The sellers had no idea, but in order to do really well with them, it's either here, now, or Tokyo. And the significant Japanese buyers are all here, today, and Paris adds a certain symbolic leverage. They were made here."

"She was tiny," Hollis said, reaching out to touch a fabric-covered button, but stopping.

"Would you like to see a photograph of her wearing one?"

"Really?"

"Mere found them in the papers, in Australian city glossies. Even a bit of video."

"No, thanks," Hollis said, the eight brightly suited dress forms feeling suddenly like tomb statuary, power objects, the fetishes of a departed shamaness, occultly cocked and ready.

"There are handbags too, purses. Like new. She has them here but decided not to display them. Because they're a bit more affordable, she'd just have to show them repeatedly. Doesn't want them pawed over by the punters."

"Did Clammy tell you what I'm after, George?"

"Not exactly, but now you're here, I'm guessing it's about your jacket."

It felt odd, hearing someone outside of Bigend's circle, other than Clammy, reference Hounds. "How much do you know about that?"

"No more than Clammy, I imagine. She's very closely held, Mere is. Business like this is more about keeping secrets than advertising."

"How's that?"

"There aren't that many serious buyers. Quite a few serious dealers, though."

She'd liked him, when they'd met at Cabinet, and found she liked him now. "Clammy says that Mere knew someone, when she was at that footwear college in London," she said, deciding to trust him. As usual, she surprised herself in this, but once in, you rolled with it. "Someone associated with Gabriel Hounds."

"That may be," George said, smiling. The proportions of his skull were oddly reversed, jaw and cheekbones massive, brows heavy, forehead scarcely the width of two fingers, between a unibrow and his densely caplike haircut. "But best I don't speak of it."

"How long have you been together?"

"Bit before Clammy met her in Melbourne. Well, that's not true, but I already fancied her. She claims it wasn't mutual at all then, but I have my doubts." He smiled.

"She's living back in London? Here?"

"Melbourne."

"That's seriously long-distance."

"It is." He frowned. "Inchmale," he said, "while I have you."

"Yes?'

"He's certainly hard on Clammy, mixing the bed tracks. I've stayed well out of it."

"Yes?"

"Can you give me any advice? Anything that might make working with him easier?"

"You'll be going to Arizona soon," she said. "Tucson. There's a very small studio there, owner's Inchmale's favorite engineer. They'll do some initially very alarming things to your London bed tracks. Let them. Then you'll basically rerecord the entire album. But very quickly, almost painlessly, and I imagine you'll be extremely pleased with the result. I've already told Clammy that, but I'm not sure it got through."

"He didn't do that on the first album he produced for us, and we were a lot closer to Tucson then."

"You weren't there yet. In terms of his process. You are now. Or almost, I'd say."

"Thanks," he said, "that's good to know."

"Call me, if you're getting exasperated. You will. Clammy will, in any case. But you've jumped with him, and if you let him, he'll land on his feet, and the album with him. He's not very diplomatic at the best of times, and he gets less so, the further into the process you go with him. Any idea when Mere will be back?"

He consulted a very large wristwatch, the color of a child's toy fire engine. "Going on an hour now," he said, "but I've really no idea. Wish she'd get back myself. I'm dying for coffee."

"Café in the courtyard?"

"Indeed. Large black?"

"You got it," she said.

"You can take the lift," he said, pointing.

"Thanks."

It was German, with a brushed stainless interior, the philosophical opposite of Cabinet's, but not much larger. She pushed 1, but when it passed 0, she realized that she'd pushed -1.

The door opened on a dim, blue-lit void, and utter silence.

She stepped out.

Ancient stone groins, receding toward the street, illuminated by concealed disco floodlights, dialed down low. A small impromptu corral of what she took to be spare Salon du Vintage gear, on the bare stone floor, dwarfed by the arches. Folding chrome sample racks, a few dress forms looking Dali-esque in this light.

All quite wonderfully unexpected.

And then, at the far end of the blue arches, descending stairs, a figure. As described by Milgrim. The short-brimmed cap, short black jacket, zipped up tight.

He saw her.

She stepped back into the elevator, pressing 0.

22. FOLEY

Milgrim, with Hollis's laptop clamped firmly under his arm, bag over the other shoulder, walked rapidly along a smaller street, away from the one where her vintage clothing fair was being held.

He needed wifi. He regretted not borrowing the red dongle.

Now he neared a place called Bless, at first mistaking it for a bar. No, a place that sold clothing, he saw. There might be someone in there, he supposed, glancing in the window, who would either know about or pretend to know about Hollis's phantom jeans line.

He kept walking, simultaneously conducting an imaginary exchange with his therapist, one in which they sorted out what he was feeling. Having worked very hard to avoid feeling much of anything, for most of his adult life, recognizing even the simplest of his emotions could require remedial effort.

Angry, he decided. He was angry, though he didn't yet know who or what at. If Winnie Tung Whitaker, Special Agent, had sent the man in the foliage green pants, and hadn't told him, he thought he'd be angry with her. Disappointed, anyway. That wouldn't be getting off on the right foot, in what he thought of as a new professional relationship. Or perhaps, his therapist suggested, he was angry with himself. That would be more complicated, less amenable to self-analysis, but more familiar.

Better to be angry with the man in the foliage green pants, he thought. Mr. Foliage Green. Foley. He didn't feel kindly disposed toward Foley. Though he had absolutely no idea who Foley might be, what he was up to, or whether Foley was following him, Hollis, or the both of them. If Foley wasn't working for or with Winnie, he might be working for Blue Ant, or for Bigend more privately, or, given Bigend's apparent new attitude toward Sleight, for Sleight. Or none of the above. He might be some entirely new part of the equation.

"But is there an equation?" he asked himself, or his therapist. Though she now seemed not to be answering.

Rue du Temple, a wall plaque informed him at the corner, on a building looking as though it had been drawn by Dr. Seuss. A larger street, Temple. He turned right. Past an ornate, Victorian-looking Chinese restaurant. Discovering a smoke shop that also offered coffee, its official, spindle-shaped, red-lit TABAC sign presenting nicotine-lack as a medical emergency. Without slowing, he entered.

"Wifi?"

"Oui."

"Espresso, please." Taking a place at the authentically nonreflective zinc counter. There was a faint but definite smell of cigarette smoke, though no one was smoking. Indeed, he was the only customer here.

His therapist had suspected that his inability with Romance languages was too thorough, too tidily complete, thus somehow emotionally based, but they had been unable get to the bottom of it.

Obtaining the password ("dutemple") from the counterman, he logged on to Twitter, his password there a transliteration of the Russian for "gay dolphin," the Cyrillic loosely rendered in approximation on the Roman keyboard.

Her "Whr R U now?" had been sent "about 2 hours ago from TweetDeck."

"Paris," typed Milgrim, "man following us, seen yesterday in London. Is he yours?" He clicked the update button. Sipped at his espresso. Refreshed the window.

"Describe," this less than five seconds ago via TweetDeck.

"White, very short hair, sunglasses, twenties, medium height, athletic." He updated. Watched people passing, through the window.

Refreshed the window. Nothing but a short URL, sent forty seconds before from TweetDeck, whatever that was. He clicked on it. And there was Foley, wearing what might be the olive-drab version of the black jacket, with a black knit skullcap rather than the forage cap.

Oddly, his eyes were concealed by a black Photoshopped rectangle, as in antique porn.

Milgrim glanced at the page's header and the image's caption, something about "elite operator's equipment." He concentrated on the photograph, assuring himself that this was in fact his man. "Yes," he wrote, "who is he?" and updated.

When he refreshed, her reply was thirty seconds old. "Never mind & try not 2 let hm no ur on hm," she'd written.

Know, he thought, then typed "Bigend?"

"When U back"

"Hollis thinks we're back tomorrow."

"Ur lucky ur in paris out"

"Over," he wrote, though he wasn't sure that was right. Her telegraphese was infectious. He saved the URL of the elite operator's page to bookmarks, then logged out of Twitter, out of his webmail, and closed the computer. His Neo began to ring, its archaic dial-phone tone filling the tobacco shop. The man behind the counter was frowning.

"Yes?"

"You're lucky to be in Paris." It was Pamela Mainwaring. "Not ours."

His first thought was that she'd somehow been watching his Twitter exchange with Winnie. "Not?"

"She rang us. Definitely not. Be lovely to have a snap from Paris."

Hollis. Pamela's call constrained now by Bigend's suspicion of Sleight and the Neo. "I'll try," Milgrim said.

"Enjoy," she said, and hung up.

Milgrim hoisted his bag to the zinc counter, unzipped it, found his camera. He loaded it with a fresh card, Blue Ant having kept the one he'd used in Myrtle Beach. They always did. He checked the batteries, then put the camera in his jacket pocket. He put Hollis's laptop in his bag and zipped it shut. Leaving a few small coins on the zinc counter, he left the shop and headed back to the Salon du Vintage, walking quickly again.

Was he still angry? he wondered. He was calmer now, he decided. He knew he wouldn't be telling Bigend about Winnie. Not if he could help it, anyway.

It was warmer, the cloud burning away. Paris seemed slightly un-real, the way London always did when he first arrived. How peculiar, that these places had always existed back-to-back, as close together and as separate as the two sides of a coin, yet wormholed now by a fast train and twenty-some miles of tunnel.

At the Salon du Vintage, after paying five euros admission, he checked his bag, something he never liked doing. He'd stolen enough checked luggage himself to know this arrangement as easy pickings. On the other hand, he'd be more mobile without it. He smiled at the Japanese girl, pocketed his bag check, and entered.

He was more at home in the world of objects, his therapist said, than the world of people. The Salon du Vintage, he assured himself, was about objects. Wishing to become the person the Salon du Vintage would want him to be, hence somehow less visible, he climbed a handsomely renovated stairway to the second floor.

The first thing he saw there was that poster of a younger Hollis, looking at once nervy and naughty. This was not the actual poster, he judged, but an amateurish reproduction, oversized and lacking in de-tail. He wondered what it would be like for her, seeing that.

He had left relatively few images himself over the past decade or so, and probably Winnie had seen most of those. Had them ready, perhaps, to e-mail to someone she wanted to be able to recognize him. Most of those had been taken by the police, and he wondered whether he'd recognize them himself. He'd certainly recognize the one she'd taken in the Caffè Nero in Seven Dials, and that would be the one she'd use.

The young man in the forage cap and foliage green pants, his black jacket still zipped, emerged from a side aisle of racks, his attention cap-tured by a darting shoal of young Japanese girls. He'd removed his mir-rored wraparound sunglasses. Milgrim stepped sideways, behind a mannequin in a delirious photo-print dress, keeping his man in sight over its massively padded shoulder, and wondered what he should do. If Foley didn't already know he was here, and saw him, he'd be recog-nized from Selfridges. If not, he supposed, from South Carolina. Winnie had been there, watching him, and someone, he'd assumed Sleight, had photographed her there. Should he tell her about that? He flagged it for consideration. Foley was walking away now, toward the rear of the building. Milgrim remembered the man with the mullet, in the moth-balled restaurant. Foley didn't have that, Milgrim decided, whatever that had been, and it was a very good thing. He stepped from behind the Gaultier and followed, ready to simply keep walking if he was dis-covered. If Foley didn't notice him, that would be a plus, but the main thing was for Milgrim not to be thought to be following him. His hand in his jacket pocket, on his camera.

Now it was Foley's turn to step sideways, behind a neon-clad man-nequin. Milgrim turned, toward a nearby display of costume jewelry, conveniently finding Foley reflected, distantly, in the seller's mirror.

A red-haired girl offered to help him, in French.

"No," said Milgrim, "thank you," seeing Foley, in the mirror, step from behind his mannequin. He turned, pressing the button that ex-truded the camera's optics, raised it, and snapped two pictures of Foley's receding back. The red-haired girl was looking at him. He smiled and walked on, pocketing the camera.

23. MEREDITH

Maybe Milgrim was the one who was hallucinating here, she thought, as she climbed the Scandinavian stairway again, a tall paper cup of quadruple-shot Americain held gingerly in either hand. The coffee was steaming hot; if Milgrim's possibly imaginary stalker suddenly manifested, she thought, she could hurl the contents of both cups.

Whatever that had been, down in the deserted blue-lit disco, if it had been anything at all, it now seemed like some random frame-splice from someone else's movie: Milgrim's, Bigend's, anyone but hers. But she'd avoid that elevator, just in case, and she were still on the lookout for vaguely Nazi caps.

Milgrim had issues, clearly. Was in fact deeply peculiar. She scarcely knew him. He might well be seeing things. He looked, pretty much constantly, as though he *were* seeing things.

She carefully kept the blow-up of the Corbijn portrait out of her field of vision as she reached the second floor and the Salon du Vintage. Keeping her mind off the basement as well, she wondered exactly when coffee had gone walkabout in France. When she'd first been here, drinking coffee hadn't been a pedestrian activity. One either sat to do it, in cafés or restaurants, or stood, at bars or on railway platforms, and drank from sturdy vessels, china or glass, themselves made in France. Had Starbucks brought the takeaway cup? she wondered. She doubted it. They hadn't really had the time. More likely McDonald's.

Her antique denim dealer, intense and ponytailed, was busy with a customer, laying out a pair of ancient dungarees that seemed to have more holes than fabric. He looked as though he should have supplemental lenses hinged to the edges of his rimless rectangular spectacles. He didn't see her pass.

And here, past the inflatable orange furniture, came a funeral, and Olduvai George marching jauntily along beside it, smiling.

Four Japanese men in dark suits, unsmiling, a black coffin or body bag slung between them.

They passed her, but not George. Delighted, he took one of the coffees. "Thank you very much."

"Sugar?"

"No, thank you." He sipped hungrily.

"Who were they?" Looking over her shoulder as the four bore their somber burden out of sight, down the stairs.

He lowered the cup, wiped his mouth with the back of his startlingly furred hand. "Mere's buyer's minders. The Chanel's in that bag, all of it, packed with archival tissue. And there's Mere," he added, "with the buyer."

And two more black-suited minders. The buyer, she thought at first, was a twelve-year-old boy, costumed like a child in some archaic comic strip: tight, silky-looking yellow shorts to midthigh, a red-and-green-striped long-sleeved jersey, a yellow beanie, yellow boots like oversized baby shoes. He looked sour, petulant. And then she saw the hint of five-o'clock shadow, the jowls. He was talking with a slender young woman in jeans and a white shirt.

"Designer," George said, after another eager swallow. "Harajuku. Fabulous collection."

"Of Chanel?"

"Everything, apparently. I'm guessing it's gone well for Mere."

"How can you tell?"

"He's still alive."

The dress forms, she saw, were bare and gray.

Now the designer turned, flanked by the two remaining suits, and walked toward them.

They watched him pass.

"Are the people who buy Chanel all like that?" she asked.

"Never sold any before. Time you met Mere."

He led her past the orange bubble-furniture.

Meredith Overton was stroking the horizontal screen of an iPhone, pinching up virtual bits of information. Ash-blond, wide gray eyes. She looked up at them. "It's in the bank, in Melbourne. Direct transfer."

"Did well, I take it?" George was smiling broadly.

"Very."

"Congratulations," said Hollis.

"Hollis Henry," said George.

"Meredith Overton," taking Hollis's hand. "Mere. Pleased to meet you." Hollis guessed that her jeans were Hounds, slender and too long, worn rucked rather than rolled, and a man's rumpled white oxford shirt, though it fit too well to really be a man's.

"They didn't want the purses," Meredith said. "Just the couture. But I've backup buyers for those, dealers here at the fair." She pocketed her phone.

Hollis, out of the corner of her eyes, saw Milgrim pass them. He carried a small camera at his side, and seemed to be looking at nothing in particular. She ignored him. "Thank you for being willing to see me," she said to Meredith. "I suppose you know what it's about."

"Bloody Clammy," said Meredith, but not uncheerfully. "You're after Hounds, aren't you?"

"Not so much the product as its maker," Hollis said, watching Meredith's expression.

"You wouldn't be the first." Meredith smiled. "But there isn't much I can tell you."

"Would you like a coffee?" Offering Meredith her own cup. "I haven't touched it."

"No, thank you."

"Hollis has been extremely helpful," George said, "about Inchmale."

"Horrid man," said Meredith, to Hollis.

"He is that," Hollis agreed. "Prides himself."

"I'm less anxious, now," said George, though Hollis found it difficult to imagine him anxious at all. "Hollis understands Reg's process from experience. She puts things into perspective."

Meredith took Hollis's cup now, and sipped gingerly from the slot in the plastic lid. Wrinkled her nose. "Black," she said.

"Sugar if you want it."

"You're really leaning on me now, aren't you," Meredith said to George.

"I am," said George. "And I've waited until you're in a very good mood."

"If that little shit hadn't met my price," Meredith said, "I wouldn't be."

"True," said George, "but he did."

"I think he wears them himself," said Meredith. "Not that I think he's gay. That would make it okay, actually. He insisted on all the documentation, everything we'd collected on their original owner. Something about that's left me wanting a shower." She took another sip of hot black coffee and handed the cup back to Hollis. "You want to know who designs the Gabriel Hounds."

"I do," said Hollis.

"Nice jacket."

"A gift," Hollis said, which was at least technically true.

"You'd have a hard time finding one now. They haven't done them for a few seasons. Not that they have seasons in the ordinary sense."

"No?" Studiously avoiding the matter of who "they" were.

"When they remake the jackets, if they ever do, they'll be exactly the same, cut from exactly the same pattern. The fabric might be different, but only an otaku could tell." She began to collect the slender security cables that had secured the Chanel suits to their dress forms, until she held them in one hand like a strange bouquet, or a steel flail.

"I don't think I understand," Hollis said.

"It's about atemporality. About opting out of the industrialization of novelty. It's about deeper code."

Reminding Hollis of something Milgrim might have said, but she'd forgotten exactly what. She looked around, wondering if he was still in sight. He wasn't.

"Lose something?"

"I'm here with someone. But never mind. Please."

"I'm not sure I should help you with this. Probably I shouldn't. And actually, I can't."

"You can't?"

"Because I'm no longer in the loop. Because they've gotten that much harder to find, since I took Clammy to buy his jeans in Melbourne."

"But you could tell me what you do know." Hollis saw that George had busied himself collapsing the chrome stands of the dress forms, closing up shop.

"Were you ever a model?"

"No," said Hollis.

"I was," said Meredith, "for two years. I had a booker who loved using me. That's the key, really, your booker. New York, L.A., all over western Europe, home to Australia for more work, back to New York, back here. Intensely nomadic. George says more so than being in a band. You can cope, when you're seventeen, even when you've no money. Almost literally no money. I lived here, one winter, in a monthly-rent hotel room with three other girls. Hot plate, tiny fridge. Eighty euros a week 'pocket money.' That was what they called it. That was to live on. I couldn't afford an Orange Card for the Métro. I walked everywhere. I was in *Vogue*, but I couldn't afford to buy a copy. Fees were almost entirely eaten up before the checks found me, and the checks were always late. That's the way it works, if you're just another foot soldier, which is what I was. I slept on couches in New York, the floor of an apartment with no electricity in Milan. It became apparent to me that the industry was grossly, baroquely dysfunctional."

"Modeling?"

"Fashion. The people I met who I most got on with, aside from some of the other girls, were stylists, people who finessed little bits of trim for the shoots, adjusted things, sourced antiques, props. Some of them had been to very good art schools, and it had put them off, profoundly. They didn't want to be what they'd been groomed to be, and really it's the nature of that system that not that many people can, ever. But they came out with brilliant skill sets for being stylists. And art school had made them masters of a kind of systems analysis. Extremely good at figuring out how an industry really runs, what the real products are. Which they did constantly, without really being that aware of doing it. And I listened to them. And all of them were pickers."

Hollis nodded, remembering Pamela explaining the term.

"Constantly finding things. Value in rubbish. That ability to distinguish one thing from another. The eye for detail. And knowing where to sell it on, of course. I began to acquire that, watching, listening. Loved that, really. Meanwhile, I wore out runners, walking."

"Here?"

"All over. Lot of Milan. Listening to stylists absently lecture on the fundamental dysfunction of the fashion industry. What my friends and I were going through as models was just a reflection of something bigger, broader. *Everyone* was waiting for their check. The whole industry wobbles along, really, like a shopping cart with a missing wheel. You can only keep it moving if you lean on it a certain way and keep pushing, but if you stop, it tips over. Season to season, show to show, you keep it moving."

Which reminded Hollis of a Curfew tour, though she didn't say so. She took a sip of the unsweetened Americain, which was cooling, and listened.

"My grandmother died, I'm the only grandchild, she left a bit of money. My booker was leaving the agency, getting out of the business. I applied to Cordwainers College, London College of Fashion, accessories and footwear. Done with modeling. It was the runners."

"Sneakers?"

"The ones I wore out walking. The ugliest ones were best for walking, the best-looking fell apart. The stylists would talk about them, because I'd show up in them, at shoots. Talk about how the business worked. The factories in China, Vietnam. The big companies. And I'd started to imagine ones that weren't ugly at all, that didn't fall apart.

But somehow," and she smiled ruefully, "untainted by fashion. I'd started doing drawings. Very bad ones. But I'd already decided that I really wanted to understand shoes, their history, how they work, before I tried to do anything. Not that conscious a decision, but a decision. So I applied to Cordwainers, was accepted, moved to London. Or rather, simply stopped moving. In London. I may just have been enamored of the idea of waking up in the same town every day, but I had my mission, the mystery runners that I couldn't quite imagine."

"And you made them, in the end?"

"Two seasons. We couldn't get away from that structure. But that was only after I'd graduated. I could still make you quite a smashing pair of shoes, with my own hands, though the finishing would never get past my tutor there. But they did teach us everything. Exhaustively."

"Sneakers?"

"Not the sole-molding or the vulcanization, but I could still cut and sew your uppers. We used a lot of elk for our line. Very thick, supple. Lovely." She looked down at the security cables in her hand. "My second year, there, I met someone, a boy, Danny. American. From Chicago. Not at Cordwainers but he knew all my friends there. Skater. Well, not that he skated much. An entrepreneur, that way, but nothing too repulsive. Made films for some of the American companies. We lived together. Hackney. He had Hounds," Meredith said, looking up from the cables, "before there were Hounds."

"Yes?"

"He had a jacket quite a lot like yours, but made of a sort of canvas, off-white, plain brass buttons. Always in need of a good wash. Perfectly simple, but it was one of those things that everyone immediately wanted or, failing that, wanted the name of a designer, a brand. He'd laugh at them. Tell them it was no-name. Tell them it was 'fucking real, not fashion.' That a friend of his in Chicago had made it."

"Chicago?"

"Chicago. Where he was from."

"His friend was a designer?"

"He never called her that."

"Her?"

"That was no-name too. He wouldn't tell me her name. He never did." Looking Hollis firmly in the eye. "I don't think she'd been a girl-friend. She was older, I guessed. And more a hobbyist than a designer, from what he said. He said she did things more out of a sense of what she didn't like than what she did, if that makes any sense. And she was very good. Very. But what I got from it, really, was that I was on the right track, with what I was designing, my shoes. On a track, anyway."

"What was your track?"

"Things that weren't tied to the present moment. Not to any mo-ment, really, so not retro either."

"What happened to your line?" Hollis asked.

"Business happened. Business as usual. We weren't able to invent a new business model. Our backing wasn't sufficient to carry us through that routine dysfunction. We crashed and burned. There might be a warehouse full of our last season in Seattle. If I could find it, get my hands on it, the eBay sales would be worth more money than we ever saw from the line."

George held open a battered Galeries Lafayette bag and Mere thrust the security cables into it.

"Can I offer you dinner?" Hollis asked.

"Where are you staying?" George asked her.

"St. Germain. By the Odéon Métro."

"I know a place," said George. "I'll make reservations for eight."

"Meredith?"

Meredith considered Hollis. Then nodded.

"For four, please," Hollis said.

24. HUNCH

Milgrim sat at a table in the courtyard's busy café, camera in his lap, cycling through his four shots of Foley.

The two from behind might be useful if you wanted to send someone to follow him. The quarter profile, against a glare of Eighties color, was actually less useful. Could be anyone. Had women's clothing actually been that bright, in the Eighties?

But this one, which he'd shot blind, by reaching around, behind a hennaed German girl, was excellent. The girl had given him a dirty look, for getting too close. He'd smelled her perfume; something pointedly inorganic. The scent of coolly focused concentration, perhaps. "Sorry," he'd said, and stepped back, palming the little camera, wondering if he'd captured Foley, who now had vanished again.

He'd looked down, summoned the image. And had found Foley, zoomed, in tight focus, crookedly off-center in the frame. He'd seen how Foley's sunglasses had left slight tan lines, recalling the porn rectangle he'd worn on the link Winnie had sent. The cap's short bill effectively concealed his forehead, cutting out a good deal of emotional information. His features were smooth, as if untouched by experience, and confident, a confidence that Milgrim suspected he might not entirely be feeling. Something he'd try to project, regardless of the situation.

With the camera semiconcealed in his right hand, Milgrim had moved on, scanning the busy Salon for Foley. He'd soon found him, but simultaneously had found Hollis, who was listening intently to a younger woman in jeans and a white shirt. Hollis had seen him, he was certain. Milgrim, focused on Foley's receding back, had ignored her, avoiding eye-connect. When Foley had descended the stairs, Milgrim had followed, then had watched as Foley left the building.

He'd gone into the courtyard, ordered an espresso, and settled down to study his photographs.

Now he turned the camera off, opened the little hatch on the bottom and removed the blue card, the size of a postage stamp. When had he last used an actual postage stamp? He couldn't remember. It gave him a strange feeling to even think of one. He reached down, hiked the cuff of his new pants, and slipped the card quite far down into his sock, which he then pulled up, allowing his cuff to fall back into place.

He was not a methodical man by nature, his therapist had said, but the constant ongoing state of emergency imposed by his active addiction had shown him the practical advantages of method, which had then become habit.

He took an unused card from the inside pocket of his jacket and extracted it, with the usual difficulty, from its cardboard backing. He inserted it, closed the hatch, and slipped the camera into the side pocket of his jacket.

The Neo rang, from a different pocket. He brought it out. It looked even uglier than usual.

"Yes?"

"Just checking your phone," Sleight said, unconvincingly. "We're having trouble with the whole system." Sleight had always spoken of the Neos as a system, but Milgrim had met no one else, other than Sleight, who had one.

"Seems to be working," Milgrim said.

"How are things?"

Sleight had never made it a secret that he was able to track Milgrim with the Neo, but only referred to it obliquely, if at all. The subtext, now, being that he knew Milgrim was in Paris. Knew that Milgrim was in this courtyard of this building, perhaps, given that extra overlay of Russian GPS.

When their relationship had begun, Milgrim had been unwilling to question anything. Sleight had set the terms, in every way, and so it had been.

"It's raining," said Milgrim, looking up at blue sky, bright clouds.

A silence lengthened.

He was trying to force Sleight to admit to knowing his location, but he didn't know why. It was something to do with the anger he'd felt, was probably still feeling. Was that a good thing?

"How's New York?" Milgrim asked, losing his nerve.

"Toronto," said Sleight, "getting hot. See you." He was gone.

Milgrim looked at the Neo. Something was unfolding within him. Like a brochure, he thought, rather than the butterfly he imagined to be the more common image. An unpleasant brochure, the sort that lays out symptoms all too clearly.

Why had Sleight actually called? Had he really needed to check Milgrim's phone? Did a brief moment of live voice provide Sleight with the opportunity to manipulate the Neo in some way that he couldn't, otherwise?

If Milgrim spoke now, he wondered for the very first time, would Sleight hear him?

It suddenly seemed entirely likely to him that Sleight could.

He sat back in his white-enameled aluminum chair, aware again of that emotion he supposed was anger. He could feel the Faraday pouch, containing his passport, slung on its cord, under his shirt. Blocking radio waves. Preventing the RFID in his U.S. passport from being read.

He looked at the Neo.

Without consciously making any decision, he undid the top button of his shirt, fished the pouch out, opened it, and slid the Neo in with his passport. He tucked it back into his shirt and buttoned up.

The pouch was bulkier now, visible under his shirt.

He finished his espresso, which had cooled, and was bitter, and left some coins on the small square receipt. He stood up, buttoned his jacket over the slight bulge of the pouch, and reentered the Salon du Vintage. Still scanning for Foley, who for all he knew had returned.

He took his time, making his way up the stairs, and then stood for a while, looking up at the blowup of Hollis's poster. Then he undid his top button again, drew out the pouch, opened it, and removed the Neo, which rang immediately.

"Hello?" As he tucked the pouch back in with his free hand.

"Were you on an elevator?"

"It was filled with Japanese girls," Milgrim said, watching one pass. "Only three floors, here, but I couldn't get off."

"Just checking," said Sleight, neutrally, and hung up.

Milgrim looked at the Neo, Sleight's extension, wondering for the first time if it was really off when he turned it off. Perhaps it needed its batteries removed for that. Though, come to think it, Sleight forbade that. Or its two cards, which Milgrim was also forbidden to remove.

Sleight had noticed it going into the Faraday pouch. Milgrim had been briefly invisible, as he'd sometimes gathered he was in elevators, for similar reasons.

Given everything else Sleight had said he could do with the Neo, having it function as a bug actually seemed like a very modest capacity. And it would help explain why they'd bothered with the thing at all, cranky as it was. He'd been carrying around a wire. Would Bigend have known about that? Milgrim wondered.

Sleight had given him the Neo on their flight from Basel to London, at the end of Milgrim's treatment. He'd had it with him constantly, since then. Except, he remembered, yesterday, when Sleight had ordered him to leave it in his room. When Winnie had taken his picture. When he'd gone to Blue Ant to tell Bigend about that, and Bigend had suggested he no longer trusted Sleight. When he'd gone to the department store to have lunch with Hollis, then back to his hotel, where Winnie had been waiting. So Sleight had missed all of that, missed it because, if he was telling the truth, the company that made the Neo had gone bankrupt. "Lucky," said Milgrim, then winced, imagining Sleight, Bluetoothed, somewhere, hearing him. But if Foley was Sleight's, which was only one possibility, how had Foley known to find them at the department store? Perhaps he was following Hollis instead? But then, he reminded himself, Foley was someone else who had his picture on Winnie's wall.

The Neo rang in his hand.

"Yes?"

"Where are you?" Hollis. "I saw you walk past."

"Can you meet me? By the entrance, downstairs."

"Are you up here?"

"Downstairs."

"On my way," she said.

"Good," he said, and clicked off. Resisting the impulse to whistle for Sleight's benefit, he put his phone in his jacket pocket, then removed his jacket, wrapped it several times around the phone, tucked the resulting bundle under his arm, and headed for the stairs.

25. TINFOIL

Hollis found Milgrim giving his jacket to the Japanese girl at the bag check. "I'm finished," she said. "We can go now, if you're ready."

Milgrim turned, took her hand, and led her away from the bag check.

"Is something wrong?"

"My phone," said Milgrim, releasing her hand on the far side of the entranceway. "They're listening through it."

Tinfoil hats, people whose fillings broadcast thought-control messages. "'They' who?"

"Sleight. Bigend doesn't trust him."

"Neither do I." She never had. And now that she thought of Sleight, Milgrim didn't sound quite as automatically crazy. That was the trouble with Bigendland. People did things like that. The ones like Sleight did, anyway. Then again, Milgrim might just be crazy.

Or on drugs. What if he'd slipped? Gone back on whatever it was they'd gotten him off of in Switzerland? Where was the semi-absent character she'd met over tapas? He looked worked up, a little sweaty, maybe angry about something. He looked more like someone in particular, anyway, she realized, and that was what had been missing before. The lack of that was what had made him simultaneously so peculiar and so forgettable. She was looking into the eyes of someone experiencing the anxiety of sudden arrival. But Milgrim's arrival, she somehow knew, was from within. But all because he thought he'd seen someone? Though someone, she reminded herself, she'd thought she'd seen too, in the basement. "I saw him," she said. "Maybe."

"Where?" Milgrim stepped back, allowing a pair of spryly geriatric American men to pass, headed for the stairs.

They looked to Hollis like aged hair-metal rockers in expensive mufti, and seemed to be talking golf. Did they collect vintage Chanel? "Downstairs," she said. "I pushed the wrong button in the elevator. Then he came down the stairs. I think."

"What did you do?"

"Got back in the elevator. Up. Didn't see him again, but I was busy."

"He's here," Milgrim said.

"You saw him?"

"I took his picture. Pamela wants it. I could show you, but the card's not in my camera."

"He's here now?" She looked around.

"I saw him go out," glancing toward the entrance. "Doesn't mean he hasn't come back."

"I asked Bigend. He said they didn't have anyone watching us."

"Do you believe him?"

"Depends how much it matters to him. But we've got bad history, that way, between us. If he bullshits me again, and I find out about it, I'm gone. He understands that." She looked Milgrim in the eye. "You aren't high on anything, are you?"

"No."

"You seem different. I'm worried about you."

"I'm in recovery," said Milgrim. "I'm *supposed* to be different. If I were high, I wouldn't *be* different."

"You seem angry."

"Not with you."

"But you weren't angry, before."

"It wasn't allowed," he said, and she heard his amazement, as if in saying this he'd discovered something about himself he'd never known before. He swallowed. "I want to find out if Sleight's telling him where I am. I think I know how to do that."

"What did Bigend say about Sleight?"

"He warned me to be careful of the Neo."

"What's that?"

"My phone. The brand. They're bankrupt now."

"Who is?"

"The company who made it. Sleight always knows where I am. The phone tells him. But I've known that."

"You have?"

"I thought Bigend wanted him to. Did want him to, probably. It wasn't a secret."

"You think he listens through it?"

"He made me leave it in the hotel, yesterday. Charging. He does that when he wants to reprogram it, add or subtract applications."

"I thought he was in New York."

"He programs it from wherever he is."

"Is he listening now?"

"It's in my jacket. Over there." He pointed at the bag check. "I shouldn't leave it there for long."

"What do you want to do?"

"Did Blue Ant make the hotel reservations?"

"I did."

"By phone?"

"Through the hotel's website. I didn't tell anyone where we'd be. What do you want to do?"

"We'll get a cab. You get in first, tell the driver Galeries Lafayette. Sleight won't hear. Then I'll get in. Don't say anything about Galeries Lafayette, or about the hotel. Then I'll block the GPS."

"How?"

"I have a way. I've already tried it. He thought I was in an elevator."

"Then what?"

"I'll get out at Galeries Lafayette, you'll go on, I'll unblock my phone. And see if Foley comes to find me."

"Who's Foley?"

"Foliage green pants."

"But what if someone's here, and they just follow the cab?"

"That's a lot of people. If they have a lot of people, there's nothing we can do. They'll follow you too." He shrugged. "Where are we staying?"

"It's called the Odéon. So is the street. And it's by Odéon Métro. Easy to remember. Your room is on my credit card, and I've paid for one night. We have an eight o'clock dinner reservation, near the hotel. In my name."

"We do?"

"With Meredith and George. I learned something, upstairs, but I think we might learn more, tonight."

Milgrim blinked. "You want me there?"

"We're working together, aren't we?"

He nodded.

"Place called Les Éditeurs. George says you can see it from the hotel."

"Eight," said Milgrim. "When I get my jacket, don't forget the phone's in it. Sleight. Listening. When we get a cab, you get in first, tell the driver Galeries Lafayette."

"Why there?"

"It's big. Department stores are good."

"They are?"

"For losing people." He was at the counter now, giving the girl his ticket. She passed him his jacket and his black bag. Hollis presented hers and the girl wheeled her roll-aboard out.

"Merci," said Hollis.

Milgrim had put his jacket on and was already headed out the door.

26. MOTHER RUSSIA

Kleenex?" Milgrim asked as the cab turned right, into what he recognized as the Rue du Temple. "My sinuses are bothering me," he added, for Sleight's benefit.

Hollis, seated to his left, behind the driver, produced a pack from her purse.

"Thanks." He removed three tissues, handed the pack back, unfolded one, spread it across his knees, and took the Neo from his pocket. He showed it to her, presenting it from different angles, which made him feel something like a conjurer, though he was none too certain about what his trick might be.

The cab turned left, into another street, one that doubled back at a sharp angle. He imagined Sleight watching a cursor represent this on a screen. It seemed unlikely, though he couldn't understand why that should be. He knew that Sleight did things like that, constantly. Sleight could be watching on the screen of his own Neo.

Milgrim lay the Neo on the Kleenex, resting it in the valley between his knees, opened the other two sheets, and began to carefully polish it. When he was finished, he remembered having idly removed the back, on the flight to Atlanta. Now he opened it again, rubbing down the inside of the battery cover and the exposed face of the battery, then replacing it. When he'd finished rubbing down the outside, he carefully folded the first tissue around it and slipped it into his pocket. He crumpled the other two and wiped his palms with them.

"Have you been in Paris before?" Hollis asked.

She seemed relaxed, her purse on her lap, the dark collar of the denim jacket turned up. "Once," he said, "when I was just out of Columbia. For a month, with another graduate. We sublet an apartment."

"Did you enjoy it?"

"It was nice, to be here with someone."

She looked out the window, as if remembering something, then looked back at him. "Were you in love?"

"No."

"A couple?"

"Yes," he said, though it seemed strange to say it.

"It didn't work, for you?"

"I wasn't available," he said. "I didn't know that, but I wasn't, really. I learned that in Basel." He remembered Sleight, their hypothetical listener. He pointed at the pocket that held his tissue-wrapped Neo.

"Sorry," she said.

"It's okay."

They took a right, then left again, at an intersection where he glimpsed a sign for the Strasbourg-Saint-Denis Métro, and into heavier traffic.

They rode in silence for a few minutes. Then he undid the top button of his shirt and drew out the Faraday pouch.

"What's that?"

"Métro station," he said, for Sleight, then touched his index finger to his lips.

She nodded.

He opened the pouch, inserted the Neo, then closed it. "It blocks radio signals. Like when you're in an elevator. If he was listening, he can't hear us now. And he just lost track of where we are."

"Why do you have it?"

"He gave it to me," he said. "It's for my passport. He's worried someone will read the microchip."

"Do they do that?"

"People like Sleight do."

"How does it work?"

"It has metallic fibers. When I tested it, before, he lost me. Thought I was in an elevator."

"But if it's that easy," she said, "why did he give it to you?"

"He insisted on it," said Milgrim. "I think he really does worry about the chip-reading thing. It's something he's done himself."

"But he gave you your means of avoiding surveillance, right there."

"When I put it in the pouch, before, that was the first time I did something that I knew he wouldn't want me to do. I wasn't well, when I met him. He worked for Bigend and I did what I was told."

She looked at him. Then nodded. "I understand."

"But Sleight," he said, "really *liked* it, having someone who'd do exactly what he said."

"He would, yes."

"I don't think he imagined I'd ever get to the point where I'd use the pouch on the Neo. He would've enjoyed being able to count on that."

"What will you do at Galeries Lafayette?"

"Wait till you're gone, then take it out of the pouch. Then see who turns up."

"But what if someone's following us now, the old-fashioned way?"

"Have the driver take you to a Métro station. Do you know the Métro?"

"More or less."

"If you're clever, you can probably lose anyone who might try to follow you."

"We're here."

He saw that they were in Boulevard Haussmann, the driver signaling to pull over.

"Take care of yourself," she said. "If that was him I saw in the basement, I didn't like the look of him."

"I didn't get the feeling that he was that good, at the Salon," he said, checking that the strap of his bag was securely over his shoulder.

"Good?"

"Scary."

He opened the door before the cab had fully come to a halt. The driver said something in irritated French. "Sorry," he said as they stopped, and slipped out, closing the door behind him.

From the curb he looked back, saw Hollis smiling, telling the driver something. The cab pulled back into traffic.

He quickly entered Galeries Lafayette and walked on, until he was beneath the center of the soaring mercantile mosque-dome of stained glass. He stood there, looking up, briefly experiencing the reflexive country-mouse awe the architect had intended to induce. A cross between Grand Central and the atrium of the Brown Palace, Denver, structures aimed heroically into futures that had never really happened. Wide balconies ringed every level, rising toward the dome. Beyond them he could see the tops of racks of clothing, rather than any audience, but if there had been an audience, he, Milgrim, would have been standing in exactly the spot where the fat lady would ultimately sing.

He drew the Faraday pouch out, on its cord, and removed the Neo, exposing it to whatever intricate soup of signals existed here. Within its childish-looking shroud of Kleenex, it began to ring.

Sleight had arranged things so that it was impossible to turn the ring off, but Milgrim thumbed the volume down, all the way, and put it into his side jacket pocket. It vibrated a few times, then quit. He took it out again, opened the Kleenex to check the time, careful not to touch it, then put it back.

He had whatever remained of his three hundred pounds, unchanged, the euros Hollis had given, plus another thin fold of euros remaining from his Basel pocket money. He decided to invest in his own future, one much more immediate than the one the founders of Galeries Lafayette had imagined.

He found his way into the men's store, a separate building next door, and selected a pair of black French briefs, then a pair of black cotton-blend crew socks, paying for them with almost all of his Basel money. The euro bills reminded him, obscurely, of Disneyland's original Tomorrowland, where his mother had taken him as a child.

The Neo began to vibrate again, in his pocket. He let it, trying to imagine the look on Sleight's face. But Sleight knew where he was, and quite possibly had heard the cashier's side of the socks-and-underwear transaction, which Milgrim for his part had conducted nonverbally, with soft apologetic grunts. The Kleenex, he hoped, was muffling things a bit, though he supposed it didn't really matter.

He went back into the main store and rode escalators, into realms of lingerie, sportswear, little black dresses. If he were sure how much time he had, he thought, he'd look for the furniture department. The furniture departments of large department stores were oases of calm, usually. He'd often found them soothing. They were also very good places in which to determine whether or not you were being followed. But he really didn't think that he was being followed, that way.

He walked through a grove of Ralph Lauren, then a thinner one of Hilfiger, to a balustrade overlooking the central atrium. Looking down, he saw Foley crossing from the direction of Boulevard Haussmann. Take off the cap, he thought. A professional would have done that, at least, and removed the black jacket as well.

When Foley reached almost the exact spot where Milgrim himself had paused to look up, he paused as well, just as Milgrim had, taking in the dome. Milgrim stepped back, knowing Foley would scan the balustrades next, which indeed he did.

You know I'm here, Milgrim thought, but you don't know exactly where. He saw Foley speak. To Sleight, he imagined, via a headset.

A moment later, Milgrim was alone in an elevator, pressing the button for the top floor, his improv module kicking in. Open to opportunity.

The elevator stopped at the next floor. The door slid open, and was quickly held by a thick arm in charcoal gray, the arm of a large man.

"It's a shame you no longer live here in the city," said a tall blonde, in Russian, to another young woman beside her, equally tall, equally blond. The second blonde rolled a massive pram or stroller into the elevator, some sort of luxury baby-transporter on three bulbous wheels, a thing made apparently of carbon-fiber and sharkskin, everything a gray like the bodyguard's suit.

"It's shit in the suburbs," replied the pram-driver, in Russian, setting the thing's hand brake with a flick of her finger. "A villa. Two hours. Dogs. Guards. Shit."

The bodyguard stepped in, eyeing Milgrim darkly. Milgrim backed up, as far as possible, a handrail digging painfully into his spine, and looked down at the floor. The door closed and the elevator began to rise. Milgrim stole a look at the two women, instantly regretting it for the attention it cost him from their looming guardian. He looked back down. The mega-stroller looked like something from the cabin of a very expensive airplane, perhaps the drinks trolley. Whatever infant it held was entirely concealed by a sharkskin cowl or fairing, probably bulletproof. "Surely he can't have lost that much," said the first blonde.

"It was all heavily leveraged," said the pram-driver.

"What does that mean?"

"That we have no Paris apartment, and shop in Galeries Lafayette," said the pram-driver, bitterly.

Milgrim, who hadn't heard Russian since leaving Basel, felt a peculiar enchantment, in spite of the sullen presence of their guard, and the handrail in his back. The elevator stopped, the door opened, and a tall Parisian teenager stepped in. As the door closed, Milgrim noted the guard's focus on the girl, no less sullen but absolute. Slender, brunette, she looked from Milgrim to the two Russian women with a sort of benign disdain, ignoring the guard.

When the elevator stopped again, and the door opened, Milgrim took the Neo from his jacket pocket and tucked it into a sharkskin pocket on the front of the super-pram, feeling it fall into the company of what he guessed were toys, tins of balm or perhaps caviar, or whatever else one needed for an infant oligarch. Doing it, as a pickpocket had once advised him, as if it were not only the expected but the only thing to do. He looked up at the guard, whose eyes were still locked on the brunette. Who turned, then, gazelle-like and justifiably bored, and stepped out, past the guard, as the pram-driver flicked the brake switch off and dragged the thing back out of the elevator like a parts cart in a tank factory.

The guard noticed Milgrim again, but stepped quickly out of the elevator, unwilling to lose sight of his charges.

Milgrim remained where he was as the door closed and the elevator rose again.

"Dogs," he said, to Sleight, who could no longer hear him. "Guards."

27. JAPANESE BASEBALL

How's Paris?" The image that came up for Heidi's call, on the iPhone, was a decade old, black-and-white, gritty. Jimmy's white Fender bass, out of focus in the foreground.

"I don't know," Hollis said. She was in Sèvres-Babylone, walking between platforms, her bag's trick wheel ticking steadily, like a personal metronome. She had decided to give Milgrim's worries the benefit of the doubt, taking a random course through the Métro, short hops, line changes, abrupt reversals. If anyone was following her, she hadn't noticed them. But it was crowded now, tiring, and she'd just decided to head for Odéon, and the hotel, when Heidi called. "I think I've found something, but someone may have found me."

"Meaning?"

"Milgrim thought he saw someone, here, who he'd seen in London. At Selfridges, when you were getting your hair cut."

"You said he was bugfuck."

"I said he seemed unfocused. Anyway, he seems more focused now. Though maybe bugfuck too." At least her bag wasn't too heavy, minus the copy of her book that she'd given Milgrim. And her Air, she remembered: He still had that.

"Does Bigend have people there for you?"

"I didn't want that. I didn't tell them where I was staying."

"Where are you staying?"

"Latin Quarter." She hesitated. "A hotel where I stayed with Garreth."

Heidi pounced. "Really. And was that Garreth's choice, then, or yours?"

"His." As she reached her platform, and the waiting crowd.

"And which hand are you carrying this torch in?"

"I'm not."

"My hairy ass you're not."

"You don't. Have one."

"Don't be so sure," Heidi said. "Marriage."

"What about it?"

"Does things to you."

"And how's fuckstick?"

"Out on bond now. Not that much media. Ponzi's under a half a billion total. Current climate, they're embarrassed to offer the story to the public. Petty sums. Like foreign serial killers."

"What about them?" The train was pulling in.

"America's the capital of serial murder. Foreign serial murder's like Japanese baseball."

"How are you, Heidi?"

"Found a gym. Hacky."

"Hack*ney*."

The doors opened and the crowd moved forward, taking Hollis with it.

"Thought it was where they invented the sack." Disappointed. "Kind of like Silverlake. Fixed-up. Creatives. But the gym's old-school. MMA."

The doors closed behind her, the embrace of the crowd, mildly personal smells, the roll-aboard against her leg. "What's that?"

"Mixed martial arts," said Heidi, as if pleased with a dessert menu.

"Don't," advised Hollis. "Remember the boxers." The train began to move. "Gotta go."

"Fine," said Heidi, and was gone.

Six minutes on Line 10 and she was on another platform, Odéon, wheel ticking. Then telescoping the bag's handle to carry it up the stairs, into slanting sunlight and the sound and smell of the traffic on St. Germain, all of this entirely too familiar, as though she'd never left, and now the fear surfacing, acknowledgement that Heidi was right, that she'd tricked herself into revisiting the scene of a perfect crime. Dreamlike reactivation of passion. The smell of his neck. His library of scars, hieroglyphic, waiting to be traced.

"Oh, please," she said. Snapping out the bag's handle, trundling it across wheel-eating cobbles, toward the hotel. Past the candyseller's wagon. Then the window offering fancy dress. Satin capes, plague-doctor masks with penile noses. The smart little drugstore at the angle of two streets, offering hydraulic breast-massage devices and Swiss skin serums packaged like the latest in vaccines.

Into the hotel, where the man at the desk recognized but didn't greet her. Discretion rather than a lack of friendliness. She gave her name, signed in, confirmed that Milgrim's room was on her card, received her key on a heavy brass medallion cast with the head of a lion. Then into the elevator, smaller even than the one at Cabinet but more modern, like a pale bronze telephone booth. The feeling of being in a telephone booth almost forgotten now. How things went away.

In the third-floor hallway, massive crooked timbers stood exposed. A maid's cart with towels and miniature soaps. Unlocking the door to her room.

Which to her considerable relief was neither of the two she'd stayed in with Garreth, though the view was virtually identical. A room the size of the bathroom at Cabinet, smaller perhaps. All dark reds and black and Chinese gold; some weird chinoiserie that Cabinet's decorators would have supercharged with busts of Mao and heroic proletarian posters.

It seemed odd, to not be in Cabinet, and that struck her as a bad sign.

I should find a flat, she said to herself, realizing she had no idea what country she should find it in, let alone which city. Putting her bag on the bed. Scarcely room to walk, here, except for a narrow circuit around the bed. Reflexively ducking the determinedly nondigital television slung in its white-painted bracket from the ceiling. Garreth had cut his head on one.

She sighed.

Looking across at the buildings opposite, remembering.

Don't. She turned back to the bed and her bag, unzipping it. She'd packed as lightly as possible. Toiletries, makeup, a dress, hose, dressier shoes, underwear. Taking out the dress, to hang it up, she discovered the Blue Ant figurine, which she was certain she hadn't packed, grinning perkily up at her. She remembered missing it, on the counter, beside the sink, in Cabinet.

"Hello," she said, the tension in her voice startling her, as she picked it up.

Its grin becoming the Mona Lisa's smile, as she'd stood with Garreth, hand in his.

Looking up at him, she'd seen that he wasn't looking at the Mona Lisa at all, but rather at its plexi-shield, its mountings, and whatever of the Louvre's invisible security devices were somehow evident to him.

"You're imagining stealing it, aren't you?"

"Only academically. That laminated ledge, just beneath it? That's interesting. You'd want to know exactly what's inside. Quite thick, isn't it? Good foot thick. Something's in there. A surprise."

"You're terrible."

"Absolutely," he'd said, releasing her hand, caressing the back of her neck. "I am."

She put the figurine on the built-in bedside table, much smaller than the Mona Lisa's defensive ledge, and forced herself to unpack the rest of her things.

28. WHITE PEAR TEA

The cost of wifi was white pear tea.

Milgrim looked at the two-cup glass tea press on the round white table, beyond the matte aluminum rectangle of Hollis's laptop. He wasn't sure why he'd chosen white pear. Probably because he wasn't very fond of tea, and because almost everything else here was white. He decided to let it steep awhile longer.

He was alone, in this narrow white shop, with a great deal of tea and a girl in a nicely fitting, crisply starched cotton dress, faintly pin-striped in gray, not unlike a tennis dress. He hadn't thought of Parisians as tea drinkers, but if this place was any indication, they preferred it in ultrafragile glass pots. Walls lined with shallow white shelves, modernist apothecary jars filled with dried vegetable matter, plus a glittering, halogen-spotted assortment of these pots and presses. Equally minimalist cozies, in thick gray felt. A few green plants. Three small tables, each with two chairs.

From outside, the occasional whine and sputter of passing scoot-ers. The street was almost too narrow for cars. Somewhere in the Latin Quarter, if the cabdriver had understood him.

Now the girl began to give the apothecary jars the once-over with a feather duster. Like performance art, or some highly conceptual species of pornography. The sort of thing that turned out to mainly be about the pinstripes. Or the tea.

He opened the pencil-thin laptop and turned it on.

Hollis's desktop was a digital representation of interstellar space. Mauve galactic clouds. Was she interested in astronomy, he wondered, or was this something from Apple? He imagined the laptop displaying an image of itself instead, and of the tea press, on the white laminate. And in that imagined screen, another, identical image. Tunneling down, Escher-style, to a few pixels. He thought of the art in Hollis's book, and of the Neo, which he now assumed was on its way to some forbiddingly upscale suburb, or there already, his own small effort in GPS art.

He noted that he felt remarkably calm about that, about what he'd done. The main thing, it seemed, was that he'd done it. It was done. But noting this caused him to start to remember Sleight.

After his cab ride from Galeries Lafayette, to a randomly chosen intersection near here, he'd felt relatively certain that he was off Sleight's map. Now he considered Hollis's laptop, wondering if Sleight might not have been at that as well. Though Hollis said she was new in Bigend's employ, this time at least.

He opened the browser, then his webmail. Could Sleight see him do that? he wondered. His address, the first and only e-mail address he'd had, was a Blue Ant address. He opened Twitter. If he understood this correctly, Sleight might be able to know what he had opened, but would be unable to see what he was doing there. He entered his user name and password.

And Winnie was there. Or had been. "Whr R U?" An hour ago.

"Still Paris. Need to talk."

He refreshed the browser. No reply.

The girl in the cotton dress, having finished dusting, was looking at him. Reminding him, as he found certain young people did, of one of those otherwise fairly realistic Japanese cartoon characters, the ones with oversized Disney eyes. What was that about? It seemed to be international, whatever it was, though not yet universal. This was the sort of thing he'd gotten used to being able to ask Bigend about. Bigend actively encouraged this, because, he said, he valued Milgrim's questions. Milgrim had arrived from a decadelong low-grade brownout, and was, according to Bigend, like someone stepping from a lost space capsule. Smooth clay, awaiting the telltale imprint of a new century.

"It is the Mac Air?" the girl asked.

Milgrim had to check the branding, at the bottom of the screen. "Yes," he said.

"It is very nice."

"Thank you," said Milgrim. Self-consciously, he carefully plunged the rod-and-ball atop the tea press, forcing clear fluid through a surgical grade of white nylon mesh. He poured some out, into the even more fragile-looking glass cup. Took a sip. Complexly metallic. Not much like tea. Though perhaps in a good way. "Do you have croissants?"

"*Non*," said the girl, "*petites madeleines.*"

"Please," said Milgrim, gesturing to his white table.

Proust cookies. It was literally all he knew of Proust, though he'd once had to listen to someone's lengthy argument that Proust had either described madeleines incorrectly or been describing something else entirely.

It was time for his medication. While the girl fetched his madeleines, from the rear of the shop, he took the bubble-pack from his bag and popped the day's ration of white capsules through the foil at the back of their individual bubbles. Out of long habit, he held them concealed in his palm. He'd replaced the bubble-pack by the time she returned, his three cookies on a square white plate. One plain, one lightly drizzled with something white, another with dark chocolate.

"Thank you," he said. He dunked the plain one briefly in his tea, perhaps out of some vague, Proust-related superstition, then quickly ate them all, as is. They were very good, and the white-drizzled one was almond. Finished, he washed the capsules from Basel down with white pear tea.

Then he remembered to refresh the browser again.

"R U there?" Two minutes ago.

"Yes. Sorry."

Refresh.

"Ur phons nt secure"

"Borrowed laptop. Lost phone." He hesitated. "I think Sleight was tracking me with it."

Refresh.

"U lost?"

"Got rid of it."

Refresh.

"Why??"

He had to think about that. "S was telling follower where I was."

Refresh.

"So??"

"Tired of it."

Refresh.

"No jack moves OK? B cool"

"Didn't want him to know where we're staying."

Refresh.

"Where R U?"

"Staying," he completed, aloud, then wrote: "Hotel Odeon, by Odeon Metro."

Refresh.

"Bak nxt AM?"

"As far as I know."

Refresh.

"Whts yr partner want??"

"Jeans."

Refresh.

"LOL! B cool B N touch bye"

"Bye," said Milgrim, less than impressed with his new federal agent handler. It felt like having a disinterested young mother.

He logged out of Twitter and went to the bookmarks, clicking for the page he'd marked earlier. Foley modeling a zip-front jacket and an old-fashioned porn rectangle. What was that about? He skipped through the site, things starting to come together. Remembering another of the French girl's PowerPoint presentations, back in Soho. The market's fetishization of elite special forces, "operators." She'd cited the Vietnam War as the tipping point for this, and had illustrated her argument with collages of small ads from the back pages of long-extinct Fifties mens' magazines, *True* and *Argosy*: hernia aids, mail-order monkeys huddled in tea cups, courses in lawn mower repair, X-Ray Specs . . . These ads, she'd said, constituted a core sample of the mass unconscious of the American male, shortly after WWII. Aside from the ubiquitous trusses and truss substitutes (and what, Milgrim had wondered, had accounted for that epidemic of herniation among postwar American men?), this record differed very little from the equivalent record to be found in the back pages of comic books of the same era. While pointing out that anyone, then, could order exactly the same Italian surplus rifle that had later been used to assassinate JFK (for under fifteen dollars, including postage), she'd said that the postwar American male's valorization of things military could be assumed to have been balanced by recent actual memories of the reality of war, though one that been quite definitively won. Vietnam had changed that, she'd said, as she'd moved into a new set of collages. Vietnam had shifted something in the American male psyche. Milgrim couldn't remember exactly what that was supposed to have been, but he knew she'd connected it with what he assumed to be the culture that produced websites like this one.

Foley was wearing his black porn rectangle to protect his identity, the assumption on the viewer's part intended to be that Foley himself was a member of some military elite. She'd actually mentioned that as a marketing technique.

He went back to the image of Foley. Foley wasn't particularly scary. Milgrim knew a number of kinds of scary, from his decade on the street. The man with the mullet, in the mothballed restaurant outside of Conway, had been quite a special kind of scary. That kind of scary, which he had no name for, was difficult to conceal, and impossible to fake. He'd first seen it in New York, in a young Albanian in the heroin business. Suggestions of a military background, other things. A similar calm, the same utter lack of wasted motion. Foley, he began to suspect, studying the mouth under the black rectangle, might be the kind of scary that was about meanness, rather than strength. Though he'd also seen the two coexist, more or less, in the same individual, and that hadn't been good at all.

He clicked back through the site. Bigend would be interested in this, though probably his team had already shown it to him. It was exactly the sort of thing they were looking at. Noticing neither a brand name nor prices. The site's URL a string of letters and numbers. Not a site so much as a dummy, a mockup? The "About Us" page blank, also the "Order" page.

A deeper throbbing of exhaust, outside. He looked up to see a black motorcycle pass, slowly, the rider's yellow helmet turning a smooth sweep of dark plastic visor his way, then forward again, rolling on. Revealing, for an instant, on the helmet's back, broad, white diagonal scratches in the yellow gel-coat.

Exactly the kind of detail that Bigend would congratulate him for noticing.

29. SHIVER

leight," Bigend said, as though the name tired him, "is asking about Milgrim. Is he with you?"

"No," Hollis said, stretched on the bed, post-shower, partially wrapped in several of the hotel's not-so-large white towels. "Isn't he in New York? Sleight, I mean."

"Toronto," said Bigend. "He keeps track of Milgrim."

"He does?" She looked at the iPhone. She had no iconic image for Bigend. Maybe a blank rectangle of Klein Blue?

"Milgrim initially required quite a lot of keeping track of. That fell to Sleight, for the most part."

"Does he keep track of me?" She looked over at the blue figurine.

"Would you like him to?"

"No. It would be, in fact, a deal-breaker. For you and me."

"That was my understanding, of course. Where did you buy your phone?"

"The Apple Store. SoHo. New York SoHo. Why?"

"I'd like to give you another one."

"Why do you care where I bought this one?"

"Making certain you bought it yourself."

"The last phone you gave me let you keep track of where I was, Hubertus."

"I won't do that again."

"Not with a phone, anyway."

"I don't understand."

She gave the figurine a flick with her finger. It wobbled on its round base.

"You know my concerns with integrity of communication," he said.

"I don't know where Milgrim is," she said. "Is that all you wanted?"

"Sleight's suggesting he's left Paris. Done a runner, perhaps. Do you think that likely?"

"He's not that easy to read. Not for me."

"He's changing," Bigend said. "That's the interesting thing, about someone in his situation. There's always more of him arriving, coming online."

"Maybe something's arrived that doesn't want Sleight knowing where it is."

"If you see him," Bigend said, "would you ask him to ring me, please?"

"Yes," she said, "goodbye."

"Goodbye, Hollis."

She picked up the figurine. It weighed no more than she recalled it having weighed before, which was very little. It was hollow, and apparently seamless. There was no way to see what might be inside it.

She sat up on the bed, wrapped in slightly damp towels, as her phone rang again. The black-and-white photo of Heidi. "Heidi?"

"I'm at the gym. Hackney."

"Yes?"

"One of my sparring partners here, he says he knows about your guy."

The gold squiggles of bullshit faux-Chinese calligraphy on the wall opposite seemed to shimmer and detach, drifting toward her. She blinked. "He does?"

"You never told me his last name."

"No," said Hollis.

"Begins with *W*, ends with *s*?"

"Yes."

An uncharacteristic pause. Heidi never thought about what she was going to say. "When did you last hear from him?"

"Around the time of my U.K. book launch. Why?"

"When are you back here?"

"Tomorrow. What's this about?"

"Making sure Ajay and I are talking about the same guy."

"Ajay?"

"He's Indian. Well, English. I'll find out what I can, then you and I will talk." And she hung up.

Hollis wiped her eyes with the corner of one of the towels, restoring the golden brushwork to its place on the blood-colored wallpaper, and shivered.

30. SIGHTING

Milgrim left the white tea shop, walking in what he imagined as the direction of the Seine, favoring streets that ran approximately perpendicular to the one where he'd had his tea. Wondering exactly how he'd been followed here from the Salon du Vintage. Directly, quite likely, on a motorcycle.

If the yellow helmet was really the one he'd seen in London, his motorcyclist was the dispatch rider who'd delivered the printout of Winnie, the photo he'd assumed Sleight had taken in Myrtle Beach. Pamela had sent it, after he'd seen Bigend, on the way back to the hotel. Did they know who Winnie was, he wondered, or what she was? They all took pictures of one another, and now they had him doing it as well.

Now he seemed to have found a street of expensive-looking African folk art. Big dark wooden statues, in small galleries, beautifully lit. Nail-studded fetishes, suggesting terrible emotional states.

But here was a small camera shop as well. He went in, bought a Chinese card-reader from a pleasant Persian man in gold-rimmed glasses and a natty gray cardigan. Put it in his bag with Hollis's laptop and her book. Continued on.

He began to feel less anxious, somehow, though the elation he'd felt after giving the Neo the slip wasn't likely to return.

The question now, he decided, was whether the motorcyclist, if he hadn't been mistaken about the helmet, worked for Sleight or Bigend, or both. Had Bigend sent him here, or Sleight? For that matter, how to be certain that Bigend really mistrusted Sleight? Bigend, as far as he knew, had never lied to him, and Sleight had always seemed fundamentally untrustworthy. Built from the ground up for betrayal.

He thought of his therapist. If she were here, he told himself, she'd remind him that this situation, however complexly threatening or dangerous, was external, hence entirely preferable to the one he'd been in when he'd arrived in Basel, a situation both internal and seemingly inescapable. "Do not internalize the threat. When you do, the system floods with adrenaline, cortisol. Crippling you."

He reached for the Neo to check the time. It was no longer there.

He walked on, shortly finding himself in what an enameled wall-sign informed him was the Rue Git-le-Coeur. Narrower, possibly more medieval. A few drops of rain began to fall, the sky having clouded over while he'd been having his tea. He checked reflections for a yellow helmet, though of course a professional might park the bike, leave the helmet behind. Or, more likely, be part of a team. He saw a magical-looking bookshop, stock piled like a mad professor's study in a film, and swerved, craving the escape into text. But these seemed not only comics, unable to provide his needed hit of words-in-row, but in French as well. Some of the them, he saw, were the French kind, very literary-looking, but just as many seemed to be the ones where everyone looked something like the girl in the tea shop, slender and big-eyed. Still, a bookstore. He had a powerful urge to burrow. Work his way back into the stacks. Pull a few piles over behind him and hope never to be found.

He sighed and hurried on.

When Git-le-Coeur ended, he found a pedestrian light and crossed the heavy traffic of what he now remembered was the Quai des Grands Augustins, then hurried down a tall steep flight of stone steps. Which he also remembered. A sunny day, years before.

There was a narrow walkway directly beside the river. Once on this, one could only be seen from above by someone craning over. He looked up, waiting, anticipating the appearance of a helmet, head, or heads.

He became aware of an engine, on the water. He turned. A dark wooden sailboat with green trim was passing, its mast horizontal, piloted by a woman in shorts, a yellow slicker, and sunglasses, looking very alert at the wheel.

He looked back up at the balustrade. Nothing. The stairs were still vacant as well.

Noticing a shallow recess, he sheltered there from the increasingly insistent rain.

And then a longer, wider boat emerged, from an archway beneath a bridge whose name he no longer remembered. Like the boats that carried tourists, for Parisian children to spit on from the bridges, but this one equipped with a long plasma screen, running almost its full length, and perhaps a dozen feet high. And on this screen, as it passed, he saw the agreeably simian-looking young man Hollis had been talking with at the Salon Du Vintage, his features unmistakable, playing an organ or piano, his deep-set eyes shadowed in stage lighting, part of a band. There was no sound, other than the quiet drumming of the boat's engine, and then the pixels spasmed, collapsing the image, then unfolding it again, to reveal those two tedious Icelandic blondes, the twins Bigend sometimes mysteriously appeared with. The Dottirs, contorting in sequined sheathes on the rain-wet screen, mouths open as in silent screams.

He set his bag down, carefully, on the paving beneath the archway, and stretched his aching shoulder, watching the Dottirs pass, mysteriously, on the dark water.

When the rain stopped, and still no one had appeared, he shifted the bag to his other shoulder and walked on, toward the bridge. He trudged up a different but equally long stone stair, then recrossed the busy Grands Augustins and reentered the Latin Quarter, headed in the approximate direction he had come.

The cobbles were slick and shining, the street furniture semi-unfamiliar, evening settling rapidly in. And it was here, nearing another randomly angled intersection, that he had the experience.

In a setting, as they had said, of clear reality.

He had always been repulsed by the idea of hallucinogens, psychedelics, deliriants. His idea of a desirable drug had been a one that made things more familiar, more immediately recognizable.

In Basel, they had questioned him closely, during early withdrawal, about hallucinations. Had he been having any? No, he'd said. No . . . bugs? No bugs, he'd assured them. They'd explained that a possible symptom of his withdrawal might be what they called "hallucinations in a setting of clear reality," though he'd wondered how they could assume that his reality, at that point, was clear. The bugs, whatever those might have been, had never come, to his considerable relief, but now he saw, however briefly but with peculiar clarity, an aerial penguin cross the intersection ahead of him.

Something wholly penguin-shaped, apparently four or five feet long, from beak-tip to trailing feet, and made, it seemed, of mercury. A penguin wrapped in fluid mirror, reflecting a bit of neon from the street below. Swimming. Moving as a penguin moves underwater, but through the Latin Quarter air, at just above the height of second-story windows. Moving down the center of the street that crossed the one he walked on. So that it was revealed only as it crossed the intersection. Swimming. Propelling itself, in a gracefully determined but efficient fashion, with its quicksilver flippers. Then a bicycle crossed, on the street, going in the opposite direction.

"Did you see that?" Milgrim asked the cyclist, who of course was already gone, and in any case could never have heard him.

31. SECRET MACHINERIES

She did her best to put away the clinging unease, after the conversation with Heidi. Put on hose, the dress she'd brought, shoes, makeup. The bathroom was no more than a sort of alcove, less floor space than the Wellsian shower in Cabinet.

Worrying about Garreth's safety, she'd wisely told herself when they'd started, was something best not begun, lest it never end. Doing very dangerous things was his avocation. Where he lacked the bits and pieces of income afforded a retired musician, once somewhat popular, he had the old man, looking not unlike the later portraits of Samuel Beckett, eyes of a similarly startling ferocity, possibly mad. The old man, who had supposedly once been something, never specified, in the American intelligence community, was Garreth's producer-director, in an ongoing sequence of covert performance-art pieces. Financed, she'd been allowed to dimly gather, by other retired members of that community. Some rogue geezerhood, evidently brought into focus by a shared distaste for certain policies and proclivities of the government. She'd never seen him again, after Vancouver, but he'd remained a background presence throughout her time with Garreth, like a radio playing quietly in a nearby room. The most frequent voice on any one of Garreth's short-lived phones.

The old man would not, Hollis imagined, have approved of their involvement, but the multiskilled Garreth would have been impossible to replace. A man whose idea of fun was to fling himself off skyscrapers in a nylon suit with airfoil membranes sewn between the legs, and arms-to-thighs; a human flying squirrel, amid lethally unforgiving uprights of glass and steel. None of that had been Hollis at all, as Heidi had pointed out at the time. Not her taste, ever. Athletes, soldiers, never. She'd favored artboys, of any stripe, and unfortunately the dodgy hybrids as well, artboy-businessmen, with personalities as demanding as ambitiously crossbred dogs. That was what she'd known, before, and in various generally unhappy ways had understood. Not base-jumping madmen from Bristol, who wore turtlenecks without having to first consider the implications, and quoted the less popular poems of Dylan Thomas in their entirety. Because, he'd said, he couldn't sing. All while scrawling graffiti on the secret machineries of history. Garreth. Whom, she now obliquely accepted, in the descending bronze elevator-booth, she did truly love. Repacking this swiftly, however, before the jolt announced the Odéon's lobby.

She was wearing the Hounds, open, over her dress, hoping that its darkness might allow it to pass for a sort of bolero. How many seasons until this kind of mismatching would read, on her, as bag lady, she wondered. That worry would be Bigend's, she guessed, and his talk of aging bohemians.

Nodding to the man at the desk, who was reading a novel, she popped the jacket's collar, producing a faint jungle whiff of indigo, which she left to hover in the hotel's lobby.

Outside, the air had been scrubbed by rain, pavements glittering. Ten to eight, by her iPhone. She could, as either George or Meredith had said, see Les Éditeurs across the way, not this street but the next one over, angled. She walked right, past the fancy little drugstore, then right again, not wanting to be early. This much narrower street, angling sharply back, behind the hotel, was home to an English-language secondhand bookshop, a cocktail bar, a serious-looking sushi restaurant, a bookbinder, and a place that seemed to specialize in Chinese reflexology equipment: sadistic-looking massage devices, instruction manuals, models of bodies and body parts marked with meridians and pressure points. Here, for instance, was a very large china ear, apparently identical to the one in Heidi's room at Cabinet. She'd known she'd seen one before.

She turned, walked back to the bookbinder's smaller window. Wondered about its clientele. Who paid whatever this cost, to have old books rebound, to this high a standard of workmanship, exquisite cobbling for ancient thoughts? Bigend might, she supposed, though any bibliophile tendencies of his were well concealed. She'd yet to see a book in any Bigendian environment. He was a creature of screens, of bare expanses of desk or table, empty shelves. He owned, as far as she knew, no art. In some way, she suspected, he regarded it as competition, noise to his signal.

One of the books in the window was shaped like a fan, or like a wedge of gilt-embossed ivory calfskin pie, the apex bitten neatly, concavely off.

The street was completely deserted. She said a silent prayer for Garreth. To what, she didn't know. Unreliable universe. Or those machineries upon which he painted. Please.

The book-fan regarded her smugly, immaculate, its contents unread perhaps for centuries.

She turned and walked toward Odéon. Crossed it, continuing on toward the restaurant.

Outside of which, some residual celebrity-sense now told her, were paparazzi. She blinked, kept walking. Yes, there were. She knew the body language, that nervy-but-negligent pretending-not-to-care. A sort of rage, born of boredom, waiting. Untouched drinks on the red tablecloths, whatever was cheapest. Phones to ears. A few with sunglasses. They watched her approach.

Instinctively, she waited for the first one to raise a camera. For the sound of machine-driven image-collection. Tightening the muscles in her pelvic floor. Prepared either to flee or look her best.

Yet no one shot her. Though they watched as she came on. She was not the target. Had not been, for years. But temporarily a person of interest now, by virtue of turning up here. Why?

Inside, Les Éditeurs was Deco, but not the chrome and faux-onyx kind. Red leather, the color of Fifties fingernails, midbrown varnished wood, books-by-the-yard, framed black-and-white portraits of French faces she didn't recognize.

"He didn't need to send you," said Rausch, her onetime editor on Bigend's nonexistent *Node*, the phantom digest of digital culture. "It's all going very smoothly."

He was glaring at her over the tops of heavy black frames, glasses that looked as though they had been cranked almost shut around whatever would be left of his field of vision. His black hair looked as though his skull had been flocked.

"No one sent me. What are you doing here?"

"If he didn't send you, why are you here?"

"I'm meeting someone for dinner. In Paris on Hubertus's business, but nothing to do with you. Your turn."

Rausch palmed his forehead, ran fingers exasperatedly back through locks he didn't have. "Fridrika. The Dottirs. They're launching the new album this week. She's here with Bram." He winced, reflexively.

"Who's Bram?"

"Bram, from the Stokers. It's that vampire thing." He actually looked embarrassed. "Eydis is supposed to have been hot for him, now he's with Fridrika. In the States, *People*'s taking Fridrika's side, *Us* is Eydis. Over here, we don't have that clean a break yet, but we should by tomorrow."

"Isn't that tactic kind of ancient?"

Rausch twitched. "Bigend says that's the point. He says it's a double-reverse, so corny it's new. Well, not new, but comforting. Familiar."

"Is that why he's always with them? They're Blue Ant clients?"

"He's tight with their father," Rausch said, lowering his voice, "all I know."

"Who's their father?" It seemed odd to her that the twins had a father. She'd thought of them as having been decanted from something.

"Big deal in Iceland. Seriously, Hollis, he really didn't send you?"

"Who decided they'd come here?" She'd spotted one twin's silver hair across Les Éditeurs, but she'd already forgotten which one Rausch had said was here. Seated at a table with a tall broad-shouldered young man, very pale, one eye concealed by a heavy, dusty-looking flop of black hair.

"I did. It's not too hip. Looks like they chose it at random. Won't detract from the narrative."

"Then unless one of the people I'm having dinner with is a Bigend plant, it's a coincidence."

Rausch glowered at her, which actually meant, she knew, that he was frightened. "Really?"

"Really." Maître d' hovering now, impatient. "Overton," Hollis said to him, "table for four." When she turned back to Rausch, he was gone. She followed the man through the crowded restaurant, to where George and Meredith were seated.

George half rose, doing the air-kiss thing. He was wearing a dark suit, no tie, white shirt. A small triangle of ultradense chest hair, at the open collar, made it look as though he were wearing a black T-shirt. She thought his stubble had lengthened, since she'd last seen him. He smiled ruefully, white teeth seemingly the size and thickness of dominoes. "Sorry about this. I had no idea. I actually chose the place so we could talk, and not be distracted by the food." He sat back down as the maître d' held her chair for her.

When he'd gone, leaving thickly bound menus, Meredith said, "We could have been across the street, at Comptoir. That would have distracted us thoroughly."

"Sorry," said George. "The food here is rather good. Unfortunately, it looks like poor Bram's the main course."

"You know him?"

"To speak to. He's talented. There but for fortune, I suppose."

"Studio time with Reg not looking quite so dire?"

"Not since our conversation this afternoon, really." Big solid teeth appearing again. She could certainly see why Meredith liked him. Indeed, she could see that Meredith very definitely did. They gave off that contact-pleasantness she expected from couples who liked one another in some genuine but nonmanic way. She wondered if she'd ever been half of one of those. "Your friend is with Fridrika Brandsdottir," she said, the name coming back.

"Evidently," George agreed.

"Not in any biblical sense, I hope," said Meredith, peering over her open menu at the Bram/Brandsdottir table.

"None whatever," said George. "He's gay."

"That must make it even more embarrassing," said Hollis, opening her menu.

"He'll do what he has to," said George. "He's looking for a way out of the vampire thing. Tricky."

Milgrim appeared, his hair looking damp, the maître d' fussing officiously behind him.

"Hello, Milgrim," Hollis said, "have a seat."

Assured that Milgrim was meant to be there, though clearly none too pleased to have him there, the maître d' retreated. Milgrim unslung his shoulder bag, lowered it to the floor by its strap, beside the remaining chair, and seated himself.

"This is my colleague, Milgrim," Hollis said. "Milgrim, Meredith Overton and George. Like you, George has only the one name."

"Hello," said Milgrim. "I saw you at the clothing show."

"Hello," said George. Meredith looked at Hollis.

"Milgrim and I," Hollis said to Meredith, "are both interested in Gabriel Hounds."

"Unidentified flying objects," Milgrim said, to George. "Do you believe in them?"

George's eyes narrowed beneath his unibrow. "I believe that what appear to be objects, flying, sometimes appear to be seen. And may be unknown."

"You haven't seen one?" Milgrim leaned sideways and down, to scoot his bag farther under his chair. He looked up, from very close to the tablecloth, at George. "Yourself?"

"No," said George, with careful neutrality. "Have you?"

Milgrim straightened up. Nodded in the affirmative.

"Let's order, shall we," said Hollis, quickly, hugely grateful for the arrival of their waitress.

32. POST-ACUTE

The waitress was departing with orders, taking the hardbound menus with her, when a disturbance broke out at a table on the opposite side of the room.

Raised voices. A tall, broad-shouldered, black-clad young man, pale features grimly set, suddenly standing, knocking over his chair. Milgrim watched as this one swept for the door, slamming out of Les Éditeurs. To be met by a tide of electronic flash, flinging up his arm to protect his eyes or hide his face.

"That didn't take long," said George, who was buttering a round of sliced baguette. He had elegantly hairy hands, like some expensive Austrian stuffed animal. He bit off half of the buttered bread with his large white teeth.

"All he could stand," said Meredith, someone whose intelligence protruded through her beauty, Milgrim felt, like the outline of unforgiving machinery pressing against a taut silk scarf.

Craning his neck, Milgrim made out one of the Dottirs, silver hair unmistakable, at the table the young man had deserted. After the liquid metal penguin, this didn't seem so odd. He felt as though he were on some kind of roll today. She was collecting her things, he saw. She checked the dial of her enormous gold wristwatch. "Saw them," he said, "the Dottirs. On the river. In a video." He turned back to George. "I saw you, too."

"It's about an album launch," said George. "They have a new release. We don't, but share a label."

"Who was that who left?"

"Bram," said Hollis, "the singer from the Stokers."

"Don't know him," said Milgrim, picking up one of the rounds of bread in order to give his hands something to do.

"You aren't thirteen," said Meredith, "are you?"

"No," agreed Milgrim, putting the slice of bread, whole, into his mouth. Oral, his therapist called that. She'd said he was very lucky to never have taken up smoking. The bread was firm, springy. He held it there a moment before he began to chew. Meredith was staring at him. He looked back at the Brandsdottir table, where someone was holding whichever Dottir's chair as she rose.

That person was Rausch, he saw, and almost spat out the bread.

Desperately, he found Hollis's eye. She winked, the sort of effortless wink that involves no other features, a wink that Milgrim himself could never have managed, and took a sip of wine. "George is in a band, Milgrim," she said, and he knew that she spoke to calm him. "The Bollards. Reg Inchmale, who was the guitarist in the Curfew with me, is producing their new album."

Milgrim, chewing and swallowing the suddenly dry bread, nodded. Took a sip of water. Coughed into his crisp cloth napkin. What was Rausch doing here? He glanced back, but didn't see Rausch. The Dottir, reaching the door, triggered a second wave of strobing, a raggedly cumulative brilliance, the color of her hair. He looked back to Hollis. She nodded, almost invisibly.

George and Meredith, he guessed, were unaware of her connection with Blue Ant or, for that matter, of his own. The Dottirs, he knew, were Blue Ant clients. Or, rather, their father, whom Milgrim had never seen, was some kind of major Bigend project. Possibly even partner. Some people, Rausch included, assumed Bigend's interest in the sisters was sexual. But Milgrim, from his intermittently privileged position as Bigend's conversational foil, guessed that not to be the case. Bigend cheerfully squired the twins through London as though they were a pair of tedious but astronomically valuable dogs, the property of someone he wished above most things to favorably impress.

"The Stokers are on a different label," explained George, "but one owned by the same firm. The publicists have set up a fake romance, between Bram and Fridrika, but have also floated the rumor that Bram and Eydis are involved."

"It's a very old tactic," said Meredith, "and particularly obvious with identical twins."

"Though new to their audience, and Bram's," said George, "who as you point out are thirteen years old."

Milgrim looked at Hollis. She looked back. Smiled. Telling Milgrim that this was not the time to ask questions. She shrugged out of her Hounds jacket, leaving it draped stiffly across the back of her chair. She was wearing a dress the color of weathered coal, a gray that was almost black. A clingy knit. He looked at Meredith's dress for the first time. It was black, a thick shiny fabric, the detailing sewn like an antique workshirt. He didn't understand women's clothing, but he thought he recognized something. "Your dress," he said to Meredith, "it's very nice."

"Thank you."

"Is it Gabriel Hounds?"

Meredith's eyebrows rose, fractionally. She looked from Milgrim to Hollis, then back to Milgrim. "Yes," she said, "it is."

"It's lovely," said Hollis. "This season's?"

"They don't do seasons."

"But recent?" Hollis looking very seriously at Meredith over the rim of her upraised wineglass.

"Dropped last month."

"Melbourne?"

"Tokyo."

"Another art fair?" Hollis finished the wine in her glass. George poured for her. Pointed the neck of the bottle questioningly at Milgrim, then saw Milgrim's inverted glass.

"A bar. Tibetan-themed micro-bistro. I never quite grasped where. Basement of an office building. Owner sleeps up above the fake rafters he put in, though that's a secret. Hounds haven't often done things specifically for women. A knit skirt that nobody's ever been able to copy, though everyone tries. Your jacket's unisex, though you'd never know it, on. Something to do with those elastic straps in the shoulders." She looked annoyed, Milgrim thought, but very much in control.

"Would it be out of line to ask how you knew to be there?"

Their first courses arrived, and Meredith waited for the waitress to leave before answering. When she did, she seemed more relaxed. "I'm not directly connected," she said to Hollis. "I've been out of touch with that friend I told you about, the one I knew at Cordwainers, for a few years now. But he'd introduced me to someone else. I'm not in touch with them either, and don't know how to contact them. But they put me on a mailing list. I get an e-mail, if there's going to be a drop. I don't know that I get them for every drop, but there's no way of knowing that. They aren't frequent. Since I took Clammy to buy his jeans, in Melbourne, there've only been two e-mails. Prague, and Tokyo. I happened to be in Tokyo. Well, Osaka. I went along."

"What were they offering?"

"Let's eat," said Meredith, "shall we?"

"Of course," said Hollis.

Milgrim's was salmon, and very good. The waitress had let him order from an English translation of the menu. He looked around, trying to spot Rausch again, but didn't see him. A shift in clientele was still under way as people who'd actually only been there, he guessed, for Bram's exit, signaled for their bills and departed, some leaving untouched food. Tables were being quickly cleared, reset, and reseated. The noise level was going up.

"I wouldn't want either of you to think I'll be any less willing to help you with Inchmale," said Hollis, "regardless of what you may or may not be able to tell me about Hounds."

Milgrim saw George glance quickly at Meredith. "We appreciate that," George said, though Milgrim wasn't sure that Meredith did. Perhaps George was using the band "we."

"All you really need with Inchmale is someone to tell you where you are in his process," Hollis said. "And that's all I can do, anyway. You can't change the process, and if you try hard enough, long enough, he'll leave. So far, you're right on track."

None of this meaning anything to Milgrim, who was enjoying the salmon, in some light chilled sauce.

"I'm sorry," Meredith said, "but you're going to have to tell us who you're working for."

"If I were better at this sort of thing," said Hollis, "I'd start by telling you about my book. It's about locative art."

"I don't know the term," Meredith said.

"It's what they're calling augmented reality now," said Hollis, "but art. It's been around since before the iPhone started to become the default platform. That was when I wrote about it. But I meant that if I were going to lie to you, I'd tell you about that, then tell you that I was writing another, on esoteric denim, or mad marketing strategies. But I won't. I'm working for Hubertus Bigend."

The last bite of salmon caught in Milgrim's throat. He drank water, coughed into his napkin.

"Are you choking?" asked George, who looked as though he could perform a really optimal Heimlich maneuver.

"No, thanks," said Milgrim.

"Blue Ant?" asked Meredith.

"No," said Hollis. "We're freelance. Bigend wants to know who's behind Gabriel Hounds."

"Why?" Meredith had put down her fork.

"Possibly because he thinks someone's outdoing him at something he considers to have been his own game. Or so he suggested. Do you know him?"

"Only by reputation," said Meredith.

"Is Blue Ant doing your band's publicity?" Milgrim asked George, after some more water.

"Not that I know of," said George. "Too small a world already."

"I'm not a Blue Ant employee," said Hollis. "Bigend's hired me to look into Gabriel Hounds. He wants to know who designs it, how their antimarketing scheme works. I'm only prepared to go so far. I'm not prepared to lie to you about it."

"How about you?" Meredith asked Milgrim.

"I don't have a badge," Milgrim said.

"What do you mean?"

"To open the door," Milgrim said. "At Blue Ant. Employees have those badges. I'm not on salary."

First-course dishes were removed. Second courses arrived. Milgrim's was pork tenderloin, stacked like a corpulent chess piece, a rook of pork. It toppled as he began to eat it.

"How badly does Bigend want to know?" Meredith's knife and fork were poised.

"He wants to know *everything*, basically," said Hollis, "all the time. Right now, he wants to know this quite badly. Next month? Maybe not so much."

"He must have a lot of resources. For information." Meredith cut into her roundel of beef.

"Prides himself on it," Hollis said.

"I mentioned that I believe most of my last season of shoes are in a warehouse in Seattle. Tacoma, possibly."

"Yes?"

"I don't know where. Can't find them. The lawyers say they could make a very convincing case for my ownership, if we could locate them. We're fairly certain they haven't been sold off, otherwise at least a few would have surfaced on eBay. None have. Could Bigend find them for me?"

"I don't know," said Hollis. "But if he couldn't, I don't know who could."

"I don't know what I could find out for you," said Meredith, "but assuming I found something, I'd consider an exchange. Otherwise, not."

Milgrim looked from Meredith to Hollis, back.

"I'm not authorized to make that sort of deal," said Hollis, "but I can certainly take him the proposal."

This reminded Milgrim of the closing rhythm of certain very backstage drug deals, the kind in which one party may know of someone with an Aerostar van, full of some precursor chemical, while another is aware of the approximate whereabouts of a really efficient pill-pressing machine.

"Please do," said Meredith, smiling, then taking a first sip of her wine.

"That was very good," Milgrim said to Hollis, after saying good night to Meredith and George outside the restaurant. "The timing. When you told them about Bigend."

"What choice did I have? If I'd told them otherwise, I'd already have been lying to them. The hotel's this way."

"I was never good at that sort of timing," said Milgrim, then remembered the penguin, and glanced up.

"What was that about UFOs, when you first walked in?"

"I don't know," said Milgrim. "I thought I'd seen something. It's been a long day. I have your computer. Would you mind if I kept it overnight? I have to check something."

"It doesn't matter," said Hollis. "I only have it for a book I haven't started writing. I have my iPhone. What did you think you saw?"

"It looked like a penguin."

Hollis stopped. "A penguin? Where?"

"In the street. That way." He pointed.

"In the street?"

"Flying."

"They can't fly, Milgrim."

"Swimming. Through the air. Level with the second-story windows. Using its flippers to propel itself. But it looked more like a penguin-shaped blob of mercury. It reflected the lights. Distorted them. It may have been a hallucination."

"Do you get those?"

"P-A-W-S," said Milgrim, spelling it out.

"Paws?"

"Post acute withdrawal syndrome." He shrugged, started for the hotel again, Hollis following. "They were worried about that."

"Who were?"

"The doctors. In the clinic. In Basel."

"What about the man at the Salon? The one in the pants? The one you thought you'd seen in Selfridges? Did he follow you?"

"Yes. Sleight was telling him where I was."

"What happened?"

"I don't know."

"Why not?"

"I left the Neo with someone else. He followed them." He needed to clean his teeth. There was pear galette between his upper rear molars. It still tasted good.

"It's been a long day," said Hollis as they reached what he took to be their hotel. "I spoke with Hubertus. He wants you to call him. Sleight thinks you've run away."

"I feel like I have." He held the door for her.

"Thank you," she said.

"Monsieur Milgrim?" A man, behind a vaguely pulpit-like counter.

"Mister Milgrim's room is on my card," said Hollis.

"Yes," said the clerk, "but he must still register." He produced a printed white card and a pen. "Your passport, please."

Milgrim brought out his Faraday pouch, then his passport.

"I'll call you in the morning, in time for breakfast here, then the train," said Hollis. "Good night." And she was gone, around a corner.

"I will photocopy this," said the clerk, "and return it to you when you are finished in the lobby." He gestured with his head, to Milgrim's right.

"The lobby?"

"Where the young lady is waiting."

"Young lady?"

But the clerk had vanished, through a narrow doorway behind the counter.

The lights were out in the small lobby. Folding wooden panels partially screened it from the reception area. Streetlight reflected on china, set out for breakfast service. And on the yellow curve of the helmet, from the low oval of a glass coffee table. A small figure rose smoothly to its feet, in a complex rustle of waterproof membranes and cycle-armor. "I'm Fiona," she said sternly, her jawline delicate above the stiff buckled collar. She stuck out her hand. Milgrim shook it automatically. It was small, warm, strong, and callused.

"Milgrim."

"I know that." She didn't sound British.

"Are you American?"

"Technically. You too. We both work for Bigend."

"He told Hollis he wasn't sending anybody."

"Blue Ant didn't send anybody. I work for him. So do you."

"How do I know you really work for Bigend?"

She tapped the face of a phone like Hollis's, listened, handed it to him.

"Hello?" said Bigend. "Milgrim?"

"Yes?"

"How are you?"

Milgrim considered. "It's been a long day."

"Run it past Fiona after we've spoken. She'll relay it to me."

"Did you have Sleight tracking me with the Neo?"

"It's part of what he does. He called from Toronto, said you'd left Paris."

"I slipped someone the phone."

"Sleight's wrong," Bigend said.

"Not about the phone leaving Paris."

"That's not what I mean. He's wrong."

"Okay," said Milgrim. "Who's right?"

"Pamela," said Bigend. "Fiona, whom you've just met. We'll be keeping it at that until the situation sorts itself out."

"Is Hollis?"

"Hollis is unaware of any of this."

"Am I?"

There was a silence. "Interesting question," said Bigend, finally. "What do you think?"

"I don't like Sleight. Don't like the man he had following me."

"You're doing well. More proactive than I asked for, but that's interesting."

"I saw a penguin. Penguin-shaped. Something. I may need to go back to the clinic."

"That's our Festo air penguin," Bigend said, after a pause. "We're experimenting with it as an urban video surveillance platform."

"Festive?"

"Festo. They're German."

"What's going on? Please?"

"Something that happens periodically. It has to do with the kind of talent Blue Ant requires. If they're any good at what I hire them for, they tend to have an innate tendency to go rogue. That or sell out to someone who already has. I expect this to happen. It can actually be quite productive. Fiona was on the train with you, this morning. She'll be on the train back, tomorrow. Put Hollis in a cab to Cabinet."

"What's that?"

"Where she's staying. Then wait near the cab rank. Fiona will bring you to me. Give her a rundown of your day now, then get some sleep."

"Okay," Milgrim said, then realized Bigend was gone. He handed the phone back to Fiona, noticing that she wore something on her left wrist, about six inches long, that looked like a doll's computer keyboard. "What's that?"

"Controls the penguin," she said. "But we're switching over to iPhones for that."

33. BURJ

She got the iPhone out of her purse in the little bronze elevator, hit Heidi's cell number as she stepped out. It was ringing as she walked along the hallway, doors to her right, weird twisted brown medieval timbers to her left. Heidi picked up as she was fiddling the key into the lock.

"Fuck—" Against a wash of what sounded to Hollis like exclusively male pub ruckus.

"Tell me what's happened to Garreth. Now." She opened the door. Saw white towels where she'd left them on the bed, the Blue Ant figurine on the built-in bedside table, big crazy gold fake Chinese scribbles on the blood-red walls. It was like stepping into a life-size Barbie's Shanghai Brothel kit.

"Hold on. Get the fuck over! Not you. Had to get out of that bench thing."

"I thought you weren't drinking."

"Red Bull. Cutting it with ginger ale."

"Tell me. Now."

"Don't look on YouTube."

"At what, on YouTube?"

"Burj Khalifa world-championship base jump."

"That hotel? Looks like an Arabian Nights sailboat? What happened?"

"That's Burj Al Arab. Burj Khalifa's the world's tallest building—"

"Shit—"

"The jump on YouTube, that wasn't him. That was earlier. That guy high-pulled, they say here. That's when—"

"What happened to Garreth?"

"The guy on YouTube holds the world's record now for jumping out of a building. Your boy figured a way to get in and go off it higher up. They still hadn't finished closing all the windows at the top. There was this crane—"

"Oh God—"

"And the security had of course gotten lots tighter, since YouTube guy did his, but your boy's an expert at—"

"Tell me!"

"He was on the way up, however he was managing that, and they got onto him. He got up to the point where the windows weren't installed, and went off from there. Actually a little lower than You-Tube guy—"

"Heidi!"

"Did the bat-suit thing. Took it really far out, really low, probably pissed that he'd jumped from below the record point. Trying for points on style."

Hollis was crying now.

"Had to come down on a freeway. Four in the morning, there was a vintage Lotus Elan—"

Hollis started sobbing. She was sitting on the bed now, but didn't know how she'd gotten there.

"He's okay! Well, he's alive, okay? My boy says he must've been super well connected, because the ambulance that picked him up put him straight on an air ambulance, a jet, into a high-end trauma center in Singapore. Where you go, there, if you need shit-hot medical attention."

"He's alive? Alive?"

"Fuck yes. I told you already. Leg's messed up. I know he was in Singapore, six weeks, then it gets fuzzy. Some people say he went to the States from there, to get stuff done they couldn't do in Singapore. Military doctors. You said he wasn't military."

"Connected. The old man . . ."

"Story is, that air ambulance had some kind of local royal crest."

"Where is he?"

"These boys at my gym, they're ex-military. Maybe ex-. Fuzzy. Doesn't matter how much they drink, the story just trails off, at a certain point. Runs up against some prime directive. They know who he is, but from the jumping. They're big fans of that. Also because he's English. Tribal thing. That secret-life shit you told me about, I don't think they'd get that. Or maybe they would. They're all batshit in their own way."

Hollis was wiping her face, mechanically, with a towel smeared with makeup. "He's alive. Say he's alive."

"They think he went into some funny arrangement, Stateside, where they work on messed-up Delta Force guys, like that. That impresses them deeply. Then they order another round, talk football, and I fall asleep."

"That's all you've been able to find out?"

"All? I've done everything short of trying to fuck it out of them, and I wouldn't say they'd made it exceptionally easy not to do that either. You were the one told me to leave the civilians alone, weren't you?"

"Sorry, Heidi."

"It's okay. They never ran into anybody thought they were civilians before. Kind of worth it. You know how to get in touch with him?"

"Maybe."

"Now you've got an excuse. Gotta go. They want me to throw darts. They bet. Take care of yourself. You back tomorrow? We'll have dinner."

"You're sure he's alive?"

"I think these guys would know, if he wasn't. He's like a football player to them. They'd hear. Where are you?"

"At the hotel."

"Get some sleep. Tomorrow."

"Bye, Heidi."

The pale gold bullshit ideograms still swimming in tears.

34. THE ORDER FLOW

Milgrim woke as some large vehicle groaned past in the street, or perhaps in dream, chains rattling. He'd slept with the windows open.

He sat up and looked at the blank screen of Hollis's laptop, on the cushioned ledge beneath the windows. The battery needed a charge, but she hadn't given him the charger. He guessed he had enough power left to check for Winnie's reply to his message of the night before. He'd intended to send Pamela the photos of Foley as well, and had bought the cable he'd need to do that, but after his conversation with Bigend he wasn't sure about Blue Ant's e-mail system. He imagined Sleight had been in charge of all of that. How complicated could that ultimately become, for Bigend?

With no Neo, and the laptop off, he had no way of knowing the time. The television suspended from the ceiling could tell him, he supposed, but he decided to shower instead. If it was time to go, Hollis would call him.

The shower was one of those telephone-handle arrangements, the stall largely conceptual. He brushed his teeth with one hand while rinsing his torso with the other, his battery-powered toothbrush loud in the small space. Toweling off, he thought of how Bigend seemed to regard what was going on in Blue Ant as a sort of expected burn-off, like some brushfire on the Nature Channel, brought on by an otherwise essential excess of intelligence and ambition.

He put on his new socks and underwear from Galeries Lafayette, and an unworn but creased shirt from Hackett. He remembered the

Russians in the elevator. Foley. Winced. He tucked the memory card, with his pictures of Foley on it, down into the top of his left sock.

He edged around the bed, stood looking down at Parisians passing on the sidewalk opposite. A graying, leonine man in a long dark coat. Then a tall girl in very nice boots. He looked for Fiona, half expecting to see her astride her motorcycle, keeping watch. He looked up then, but didn't see the penguin either.

A tiny garret window popped open, on a building opposite, and a girl with short dark hair thrust her head and shoulders through, into the morning, a cigarette between her lips. Milgrim nodded. Addictions were being serviced. He sat down on the padded bench and checked his Twitter. No Winnie. It was five after seven, he saw, earlier than he'd thought.

He packed his bag, putting the laptop in last. What would he do, once he'd returned it? How would he keep in touch with Winnie? The fact of Winnie made his knowledge of Blue Ant's internal brushfire feel awkward. Otherwise, he imagined, without her, it would mainly have been interesting, as Bigend didn't seem particularly worried. Though he'd never seen Bigend worried about anything. Where most people got worried, Bigend seemed to become interested, and Milgrim knew that that could be strangely contagious. Imagining explaining that to Winnie made him uneasy.

He made a last pass for misplaced property, discovering one of his socks under the edge of the bed. He put it in his bag, put the strap over his shoulder, and left the room, leaving the door unlocked. Maids were afoot but he didn't see them, only their metal carts stacked with towels and tiny plastic bottles of shampoo. He saw the building's original stairway, winding down, beyond big twisted brown-stained timbers that couldn't possibly have been as old, in America, as they no doubt were, here.

He descended, passing windows, on each floor, overlooking a courtyard the morning hadn't reached yet. Scooters and bicycles were parked there, at the bottom of a well of shadow.

On the ground floor he found his brief way around to the lobby, where china was rattling. No Hollis. He took a seat at a table for two, beside the windows, and asked for coffee and a croissant. The Tunisian waitress went away. Someone else brought the coffee immediately, with a small pitcher of hot milk. He was stirring his coffee when Hollis arrived, looking red-eyed and exhausted, the Hounds jacket draped across her shoulders like a short cape.

She sat down, a crumpled tissue in one hand.

"Is something wrong?" asked Milgrim, seized by some substrate of his own childhood fear, sorrow, the cup halfway to his mouth.

"I haven't slept," she said. "Found out a friend's been in an accident. Not in very good shape. Sorry."

"Your friend? Not in good shape?" He'd set the cup in its saucer. The waitress arrived with his croissant, butter, a miniature jar of jam.

"Coffee, please," she said to the waitress. "Not a recent accident. I only heard last night."

"How is she?" Milgrim was having one of those experiences of feeling, as he'd explained to his therapist, that he was emulating a kind of social being that he fundamentally wasn't. Not that he was unconcerned with the pain he saw in Hollis's eyes, or with the fate of her friend, but that there was some language required here that he'd never learned.

"He," corrected Hollis as her coffee arrived.

"What happened?"

"He jumped off the tallest building in the world." Her eyes widened, as if at the absurdity of what she'd just said, then closed, tightly.

"In Chicago?" asked Milgrim.

"It hasn't been Chicago for years," she said, opening her eyes, "has it? Dubai." She poured milk into her coffee, her movements determinedly businesslike now, precise.

"How is he?"

"I don't know," she said. "Flown to a hospital in Singapore. His leg. A car hit him. I don't know where he is."

"You said he jumped off a building," said Milgrim, sounding accusing, though he hadn't intended to.

"He glided down, then opened a chute. Came down in traffic."

"Why?" Milgrim shifted uneasily in his seat, knowing he was somehow off-script now.

"He'd need somewhere clear, flat, no wires."

"I mean, why did he jump?"

She frowned. Sipped some coffee. "He says it's like walking through walls. Nobody can, but if you could, he says, it would feel like that. He says the wall is inside, though, and you do have to walk through it."

"I'm afraid of heights."

"So's he. He says. Said. I haven't seen him for a while."

"Was he your boyfriend?" Milgrim had no idea where this came from, but his therapist had had a lot to say about his relative inability to trust certain kinds of instinct.

She looked at him. "Yes," she said.

"Do you know where he is?"

"No."

"Do you know how to get in touch with him?"

"I have a number," she said, "but I'm only supposed to call it if I'm in trouble."

"Aren't you?"

"I'm unhappy now. Anxious. Sad. That's not the same."

"But do you want to stay that way?" Milgrim felt as though he'd become his therapist, in some weird role-flip, or rather Hollis's. "How can you expect to feel better if you don't find out how he is?"

"You should eat that," Hollis said, sharply, indicating his croissant. "We have a cab coming."

"I'm sorry," he said, feeling suddenly miserable. "It's none of my business." He fumbled with the paper seal on the lid of the tiny jam jar.

"No, I'm sorry. You're just trying to help. It's complicated, for me. And I haven't slept. And I'd been managing not to think about him, for quite a while."

"You were good, last night, with Meredith," Milgrim said, tearing his croissant in half and troweling butter and jam inside both pieces. He bit into one of the halves.

"Now I don't know whether I can go on with that. I have to find him."

"Call him. Not knowing is affecting your work. That's trouble."

"I'm afraid. Afraid that might not work. Afraid he might not want to hear from me."

"Use Hubertus," Milgrim said, around a mouthful of croissant, covering his mouth with his hand. "He can find anyone."

Her eyebrows rose.

"Like Meredith's sneakers," he said. "The price of admission."

"Meredith's sneakers wouldn't be unhappy to be found by Hubertus. My friend would be unhappy to be found by anyone."

"Would he have to know?"

"Did you learn to think this way from Bigend?"

"I learned it being an addict. Constantly requiring something I wasn't legally allowed to possess, and which I couldn't afford. I learned leverage. What you did last night, with Meredith. You could do that with Hubertus, and find your friend."

She frowned.

"There was someone here, last night," he said. "From Hubertus. After you went up."

"Who?"

"Fiona. A girl on a motorcycle. Not someone I'd seen at Blue Ant. Well, I'd *seen* her. On her motorcycle. Delivering something for Pamela. But I didn't know she was a girl."

"Why was she here?"

"So that I could speak with Hubertus, on her phone. He told me that Sleight is either working for or with someone else. He told me that I should regard everyone other than Pamela, and Fiona, as suspect. And you. He said you didn't know about it. But you do now."

"How did he seem to be taking that?"

"He seemed . . . interested? He wants you to take a cab to your hotel when we arrive. Fiona will take me to meet him then."

"Isn't she in Paris?"

"She'll be on the train we take."

"He cultivates this stuff," she said. "Makes sure it's in the mix. Hires people who'll go off the reservation, lead him somewhere new. Harnessing chaos, Garreth said."

"Who's Garreth?"

"My friend. He enjoyed hearing about Hubertus. I think Hubertus made a lot of sense to him. I thought it might be the jumping-off thing. That Hubertus erects his life, and his business, in a way guaranteed to continually take him over the edge. Guaranteed to produce a new edge he'll have to go over."

"He believes that stasis is the real enemy," Milgrim said, glad to put any space at all between himself and Hollis's moment of crossness. "Stability's the beginning of the end. We only walk by continually beginning to fall forward. He told me," remembering, "that that would be the problem with being able to perceive the order flow. The potential for stasis."

"The what?'

"The order flow. He was talking about secrets, once. In Vancouver, when I first met him. He loves secrets."

"I know," said Hollis.

"But not all secrets are information people are trying to conceal. Some secrets are information that's *there*, but people can't have it."

"There where?"

"It just *is*, in the world. I'd asked him what piece of information he'd most want to have, that he didn't have, if he could learn any secret. And he said that he'd want something nobody had ever been able to have."

"Yes?'

"The next day's order flow. Or really the next hour's, or the next minute's."

"But what is it?"

"It's the aggregate of all the orders in the market. Everything anyone is about to buy or sell, all of it. Stocks, bonds, gold, anything. If I understood him, that information exists, at any given moment, but there's no aggregator. It exists, constantly, but is unknowable. If someone were able to aggregate that, the market would cease to be real."

"Why?" She looked out the window, over the taut black wire supporting its gray linen curtain. "Our cab's here."

"Because the market *is* the inability to aggregate the order flow at any given moment." He pushed his chair back, stood, and popped the last of the croissant into his mouth. Chewing, he bent and picked up his bag. He swallowed, then drank off what was left of his coffee. "I'll give you your computer on the train."

She was leaving some change on the tablecloth. "You can have it, if you need it."

"But it's yours."

"I bought it three months ago, thinking I might start another book," she said, standing. "I've opened it about three times. I have a little e-mail on it, but I'll put that on a thumb drive. If I need a computer, Blue Ant can pay for it." She started for the desk, where she'd left her bag.

Milgrim followed, order flow forgotten in his surprise at being offered such a gift. Since he'd been with Hubertus, he'd been provided with things, but they all felt like equipment. It wasn't personal. Hollis was offering him something that he'd thought of as hers.

And she'd already given him her art book, he remembered. He could read more of it on the train to London.

They gave their keys to the man at the desk, and went out to the waiting cab.

35. DONGLE

As the train pulled out of the Gare du Nord, past rain-streaked concrete and intricate calligraphies of spray-paint, she gave Milgrim the Air's white charger, and two other white cables whose purpose she'd never been sure of. Then she cleaned out what little e-mail she had, copying it to the USB drive on her key ring, shaped like an actual key, purchased in the West Hollywood Staples when she began her book. She changed the machine's name to "Milgrim's Mac," wrote its password on a slip of paper for him, and loaned him the USB modem that Inchmale had talked her into signing up for the month before. She didn't know how to remove her e-mail account, but she hadn't given him the password for that, and she could get it sorted in London.

His delight in the gift had a direct and childlike simplicity that saddened her. She suspected he'd not been given a gift in a long time. She'd have to remember to get the dongle back, though, or she'd be paying for his cellular time.

She watched as he sank instantly into whatever it was that he did on the Net, like a stone into water. He was elsewhere, the way people were before their screens, his expression that of someone piloting something, looking into a middle distance that had nothing to do with geography.

She sat back, staring at French vegetation hurtling past, punctuated by a dark staccato of power poles. Bigend wanted her to go straight to Cabinet. That was good. She needed to see Heidi, needed Heidi to get her over the hump, get her to phone Garreth's emergency number. And if phoning produced no result, she'd do what Milgrim suggested, cut a deal with Bigend. Bigend drove a hard bargain. She couldn't imagine what she might have that he most wanted, but she didn't want to find out. And Garreth, she was fairly certain, would be unhappy to have Bigend aware of him. She'd never told anyone anything at all about Garreth, other than Heidi, and now Milgrim. What Garreth and the old man did, insofar as she understood it, was just too peculiarly up Bigend's alley, she'd always thought. It seemed a bad idea, putting Bigend and Garreth together in any way, and she hoped she could avoid it.

She looked over at Milgrim, lost in whatever he was doing. Whatever he was, she found she trusted him. He seemed peeled, somehow, transparent, strangely free of underlying motive. Seemed used as well. Bigend had created him, or would feel that he had; had cobbled him up from whatever wreckage he'd initially presented. That was what Bigend did, she thought, putting her head back and closing her eyes. She supposed it was what he was doing with her as well, or would, if he could.

She was asleep before they reached the tunnel.

36. VINEGAR AND BROWN PAPER

Milgrim didn't open Twitter as he settled, opposite Hollis, in their business-class carriage, into what he still thought of as her computer. Instead, he opened the bookmarks menu and selected the URL for the page with the photograph of Foley modeling an olive drab jacket and a black porn-rectangle.

He scrolled down, past other jackets, modeled by other young men with rectangles, to a shot of black-gloved hands. "Kevlar knit liners," read the description, "for increased cut-resistance, Velcro closure strap with embossed logo. Superior grip for apprehension and control."

Having sometimes been an apprehended suspect himself, he blinked. Frowned. Though the gloves actually reminded him more of Fiona, her armor. He saw her pale jawline above the upright belted collar of her black jacket. As if a wing had grazed him.

He glanced guiltily across the table at Hollis, but found her apparently asleep, her eyes swollen. He tried to imagine her boyfriend, jumping off the world's tallest building, wherever she'd said that was.

He looked back at the specialized apprehender gloves. What would the embossed logo be, exactly? It didn't say. The whole site was like that. No-name. Sketchy. Half-finished. No contact information. Why was Foley there? How had Winnie known where to find him? He'd heard Bigend refer to "ghost sites," the sites of defunct businesses or product lines, still sitting there, forgotten, unvisited. Was this one of those, or something unfinished? There was something unconvincing about it, amateurish.

He went to Google, typed in "Winnie Tung Whitaker." Stopped.

Remembering Bigend and Sleight talking about the collection of search terms, about access to that. He imagined Winnie's PDA alerting her to the fact of someone just having Googled her. Was that possible? On being introduced by Bigend to the current iteration of the internet, Milgrim had decided it was best to assume that anything was possible. Often, he'd been disappointed to learn that something wasn't. Otherwise, better safe than sorry.

He logged out of Twitter, without checking to see if there was a message from Winnie. He didn't want to have to see her, not upon arrival in London, anyway. He had his appointment with Bigend. He logged out of his webmail. Stared at Hollis's interstellar vista. Changed that to a plain medium gray. That was better.

The train entered the tunnel.

He watched as the red dongle launched a window, informing him that the signal was lost.

He couldn't be reached. Not electronically.

Hollis's face was scrunched against the side of her headrest now, but her forehead was relaxed. He saw that the Hounds jacket had fallen to the floor. He bent, picking it up. It was heavier than he would have expected, more substantial, stiffer. He buttoned it. Folded it carefully, the way someone in a store would refold a shirt. It lay on his lap, the focus of one of Bigend's mysteries. A secret.

The rectangular label was made of heavy, stiff, tan leather, branded with some four-legged animal, its head wrong.

He closed his eyes. Put his head back. He was hurtling through a tube, under the English Channel. Did the French call it that? He didn't know. Why were these giant projects so relatively common in Europe? He'd grown up with the unquestioned assumption that America was the home of heroic infrastructure, but was it, now? He didn't think so. How did they pay for these things here? Taxes?

He reminded himself to ask Bigend.

> > >

"You don't know where you're going?" Hollis asked, from the cab, as he lifted her bag in.

"No," said Milgrim, "I'm supposed to wait here."

"You've got my number," she said. "And thank you. I wouldn't have wanted to do that alone."

"Thank you," said Milgrim. "And for the laptop. I'm still not—"

"Never mind," she said. "It's yours. Be careful." She smiled and pulled the door shut.

He watched the cab pull away, another taking its place. He stepped back, gesturing for the couple behind him to go ahead. "I'm meeting someone," he said, to no one in particular, glancing around. As Fiona's horn pipped, just beyond the cab's black fender. She gestured, urgently, the yellow helmet jerking, astride a large, dirty, gray bike.

She took his bag as he reached her, and began securing it to the gas tank with elastic cords, shoving a black helmet into his hands. The visor of her helmet was up. "Put that on. I'm not supposed to be in here. Get on behind and hold on." She flipped the visor down.

He fumbled the helmet over his head. It smelled of something. Hairspray? The transparent visor was scratched and thumb-printed, greasy. He didn't know how to fasten the under-chin thing. Padding rested uncomfortably on the crown of his head.

"Put your arms around me, lean forward, hold on!"

Milgrim did.

She sounded her horn again as they rolled forward, Milgrim unsure where to put his feet. He shifted, trying to look down. Heard her yell something. Found muddy pegs for passenger feet. Saw a rapidly strolling pigeon framed for an instant in the narrow, smudged field the jiggling helmet allowed his vision.

Fiona felt like a very determined child, encased in layers of ballistic nylon and an indeterminate number of armored plates. Milgrim locked his fingers together, instinctively, and leaned into her back. Hard automotive protrusions, some chromed, were zipping past his knees, either side.

He had no idea where they'd emerged from the station, what street they were on, or which direction they might be going. The hairspray smell was giving him a headache. When she stopped for a light, he kept his feet on the pegs, dubious about finding them again.

Pentonville Road, on a sign, though he didn't know whether they were on it or near it. Midmorning traffic, though he'd never seen it from a motorcycle. His jacket, unbuttoned, flapped energetically in the wind, making him glad of the Faraday pouch. His money, what was left of it, was in his right front pocket, the memory card with the photographs of Foley tucked down into his right sock.

More signs, blurry through the plastic: King's Cross Road, Farringdon Road. He thought the hairspray fumes were making his eyes sting now, but no way to rub them. He blinked repeatedly.

Eventually, a bridge, low railings, red and white paint. Blackfriars, he guessed, remembering the colors. Yes, there were the tops of the very formal iron columns that had once supported another bridge, beside it, their red paint slightly faded. He'd come this way once with Sleight, to meet Bigend in an archaic diner, for one of those big greasy breakfasts. He'd asked Sleight about the columns. Sleight hadn't been interested, but Bigend had told him about the railway bridge that had stood beside Blackfriars. When Bigend talked about London, it felt to Milgrim that he was describing some intricate antique toy he'd bought at auction.

Leaving the bridge, she turned, deftly negotiating smaller streets. Then she slowed, turned again, and they rode up on oil-stained concrete, into a workyard full of motorcycles, big ugly ones, their fairings patched with tape. Almost stopping, she dropped her booted feet to the ground and supported the motorcycle with her legs, walking with it as she crept it forward, between the others, past a man in a filthy one-piece orange suit and a backward baseball cap, a gleaming socket wrench in his hand. Through a wide opening and into an interior littered with tools, disassembled cycles and their engines, white foam cups, crumpled food wrappers.

She cut the engine, put down the kickstand, and swatted at Milgrim's hands, which he quickly withdrew. The sudden silence was disorienting. He struggled off, knees stiff, and removed the helmet. "Where are we?" He looked up at the high, soot-blackened ceiling, hung with shattered fiberglass fairings.

Now she dismounted, swinging one multibuckled boot over the seat. "Suthuk," she said, after removing the scarred yellow helmet.

"What?"

"South-wark. South of the river. Suth-uk." She set the helmet on a cluttered tool cart, and began to undo the elastic net that held Milgrim's bag atop her gas tank.

"What is this place?"

"A roll-in. Vinegar and brown paper. Quick and dirty repairs. No appointment necessary. For couriers."

Milgrim raised the helmet, sniffed at its interior, put it on the motorcycle where he'd sat. She handed him his bag.

After various rippings of Velcro, the zipper down the front of her jacket made its own loud noise. "You hadn't ridden a motorcycle before?"

"A scooter, once."

"There's a center-of-gravity concept you're missing. You need passenger lessons."

"Sorry," said Milgrim, and he was.

"Not a problem." Her hair was a pale brown. He hadn't been able to tell in Paris, in the darkened hotel lobby. The helmet had made it stick up in back. He wanted to smooth it down.

The man in the once-orange boiler suit came to the entrance. "Himself is on the bridge," he said to Fiona. He sounded Irish, but looked to Milgrim to be of some other, darker ethnicity, his face battered and immobile. He took a cigarette from behind his ear and lit it, using a small transparent lighter. Put the lighter in a side pocket and absently wiped his hands on the stained orange fabric. "You could wait in the room," he said, and smiled at Fiona, "for all that's good in it." His two front teeth were framed in gold, and protruded at an unusual angle, like the roof of a tiny porch. He drew on his cigarette.

"Is there tea, Benny?"

"I'll send the boy," the man said.

"Carburetors aren't right," she said, looking at her bike.

"I told you not to go with the Kawasaki, didn't I?" said Benny, pinching the cigarette for a final fierce drag, then letting it drop, to crush it with a battered, grease-soaked toe, through which dull steel showed. "Carbs wear out. Dear to replace. Carbs on the GT550've been very good to me."

"Have a look at it for me?"

Benny smirked. "Not like I've real couriers needing repairs. Family men, working for a guarantee."

"Or home in bed, radio on, skiving," said Fiona, taking off her jacket. She looked suddenly smaller, in a gray turtleneck jersey. "More your usual description."

"I'll have Saad look into it," Benny said, turning and walking out.

"Is Benny Irish?"

"Dublin," she said, "father's Tunisian."

"And you work for Hubertus?"

"As do you," she said, slinging the heavy jacket over her shoulder. "This way."

He followed her, avoiding oil-soaked rags and white foam cups, some half filled with what he assumed had once been tea, past a sort of giant red toolbox on wheels, to a battered door. She fished a small ring of keys from her trousers, which looked as heavy, and nearly as well armored, as her jacket.

"Did you want to?" he asked as she unlocked the door.

"Want to what?"

"Work for Hubertus. I didn't. Didn't plan to, I mean. It was his idea."

"Now that you mention it," she said, over her shoulder, "it was his idea."

Milgrim stepped through after her, into a tidy white space perhaps fifteen feet on a side. The walls were recently painted brick, the concrete floor a glossier white, nearly as clean. A small square table and four chairs, matte steel tubing and bent, unpainted plywood, expensively simple. An enormous light glowed softly, something on a clinical-looking metallic pedestal, a sort of white parabolic umbrella, angled up. It looked to Milgrim like a very small art gallery between shows. "What's this?" he asked, looking from one blank wall to another.

"One of his Vegas cubes," she said. "Haven't you seen one before?" She went to the light and did something, dialing the illumination up.

"No."

"He doesn't understand gambling," she said, "the ordinary kind, but he loves Las Vegas casinos. The sort of thought that goes into them. How they enforce a temporal isolation. No clocks, no windows, artificial light. He likes to think in environments like that. Like this. No interruptions. And he likes them to be secret."

"He likes secrets," Milgrim agreed, putting his bag on the table.

A boy with an almost-shaven head came in, a tall white foam cup in either grimy hand, and placed them on the table. "Thanks," said Fiona. He left without a word. Fiona picked up one of the cups, sipped through the hole in the white plastic lid. "Builder's tea," she said.

Milgrim tried his. Shuddered. Sweet, stewed.

"I'm not his daughter," Fiona said.

Milgrim blinked. "Whose?"

"Bigend's. In spite of rumors to the contrary. Not the case." She sipped her tea.

"I wouldn't have thought that."

"My mother was his girlfriend. That's where the story started. I was already around, so it actually doesn't make any sense. Though I did wind up here, working for him." She gave Milgrim a look he couldn't read. "Just to get that straight."

Milgrim sucked down some tea, mainly to cover his inability to think of anything to say. It was very hot. "Did he train you," he asked, "to ride motorcycles?"

"No," she said, "I was already a courier. That's where I know Benny from. I could walk out on Bigend today, have a job in an hour. It's like that, being a courier. If you want the day off, you quit. But it was driving my mother crazy. Worried about the danger."

"Is it dangerous?"

"Average career's all of two years. So she talked to Bigend. Wanted him to take me on at Blue Ant. Do something there. Instead, he decided to have his own courier."

"That's less dangerous?"

"Not really, but I tell her it is. She doesn't know the extent of the job. She's busy."

"Good morning," said Bigend, behind them.

Milgrim turned. Bigend was wearing his blue suit, over a black knit shirt, no tie.

"Do you like them?" Bigend asked Milgrim.

"Like what?"

"Our Festos," said Bigend, raising his index finger to point straight up.

Milgrim looked up. The ceiling here, as white as the walls, was a good ten ten feet higher than it was in the adjacent space. Against it floated confusing shapes, silver, black. "Is that the penguin? From Paris?"

"It's like the one in Paris," she said.

"What's the other?"

"Manta. Ray," said Bigend. "Our first custom order. They're ordinarily in the silver Mylar."

"What do you do with them?" Though he already knew.

"Surveillance platforms," Bigend said. He turned to Fiona. "How was it, in Paris?"

"Good," she said, "except that he saw it. But that's the silver, and daytime operation." She shrugged.

"I thought I was hallucinating," Milgrim said.

"Yes," Bigend said, "people do. In Crouch End, though, when we first tried the penguin at night, we triggered a mini-wave of UFO reports. The *Times* suggested people were actually seeing Venus. Have a seat." He drew out one of the chairs.

Milgrim sat. Held the tall cup of hot tea in his hands, its warmth comforting.

When Bigend and Fiona were seated as well, Bigend said, "Fiona's told me what you told her last night. You said that you photographed the man who was following you, or perhaps following Hollis. Do you have the photographs?"

"Yes," said Milgrim, bending to fish in his sock top. "But he was following me. Sleight was telling him where I was." He put the camera card on the table, opened his bag, brought out the Air, found the card reader he'd bought from the Persian man in the camera shop, and put them together.

"But Sleight may simply have assumed you'd be with Hollis," Bigend said as the first of the photographs of Foley came up.

"Foley," Milgrim said.

"Why do you call him that?"

"Because he was wearing foliage green pants. That was what I first noticed about him."

"Have you seen him?" Bigend asked Fiona.

"Yes," Fiona said. "He was in and out of the old-clothes fair. Busy. I could see he was doing something. Or wanting to."

"Was he alone?"

"He seemed to be. But talking to himself. You know: not to himself. An earpiece."

"Sleight," said Milgrim.

"Yes," agreed Bigend. "We'll call him Foley, then. We have no idea what he goes by at the moment. These people have access to quite a bit of documentation."

"What people?" asked Milgrim.

"Foley," said Bigend, "knows the man whose trousers you documented for us in South Carolina."

"Is Foley . . . a spy?" asked Milgrim.

"Only to the extent that he's a clothing designer, or wants to be," said Bigend. "Though he's probably a fantasist as well. When you slipped your phone into that Russian woman's pram, what was your intention?"

"I knew that Sleight was tracking it, telling Foley where I was. Foley would follow the Russians instead. Out of town. They mentioned a suburb."

Bigend nodded. "Just because a man wants to be a clothing designer," Bigend said, "and is a fantasist, doesn't mean that he isn't dangerous. If you should see Mr. Foley again, you'll want to stay well away from him."

Milgrim nodded.

"I'll need to know, immediately, if that happens."

"What about Sleight?"

"Sleight," said Bigend, "is behaving as though absolutely nothing has happened. He's still very much at the center of things, as far as Blue Ant goes."

"I thought he was in Toronto."

"He's in a post-geographical position," said Bigend. "Where did you get this laptop?"

"Hollis gave it to me."

"Do you know where she got it?"

"She said she bought it, to write on."

"We'll have Voytek give it a once-over."

"Who?"

"He predates Sleight. Someone I've kept out of the loop, in case something like this should happen. My IT backup, you might say. Have you had breakfast?"

"A croissant. In Paris."

"Fancy the full English? Fiona?"

"Could do. Saad's looking at my carbs."

They looked at Milgrim. He nodded. Then looked up at the silver penguin and the black ray, floating against the bright white ceiling. He tried to imagine the black ray above a Left Bank intersection. "What's it like, flying those?"

"It's like being one," said Fiona, "when you get into it. The iPhone app's made a huge difference. The one in Paris hasn't had the upgrade yet."

37. AJAY

Inchmale's spirit-beast, the narcoleptic stuffed ferret, still frozen in nightmarish dream-waltz amid the game birds, was waiting near Cabinet's grumbling lift.

Robert had said, on being asked just now, that "Miss Hyde" was in. He seemed to have entirely forgotten any discomfort experienced on Heidi's arrival, and in fact showed every sign of having become an enthusiast. This, Hollis knew, was all too likely to happen. Men who didn't permanently flee at the onset tended to become devotees.

She entered the familiar cage, pulled her bag in after her, shut the cage's door, and pushed the button. Once and only briefly, so as not to confuse it.

In the hallway, upstairs, she avoided looking at the watercolors, opened the door to Number Four, entered, put her bag on the bed. Everything was as she remembered it, except for a few unfamiliar dust jackets in the birdcage. She opened her bag, took out the Blue Ant figurine, and went next door, to Heidi's room.

She knocked.

"Who is it?" asked a male voice.

"Hollis," she said.

It opened, a crack. "Let her in," said Heidi.

The door was opened by a beautiful, supremely fit-looking young man, like a Bollywood dancer, whose translucently short haircut became a sort of short black waterfall on top. As if to balance this prettiness, though, it looked as though someone had struck the bridge of his nose with something hard and narrow, leaving the suggestion of a notch, pale at the center. He wore a bright blue tracksuit under Heidi's faded leather tour jacket.

"That's Ajay," said Heidi as Hollis stepped in.

"Hullo," said Ajay.

"Hello," said Hollis. The room was confusingly tidy now, with almost no sign of Heidi's characteristic luggage-explosion, though Hollis noted that the bed, where Heidi reclined in a Gold's Gym tank top and kneeless jeans, was very thoroughly unmade. "What happened to your stuff?"

"They helped me sort it out, stored what I wanted to keep. They're nice here."

Hollis couldn't remember ever having heard Heidi say that about any hotel staff anywhere. She suspected Inchmale in the mix, advising Cabinet on how best to deal with Heidi, distributing bribes, though in fact the Cabinet people actually were very good at what they did.

"What the fuck is that?" asked Heidi, much more in character, indicating the blue figurine.

"A Blue Ant marketing toy. It's hollow"—she showed Heidi the bottom of its base—"and I think it might have some sort of tracking bug in it."

"Really?" said Ajay.

"Really," said Hollis, passing it to him.

"Why would you think that?" He held it to his ear, shook it, smiled.

"Long story."

"The only way to tell would be to cut it open . . ." He'd padded to the window, moving like a cat, and was peering closely at the base. "But someone already has," he said, looking up at her. "Been sliced off here, glued back on, then sanded out."

"Ajay's handy," said Heidi.

"I'm not interrupting you, am I?" Hollis asked.

Ajay grinned.

"We were waiting for you," Heidi said. "If you didn't turn up, we were going to the gym. Ajay's the one who told me about your boyfriend."

"An absolutely blinding 'chutist," said Ajay, solemnly, lowering the figurine. "Seen him twice, 'round the pubs. Regret to say I haven't had the pleasure."

"Do you know where he is?" Hollis asked. "How he is? I've just learned about his accident. I'm terribly worried."

"Neither, really, sorry," said Ajay. "Though if there had been further bad news, we'd have heard something. He's very well-thought-of, your man. Has his fan base."

"Do you know any way that I might find out?"

"He's private. Not at all clear what he does, aside from the odd jump. Do you want me to open this?" Holding up the ant. "Heidi's got the perfect set of tools for it. Building her Breast Chaser." He grinned.

"Your what?" Hollis asked Heidi.

"It's therapy," Heidi said, crossly. "My psychiatrist taught me."

"What is?"

"Plastic models," said Heidi. She sat up, put her feet on the floor, toenails freshly and glossily blackened.

"Your psychiatrist taught you to build models?"

"He's Japanese," Heidi said. "You can't make a living as a psychiatrist in Japan. They don't really believe in it. So he came to L.A. Office near fuckstick's, Century City."

Ajay had crossed to the intricately inlaid vanity, on which Hollis now saw small tools, plastic parts still attached to their molding-trees, miniature cans of spray paint, narrow-tipped brushes. All of this spread over a thick layering of newspaper. "This'll do it," he said, seating himself on the low stool, and raising a thin rod of aluminum, tipped with a small isosceles blade. Hollis peered over his shoulder. Saw a brightly colored box standing against the mirror, printed with a painting of a very militant-looking robot warrior in a sort of Aztec headdress, the words BREAST CHASER in sans serif caps. The rest of the writing was in Japanese.

"Why do they call it that?" Hollis asked.

"'Engrish,'" said Heidi, with a shrug. "'Beast,' maybe? Or sometimes they just like the shape of the letters. It's a beginner's kit." This last addressed to Ajay, accusingly. "I ask him to get me a kit by Bandai, something in their Gundam series, expert-grade. Gold standard of figure kits. He brings me fucking Breast Chaser Galvion. Thinks it's funny. Not Bandai, not Gundam. A kid's kit."

"Sorry," said Ajay, who'd obviously heard about this before.

"You build them?" Hollis asked.

"Helps me focus. Calms me down. Fujiwara says it's the only thing that works, for some people. Only thing that works for him."

"He does it himself?"

"He's a master. Incredible airbrush technique. Scratch-built modifications."

"Do you want me to open this?" Ajay jiggled the tip of the razor knife.

"Yes," said Hollis.

"If it's full of anthrax, we'll all be sorry." He winked.

Heidi got up from the bed and came over. "Hey. Don't blunt that."

"It's vinyl," said Ajay, laying the ant down, on its back, and deftly wielding the razor knife. Hollis watched the tip of the blade slide smoothly into the side of the round base. "Yes. Been cut, glued. Easy. There." The bottom of the base lay flat on the newsprint, a round of blue a few millimeters thick. "Well," said Ajay, peering into the twin small tunnels of the ant's hollow legs, "what's this, then?" He put down the knife, picked up a long, slender pair of tweezers, with canted tips, and inserted them into one leg. He looked up at Hollis. "Watch. I'm going to pull out . . . a rabbit!" He produced, gradually, a spongy sheet of thin yellow foam. Displayed it dangling limply from the tweezers' sharp jaws, five inches square. "Rabbit," he said, dropping it. "And for my next trick . . ." He inserted the tweezers again. Felt around with them. And slowly, carefully, drew out a two-inch length of narrow, transparent flexible tubing, plugged at either end with a tiny red cork. "Looks like very professional funny business to me." There were various differently cylindrical bits of metal and plastic inside the tube, like a section of a hippie-techno necklace. He looked at it more closely, then looked up at Hollis, raising his eyebrows.

"Huh," said Heidi, "ant's been LoJacked. Bigend."

"I'm not sure," said Hollis. "Can they hear us?" she asked Ajay, suddenly afraid.

"No," he said. "It was sealed in the doll. The foam was to keep it from rattling. You'd never set up an audio bug that way. You'd want a little needle mike, through the vinyl, for that. This is a transponder and a battery. What do you want to do with it?"

"I don't know."

"I can replace it. Reglue the base. I'll bet Heidi can fix it so you'd never know we opened it."

"I'm much more concerned with Garreth at the moment," said Hollis.

"We've discussed that," said Heidi. "You have to call that number. That's all. If that doesn't get him, plan B."

"Or," said Ajay, still considering the tracker bug, "you could keep this, but reglue your ant. That would give you a degree of lateral control."

"How do you mean?"

"If you keep the bug hidden in the vicinity of the ant, rather than *in* the ant, they'll think it's still in the ant. So they'll assume the bug is where the ant is. It has possibilities. Bit of wiggle room." He shrugged.

"I've had it since Vancouver," Hollis said to Heidi. "Hubertus gave it to me. I thought I'd left it there, deliberately, but then I found it in my luggage, in New York. Somebody here put it in my bag before I went to Paris."

"Do what Ajay says," Heidi said, tousling his waterfall. "He's handy. Now come with me."

"Where?"

"Your room. You're going to make that call. I'll be your witness."

38. GETTING HOTTER

Bigend was having the No. 7 Breakfast: two fried eggs, black pudding, two slices of bacon, two slices of bread, and a mug of tea. "They get the black pudding right, here," he said. "It's so often overcooked. Dry."

Milgrim and Fiona were having Thai noodle dishes, which Milgrim found an unexpected option in a place serving the sort of breakfast Bigend was having, but Fiona had explained that the Thais had quite seamlessly integrated the two, much in the way Italians had once learned to offer the full English, in a setting of pasta, but even more convincingly.

It was a tiny place, crowded, not much larger than Bigend's Vegas cube, the clientele a mixture of office workers, builders, and the arts-oriented, consuming lunch or late breakfast. The china and tableware were random, unmatched, and Bigend's mug of tea bore a smiling teddy bear.

"You don't think Foley was following me in Paris?"

"You went back to the hotel," Bigend said. "I phoned and said that Aldous would be picking you up. You were using a phone Sleight gave you, but I didn't say where you were going, or who you were meeting. Fiona followed the Hilux." He nodded in her direction.

"No tails," said Fiona.

"But I'd phoned Hollis first," Bigend said, "to find out where she'd be, in order to send you there. They might have overheard that. But if your Foley was there just as you arrived, I imagine he either followed Hollis to Selfridges or knew that she'd be going there."

"Why would they be interested in Hollis? What does she have to do with Myrtle Beach and those army pants?"

"You," said Bigend, "and me. They may have seen us all together at lunch, the day before. Sleight has allies within Blue Ant, almost certainly. They would assume that Hollis may be involved with our contracting project. And she is, of course." Bigend forked a large piece of bacon into his mouth, and chewed.

"She is?"

Bigend swallowed, drank tea. "I'd like to see what the Gabriel Hounds designer could do for us for military contracting."

Milgrim glanced at Fiona, curious to see whether she'd respond to the mention of the brand, but she was deftly picking shrimp from her noodles with chopsticks. "Hollis is upset," Milgrim said to Bigend. "Her boyfriend."

"Really? She has one?"

"Had," said Milgrim. "They aren't together. But she's learned he was in an accident."

"What kind of accident?"

"Automobile," said Milgrim, which was literally true.

"Nothing serious, I hope," said Bigend, tearing a slice of bread in half.

"She thinks it may have been," said Milgrim.

"I can keep her on track," said Bigend, sopping up yolk.

Milgrim looked at Fiona, who was looking at Bigend quite coldly now, he thought, but then went back to her noodles.

"You want the Gabriel Hounds designer to design for the U.S. military?"

"If a great deal of men's clothing today is descended from U.S. military designs, and it is, and the U.S. military is having trouble living up to their heritage, and they are, someone whose genius lies in some recombinant grasp of the semiotics of mass-produced American clothing . . . Foolish not to look at the possibilities. In any case, it's getting hot now," said Bigend.

"What is?"

"The situation. The flow of events. It always does, when people like Sleight decide to have a go. And the person in my position is expected to focus, narrowly, on the situation at hand. Terrible waste, tactically. You can often make a killing in the market, while an attempted coup is under way." He wiped up yolk and grease with his final bit of bread and popped it into his mouth, leaving his plate perfectly clean.

Fiona put down her chopsticks, having picked a last shrimp from her noodles. "And where will I be taking Mr. Milgrim?"

"Holiday Inn, Camden Lock," said Bigend. "Everyone seems to know about Covent Garden."

"I saw one of the Dottirs, in Paris, at the restaurant," said Milgrim, "and Rausch."

"I know," said Bigend. "You told Fiona, last night."

"But was it an accident that we were there? When they were?"

"It appears to have been," said Bigend, cheerfully, wiping his fingers with a paper napkin. "But you know what they say."

"What?"

"Even the delusionally paranoid have enemies."

>>>

"He's put you in the Holiday Inn," said Fiona as they walked back to the repair yard along what she'd said, when he'd asked, was lower Marsh Street.

"Yes?"

"Certainly not as posh," she said, "but where you were has a lot of inherent security, simply in the ground plan. Stars have ridden out serious press-sieges there. Nothing wrong with the Camden Holiday Inn, but it's not that tight."

"He thinks too many people know where I've been staying," Milgrim said.

"I don't know what he thinks," said Fiona, "but you'd better watch yourself."

I do, thought Milgrim. Or rather, he had. Pathologically, his therapist had said. "You were going to explain what I need to do in order to be a better passenger," he said.

"Was I?"

"You said I needed a passenger lesson."

"You need to sit closer to me, and hold on tight. Our mass needs to be as one."

"It does?"

"Yes. And you need to stay with me, lean with me, on the turns. But not too much. It's like dancing."

Milgrim coughed. "I'll try," he said.

39. THE NUMBER

Heidi perched on the edge of the Piblokto Madness bed, like an expensively coiffed gargoyle, pale knees protruding through the holes in her jeans, long pale black-nailed toes extended over the scrimshawed trim. "Number's in your phone?"

"No," said Hollis, standing in the middle of the room, feeling trapped. The insectoid wallpaper seemed to have closed in. All the various busts and masks and two-eyed representations staring.

"Bad sign," said Heidi. "Where is it?"

"In my wallet."

"You never memorized it."

"No."

"It was for emergencies."

"I never really expected to need it."

"You just wanted to carry it around. Because he wrote it."

Hollis looked away, through the open door to the vast bathroom, where fresh towels were hung, warming, on the horizontal pipes of the Time Machine shower.

"Let's see it," said Heidi.

Hollis got her wallet out of her purse, her iPhone with it. The little strip of paper, which he'd neatly torn from the bottom of a sheet of Tribeca Grand notepaper, was still there, behind the Amex card she only used for emergencies. She drew it out, unfolded it, and passed it to Heidi.

"American area code?"

"It'll be a cell. It could be anywhere."

Heidi dug in a back jeans pocket with her other hand, came up with her own iPhone.

"What are you doing?"

"I'm putting it in my phone." When she'd finished, she handed the strip of paper back to Hollis. "Have you thought about what you'll say?"

"No," said Hollis. "I can't think about it."

"That's good," said Heidi. "Now do it. But put your phone on speaker."

"Why?"

"Because I need to hear it. Because you may not remember what you say. I will."

"Shit," said Hollis, sitting down on the bed, nearer its foot, and switching on the speaker.

"No shit," agreed Heidi. "Call him."

Hollis blankly entered the number.

"Put his name on it," Heidi said. "Add it to your numbers."

Hollis did.

"Give it a speed-dial code," said Heidi.

"I never use that."

Heidi snorted. "Call him."

Hollis did. Almost immediately, the room filled with the sound of a ring tone, unfamiliar. Five rings.

"He's not there," said Hollis, looking up at Heidi.

"Let it ring."

After the tenth ring, there was a small, nondescript digital sound. Someone, perhaps a very old woman, began to chatter fiercely, demonstratively, in what might have been an oriental language. She seemed to make three firm statements, increasingly brief. Then silence. Then the record tone.

"Hello?" Hollis winced. "Hello! This is Hollis Henry, phoning for Garreth." She swallowed, almost coughed. "I just heard about your accident. I'm sorry. I'm worried. Could you call me, please? I hope you get this. I'm in London." She recited her number. "I—" The record tone sounded again, causing her to jerk.

"Hang up," said Heidi.

Hollis did.

"That was good," said Heidi, punching her shoulder softly.

"I feel like throwing up," said Hollis. "What if he doesn't call?"

"What if he does?"

"Exactly," said Hollis.

"Either way, we've moved it forward. But he will."

"I'm not so sure."

"If you felt like he wouldn't, you wouldn't be going through this. You wouldn't need to."

Hollis sighed, shakily, and looked at the phone in her hand, which now seemed to have taken on a life of its own.

"I'm not doing Ajay," Heidi said.

"I wondered," said Hollis.

"What I *am* doing, very actively, is not doing Ajay." She sighed. "Best sparring partner I've ever had. You wouldn't believe the way those squaddies can mix it."

"What are 'squaddies'?"

"I don't know." Heidi grinned. "I think it might just mean regular soldiers, in which case it's a joke, because they aren't that."

"Where did you find them?"

"The gym. Hackney. Your boy at the front door found it for me. Robert. He's cute. I went over there in a cab. They laughed at me. Don't get women there. I had to put some whup-ass on Ajay. Which was not easy. Picked him 'cause he was smallest."

"What are they?"

"Something. Military. Listening to them, you can't tell whether they're still in or not. Bouncers, bodyguards, like that. Moonlighting? Between assignments? Fuck if I know."

Hollis was still looking at the iPhone.

"You think that was Korean? On his voice mail?"

"I don't know," said Hollis. The phone rang.

"There you go," said Heidi, and winked.

"Hello?"

"Welcome back." Bigend's voice filled the room. "I'm on my way back to the office. Can you join me there, please? We should talk."

Hollis looked up at Heidi, tears starting to come. Then back down at the phone.

"Hello?" said Bigend. "Are you there?"

40. ENIGMA ROTORS

His room here overlooked a canal. He'd only been vaguely aware of London having canals, before. It didn't have them to the extent that Amsterdam did, or Venice, but it did have them. They were a sort of backdoor territory, evidently. Shops and houses didn't seem to have faced them. Like a system of aquatic alleys, originally for heavy transport. Now, to judge by the view from his window, they were repurposed as civic and tourist space. Turned into a framework for boat rides, with paths for jogging and cycling. He thought of the boat on the Seine, with its video screen, the Dottirs and George's band, the Bollards. The boat he'd seen here, earlier, had been much smaller.

The room phone rang. He left the bathroom to answer it. "Hello?"

"I am Voytek," a man said, with some accent that caused Milgrim, on the off chance, to repeat himself in Russian.

"Russian? I am not Russian. You are?"

"Milgrim."

"You are American."

"I know," said Milgrim.

"My shop," said Voytek, whose name Milgrim now remembered from brunch in Southwark, "is in market, near your hotel. Under, in old stables. You bring your unit now."

"What's the name of your shop?"

"Biro Shack."

"Biro Shack? Like the pen?"

"Biro Shack. And son. Goodbye."

"Goodbye." Milgrim returned the phone to its cradle.

He sat down at the desk and logged into his Twitter account.

"Get n touch," Winnie had posted, an hour earlier.

"Camden Town Holiday Inn," he typed, then added his room number and the telephone number of the hotel. He updated. Refreshed. Nothing.

The phone rang.

"Hello?"

"Welcome back," said Winnie. "I'm coming over there."

"I'm just going out," said Milgrim. "It's work. I don't know how long it's going to take."

"How's your evening look?"

"Nothing scheduled yet."

"Keep it open for me."

"I'll try."

"I'm not that far away. Heading for the general vicinity now."

"Goodbye," Milgrim said to the phone, though she was already gone. He sighed.

He'd forgotten to return Hollis's red dongle, but he didn't need it here. He'd give it back to her the next time he saw her.

He closed the laptop and put it in his bag, which he'd unpacked on arrival. Bigend had wanted the memory card with the pictures of Foley, and he didn't have another, so he wouldn't bother taking the camera.

Walking from his room to the elevator, he wondered why they had decided to build a Holiday Inn here, beside this canal.

In the lobby, he waited at the concierge desk while two young American men received directions to the Victoria and Albert. He looked at them the way he imagined Blue Ant's young French fashion analyst might. Everything they were wearing, he decided, qualified as what she'd call "iconic," but had originally become that way through its ability to gracefully patinate. She was big on patination. That was how quality wore in, she said, as opposed to out. Distressing, on the other hand, was the faking of patination, and was actually a way of concealing a lack of quality. Until he'd found himself in Bigend's apparel-design push, he hadn't known that anyone thought about clothing that way. He didn't imagine that anything these two wore was liable to acquire any patina, except under different and later ownership.

When they'd moved on, he asked for directions to Voytek's Biro Shack, explaining where he'd been told it was.

"I don't see it listed, sir," said the concierge, clicking his mouse, "but you aren't far, if it's where they told you it would be." He ballpointed a map in a colored brochure and handed it to Milgrim.

"Thanks."

Outside, the air smelled differently of exhaust. More diesel? The neighborhood felt theme-parky but downscale, a little like a state fairground before the evening crowds arrive. He passed two Japanese girls eating what seemed to be corn dogs, which heightened the effect.

He was keeping an eye out for Winnie, but if she'd arrived he didn't see her.

Following the ballpoint line on the concierge's map, he found himself in a brick-arched under-mall, some Victorian retrofit, stocked mostly with merchandise that reminded him of St. Mark's Place, though with an odd, semi-Japanese feel, perhaps an appeal to foreign youth-tourism. Further back in this, glassed behind half a brick archway, floridly Victorian gilt lettering announced BIROSHAK & SON. A surname, then. As he entered, a bell tinked, bouncing on a long Art Nouveau lily stem of brass, attached to the door.

The shop was densely but tidily packed with small, largely featureless boxes, like old-fashioned TV-top cable units, arrayed on glass shelves. A tall, balding man, about Milgrim's age, turned and nodded. "You are Milgrim," he said. "I am Voytek." There was a battered plastic pennant behind the counter: AMSTRAD, both the name and the logo unfamiliar.

Voytek wore a wool cardigan pieced together from perhaps half a dozen donors, one sleeve plain camel, the other plaid. Under it a silky ecru T-shirt with too many pearl buttons. He blinked behind harsh-looking steel-framed glasses.

Milgrim put his bag on the counter. "Will it take long?" he asked.

"Assuming I find nothing, ten minutes. Leave it."

"I'd rather stay."

Voytek frowned, then shrugged. "You think I will put something in it."

"Do you do that?"

"Some people do," said Voytek. "PC?"

"Mac," said Milgrim, unzipping his bag and bringing it out.

"Put it on the counter. I lock up." He came from behind the counter, wearing those gray felt clogs that reminded Milgrim of the feet of toy animals. He went to the door, slid a bolt into place, and returned. "I hate these Air," he said, amiably enough, turning the laptop over and producing the first of a number of tiny, very expensive-looking screwdrivers. "They are very bitch, to open."

"What are all these boxes?" Milgrim asked, indicating the shelves.

"They are computers. Real ones. From the dawn." He removed the bottom of the Air, with no evident difficulty at all.

"Are they valuable?"

"Valuable? What is true worth?" He put on an elaborate pair of magnifying glasses, with clear colorless frames.

"That's what I asked you."

"True worth." LEDs in the clear temples illuminated the elegantly compacted guts of the Air. "You put a price on romance?"

"Romance?"

"These true computers are the root code. The Eden."

Milgrim saw that there were still older machines, some actually housed in wood, locked in a large, really quite seriously expensive-looking glass case, rising a good six feet from the floor. The wood-cased typewriter-y device nearest him bore an eye-shaped silk-screened ENIGMA logo. "What are those, then?"

"*Before* the Eden. Enigma encryption. As called forth by Alan Turing. To birth the Eden. Also on offer, U.S. Army M-209B cipher machine with original canvas field case, Soviet M-125-3MN Fialka cipher machine, Soviet clandestine pocket-sized nonelectronic burst encoder and keyer. You are interested?"

"What's a burst encoder?"

"Enter message, encrypt, send with inhuman speed as Morse

code. Spring-winder. Twelve hundred pounds. Discount for Blue Ant employee, one thousand."

Someone rapped on the door. A young man with a massive diagonal forelock, wrapped in what appeared to be a bathrobe. He was grimacing with impatience. Voytek sighed, put down the Air, on a battered foam pad that bore the Amstrad logo, and went to open the door, still wearing the illuminated magnifying glasses. The bathrobed boy—Milgrim saw that it was a very thin, very wrinkled sort of overcoat, perhaps cashmere—swept past Voytek without eye contact, to the rear of the shop, and through a door Milgrim hadn't previously noticed. "Cunt," said Voytek, neutrally, relocking the door and returning to the Air and the task at hand.

"Your son?" asked Milgrim.

"Son?" He frowned. "It is Shombo."

"Is what?"

"Is arse-pain. Nightmare. Bigend." He'd picked up the Air now and was peering savagely into it from a few inches away.

"Bigend is?" Milgrim was not unfamiliar with the opinion, if the man meant Bigend.

"Shombo. I must keep him here, take him home. I lose track of the months." He tapped the little Mac with a screwdriver. "Nothing has been added here." He began to smoothly reassemble it, his efficiency fueled, Milgrim sensed, with resentment. Of gray-robed Shombo, Milgrim hoped.

"Is that all you need to do?"

"All? My family is living with this person."

"To my computer."

"Now software analysis." He produced a battered black Dell from beneath the counter and cabled it to the Air. "Is password?"

"Locative," Milgrim said, and spelled it. "Lowercase. Dot. One." He went to the showcase to look more closely at the Enigma machine. "Does patination make them more valuable?"

"What?" LEDs flashed in his direction from the plastic glasses.

"If they're worn. Evidence of use."

"Most valuable," said Voytek, staring at him over the tops of the glasses, "is mint."

"What are these things?" Black, shark-toothed gears, the size of the bottom of a beer bottle. Each one stamped with a multidigit number, into which white paint had been rubbed.

"For you, same as burst encoder: one thousand pounds."

"I mean what are they for?"

"They set encryption. Receiving machine must have day's identical rotor."

A single rap on the door, tinkling the lily bells. It was the other driver, the one who'd driven Milgrim in from Heathrow.

"Shit-persons," said Voytek in resignation, and went to unlock the door again.

"Urine specimen," the driver said, producing a fresh brown paper bag.

"The fuck," said Voytek.

"I'll need to use your bathroom," Milgrim said.

"Bath? I have no bath."

"Toilet. Loo."

"In back. With Shombo."

"He'll have to watch," Milgrim said, indicating the driver.

"I don't want to know," said Voytek. He rapped on the door through which Shombo had vanished. "Shombo! Men need loo!"

"Fuck off," said Shombo, muffled by the door.

Milgrim, closely followed by the driver, approached it, tried the knob. It opened.

"Fuck off," said Shombo again, but abstractedly, from a multi-screened rat's-nest quite far back in a larger, darker space than Milgrim had expected. The screens were covered with dense columns of what Milgrim took to be figures, rather than written language.

With the driver behind him, Milgrim headed for the plywood-walled toilet cubicle, illuminated by a single bare bulb. There wouldn't have been room for the driver, who simply loomed in the doorway, passing Milgrim the paper bag. Milgrim opened it, removed the sandwich bag, opened that, removed the blue-topped bottle. He broke the paper seal, removed the lid, and unzipped his fly.

"Piss off," muttered Shombo, without a trace of irony.

Milgrim sighed, filled the bottle, capped it, finished in the grimy toilet, flushed by pulling a chain, then put the bottle in the sandwich bag, the sandwich bag in the paper bag, handed the paper bag to the driver, then washed his hands in cold water. There didn't seem to be any soap.

As they left the room, Milgrim saw the reflection of the bright screens in Shombo's eyes.

He closed the door carefully behind him.

The driver handed Milgrim a crisp manila envelope of a pattern suggesting deeply traditional banking practices. Within it, Milgrim felt the sealed bubble-pack containing his medication.

"Thanks," said Milgrim.

The driver, without a word, took his leave, Voytek bustling irritably to lock the door behind him.

41. GEAR-QUEER

He'll be right down," said Jacob, smiling and luxuriantly bearded as ever, when he met her at Blue Ant's entrance. "How was Paris? Would you like coffee?"

"Fine, thanks. No coffee." She felt ragged, and assumed she looked it, but also better, since Heidi had forced her to make the call. Looking up at the lobby's used-eyeglasses chandelier, she welcomed whatever distraction or annoyance Bigend might be able to provide.

And here he suddenly came, the optically challenging blue suit muted, if that could be the word for it, by a black polo shirt. Behind him, silent and alert, his two umbrella-bearing minders. Leaving Jacob behind, he took Hollis's arm and steered her back out the door, followed by the minders. "Not *good*, Jacob," he said to her, quietly. "Sleight's."

"Really?"

"Not entirely positive yet," he said, leading her left, then left again at the corner. "But it looks likely."

"Where are we going?"

"Not far. I'm no longer conducting important conversations on Blue Ant premises."

"What's happening?"

"I should have the whole phenomenon modeled. Have some good CG visualizations done. It's not clockwork, of course, but it's familiar. I'd guess it takes a good five or six years to cycle through."

"Milgrim made it sound like a palace coup, some kind of takeover."

"Overly dramatic. A few of my brightest employees are quitting.

Those who haven't gotten where they'd hoped to, with Blue Ant. So few do, really. Someone like Sleight tries to quit with optimal benefits, of course. Builds his own golden parachute. Robs me blind, if he can. Information flows out, before these parties depart, to the highest bidders. Always more than one golden parachutist." He took her arm again and crossed the narrow street, in the wake of a passing Mercedes. "Too many moving parts for a solo operator. Sleight, probably Jacob, two or three more."

"You don't seem that alarmed."

"I expect it. It's always interesting. It can shake other things out. Reveal things. When you want to know how things really work, study them when they're coming apart."

"What does that mean?"

"Increased risk. Increased opportunity. This one comes at an inopportune time, but then they do seem to. Here we are." He'd stopped in front of a narrow Soho shopfront, one whose austerely minimalist signage announced TANKY & TOJO in brushed aluminum capitals. She looked in the window. An antique tailor's dummy, kitted out in waxed cotton, tweed, corduroy, harness leather.

He held the door for her.

"Welcome," said a small Japanese man with round gold-framed glasses. There was no one else in the shop.

"We'll be in back," said Bigend, leading Hollis past him.

"Of course. I'll see that you aren't disturbed."

Hollis smiled at the man, nodded. He bowed to her. He wore a tweed hacking jacket with sleeves made partially of waxed cotton.

The back office in Tanky & Tojo was tidier, less shabby than she expected spaces like this to be. There was no evidence of employees attempting to alleviate boredom, no stabs at humor, no wistful pockets of nonwork affect. The walls were freshly painted gray. Cheap white shelving was piled with plastic-wrapped stock, shoe boxes, books of fabric samples.

"Milgrim and Sleight were in South Carolina," said Bigend, seating himself behind the small white Ikea desk. One of its corners, facing her, was chipped, revealing some core material that resembled compacted granola. She sat on a very Eighties-looking vanity stool, pale violet velour, bulbous, possibly the last survivor of some previous business here. "Sleight had arranged for us to have a look at a garment prototype. We'd picked up interesting industry buzz about it, though when we got the photos and tracings, really, we couldn't see why. Our best analyst thinks it's not a tactical design. Something for mall ninjas."

"For what?"

"The new Mitty demographic."

"I'm lost."

"Young men who dress to feel they'll be mistaken for having special capability. A species of cosplay, really. Endemic. Lots of boys are playing soldier now. The men who run the world aren't, and neither are the boys most effectively bent on running it next. Or the ones who're actually having to *be* soldiers, of course. But many of the rest have gone gear-queer, to one extent or another."

"'Gear-queer'?"

Bigend's teeth showed. "We had a team of cultural anthropologists interview American soldiers returning from Iraq. That's where we first heard it. It's not wholly derogatory, mind you. There are actual professionals who genuinely require these things—some of them, anyway. Though they generally seem to be far less *fascinated* with them. But it's that fascination that interests us, of course."

"It is?"

"It's an obsession with the idea not just of the right stuff, but of the special stuff. Equipment fetishism. The costume and semiotics of achingly elite police and military units. Intense desire to possess same, of course, and in turn to be associated with that world. With its competence, its cocksure exclusivity."

"Sounds like fashion, to me."

"Exactly. Pants, but only just the right ones. We could never have engineered so powerful a locus of consumer desire. It's like sex in a bottle."

"Not for me."

"You're female."

"They want to be soldiers?"

"Not to *be*. To self-identify as. However secretly. To imagine they may be mistaken for, or at least associated with. Virtually *none* of these products will ever be used for anything remotely like what they were designed for. Of course that's true of most of the contents of your traditional army-navy store. Whole universes of wistful male fantasy in those places. But the level of consumer motivation we're seeing, the fact that these are often what amount to luxury goods, and priced accordingly. That's new. I felt like a neurosurgeon, when this was brought to my attention, discovering a patient whose nervous system is congenitally and fully exposed. It's just so nakedly obvious. Fantastic, really."

"And it ties into military contracting?"

"Deeply, though not simply. A lot of the same players, where the stuff actually originates. But your civilian buyer, your twenty-first-century Walter Mitty, needs it the way a mod, in this street, in 1965, needed the right depth of vent on a suitcoat."

"It sounds ridiculous to me."

"Almost exclusively a boy thing."

"Almost," she agreed, remembering Heidi's IDF bra.

"Milgrim and Sleight were in South Carolina because it seemed someone there might be on the brink of a Department of Defense contract. For pants. Since it's something we've been looking to get into ourselves, quite actively, we decided to have a closer look at their product."

"'They' who?"

"We're still looking into that."

"It's not the sort of thing I'd have ever imagined you doing. Military contracts, I mean. I don't get it."

"It's the one garment industry with none of the fantastic dysfunction of fashion. And hugely better profit margins. But at the same time everything that works, in fashion, also works in military contracting."

"Not everything, surely."

"More than you imagine. The military, if you think about it, largely invented branding. The whole idea of being 'in uniform.' The global fashion industry is based on that. But the people whose prototype we had Milgrim photograph and make rubbings of, in South Carolina, have evidently turned Sleight. And here we are."

"Where?"

"In a position," he said, firmly, "of possible danger."

"Because Sleight's your personal IT man?"

"Because of who and what *they* seem to be. I've had a more genuinely personal IT man looking out for me, keeping track of Sleight and the various architectures he's been erecting, both those he's told me about and those he hasn't. I did say I've been through this before. So in most cases, I wouldn't be as concerned, and not in this way. But one of these people was here, in London. He followed you and Milgrim to Paris, with Sleight's help."

"Foley, Milgrim calls him."

"We must assume that Foley, so-called, was following you as well. That overlap I mentioned, between the actual elite and the mall ninjas. That can be a problematic segment, in this particular Venn diagram."

"I saw him," Hollis said. "He followed me into the basement of the building where I'd gone to—" She hesitated.

"Meet Meredith Overton. I had Milgrim debriefed last night, in Paris. He was particularly unnerved to have run into Rausch."

"So was I, though Rausch was more rattled to see me, it seemed to me. He thought you were checking up on him. Is he with Sleight?"

"I doubt it," said Bigend. "He's not that fast. Do you know who designs Gabriel Hounds yet?"

"No. But either Meredith already does, or she thinks she can find out."

"And what do you judge it will take to induce her to tell us, or to find out and tell us?"

"She had a shoe line. It failed financially, and somehow the bulk of the final season was misplaced."

"Yes. We're looking at her now. That was a good line. She prefigured the best of the back-of-Harajuku tendencies."

"She thinks they're in a warehouse in Seattle. Tacoma. Somewhere. She imagines Blue Ant might be able to locate something like that. If they're found, she believes, she's in a position to legally claim them."

"And then?"

"She'd sell them. On eBay, she said. They're worth more now, evidently."

"But mainly as a relaunch strategy," said Bigend. "The eBay sales would attract coolhunters, generate attention in the industry."

"She didn't mention that."

"She wouldn't. She needs to leverage fresh financing. Either to relaunch the line herself or sell it to the ghostbranders."

"The what?"

"Ghostbranders. They find brands, sometimes extinct ones, with iconic optics or a viable narrative, buy them, then put out denatured product under the old label. Meredith's shoes probably have enough cult cachet to warrant that, on an interestingly small scale."

"Is something like that why you're after Gabriel Hounds?"

"I'm more interested in their reinvention of exclusivity. Far ahead, say, of the Burberry label you can only buy in one special outlet in Tokyo, but not here, and not on the web. That's old-school geograph-ical exclusivity. Gabriel Hounds is something else. There's something spectral about it. What did Overton tell you?"

She saw Ajay slipping the little blade into the base of the Blue Ant figurine, back in Number Four. "She knew someone, in fashion school here, or around it, who knew someone in Chicago. She believes that that person, in Chicago, then, is the Hounds designer."

"You don't think she knows?"

"She may not. She says she wound up on an e-mail list announcing Hounds drops."

"We assumed there must be one," he said. "We've put a fair bit of effort into finding it. Nothing."

She took one of the books of swatches from where it lay on the shelf nearest her. It was amazingly heavy, its cover plain heavy brown card, marked with a long number in chisel-tipped black felt pen. She opened it. Thick, wholly synthetic materials, strangely buttery to the touch, like samples of the hides of robotic whales. "What is this?"

"They make Zodiacs out of it," he said. "The inflatable boats."

She put it back on the shelf, deciding as she did that this was not the time to be bringing up the bug in the figurine, if in fact she was going to.

"Foley himself," said Bigend, "may not be that dangerous, though we don't know. A fantasist, designing for fantasist consumers. But the person who's employing him is another matter. I haven't been able to find out as much as I'd like. Currently, I'm having to go outside Blue Ant, bypass Sleight and his architecture, for even basic intelligence."

"How do you mean, dangerous?"

"Not good to know," said Bigend, "or to be known by. Not good to be seen as being in competition with. That little bit of industrial espionage in South Carolina, as it happened, put Sleight in their camp. Given what I've managed to learn so far, we are likely regarded, now, as the enemy."

"Who are they?"

"They were, at some point, usually, the people our new demographic imagines being. What are you looking at?"

"Your suit."

"It's by Mr. Fish."

"It is not. You told me nobody could find him."

"He may be selling furniture in California. Antiques. That's one story. But I found his cutter."

"You're really worried about these contracting people? Foley?"

"Contractors, that would be. In that other, more recently newsworthy sense. I have an unusual amount on my plate now, Hollis. One of my long-term projects, something that runs in the background, has recently been showing strong signs of possible fruition. It's frustrating, to be distracted now, but I'm determined not to drop any balls. Your getting hurt would constitute a dropped ball." He was looking at her, now, with something she took to be the artful emulation of actual human concern, but she understood that that indicated there really might be something to be afraid of. She shivered on the ridiculous velour toadstool.

"Florence," he said. "I have a flat there. Lovely. I'll send you there. Today."

"I have Meredith in play. She's coming back here with George. Probably here already. Reg needs him in the studio. You can't assign me that specific a task, then send me away when I'm about to complete it. I'm not working for you that way." All of which was true, but having gotten as far as Garreth's voice mail, she felt she needed to be here, where she'd told him she was, at least until she discovered where he was.

Bigend nodded. "I understand. And I do want the identity of the Hounds designer. But you need to be careful. We all do."

"Who's Tanky, Hubertus? Assuming that's Tojo out front."

"I suppose I am," he said.

42. ELVIS, GRACELAND

Winnie Tung Whitaker was wearing a pale blue iteration of the sweatshirt with the South Carolina state flag monogram. Milgrim imagined her buying the full color-range at some outlet mall, off the highway to Edge City Family Restaurant. The blue made her look more like a young mother, which she evidently was, than a bad-ass, which she'd just told him she was. He really didn't doubt that she was either. The bad-ass part was currently expressed by a pair of really impressively ugly wraparound sunglasses with matte alloy frames, worn pushed up over her smooth black hair, though more so by something about the look in her eyes. "How did you know about this place?" asked Milgrim. Their starters had just arrived, in a small Vietnamese café.

"Google," she said. "You don't believe I'm a bad-ass?"

"I do," said Milgrim, rattled. He hurriedly tried his chili squid.

"How is it?"

"Good," said Milgrim.

"You want a dumpling?"

"No, thanks."

"They're great. Had them when I was here before."

"You were here before?"

"I'm staying near here. Called Kentish Town."

"The hotel?"

"The neighborhood. I'm staying with a retired detective. Scotland Yard. Seriously." She grinned. "There's a club, the International Police Association. Hooks us up with lodging in members' homes. Saves money."

"Nice," said Milgrim.

"He has doilies." She smiled. "Lace. They kind of scare me. And I'm a clean-freak myself. Otherwise, I couldn't afford to be here."

Milgrim blinked. "You couldn't?"

"We're not a big agency. I'm covered for a hundred and thirty-six dollars per day, meals and incidentals. More for a hotel, but here, not really enough. This is the most expensive place I've ever seen."

"But you're a special agent."

"Not *that* kind of special. And I've already got pressure going on, from my boss."

"You do?"

"He doesn't see the cooperation via the legate and the Brits going anywhere. And he's right, it isn't. He isn't crazy about me running around London on per diem, conducting investigations outside U.S. territory, without the proper coordination. He wants me back."

"You're leaving?"

"That's bad for you?" She looked as though she were about to laugh.

"I don't know," he said, "is it?"

"Relax," she said, "you aren't rid of me that easily. I'm supposed to go home and work through the FBI to get the Brits on board, which would be slow as molasses even if it worked. The guy I've got the really serious hard-on for, though, he'd be gone anyway." Thinking about this person, Milgrim noticed, made her eyes look beady, and that brought back his initial reaction to her in Covent Garden. "Recruiting a U.S. citizen in the U.K. is okay," she said, "but interacting with non-U.S. citizens, in furtherance of a criminal investigation or a national security matter? Not so much."

"No?" Milgrim had the feeling, somehow, that he'd just penetrated some worryingly familiar modality, one that felt remarkably like a drug deal. Things were going seriously *transactional*. He looked around at the other diners. One of them, seated alone, was reading a book. It was that kind of place.

"If I did that," she said, "the Brits would get very upset. Fast."

"I guess you wouldn't want that."

"Neither would you."

"No."

"Your tasking is about to get a lot more specific."

"Tasking?"

"How's your memory?"

"The past ten years or so, nonlinear. I'm still putting it together."

"But if I tell you a story, a fairly complicated one, now, you'd retain the general outline, and some of the detail?"

"Hubertus says I'm good with detail."

"And you won't inflate it, distort it, make up crazy shit when you tell it to someone else later?"

"Why would I do that?"

"Because that's what the people we tend to work with do."

"Why?"

"Because they're pathological liars, narcissists, serial imposters, alcoholics, drug addicts, chronic losers, and shitbirds. But you're not going to be like that, are you?"

"No," said Milgrim.

The waitress arrived with their bowls of pho.

"Curriculum vitae," she said, and blew on her pho, the shaved beef still bright pink. "Forty-five years old."

"Who is?"

"Just listen. 2004, he resigns his commission, fifteen years an officer in the U.S. Army. Rank of major. Last ten years of that, he was with First Special Forces Group in Okinawa, Fort Lewis near Tacoma. Spent most of his career deploying in Asia. Lots of experience in the Philippines. After 9/11, he does deployments to Iraq and Afghanistan. But *before* the Army figures out how to do counterinsurgency. Resigns because he's a classic self-promoter. Believes he has a good chance at striking it rich as a consultant."

Milgrim listened intently, methodically sipping broth from the white china spoon. It gave him something to do, and that was very welcome.

"2005 through 2006, he tries to get work as a civilian contractor with CIA, interrogations and whatnot."

"Whatnot?"

She nodded, gravely. "They see, to their credit, that his talents and expertise don't really go that way. He knocks around the Gulf region for two years, pitching security consulting services for oil companies, other big corporations in Saudi, UAE, Kuwait. Tries to get his foot in the door as a consultant with the rich Arab governments, but by this time the big dogs in that industry are up and running. No takers."

"This is Foley?"

"Who's Foley?"

"The man who followed us in Paris."

"Did he look forty-five to you? You might not make such a good informant after all."

"Sorry."

"2006 to present. This is where it gets good. Going back to what he knew best before 9/11, he exploits old contacts in the Philippines and Indonesia. Moves his business to Southeast Asia, which is a gold mine for him. The big companies are more focused on the Middle East at this point, and smaller operators can pick up more cash in Southeast Asia. He starts by doing the same security consulting work for corporate clients in Indonesia, Malaysia, Singapore, and the Philippines. Hotel chains, banks . . . He games the political connections of those corporate clients into consulting work for those governments. Now he's teaching tactics, counterinsurgency strategies, which he's maybe only barely qualified to do. Interrogation, which he's not qualified to do. And more. Whatnot. Instructing police units, probably the military too, and here's where he starts to seriously get into arms procurement."

"Is that illegal?"

"Depends how you do it." She shrugged. "Of course, he also has some former service buddies working for him by this point. While he's teaching tactics, he's also specifying the equipment these outfits will need. He starts small, outfitting counterterrorist police squads with special weapons and body armor. Stuff sourced from American companies where he has ties of friendship. But if general officers of these countries' militaries get visibility on what he's doing, and get a chubby from it, which some of them are highly disposed to do, and are also impressed by his Rambo routine, your classic multitalented

American commando but with more business acumen, they can start talking to him about equipment needed by their militaries' conventional forces." She put her spoon down. "So here's where we start talking real money."

"He's selling arms?"

"Not quite. He becomes a hookup artist. He's hooking up deals with contacts in the United States, people who work for companies that build tactical vehicles, UAVs, EOD robots, mine detection and removal equipment . . ." She sat back, picking up her spoon again. "And uniforms."

"Uniforms?"

"What did your Blue Ant guys think they'd picked up on in South Carolina?"

"An Army contract?"

"Right, but the wrong army. At this point, anyway. And at this point, the man I've just described to you regards your employers as direct and aggressive competitors. Those pants are his first shot at contracting equipment himself. He won't just be the hookup."

"I don't like the way this sounds," Milgrim said.

"Good. What you need to remember, with these guys, is that they don't *know* they're con men. They're wildly overconfident. Omnipotence, omniscience—that's part of the mythology that surrounds the Special Forces. I had those guys hitting on me every last day in Baghdad." She held up her fist, showing Milgrim her plain gold wedding band. "Your guy can walk in the door and promise training in something he personally doesn't know how to do, and not even realize he's bullshitting about his own capabilities. It's a special kind of gullibility, a kind of psychic tactical equipment, that he had installed during training. The Army put him through *schools* that promised to teach him how to do *everything*, everything that matters. And he believed them. And that's who your Mr. Bigend has interested in his ass today, if not seriously after it."

Milgrim swallowed. "So who's Foley?"

"The designer. You can't make uniforms without a designer. He was at Parsons, the New School for Design."

"In New York?"

"Kind of doubt he fit in. But never mind him. Michael Preston Gracie's who I'm after."

"The major? I don't understand what it is he's done."

"Crimes that involve lots of official acronyms. Crimes that would take me all night to explain accurately. I hunt in an underbrush of regulations. But the good thing about these guys, for me, is that the smaller the transgression, the sloppier they'll handle it. I watch the underbrush for twigs they've broken. That was Dermo, in this case."

"Dermo?"

"D-R-M-O. Defense Reutilization and Marketing Offices. They sell off old equipment. He manipulates old Army buddies. Illegally. Equipment's sold on to foreign entities, be they companies or governments. ICE notices a shipment, all curiously shiny-new. No ITAR violations but they note the shiny, the new. I look into it, turns out those radios were never meant to be sent to DRMO at all. Look a little closer and the DRMO buy wasn't right either. See he's involved in lots of these purchases, lots of contracts. Nothing huge, but the money seriously adds up. Those pants of yours look to me like the start of a legitimization phase. Like he's started listening to lawyers. Might even be a money-laundering angle there. What did I tell you his name was?"

"Gracie."

"First name?"

"Peter."

"I'll give you a mnemonic: Elvis, Graceland."

"'Elvis, Graceland'?"

"Preston, Gracie. Presley, Graceland. What's his name?"

"Preston Gracie. *Mike*."

She smiled.

"What am I supposed to do with this?"

"Tell Bigend."

"But then he'll know about you."

"Only as much as you tell him. If we were back in the States, I'd play this another way. But you're my only resource here, and I'm out of time. Tell Bigend there's this hard-ass federal agent who wants him made aware of Gracie. Bigend has money, connections, lawyers. If Gracie fucks with him, let's make sure he knows who to fuck back *at*."

"You're doing what Bigend does," Milgrim said, more accusingly than he intended. "You're just doing this *to see what happens*."

"I'm doing it," she said, "because I find myself in a position to. Maybe, somehow, it'll cause Michael Preston Gracie to fuck up. Or get fucked up. Sadly, it's just a gesture. A gesture in the face of the shitbird universe, on behalf of my ongoing frustration with its inhabitants. But you need to tell Bigend, fast."

"Why?"

"Because I've got Gracie's flight schedule on APIS, via CBP. He's on his way here. Atlanta by way of Geneva. Looks like he's laying over for a meeting there, four hours on the ground. Then he's into Heathrow."

"And you're leaving?"

"It's a piss-off, but yeah. And my kids and husband miss me. I'm homesick. I guess it's time." She put down her spoon, switching to chopsticks. "Tell Bigend. Tonight."

43. ICHINOMIYA

Thanks for meeting on such short notice," said Meredith Overton, seated in the armchair directly beneath the rack of narwhale tusks. She wore a tweed jacket that might have come from Tanky & Tojo, if they cut things for women. She'd phoned on Hollis's way back from her meeting with Bigend, in the strange, high, surgically clean silver pickup driven by Aldous, one of the tall black minders.

"It's perfect timing," Hollis said. "I've just seen him. He'd be delighted to have a team of Blue Ant researchers look for your shoes."

"Provided I give him the identity of the Gabriel Hounds designer."

"Yes," said Hollis.

"I can't," said Meredith. "That's why I'm here."

"You can't?"

"Sorry. Attack of conscience. Well, not an attack. My conscience is in fairly decent shape. That's the problem. I was trying to do a run around it, because I want my shoes. George and I were up all night, discussing it, and it became apparent that it's just not something I'm willing to do. George agrees, of course. As much as he wants your advice about working with Inchmale."

"He has that," Hollis said. "I thought I'd made that clear, in Paris. I'm a one-woman sisterhood that way. Counseling the stricken."

Meredith smiled. The Italian girl arrived with coffee. It was something like the cocktail hour now, Hollis supposed, and the room, while not crowded, was filling with a peculiar murmur, leaning by undetectable increments toward the later evening's full rout. "That's kind of you," Meredith said. "Do you know Japan?"

"Tokyo, mainly. We played there. Huge venues."

"I went there when I was putting my second season together. The first season, all the shoes had been leather. I was more comfortable with that. For the second season, I wanted to do some in fabric. A classic summer sneaker. I needed some kind of artisanal canvas. Dense, long-wearing, but a great hand. Special."

"Hand?"

"How it feels, to the touch. Someone had suggested I talk to this couple in Nagoya. They had an atelier there, above a little warehouse on the outskirts of a place called Ichinomiya. I can tell you that because they're no longer there. They were making jeans there, in deadstock fabric from a mill in Okayama. Depending on the length of the roll, they might get three pairs of jeans, they might get twenty, and once the roll was gone, it was gone. I'd heard they'd also been buying canvas from that same mill, Sixties stuff. I wanted to see it and, if it was good, talk them into selling me a few rolls. They'd tried it for jeans, but it was too heavy. They were lovely people. There were stacks of samples of their jeans. Old photographs of American men in workwear. All of their machines were vintage, except the one they used for riveting. They had a German Union Special chain-stitching machine. A 1920s belt-loop machine." She smiled. "Designers become machine nerds. Machines define what you can do. That and finding the right operators for them." She added sugar to her black coffee, stirred it. "So I'm up in the loft, very top of the building, where they had these rolls of canvas, on shelves, lots of them. They're all different, the light's not great, and I realize I'm not alone. The Japanese couple are downstairs, on the second floor, making jeans, and they haven't said anything about anyone else being there. I can hear the machines they're using. Below them, there's a place that makes cardboard cartons. They have machines too, a sort of distant thumping undertone. But I can hear a woman singing, like she's singing to herself. Not loud. But close. From toward the back of the building. Up in the loft, with me. The jeans people haven't said anything about anybody else, but they barely speak English. Absolute focus on their work. They make two or three pairs a day, just the two of them. Self-taught. So I put the roll I'm looking at back on the shelf. Old metal shelves, about four feet deep, and I follow the sound of her singing." She took a sip of her coffee. "And at the very back of the loft, there's light, good light, over a table. Actually it's a hollow-core door, on a couple of big cardboard cartons. She's working on a pattern. Big sheets of tissue, pencils. Singing. Black jeans, a black T-shirt, and one of those jackets you're wearing. She looks up, sees me, stops singing. Dark hair, but she's not Japanese. Sorry, I say, I didn't know anyone was here. That's okay, she says, American accent. Asks me who I am. I tell her, and tell her I'm there to look at canvas. What for? Shoes, I tell her. Are you a designer? Yes, I say, and show her the ones I'm wearing. Which are my shoes, from the first season, cowhide, from the Horween factory, Chicago, big white vulcanization, like deck shoes, but really they're like the very first skate shoes, the ones the first Vans took off from. And she smiles at me, and steps out from behind the table, so I can see she's wearing them, the same shoes, my shoes, but in the black. And she tells me her name."

Hollis was holding her coffee with both hands, leaning forward in her chair, across the low table.

"Which I now know I can't tell you," Meredith said. "And if you go there, the couple aren't there, and neither is she."

"She liked your shoes."

"She really got them. I'm not sure anyone else ever did, to the same extent. She got what I was trying to get away from. The seasons, the bullshit, the stuff that wore out, fell apart, wasn't real. I'd been that girl, walking across Paris, to the next shoot, no money for a Métro card, and I'd imagined those shoes. And when you imagine something like that, you imagine a world. You imagine the world those shoes come from, and you wonder if they could happen here, in this world, the one with all the bullshit. And sometimes they can. For a season or two."

Hollis put her cup down. "I want you to know," she said, "that it's okay not to tell me any more. I'll understand."

Meredith shook her head. "We wound up having dinner, drinking

sake, in this little place down the street. All the sake cups were differ-
ent, used, old, like someone had chosen them from a charity shop.
That was after she'd helped me choose my canvas. That was the
Hounds designer. She doesn't need anyone like your Mr. Bigend."

"He's not my Mr. Bigend."

"Of all the people in the world, she doesn't need that."

"Okay."

"And that's why I can't trade her name for my shoes. As much as
I want my shoes."

"If I tell him you won't tell me, he'll try to find those shoes himself. And when he has them, he'll send someone else, to negotiate. Or
come himself."

"I've thought of that. It's my own fault, really. For having considered betraying a friend." She looked at Hollis. "I haven't seen her
since. Or been in touch, really. Just those e-mails announcing drops.
I sent her a pair of the shoes she helped choose the canvas for. To the
place in Ichinomiya. So I just can't do it."

"I wouldn't either," Hollis said. "Look, this is just a job for me, one
I wish I didn't have. Not even a job. Just Bigend bribing me to do
something for him. The best thing, for you, would be for me not to tell
him we've had this conversation. You've stopped returning my calls.
Have George tell Reg to tell Bigend to leave you alone."

"Would that work?"

"It might," said Hollis. "Bigend values Reg's take on certain things.
Reg advises him on music. I think Reg actually likes him. If he thinks
Bigend's unsettling you, which in turn unsettles George, jeopardizing
the next Bollards album, he'll do everything he can to get Bigend to
back off. But that's not only my best plan, it's my only one."

"What will you do?"

"I'll tell him I've been unable to contact you."

"That's not what I mean," said Meredith. "Will you still be looking
for her?"

"That's a good question," said Hollis.

44. THE VERBALS

Milgrim stood at the window of his room, watching someone on the canal path being given what Aldous would call the verbals. Which was to say harsh criticism, pointed verbal violence, probably with added threat of the physical. The recipient, whom Milgrim instinctively identified with, was an insubstantial figure in a pale grubby thigh-length raincoat, his verbalizer a slablike individual in a bright green exercise suit, one of those silky two-piece outfits sometimes still worn here, Milgrim guessed, out of nostalgia for an extinct American style of triumphal ghetto criminality. The verbals, Milgrim now saw, were being punctuated with fisted thumb-jabs to the smaller man's ribs and sternum. Milgrim forced himself to turn away, absently rubbing a hand across his own ribs.

He'd walked with Winnie down the street called Parkway (wasn't that in Monopoly?) to the High Street and the station, quizzed by her along the way on Michael Preston Gracie, and then she'd said goodbye, handshake firm, and ridden off down a very long escalator.

He'd continued back along the High Street, looking still more like a fair midway in some state in which youth-market footwear and alcohol were the main products, through buzzing young throngs outside several pubs, and home to the Holiday Inn.

He didn't want to call Bigend, but Winnie had specifically ordered him to do that, and he'd said he would. He opened the envelope the driver had given him earlier, looked at the variously sized white capsules in their foil-backed transparent bubbles, the tiny, maniacally precise hand-labeling in purple Rapidograph ink, an hour and date and day of the week for each bubble. He had no more idea who had prepared this than he had of what the capsules contained. He felt as though he were between two worlds, vast and grinding spheres of influence, Bigend's and Winnie's, a wobbly little moon, trying to do as he'd been told by both. Trying, he supposed, to avoid the verbals.

He should call Bigend now. But no longer had the Neo, he remembered, and that meant he no longer had a number for him. He could look up Blue Ant and try to go through the switchboard, but under current circumstances that didn't seem a good idea. A reprieve, of sorts. He went into the bathroom instead, and prepared to clean his teeth, the full four-stage operation, noting that he was still without the special mouthwash. He'd just inserted a fresh conical brush tip between his rearmost upper right molars when the room's phone rang. Unwilling to remove the brush, he left the bathroom with it still in place, and answered the phone.

"Hello?"

"Why do you sound that way?" asked Bigend.

"Sorry," Milgrim said, extracting the brush, "something in my mouth."

"Go down to the lobby. Aldous will be there shortly. You'll pick up Hollis on your way to me. We need to talk."

"Good," said Milgrim, before Bigend could hang up, but then began to worry about whether he could deliver Winnie's message about Gracie in front of Hollis.

He went back into the bathroom, to finish cleaning his teeth.

45. SHRAPNEL, SUPERSONIC

Heidi, legs strong and white in black cyclist's shorts, shoulders square in her more complexly black majorette jacket, once again crouched gargoyle-fashion on the edge of the Piblokto Madness bed, black-nailed toes prehensile. Two pale silvery darts were tucked like bullets in a bandolier, into the thick cording of the jacket's frogged front, their blood-red, paper-thin plastic flights pointing toward Number Four's ceiling.

She rolled a third between thumb and forefinger, as if she might decide to smoke it. "Tungsten," she said, "and rhenium. Alloyed, they're superheavy." She sighted along the dart's black tip, almost invisible in this light. The heavy, multilayered drapes were drawn against the night, and only the tiny, focused, supernally brilliant Swiss bulbs, in the birdcage library, lit the room and its artifacts. "Place Ajay knows. Cost a hundred pounds apiece. You want to make supersonic shrapnel, you make it with this stuff."

"Why would you?" asked Hollis, barefoot as well, from the striped armchair nearest the foot of the bed.

"Penetration," said Heidi, flicking the dart past Hollis and into the eye, ten feet away, of a glossy black Congolese fetish.

"Don't," said Hollis. "I wouldn't want to have to pay for that. I think it's ebony."

"Dense," said Heidi, "but no match for wolfram. Old name for tungsten. Should've been a metal band: Wolfram. They wind the strings of some instruments with it. Need the density. Jimmy told me."

The name of their dead friend and bandmate hung momentarily in the air.

"I don't think this job with Bigend is working out," Hollis said.

"No?" Heidi drew a second dart, which she held up like a fairy sword, between her eye and the birdcage lights, admiring the point.

"Don't throw that," Hollis warned. "I'm supposed to find someone for him. The woman who designed this jacket. Though he may not know she's a woman."

"So you have? Found her?"

"I've found someone who met her. Meredith, George's girlfriend."

Heidi arched an eyebrow. "Small world."

"Sometimes," Hollis said, "I think something about Bigend condenses things, pulls them together . . ."

"Reg," said Heidi, drawing the dart's black tip perilously close to her eye, "just says Bigend's a producer. The Hollywood kind, not the music kind. A giant version of what fuckstick said he'd like to be, but without the hassle of having to make movies." She lowered the second dart, looked seriously at Hollis. "Maybe that was what he was thinking of with the Ponzi scheme, huh?"

"You had no idea he was doing that?"

"I don't think he did either, most of the time. He was good at delegation. Delegated that to some module of himself he didn't have to hear from too often. Reg says he embodied the decade that way."

"Have you seen Reg yet?"

"We had lunch when you were in Paris."

"How was that?"

Heidi shrugged, the jacket's black-fringed left epaulet rising half an inch, falling back. "Okay. I don't usually have too much trouble with Reg. There's a trick to that."

"What is it?"

"I ignore everything he says," said Heidi, with an uncharacteristically upbeat seriousness. "Dr. Fujiwara taught me." Then she frowned. "But Reg, he had his doubts about you working for Bigend."

"But he was the one who suggested it. It was his idea."

"That was before he decided Bigend's up to something."

"Bigend's *defined* by being up to something."

"This is different," said Heidi. "Inchmale doesn't know what it is, right? Otherwise, he'd tell. Can't keep a secret. But his wife's been getting the signals at work, some kind of London PR hive-mind thing. Wires are humming, she says. Wires are *hot*, but there's no actual *signal*. Kind of subsonic buzz. PR people dreaming of Bigend. Imagining they see his face on coins. Saying his name when they mean someone else. Omens, Reg says. Like before a quake. He wants to talk to you about that. Just not on the phone."

"There's something going on at Blue Ant. Corporate spook stuff. Hubertus doesn't seem that concerned about it." She remembered what he'd said about a long-term project nearing fruition, his frustration with the timing of Sleight's apparent defection.

"You don't want to tell him who makes those jackets?"

"Fortunately, I don't know who she is. But I've already told him that Meredith knows. If she won't tell me, and she won't, because she doesn't want to, and I don't want her to, he'll go after her. He already has something she really wants, or he could have it, if he hasn't found it already."

"Something changed your mind?"

"Something changed hers. She was going to do it, tell me. Then she decided not to. Then she told me why. Told me a story." It was Hollis's turn to shrug. "Just like that, sometimes." She put her feet down on the carpet and stood, stretching. Walked to the shelf, where the dart was centered perfectly, an instant and quite convincing Dadaist assemblage, in one deep orbit of the rectilinear ebony head. When she tried to pull it out, the head moved toward the edge of the shelf. "That's really in there." She steadied the sculpture with her left hand, twisting the dart out with her right.

"It's the mass. Behind a force-localizer."

Hollis bent, peering into the head's left eye socket. A tiny round hole. "How did you learn to do that?"

"I didn't. I don't. It wants to happen. I get out of the way. I told Ajay that, he said he loves me."

"Does he?" Hollis looked at the dart's black tip.

"He loves that. How about your boyfriend?"

"Obviously," Hollis said, "he hasn't called."

"Call him again."

"Doesn't feel right." She crossed to the bed, offered Heidi the dart. Heidi took it.

"You fight with him?"

"No. I'd say we drifted apart, but it wasn't like that. When we were together, it was like we were both on vacation. On vacation from ourselves, maybe. But he didn't have a project. Like an actor between films. And then he did, but it was gradual. Like an atmosphere. Some kind of fog. He became harder to see. Less present. And I was starting to work on the book. I took that much more seriously than I would have expected to."

"I know," said Heidi, tucking the two darts back into the frogging, beside the third, with seemingly no regard for where the black needle-points might go. "I remember going up to see you in the Marmont. All that stuff laid out on tables. Seeing you were really doing it."

"It helped me make sense of what I'd been through. Working for Bigend, being with Garreth . . . I think there's a way in which I may be able to look at that book, one day, and make a different kind of sense out of what happened. Not that there's anything there that's about that. I told that to Reg, last month, and he said it was a palimpsest."

Heidi said nothing. Canted her head slightly, her black hair a raptor's wing, swinging a precise inch, no more.

"But not now," Hollis said. "I don't want to look at it now, and it wouldn't tell me anything if I did. And leaving him a second message would be like that. I left the first one. I did what he told me to do, except that I didn't do it because knowing him had gotten me in trouble. I did it because I heard he'd been hurt. I'm not not calling him out of some kind of pride."

"Magical thinking," said Heidi. "That's what Reg would say about that. But hey, he totally navigates by that shit. We know that."

The room phone's sclerotic mechanical cricket chirped. Again. Hollis was lifting the heavy receiver from the rosewood cube as it rang a third time. "Hello?"

"We need to talk," said Bigend.

"We just did."

"I'm sending Aldous for you, with Milgrim."

"Fine," said Hollis, deciding she might as well use this as an opportunity to quit. She hung up.

"Muskrat man," said Heidi.

"I have to meet him," Hollis said, "but I'm going to quit."

"Okay," said Heidi, rolling back, then over and off the bed, straightening smoothly to her full height. "Take me."

"I don't think he'd like that," said Hollis.

"Good," said Heidi. "You want to quit? I'll get your ass fired."

Hollis looked at her. "Okay," she said.

46. TORTOISESHELL AND PINSTRIPES

This hotel where Hollis was staying, which had no sign at all, had an antique desk carved with a naked girl, apparently feeling up a horse, though the work was so intricate that it was hard to tell, exactly, what was going on, and Milgrim didn't want to seem to be staring. Otherwise, there were dark paneled walls, a pair of curving marble stairways, and the unfriendly regard of the young man seated behind the desk, peering coldly up through nonprescription lenses in tortoiseshell frames. Not to mention his tall, sturdy, pinstriped associate, who'd asked if he could help Milgrim. Help him, Milgrim had felt, to turn right around and get back on the street where he belonged. "Hollis Henry," Milgrim had said, managing what he'd felt had been a good approximation of a neutral tone he'd heard a lot of around Blue Ant, in similar circumstances.

"Yes?"

"Her car's here." Truck had seemed too specific. "Can you let her know, please?"

"You'll want the desk," the tall young man had said, turning and walking back to what Milgrim now assumed to be his station by the door.

There hadn't seemed to be any, or not in the stand-up, pigeon-holes-behind sense, so Milgrim had continued on, another ten feet or so, to where this other, smaller, similarly suited young man was seated. "Hollis Henry," he'd said, trying his neutral tone again, though it hadn't come out very well. He'd thought it sounded rather dirty, somehow, though perhaps that was the carving, which he'd noticed as he spoke.

"Name?"

"Milgrim."

"Are you expected?"

"Yes."

Milgrim, viewed through what he imagined were probably parts of the actual exoskeleton of a dead if not extinct animal, held his ground while a very elegantly ancient-looking telephone was brought into play. "She doesn't appear to be in."

From somewhere beyond the stair came a complex rattle of metal, and then the sound of Hollis's voice.

"That would be her now," said Milgrim.

Then Hollis appeared, beside a tall, pale, hawk-nosed, ferocious-looking woman who might have been captain of the guard at some Goth queen's palace, to judge by her tight short jacket, with its fringed epaulets and ornate frogs, every shade from charcoal to midnight. She needs a saber, Milgrim thought, delighted.

"Your car is here, Miss Henry," said Tortoiseshell, Milgrim having apparently become invisible.

"This is Heidi, Milgrim." Hollis sounded tired.

The tall woman's large, startlingly strong hand effortlessly captured Milgrim's, giving it a brisk, rhythmic shake, possibly half of some covert recognition system. Milgrim's hand was allowed to escape.

"She's coming with us."

"Of course," said Milgrim as the tall one, Heidi, headed for the door, her stride long and determined.

"Good evening, Miss Hyde, Miss Henry," said Pinstripes.

"Honey," said Heidi.

"Robert," said Hollis.

He opened and held the door for them.

"Now, that's a ride," said Heidi, catching sight of the Hilux. "Lose your rocket launcher?"

Milgrim looked back as Pinstripes closed the door behind them. Was there such a thing as a private hotel? He knew that there were private parks here. "What's this hotel called?" he asked.

"Cabinet," said Hollis. "Let's go."

47. IN THE CUISINART ATRIUM

Heidi, for some reason, knew a great deal about custom vehicular armor. Perhaps it was a Beverly Hills thing, Hollis thought, as Aldous wound them deeper into the City, or a Ponzi scheme thing, or both. Heidi and Aldous, with whom Hollis could see Heidi was flirting, though still at a level of solid deniability, were deep in a discussion of whether or not Bigend had been wise to insist on power windows for the front set of doors, which had meant forgoing a bulletproof documentation slot on the driver's side, through which papers might be presented without opening either the door or the window. The power windows, Heidi maintained, meant that the doors were necessarily armored to a lower standard, with Aldous firmly insisting that this was not the case.

"I wish I didn't have to see him now," said Milgrim, beside Hollis in the back seat. "I have to tell him something."

"So do I," said Hollis, not caring whether Aldous heard, though she doubted that he did. "I'm quitting."

"You are?" Milgrim looked suddenly bereft.

"Meredith's changed her mind about telling me who the Hounds designer is. Her reason for doing that left me thinking I should let the whole thing go."

"What will you do?"

"I'll tell him I can't do it. That should be that." She wished she were as confident as she'd just sounded. "What do you have to tell him?"

"About Preston Gracie," said Milgrim, "the man Foley's working for."

"How do you know that?"

"Someone told me," said Milgrim, and actually squirmed. "Someone I met."

"Who's Preston Gracie?"

"Mike," Milgrim said. "She says they're all named Mike."

"All who?"

"Special soldiers."

"He's a soldier?"

"Not anymore. An arms dealer."

"She who?"

"Winnie," said Milgrim, his voice catching. "She's a . . . cop." This last emerging, Hollis thought, as though he were having to confess, in utmost seriousness, to having had a conversation, or perhaps some more intimate exchange, with some other species entirely. "Well, sort of a cop. Worse, probably. A DCIS agent." He pronounced this "dee-sis," and she had no idea what it meant.

"That's British?"

"No," said Milgrim, "she followed me from Myrtle Beach. What she does is about military contracts, at least it is this time. She took my picture, in Seven Dials. Then came to the hotel. Do you want your computer back?"

"Of course not," said Hollis. "Why did she follow you?"

"She thought we might be involved with Gracie. That Bigend might be. Then she talked to me, and saw that Bigend's just after the same contracts." She could barely hear him now.

"Bigend's an arms dealer?" She looked at the back of Aldous's head.

"No," said Milgrim, "but Gracie's trying to be involved in the same sort of contracting. Legitimization."

"And she told you this because . . . ?"

"She wants Bigend to know," Milgrim said, miserably.

"Then tell him."

"I shouldn't have been talking with her," Milgrim said. He'd locked his hands together, like a child desperately miming prayer. "I'm afraid."

"Of what?"

His shoulders drew further together. "I just *am*," he said. "I'm like that. But I . . . forgot."

"It'll be fine," said Hollis, immediately deciding it was a ridiculous thing to have said.

"I wish you weren't quitting," he said.

Narrow City streets, their names often basic common nouns. They had to be really old, then, she supposed. She didn't know this part of London at all. Had no idea now where they were. "How much further?" she asked Aldous.

"Almost there," said Aldous. There was little traffic. Quite a few very new buildings, recalling the boom prior to the bust. They passed one with a logo she remembered from an ad on the cab she'd taken, the night Inchmale had advised her to call Bigend.

She reached over and gave Milgrim's balled double fist a squeeze. His hands were very cold. "Relax. I'll help you. We'll do it together." She saw that his eyes were closed.

"Draw Your Brakes" briefly filled the truck. "Aldous," Aldous said into his iPhone. "Yes sir. Miss Henry, Mr. Milgrim, and Miss . . . ?" He glanced back at Hollis.

"Give me the phone."

He passed it back to her.

"Heidi's with us," she said.

"I wasn't expecting her," said Bigend, "but she can play with the balloons. We do need to talk."

"She'll understand." She handed the phone back to Aldous. He held it to his ear. "Yes sir," he said, and slipped it into his black suitcoat.

"Milgrim and I have to have a talk with Hubertus," Hollis said to Heidi.

Heidi turned. "I thought you wanted some help with that."

"I did," said Hollis, "but it's gotten more complicated." She rolled her eyes in Milgrim's direction.

"What's wrong with him?"

"Nothing," said Hollis.

"Don't let him *fuck* with you," said Heidi, reaching back to prod Milgrim in the knee, causing his eyes to snap wide with terror. "He's full of *shit*," she insisted, "they *all* are." Leaving Hollis to wonder, as Aldous pulled the truck over, who they all were. Male authority figures, she guessed, from having known Heidi. Whatever had once made her serial liaisons with professional boxers so relentlessly lively, and had required her separation, as much as had been possible, from label executives.

Aldous pressed various switches on the truck's dash, with resulting clunks and clanks. He opened his own door, climbed down, closed it, opened the one beside Hollis, and helped her down, his hand large and warm. Milgrim scrambled down behind her, flinching when Aldous heaved the door shut. Heidi, meanwhile, had opened her own door and jumped down. She was wearing gray-green leather plus-fours and knee-high black boots whose brogue-style uppers were soled with sections of tank tread, more loot from the ongoing punitive demolition of fuckstick's remaining credit cards.

Hollis looked up at the building they were parked in front of. It resembled a European countertop appliance from the Nineties, something by Cuisinart or Krups, metallic gray plastic, its corners blandly rounded. Aldous pressed something on a black key-fob, causing the truck to clunk multiply and give an almost visible shiver of heightened awareness.

They followed him to the building's entrance, where his equally tall but less-charming colleague, whose name Hollis had never gotten, waited inside.

"I hope he doesn't want a urine sample," Milgrim seemed to say, inexplicably, though she opted to pretend she hadn't heard him.

They were passed through the door, then, from one Jamaican to another, the door locked behind them, and led out into the center of the Cuisinart Building's determined but rather miniature atrium. Hollis, having some vague idea of what City real estate was worth, supposed they must have agonized over this empty, purely American volume of space, every square centimeter of which, otherwise, might have been filled with usable, windowless office-hive. As it was, it rose a mere five floors, wrapped at each level with a walk-around interior balcony of the same metallic-looking plastic, or plastic-looking metal, that sheathed the exterior. Like a model, to only partial scale, of some hotel in the Atlanta core.

Bigend, in his trench coat, stood at its center, holding an iPhone with both hands, arms extended, squinting, thumbs moving slightly.

"I need to speak with Hollis and Milgrim," Bigend said to Heidi, offering her the iPhone, "but you'll enjoy this. The controls are highly intuitive. The video-feed, of course, is from its nose-camera. Start with the manta, then try the penguin." He pointed, up. They all looked up. Near the atrium's uniformly glowing, paneled ceiling hung a penguin and a manta ray. The penguin, silvery, looked only approximately like a penguin, but the manta, merely a black, devilishly dynamic-looking blot, seemed considerably more realistic. "Try them," Bigend said. "Delightful, really. Relaxing. The only other people in the building, at the moment, are employees of mine."

Heidi craned up at the balloons, if that was what they were, then looked at the iPhone, which she now held in much the way Bigend had been holding it. Her thumbs began to move. "Damn," she said appreciatively.

"This way," said Bigend. "I've leased two floors of offices here, but they're very busy now. We can sit here . . ." He led them to an L-shaped bench of dull aluminum mesh, in the shadow of a hanging stairway, the sort of place that would have been a smoking-nest, when people smoked in office buildings. "You recall the Amsterdam dealer we bought your jacket from? His mysterious picker?"

"Vaguely."

"We've gone back to that. Or, rather, a strategic business intelligence unit I've hired in the Hague has. An example of Sleight pushing me out of my comfort zone. I've never trusted private security firms, private investigators, private intelligence firms, at all. In this case, though, they have no idea who they're working for."

"And?" Hollis, seated now, Milgrim beside her, was watching Bigend closely.

"I'm sending you both to Chicago. We think the Hounds designer is there."

"Why?"

"Our dealer has had subsequent dealings with the picker who brought him the jacket. Both picker and jacket came from Chicago."

"Are you certain?"

He shrugged.

"Who is the designer?"

"I'm sending you to find that out," said Bigend.

"Milgrim," said Hollis, "has something he needs to tell you." It was the only thing she could think of that might change the subject, give her time to think.

"Do you, Milgrim?" Bigend asked.

Milgrim made a brief, strange, high-pitched sound, like something burning out. Closed his eyes. Opened them. "The cop," he said, "in Seven Dials. The one who took my picture. The one from Myrtle Beach."

Bigend nodded.

"She's an agent. From," and he closed his eyes again, "the Defense Criminal Investigative Service." Milgrim opened his eyes, tentatively discovering himself not dead.

"Who are, I confess," said Bigend, after a pause, "entirely new to me. American, I take it?"

"It was the pants," said Milgrim. "She was watching the pants. Then we showed up, and she thought we might be involved with Foley, and Gracie."

"Which we are, of course, courtesy of Oliver."

Hollis hadn't heard Bigend use Sleight's first name for a while.

"She wants me to tell you about Gracie," said Milgrim.

"I'd like you to do that," said Bigend, "but perhaps things would be simplified by my speaking with her myself. I'm not entirely unaccustomed to dealing with Americans."

"She has to go back," said Milgrim. "She isn't going to learn what she needs to learn here. You aren't what she thought you were. You're just competition for Foley and Gracie. But she wants you to know about Gracie. That Gracie won't like it that you're competing."

"He already didn't," said Bigend. "He turned Sleight, probably at that Marine Corps trade fair in Carolina. Unless Sleight volunteered, which I regard as a possibility. And did she give you a reason for her wanting me to know all this, your unnamed, perhaps nameless federal agent?"

"Winnie Tung Whitaker," said Milgrim.

Bigend stared at him. "Hyphenated?"

"No," said Milgrim.

"Did she? Suggest why she might want me to know about this person?"

"She said that you're rich and have lawyers. That if she can roll you in front of him, she might as well. I don't think she's been getting any closer to popping him. Sounded frustrated."

"One does," agreed Bigend, leaning forward in his trench coat. "And when did you discuss all this with her?"

"She was at the hotel," Milgrim said, "after I met with you. And I had dinner with her, tonight. Vietnamese."

"And who is employing 'Foley,' then?"

"Michael Preston Gracie." Hollis saw Milgrim check to see that he'd gotten the name right. "Major, retired, U.S. Army, Special Forces. He trains police for foreign countries, arranges for them to buy equipment from friends of his. Sometimes it isn't equipment they should be able to buy. But he's moving into contracting the way you want to. Designing things, manufacturing. She said it was the legitimization stage."

"Ah," said Bigend, with a nod. "He's gotten big enough to acquire real lawyers."

"That's what she said."

"That's often problematic. A watershed. Not everyone makes it. By the time you're big enough to have lawyers willing to sufficiently make the case for legitimization, you're quite big, and highly illegitimate."

"I knew a drug dealer who bought a Saab dealership," offered Milgrim.

"Exactly," said Bigend, with a look for Hollis.

"I think she wanted you to understand that Gracie's dangerous," Milgrim said, "and that he regards competitors as enemies."

"'Listen to your enemies,'" Bigend said, "'for God is speaking.'"

"What does that mean?" Milgrim asked.

"A Yiddish proverb," Bigend said. "It rewards contemplation."

Something moved, three feet above Bigend's head. The manta, a sinuous matte-black blot, as wide, from wingtip to wingtip, as a small boy's outstretched arms.

"Fuck, this is cool," called Heidi, from across the floor of the atrium, "I heard everything you said!"

"Be a dear," Bigend called to her, not bothering to look up. "Swim it away. Try the penguin now."

The thing's wingtips silently flexed, catching the air, for all the world like a real ray, as it swam slowly up, wheeling gracefully, barely missing the hanging stairway. "Utterly addictive," Bigend said to Hollis. "Your locative art will morph again, with cheap aerial video drones."

"That doesn't look cheap to me."

"No," said Bigend, "not at all, but cheaper platforms will be in the High Street by Christmas. But the Festos are genius. We opted for their sheer strangeness, the organic movement, modeled from nature. They aren't very fast, but if people see them, their first thought is that they're hallucinating."

Milgrim nodded. "He's coming," he said. "Gracie."

"To London?"

"She said he'll be here soon."

"He has Sleight," Bigend said, "so he knows that having a look at his pants was simply basic strategic business intelligence. It isn't as though we've done anything to harm him. Or 'Foley' either, for that matter."

Milgrim looked from Bigend to Hollis, eyes wide.

"A friend of mine has been in a traffic accident," Hollis said. "I have to stay in town until I know how he is."

Bigend frowned. "Anyone I know?"

"No," said Hollis.

"That's not a problem. I wasn't planning on sending you immediately. Say four more days. Will you know by then whether or not your friend is out of the woods?"

"I hope so," said Hollis.

48. SHOTGUN

You're shotgun," Heidi said to Milgrim as they neared the truck. Milgrim saw the pink Mossberg-Taser collaboration in Bigend's gloved hands, in the office at Blue Ant, and almost said that he didn't have one. "Hollis and I need a talk," she said, clarifying things. He'd be in front with Aldous, his accustomed seat.

Aldous, alerted to their exit, had the motor running. Locks clunked open for them. Milgrim and Heidi hauled their respective doors open. He scrambled up while Heidi helped Hollis. He managed to close his door before Heidi had closed hers. The locks clunked solidly into place. Aldous had proudly pointed out the narrowness, the extreme evenness, of the gaps between the doors and the bodywork. These were too narrow for the insertion of any pry bar, he'd said, too narrow even for "the jaws of life," an expression Milgrim was unfamiliar with, but which he took to be Jamaican, some potent icon of existential dread.

He fastened his seat belt, a bulky, complicated thing, and sat back, taking stock. Where, exactly, was he now, vis à vis the snapping jaws of life? Bigend had seemed to have virtually no reaction at all to the news of Milgrim having a federal agent in his life, or for that matter to Winnie's alert regarding Gracie. Milgrim's panic attack, only his second in recovery, not counting his initial reaction to having been photographed by Winnie in the Caffè Nero, had been for naught. As indeed had been every other panic attack he'd ever suffered, his therapist had repeatedly pointed out. His limbic mind was grooved by irrational fear, a sort of permanent roller coaster, always ready for a ride. "Don't tell yourself that you're afraid," she'd advised him, "but that you *have fear*. Otherwise, you believe that you *are* fear."

"You didn't quit," said Heidi, behind him.

"No," said Hollis. "It wasn't the right time."

"You've got to try those balloons. They fucking rock."

They were rolling now, the run-flats juddering over City tarmac, not so much old as recently resurfaced, piecemeal, in the course of much building.

Milgrim sighed reflexively and let himself settle forward, slightly, into the seat belt harness. Let go of the tension, he told himself. Be, as his therapist said, in the moment.

In the moment, a shiny black car, coming in the opposite direction, swerved diagonally into their path. Aldous instantly swinging right, into a much narrower street, the City equivalent of an alley, dark windowless walls of stone or concrete. Behind them, tires squealed. Milgrim glanced back, saw headlights plunging after them. "Look sharp," advised Aldous, speeding up. Threads burst in the straps across Milgrim's lap and chest, black shapes birthing instantly, a conjurer's trick, hauling him upright.

"Mother*fuck*," observed Heidi, from the back seat, as Aldous continued to accelerate.

And Milgrim fell, amazed and unthinking, into his mysterious joy at the Hanger Lane Gyratory, lost in the basso howl of the Hilux's supercharger.

Constrained by the inflated crash-harness, he struggled to look back. Saw headlights. The black car.

Aldous stamped on the brakes, momentum whipping Milgrim around. A second set of headlights, ahead of them, approaching.

"Well, then," said Aldous, his teeth very white in the beams of the approaching vehicle.

Milgrim looked to the side, seeing a blank and ancient wall, perhaps two feet away.

"Aldous," said Hollis.

"Moment, please, Miss Henry," said Aldous.

The car in front of them was only a few feet away now. Squinting against the glare of the other's lights, Milgrim saw, through the car's windshield, two men. One, the driver, masked in a black balaclava. The other was masked in white, though weirdly and only partially. And was holding something up to the windshield in front of him. For Milgrim to see.

Milgrim's Neo.

Foley, his short-billed cap low over his bandaged head, fixed Milgrim with the one eye Milgrim could see, raised his other hand, and slowly shook an admonitory finger, his expression changing abruptly as Aldous floored the truck, popped the clutch, and crashed into the car, still accelerating. Foley's car began to move backward as its masked driver twisted the wheel, a few sparks popping as if off a grindstone, and still Aldous accelerated, the truck's unnatural mass and abnormal power, Milgrim now realized, being central to that cartel-readiness of which Aldous was so proud. Milgrim saw the other driver abandon the wheel, actually cover his eyes. The car struck the opposite wall, producing more sparks, and suddenly they were in the street at the far end, back in the world. Foley's car, patches of paint-work scoured to raw plastic, grille shattered, sat in the street, at a diagonal, its driver struggling, around an inflated airbag, with the wheel.

Aldous backed up slightly, then drove carefully, at an angle and at speed, into Foley's car. Then calmly and neatly reversed, backing up until the bed of the truck blocked the passage. Milgrim heard brakes behind them, and turned to see the black car reversing, its headlights receding. He heard it scrape the wall.

"Fiona will take you home, Miss Henry," said Aldous, as Milgrim turned to see him rapidly thumbing the screen of his iPhone.

"Fiona," said Milgrim, hopefully.

"You must all leave now, quickly," said Aldous. "The police are coming. Please go with Mr. Milgrim, Miss Hyde." He touched something on the dash, causing their inflated harnesses to simultaneously unlatch. Milgrim looked down at the thing that lay across his chest, like a rubber bat, a goth party favor. He heard the doors unlatch.

"Let's roll," said Heidi.

"Ouch," said Hollis. "Don't hit me!"

"Move!"

Milgrim did as told, shoving the door open and jumping down, managing to bite the corner of his tongue in the process. He tasted blood, metallic and scary, then knew, in some new way, that he was simply here, alive for the moment, and that that was that. He blinked.

And saw Foley lunge around the back of his ruined car, his fists balled, headed straight for him. While simultaneously, it seemed, the narrow space between them was bisected by the arrival of Fiona's duct-taped cowling, like an intrusion from another dimension, impossible but there it was. Foley seems to vanish as Fiona, in her yellow helmet, somehow slewed the big bike around in an amazingly tight circle, motor revving. Heidi stepped forward then, driving Hollis before her, then suddenly picked her up and sat her on the back of the bike, like someone putting a child on a pony. Milgrim saw Fiona toss Heidi the spare helmet, and hallucinated hairspray as Heidi popped it on Hollis's head, giving Fiona's yellow helmet a rap with her knuckles. He saw Fiona make a thumbs-up gesture without taking her hand off the throttle, and then she roared away, Hollis throwing her arms around her.

"Where's Foley?" Milgrim asked, trying to look in every direction at once.

"That way," said Heidi, pointing down the street. "His driver grabbed him. We're this way. Move." She pointed past the truck, into the passage.

"My laptop," Milgrim said, remembering. He ran around the back of the truck, reached into the cab, hauling his bag out.

"Hang tough," said Heidi to Aldous, who was lighting a cigarette now, with an elegant silver lighter. She fist-bumped his black-suited shoulder as she passed.

And for the first time, Milgrim heard the sirens, foreign, British, and so many.

As quickly as he could, he followed Heidi's tall, straight back.

49. GREAT MARLBOROUGH

All was forward, turn, forward, turn again, and a sharp smell of hairspray.

Her body remembering to lean into the turns, hugging what she took to be a strong thin girl, definitely breasts in there, through layers of armored Cordura. Very little she could see, past the smudged plastic of the visor, under wing-beat strobings of streetlight. Ahead, the yellow of the rider's helmet, scratched diagonally, as by something with three large claws. To either side a blur of abstracted London texture, as free of meaning as sampled skins in a graphics program. The awning of a Pret A Manger, brick, possibly the green round of a Starbucks sign, more brick, something in that one official shade of red. And most of it, she guessed, in the service of evasion, a route no car could follow. At least there seemed to be relatively little traffic now.

And then they slowed, stopped, the rider reversing into a parking place. When the ignition was cut, London was instantly, strangely quiet. The rider was removing her yellow helmet, so Hollis released her, then reached up and removed her own, which she now saw was black.

"You might need the loo," said the girl, twenty-something, fox-faced, pale brown hair mussed by the helmet. The hairspray wouldn't have been hers.

"Loo?"

"Downstairs," the girl said, indicating a sign: WOMEN. "Clean. Open till two. Free." She looked very serious.

"Thank you," said Hollis.

"Fiona," said the girl, over her shoulder.

"Hollis."

"I know. Hurry, please. I'll check my messages." Hollis dismounted, watched as Fiona did the same. Fiona frowned. "Please," she said, "hurry."

"I'm sorry," said Hollis, "my head's not working."

"Don't worry," said Fiona, who sounded neither British nor anything else in particular. "If you're not right back up, I'll come and find you."

"Good," said Hollis, and took the stairs, her knees behaving oddly, down into bright cheap light, white tile, the smell of some very modern disinfectant.

Seated in a stall, the door shut, she briefly considered screaming. She tried to remember if she'd hit her head on anything, because her brain felt too large for it, but she didn't think she had. It wouldn't have been possible, with what Aldous had made the seat belts do, which she recalled as having involved a sort of neck brace, as well as some biomorphically triangular cushion across her chest. If you were going to be bashing into cars, she supposed, you'd want that.

"My God," she said, remembering, "that was Foley." Milgrim's Foley, from the blue-lit grotto beneath the Salon du Vintage, simultaneously looking the worse for wear and somehow like a scarily adult version of that Diane Arbus photograph of the emotionally disturbed boy, the one with the grenade. Bandaged, as from a head injury.

They had startlingly slick toilet paper here. In a club, she'd have assumed it was deliberately retro.

Upstairs, on the small concrete island that she guessed might be a tiny public square, though it wasn't square, the girl called Fiona stood near her motorcycle, pinching at pixels on her iPhone's screen. The half-dozen other bikes parked there were all equally large and rough-looking. A pair of couriers stood on the tarmac, smoking, past the end of the row of bikes, like knights in smudged primary colors, serrated plates of carbon fiber giving their backs a Jurassic look. Shapeless hair and beards, like extras in a Robin Hood movie. Beyond

them, she recognized the mock Tudor façade of Liberty. Great Marl-
borough Street. Not so far from Portman Square. It felt like days since
she'd left there.

"Ready," said Fiona, behind her.

She turned as Fiona was slipping her phone into a pocket on the
front of her black coat. "Where are Heidi and Milgrim?"

"My next job," Fiona said, "after I run you to your hotel."

"You know where they are?"

"We can find them," Fiona said, throwing her leg over her bike.
She wore knee-high black boots, side-buckled from top to bottom,
their toes abraded to a pale gray. She held out the helmet.

"It's giving me a headache," she said.

"Sorry," said Fiona, "it's Mrs. Benny's. Borrowed it."

Hollis put it on and climbed on behind her, without waiting for
further explanation.

50. BANK-MONUMENT

Milgrim had never liked the City. It had always seemed too mono-lithic, though to some older scale of monolith. Too few hiding places. A lack of spaces in between. It had been turning its back on people like himself for centuries, and made him feel like a rat running along a baseboard devoid of holes. He felt that now, very strongly, though they weren't running. Walking, but briskly, owing to Heidi's long legs.

He was wearing a black "Sonny" jacket that Heidi had purchased off the back of an agreeable Turkish-looking office cleaner, here in Lombard Street, paying with a fold of bills. Or at least that was what it had embroidered on the left breast, in white, in an otherwise very good approximation of the Sony logo. His own jacket was stuffed into his bag, on top of his laptop. The transaction had also yielded a gray knit acrylic hat, which Heidi wore pulled very low, her black hair tucked completely out of sight. She'd turned her jacket inside out, revealing an impressive scarlet silk lining. The fringed epaulets had become padding, exaggerating her already formidable shoulders. This would be out of concern, Milgrim assumed, with being recognized, either by any remaining associates of Foley's or by the ever-watchful cameras, which Milgrim now noticed everywhere.

Immediately he regretted thinking of Foley. That had been very bad, the business with the truck and the two cars, and he couldn't help but believe it to have been his fault. That had definitely been a bandage on Foley's head, under the cap, and Milgrim could only as-sume that it had had something to do with that young Russian mother's bodyguard, in Paris. If Sleight had sent Foley after the Neo, as Milgrim had intended, he would in fact have sent him after that ominous-looking pram. And it had happened because he, Milgrim, had given in to some unfamiliar impulse to rebellion. He'd done it out of anger, really, resentment, and because he could.

Now Heidi produced her iPhone. Thumbed the screen once. Listened, then held the phone away, as if to ignore a message she'd heard before. When she put it to her mouth, she said: "Listen up, Garreth. Hollis Henry's in deep shit now. Kidnap attempt, looked to me. Call her." She tapped the phone again.

"Who was that?"

"Hollis's ex," said Heidi, "voice mail. I hope."

"The one who jumps off buildings?"

"The one who doesn't return his fucking calls," said Heidi, putting her phone away.

"Why don't we get a cab?" He'd seen several pass.

"Because they can't *stop* a train."

In the canyon of King William now, more traffic, more cabs, the strap of his bag digging into his shoulder, the Sonny jacket scented faintly and not unpleasantly with cooking spices, perhaps from a recent meal. He was hungry now, in spite of the Vietnamese with Winnie. He remembered Hollis's dongle, the cellular connection, in the Chunnel. He wondered if phones worked on the London subway. He didn't think they did in New York; he'd never had one there. If they did, he could send Winnie a message, once they were on the train. Tell her about Foley and the Hilux. Had it been an attempted kidnapping? He supposed it had, if not worse, but why would anyone attempt that on the passengers of a cartel-grade Jankel-armored truck? But then it occurred to him that graduates of Parsons School of Design probably weren't necessarily up on that sort of thing.

An entrance to Bank Station ahead, pedestrian traffic picking up around them, and that was the Central Line, they'd ride straight to Marble Arch, close to Portman Square, and walk to the hotel. Quicker than a cab, probably, and maybe he could get on Twitter.

Heidi swung suddenly around, whisking back one side of her inside-out jacket. As if to show him the large brooch he now saw she wore there, three rocketships, perhaps, nose-down, silver with crimson tails. And plucking part of this away, she flung it behind them, the entirety of her long body pivoting behind it.

Someone shrieked, as terrible a sound as Milgrim had heard, and continued to as Heidi, rough as any policeman, rushed him down the stairs and into Bank-Monument.

51. SOMEONE

Hollis lay fully dressed on the embroidered velvet spread of the Piblokto Madness bed, watching the faint oscillation of huge curved shadows thrown by the halogens in the birdcage library, dialed down until they were almost off. In some sense, she decided, she literally no longer knew where she was. In Number Four, in Cabinet, certainly, but if she'd just been one of the subjects of an abduction attempt, as Fiona seemed to believe she had, was Number Four still the same place? A matter of context. The same place, but *meaning* differently.

Fiona had insisted on bringing her up here, and then had looked in the bathroom, and in the wardrobe, where in any case there was no room to hide. If the wooden sides of the bed hadn't gone straight down to the carpet, Hollis guessed, Fiona would have looked under it as well. Put the chain on, Fiona had ordered, leaving to find Milgrim and Heidi, something she seemed relatively certain of being able to do. As far as she knew, Fiona had said, both were okay. She'd had no more idea about what the attempted truck-trapping had been about than Hollis did, it seemed, though she too had identified Milgrim's Foley, their shadow from Salon du Vintage. What had Bigend called him? A fantasist? How would he have expected to get inside Aldous's super-truck? The thing was capable of being sealed hermetically, she knew, because Aldous delighted in explaining its many features. It carried tanks of compressed air, and could be driven through clouds of tear or any other gas. He'd also told her that it could drive under-water, with a snorkel extended. A bank vault on wheels, its "glass" some hush-hush Israeli nano stuff that Aldous was particularly proud of Bigend's having been able to source. Was it possible that Foley had simply had no idea what the silver pickup was about? It looked, after all, at least to Hollis, like any other truck, of that stretched, four-door, overly masculine sort, its bed shortened by half through the extension of the cab. The bed was covered with a ribbed lid, painted to match the bodywork. Perhaps that was where they kept the air supply. And what had happened to Foley since she'd seen him in Paris? An accident? A head injury?

There was a knock at the door. Two raps, brisk, quite sharp. "Miss Henry?" A man's voice. "It's Robert, Miss Henry."

It did in fact sound like Robert. She sat up, stood up, crossed to the door. "Yes?"

"Someone to see you, Miss Henry."

This was such a singular thing for a hotel security man to say, and delivered with such an uncharacteristic cheerfulness, that she stepped back, quickly scanned the nearest shelf, and seized the same spikey ebony head that Heidi had so tidily bull's-eyed earlier that day. Inverted, it felt comfortingly heavy, its serrated hairdo adding teeth to blunt-instrument potential.

She unlocked the door, leaving the chain in place, and peered out. Robert stood there, smiling. Garreth looked up at her from about the level of Robert's waist. She couldn't put that together, and didn't, until she'd opened the door, although she never managed, subsequently, to remember closing it or undoing the chain. Nor could she ever remember what she'd said, but whatever it was, she would remember, had caused a look of relief to flash across Robert's face, and his smile to widen.

"Sorry I couldn't return your call," said Garreth.

She heard the ebony fetish hit the carpet, bounce. Saw Robert's broad back disappearing through one of the green corridor's spring-loaded doors.

He was seated in a wheelchair.

Or not a wheelchair, she saw, as the fingers of his right hand moved on a joystick, but one of those electric mobility scooters, black with gray pneumatic tires, like the offspring of a high-end Swiss office chair and some expensive 1930s toy. As it rolled forward, across the threshold, she heard herself say "Oh God."

"Not as bad as it looks," he said. "Playing the disability card for your doorman." He unclipped a black cane from the scooter's side, pressed a button. A quadrangle of rubber-tipped supports sprang open at its tip. "A bit, anyway." Using the cane for support, he stood carefully, wincing, putting no weight on his right leg.

And then her arms were around him, one of his around her, her face wet with tears. "I thought you were dead."

"Who told you that?"

"Nobody. But I imagined it as I was being told you'd jumped off that hideous building. And nobody knew where you were—"

"Munich, when you called. Intimate session with five neurosurgeons, three German, two Czech, getting some feeling restored to this leg. Why I couldn't call. Wouldn't give me the phone."

"Did it work?"

"It hurts," he said.

"I'm sorry."

"That's actually a *good* thing, in this case. Perhaps you should close the door?"

"I don't want to let go of you."

He rubbed her lower back. "Better behind a locked door."

While she was putting the chain on, he asked: "Who's this for?" She turned. He was looking down at the fetish head. "To do with this deep shit your lairy drummer says you're in?"

"Heidi?"

"Left a voice mail herself. About an hour ago."

"How did you convince Robert to bring you up here?"

"Showed him the head-mount video of the Burj jump. Handicapped access is through the rear here. Your man had to help me in. When you weren't here, I said I'd wait in the rear lobby, do some work on my laptop. He came back to check on me, of course. Saw the video, we got talking. I explained I was a friend of yours." He smiled. "Is that whiskey?"

"Want some?"

"Can't. Painkillers. Thought you might. You're looking a bit pale."

"Garreth . . ."

"Yes?"

"Missed you." It sounded incredibly stupid.

"Mutual." He wasn't smiling now. "Knew I'd fucked up, really. When the Lotus hit me, actually."

"You shouldn't have jumped."

He shook his head. "Shouldn't have left." He went slowly to the bed, supporting himself with the four-footed cane. Turned, as slowly, and carefully sat. "Himself," he said, "sends regards."

She had no idea how old the old man was. She would have thought seventy, at least. "How is he?"

"None too happy with me. I'm not likely to be that operational again for him. I think he sees the tricks are over, for both of us."

She poured herself a half-inch of whiskey, in a highball glass. "I never understood exactly what motivated him," she said.

"Some sort of seething Swiftian rage," he said, "that he can only express through perverse, fiendishly complex exploits, resembling Surrealist *gestes*." He smiled.

"And that was one, in Vancouver?"

"That was a good one. And I met you."

"And then you went off to do another, before the election?"

"Night of the election, actually. But that was different. We were simply making certain that something *didn't* happen, that time."

The whiskey burnt the back of her throat. Made her eyes water. She sat down, gingerly, beside him, fearing that she might hurt him if she made the mattress move.

He put his arm around her waist. "I feel like a schoolboy at the theater," he said. "With a date who can't stand whiskey."

"Your hair's longer," she said, touching it.

"Grows out in hospital. Quite a few procedures. Yet to murder a physiotherapist, but then I've not had my last chance." He took the glass from her, sniffed at it. "Deep shit, your Heidi said. Harsh woman. Tell me: how deep?"

"I don't know. I was in a truck tonight, in the City, leaving a meeting with Bigend, and a car cut us off. Our driver went into a passage, sort of alley, and I think we were meant to, because another car drove in at the other end, and drove right up to us. That driver had a bala-clava, pulled down. We were trapped between the two cars."

"What happened?"

"Aldous, our driver, pushed the car in front back out into the street, then crushed the front corner of it. It's an armored truck, a Toyota, like a tank."

"Hilux," he said. "Jankel-armored?"

"How did you know?"

"It's a specialty of theirs. Whose is it?"

"Bigend's."

"Thought you wanted shut of him."

"I did. Do, actually. But he came back, a few days ago, and I agreed to a job. But it's all gone sideways."

"Pear-shaped. But how exactly?"

"His IT man and security expert's defected. He has big plans for military contracting. In the United States."

"The IT man?"

"Bigend. He wants to design clothing. For the military. Says it's recession-proof."

He looked at her. "It is that," he said. "Do you know who was after your truck?"

"Someone Bigend pissed off. Another contractor. I heard the name earlier tonight but can't remember it. An American arms dealer, I think."

"Who told you that?"

"Milgrim. Someone who works for Bigend. Or is a *hobby* of his, more like it."

"Crepuscular in here," he said, looking around.

She got up, carefully, and went to the control. Turned up the halogens.

"Someone's been to a lot of boot sales," he said. "Regular Museum of Mankind in here."

"A club," she said. "Inchmale joined. It's all like this."

He looked up at the whale ribs. "Portobello Road on acid."

She saw that the right leg of his black trousers had been split neatly up the inner seam, from hem to crotch, and reclosed with small black safety pins. "Why is your leg pinned up?"

"Going goth. Difficult to find just the right black ones. Change the dressings myself, this way. Have the kit for it in back of my invalid chair." He smiled. "Sutures are already starting to itch." Then he frowned. "Not pretty, though. Best leave that." He sniffed at the whiskey again, took a tiny sip. Sighed. "That's your deep shit, then?"

"There was a tracker bug in this," she said, picking up the Blue Ant figurine from the nightstand. "It may have been there since Vancouver, or it may have been put in later." She opened a drawer and produced the bug, in its baggie. "Bigend? Sleight?"

"Who's that?"

"Bigend's IT specialist. The recent defector. Ajay left it out, when Heidi put this back together for me. Said there were more options, leaving it out."

"A.J.?"

"Ah-jay. Heidi's favorite sparring partner, at her new gym, in Hackney. He's a fan of yours. Total fanboy."

"That would be a change," he said, "wouldn't it?" Then he patted the embroidered velour beside him. "Come back and sit here. Make an old man happy."

52. THE MATTER
IN GREATER DETAIL

Heidi said there was no cellular connection on the London subway, so Milgrim hadn't bothered trying the dongle. The trip to Marble Arch had been a quick one, Milgrim seated and Heidi standing, ceaselessly eyeing the other passengers for signs of incipient Foleyism.

Heidi still had her jacket inside out. As she'd swayed in front of him, on the balls of her feet, he'd been able to look up, the jacket repeatedly swinging open, and identify what he'd earlier taken for a brooch as having been three darts, the kind they played a game with here, in pubs. He'd sometimes, on hotel television, glimpsed hypnotically tedious competitions that made golf seem like a contact sport. But now he understood what she'd done. There were two left. Not good. He supposed he should be grateful for her having done it, under the circumstances, but still, ungood. Though he noted that he didn't find *her* frightening, however little he'd want to get on her bad side.

There was a KFC adjacent the Marble Arch exit, he saw as they emerged, but it was closed. It smelled horrible, and this struck him with some full and unexpected force of nostalgia and desire. Homesickness, he thought, another feeling he'd tamped down beneath the benzos, in whatever unventilated chamber of the self, however abstract the notion of home might be.

But then Fiona pipped her bike's horn, twice, at the curb, gesturing to them. He walked over as she flipped her visor up, the particular angle at which the line of her cheekbone intersected the yellow helmet-edge striking him in some nameless but welcome way. "Coming with me," she said, offering him the black helmet. Raising her chin slightly to make eye contact with Heidi, who'd come up beside Milgrim. "I'll send a car for you."

"Fuck it," said Heidi, "I'm walking. Where's Hollis?"

"At Cabinet. I'm taking Milgrim."

"You do that," said Heidi, taking the black helmet and placing it on Milgrim's head. The hairspray was still there. She gave the helmet a sharp rap with her knuckles, in parting. Milgrim threw his leg over the seat behind Fiona and put his arms around her, conscious of girl within the armor. Blinking at the newness of that. Turned the helmet to see Heidi, dimly, through the miserable visor, marching away.

Fiona put the bike in gear.

> > >

"Faggot above a load," said Bigend, seated behind a very basic white Ikea desk. It had a broken corner and was stacked with books of fabric samples.

"Excuse me?" Milgrim was perched on a ridiculous violet stool, deeply and cheaply cushioned.

"Archaic expression," said Bigend. "Faggots, properly speaking, being pieces of firewood. When one had a faggot above a load, one was about to drop one. It meant that something was excessive, too busy."

"Foley," said Milgrim. "In the car in front of us."

"I gathered as much."

"Where's Aldous?"

"Being questioned by various species of police. He's good at that."

"Will he be arrested?"

"Unlikely. But when Fiona debriefed you, in Paris, you told her that you'd gone to Galeries Lafayette. That Foley had followed you there, as you'd guessed he would, and that you'd slipped the Neo, having determined that Sleight was using it to allow Foley to track you, into, I believe she said, a pram."

"Not a pram," said Milgrim, "exactly. More modern."

"Was there a reason for choosing that one particular pram?"

"The woman, the mother, was Russian. I'd been eavesdropping."

"What sort of a woman did you take her to be?"

"The wife of an oligarch, would-be oligarch . . ."

"Or gangster?"

Milgrim nodded.

"Accompanied by at least one bodyguard, I would imagine?"

Milgrim nodded.

Bigend stared at him. "Naughty."

"I'm sorry."

"It isn't as though I don't want you to become more proactive," said Bigend, "but now that I understand what you did, I see that you've been irresponsible. Impulsive."

"You're impulsive," said Milgrim, surprising himself.

"I'm *supposed* to be impulsive. You're supposed to be relatively circumspect." He frowned. "Or, rather, not that you're supposed to be, particularly, but that I expect it of you, on the basis of experience. Why did you do it?"

"I was tired of Sleight. I've never liked him very much."

"One doesn't," agreed Bigend.

"And I'd never really thought about the idea of his being able to track me with the Neo before. I'd taken that for granted, assumed it was something you wanted him to do, but then you were expressing distrust for him, suspicion . . ." Milgrim shrugged. "I felt impatient, angry."

Bigend studied him, the weird cathode blue of his suit seeming to float in Milgrim's retina at some special depth. "I think I understand," he said. "You're changing. They told me to expect that. I'll factor it in, in future." He took an iPhone from an inner pocket and squinted at its screen, replaced it. "The woman in Seven Dials. The federal agent. I need to know more about that. All about it."

Milgrim cleared his throat, something he tried never to do in situations like this. His bag was at his feet, the laptop in it, and now he resisted the urge to look at it. "Winnie," said Milgrim, "Tung Whitaker."

"Why are you wearing the Sonny logo?" interrupted Bigend.

"Heidi bought it from a cleaner."

"It's a Chinese brand, if one can call it a brand. Logo, rather. Used for the African market."

"I don't think he was African. Slavic."

"Jun," called Bigend, "come here."

A small man, Japanese, with round gold glasses, entered from the darkened shop. Milgrim hadn't seen him when Fiona had ushered him in, only the other driver, the urine-sample man. "Yes?"

"Milgrim needs some clothes. Put an outfit together."

"Would you mind standing, please?" asked Jun. He wore a type of pointedly British hunting cap, Milgrim thought by Kangol. Milgrim associated it with the Bronx of another era. He had a small, very neat mustache.

Milgrim stood. Jun walked around him. "A thirty-two waist," he said. "A thirty-two inseam?"

"Thirty-three."

He looked at Milgrim's shoes. "Eight?"

"Nine," said Milgrim.

"British eight," said Jun, and went back to the darkened front of the shop, where Milgrim knew the urine-sample driver was sitting, with his umbrella.

"She's not interested in you," Milgrim said. "She thought you might be Gracie's business partner. She had no way of knowing what she was watching, in Myrtle Beach. So she followed me back here. And I think . . ."

"Yes?"

"I think she wanted to see London."

Bigend raised an eyebrow.

"But the police, authorities, wouldn't really help her much with you. She said you were connected. With them."

"Really?"

"But they asked her about your truck."

"Asked her what?"

"They were curious about it."

"But what did she want from you?"

"She'd thought that by learning more about you, she'd learn more about Gracie, about Foley. But as soon as she learned that you were just a competitor, that you were interested in U.S. military contracts yourself, she stopped being interested in you."

"You told her that?"

"And she stopped being interested in you," repeated Milgrim.

There was a silence. "I see what you mean," said Bigend.

"I wasn't volunteering information. I was responding to specific questions. I didn't know what else to do."

Jun returned, his arms full of clothing, which he put down on the desk, pushing the fabric samples aside. There was a pair of very new, very bright brown shoes. "Stand, please." Milgrim stood. "Remove jacket." Milgrim unzipped the Sonny and took it off. Jun helped him on with something made of fragrant tweed, immediately removed it, tried another, equally fragrant, walked around, buttoned the jacket, nodded.

"But why didn't you tell me this at the time?" asked Bigend.

"Remove trousers, please," said Jun, "and shirt."

"I was too anxious," said Milgrim. "I have an anxiety disorder." He sat down on the horrible stool and began to remove his shoes. Taking them off, he stood and began removing his pants, grateful to have something to do. "I didn't *make* her follow me. You sent me to Myrtle Beach."

"You may have an anxiety disorder," Bigend said, "but you're definitely changing."

"Remove shirt, please," said Jun.

Milgrim did. He stood there in black socks and underpants from Galeries Lafayette, with a peculiar awareness of something just having shifted, though he wasn't clear what. Jun had been busy unbuttoning and unfolding a tattersall shirt, which he now helped Milgrim into. It had a spread collar, Milgrim saw, and as he was buttoning the front he discovered that the barrel cuffs extended nearly to his elbows, with a great many pearl buttons.

"Have you been to Florence?" asked Bigend as Milgrim was fastening those very peculiar cuffs.

"Florence?" Jun had just handed him a pair of whipcord trousers.

"Tuscany," said Bigend, "is lovely. Better this time of year. The rain. More subtle light."

"You're sending me to Italy?"

"Along with Hollis. I want you both out of here. Someone is angry with you. I'll generate deep Blue Ant traffic, to the effect that you're both in Los Angeles. Perhaps that will convince Oliver."

Milgrim heard that scream, outside of Bank Station, took a breath, but found that no words came. He zipped up his new pants. Which were oddly narrow in the ankles, and cuffed.

"Sit, please," said Jun, who was loosening the laces of the brown shoes. They were wing-tip brogues, but with a narrower toe than was traditional, and thick, cleated-looking soles. Milgrim sat. Jun knelt, helped Milgrim on with the shoes, then tightened the laces and tied them. Milgrim stood, shifting his weight. They fit, he decided, but were stiff, heavy. Jun handed him a narrow, heavy leather belt of a similar shade, with a polished brass buckle. He put it on. "Tie," said Jun, offering one in paisley silk.

"I don't wear them, thanks," said Milgrim.

Jun put the tie down on the desk, helped Milgrim into the jacket, then picked up the tie again, folded it, and tucked it into the jacket's inside breast pocket. He smiled, patted Milgrim on the shoulder, and left.

"That's better," said Bigend. "For Florence. *Bella figura*."

"Am I going back to Camden?"

"No," said Bigend. "That was why I had you give Fiona your key. She's gone 'round to pick up your things, check you out."

"Where am I going?"

"You aren't," said Bigend. "You're sleeping here."

"Here?"

"A foam mattress and a sleeping bag. We're just around the corner from Blue Ant, but they don't know."

"Know what?"

"That I'm Tanky."

"What does *that* mean?"

"Tanky and Tojo. Name of the shop. I'm Tanky, Jun's Tojo. He's amazing, really."

"He is?"

"You look," said Bigend, "like a foxhunting spiv. His grasp of contradiction is brilliantly subversive."

"Is there wifi?"

"No," said Bigend, "there isn't."

"What she most particularly wanted to convey to you," Milgrim said, "Winnie Tung Whitaker, is that Gracie believes you're his competitor. Which means, to him, that you're his enemy."

"I'm not his enemy," said Bigend.

"You had me steal the design of his pants."

"'Business intelligence.' If you hadn't thrown Foley under some random Russians, this would all be much easier. And it wouldn't be distracting me from more important things. I am, however, glad that we had this opportunity to discuss the matter in greater detail, privately."

"Bent cops are one thing," said Milgrim. "A bent former major in the Special Forces, who does illegal arms deals? I think that might be something else."

"A *businessman*. I'm one myself."

"She said he believes he can do anything," said Milgrim. "She said they sent him to *schools*."

"He wouldn't be my first arms dealer, you know," said Bigend, getting up. He straightened his suit, which Milgrim noted was in need of a pressing. "Meanwhile, you and Hollis can do the museums, enjoy the food. It's extraordinary, really."

"The food?"

"What they managed to do with you in Basel. I'm really very impressed. I see now that it's all taken a while to gel."

"That reminds me," said Milgrim.

"Of what?"

"I'm starving."

"Sandwiches," said Bigend, indicating a brown paper bag on the desk. "Chicken and bacon. Seedy bread. I'll be in touch tomorrow, when the travel's been arranged. You'll be locked in here. The alarm system will be activated. Please don't try to leave. Jun will be in at ten thirty or so. Good night."

When Bigend had gone, Milgrim ate the two sandwiches, carefully wiped his fingers, then removed his new shoes, examined the Tanky & Tojo logo stamped into the orange leather insoles, smelled them, and put them on the white desk. The gray vinyl floor was cold through his socks. The door to the front of the shop, which Bigend had closed behind him, looked cheap, hollow-core. He'd once watched a dealer called Fish chisel the thin wooden skin from one side of a door like that. It had been filled with plastic bags of counterfeit Mexican Valium. Now he pressed his ear against this one, held his breath. Nothing.

Was the urine-sample man still sitting out there with his umbrella? He doubted it, but he wanted to be sure. He found the light switch, pressed it. Stood for a moment in darkness, then opened the door.

The shop was lit, but dimly, by wonky columnar lanterns of white paper, floor lamps. The display window, from here, looked like one of those big Cibachromes in an art gallery: photograph of a blank brick wall across the street, faint ghost of graffiti. Suddenly someone passed, in a black hoodie. Milgrim swallowed. Closed the door. Turned the lights back on.

He went to the rear, no longer bothering to be quiet, opened a similar but smaller door, finding a clean little room with a very new toilet and corner sink. No other doors. No rear entrance. The neighborhood, like much of London, he guessed, not having alleys in the American sense.

He found a virginal white slab of foam, five inches thick, double-wide, rolled into a thick upright cylinder. It was secured with three bands of transparent packing tape, the Blue Ant logo repeated along them at regular intervals. Beside it was a fat, surprisingly small sausage of what appeared to be a darkly iridescent silk, and a plastic liter bottle of still spring water, from Scotland.

The desk's top drawer contained its Ikea assembly instructions and a pair of scissors with colorless transparent handles. The other two drawers were empty. He used the scissors to cut the tape, releasing the foam, which remained slightly bent, in the direction in which it had been rolled. He put the concave side down, on the cold vinyl, and picked up the silken sausage. MONT-BELL was embroidered on one side. He fumbled with the plastic lock on the draw cord, loosened it, and worked the densely compacted contents out. The sleeping bag, when he unfurled it, was very light, very thin, stretchy, and of that same iridescence, purplish-black. He unzipped it and spread it on the bed. He picked up the bottle of water and carried it to the desk, where he retrieved his bag from the floor, putting it beside the bottle. Taking Bigend's chair, he sat down, opened the bag, and pulled out his crumpled cotton jacket. He looked down at the tweed lapels of his new one, surprised to see them. The shirt cuffs were too strange, but then, you couldn't see them under a jacket. Laying his old jacket aside, he brought out the Mac Air, its power cord and U.K. adaptor plug, and Hollis's red dongle.

British electricity was some brutal other breed, their plugs three-pronged, massive, wall sockets often equipped with their own little switches, a particularly ominous belt-and-suspenders touch. "Faggot above a load," he said, plugging the power unit into the socket nearest the desk and flipping the socket switch.

He Googled "Tanky & Tojo," shortly discovering that Jun, Junya Marukawa, had his own shop in Tokyo, that Tanky & Tojo were getting lots of web coverage, and that a SoHo branch would be opening next year on Lafayette. There was no mention of Hubertus Bigend at all. Jun's style, evidently, was one Japanese take on something at least one writer called "transgressive trad."

Then he went to Twitter, logged in, saw that there was nothing new from Winnie, and started composing his message to her in his head while he got rid of the three strange girls with numbers instead of surnames, the ones who wanted to follow him.

53. CRICKET

The phone's cricket-noise woke her, though instantly she was uncertain whether she'd actually been asleep. She'd lain curled all night beside him, for the most part awake, out of some need to process the fact that he was there. He'd smelled of hospitals. Something he'd used to dress the wounds. He hadn't let her see that, describing his injured leg as "a work in progress."

He'd sat in the armchair to change the dressings, on a black garbage bag taken from the backpack slung behind the scooter-chair, undoing the safety pins down one inside leg of his trousers. She'd had to wait in the bathroom, leaning against the towel-warming pipes that caged the shower, listening to him whistling, deliberately tunelessly, to tease her. "There," he'd called, finally. "I'm decent now."

She'd emerged to find him safety-pinning the hem of his trouser leg. The black bag he'd spread across the chair was on the carpet now, something knotted into one of its corners. "Does it hurt, to do that?" she'd asked

"Not really," he'd said. "The rest of it, the reconstruction, physiotherapy, that's less fun. Do you know I've a rattan thighbone?" He grinned at her, evilly, sitting more upright.

"What's that?"

"Rattan. The stuff they weave baskets and furniture out of. They've found a way to turn it into a perfect analog of human bone."

"You're making that up."

"They're just starting to test it on humans. On me, in fact. Works a charm, on sheep."

"They can't. Turn that into bone."

"They put it in ovens. With calcium, other things. Under pressure. For a long time. Turns to bone, near enough."

"No way."

"If I'd thought of it, I'd have had them make you a basket. Brilliant thing about it, you can *build* exactly the bone you need, out of rattan. Work it as rattan. Then ossify it. Perfect replacement. Actually a bit stronger than the original. Microscopic structure allows the blood vessels to grow through it."

"Don't mess with me."

"Tell me more about what this Milgrim said, to Mr. Big End," he'd said. He always pronounced it that way, as though it were two words.

She found the receiver, feeling more absurdly massive in the dark than ever, lifted it. "I'll be there in ten minutes," said Bigend. "Be in the sitting room."

"What time is it?"

"Eight-fifteen."

"I'm asleep. Was."

"I need to see you."

"Where's Milgrim? And Heidi—"

"We'll be discussing him shortly. Heidi's no part of it." He hung up.

She squinted at the glow around the edges of the curtains. Returned the receiver as quietly as she could to its cradle. Garreth's breathing continued, unchanged.

She sat up, carefully. Made out the dark horizontals of his legs. He'd insisted on sleeping in his trousers and stocking feet. On his bare chest, she now knew, were new scars, healed but still livid, next to older ones she could have sketched from memory. She stood, padded into the bathroom, closed the door behind her, and turned on the light.

54. AIR GLOW

"Ferguson," said Winnie Tung Whitaker, "the one with the mullet. He was on Gracie's Heathrow flight, from Geneva."

In the glow of the Air's screen and backlit keyboard, Milgrim was huddled at the desk, cowled in the MontBell sleeping bag. He'd tried sleeping, but had kept getting up to check Twitter. On the sixth or seventh try, her response had been this number in the United States. On checking her card, he'd seen that it was her cell number. Some research in the paper telephone directory under the swatch books had provided the necessary dialing prefixes. "The one with the pants?" he asked, hoping he was wrong.

"*Mike* Ferguson. See? I told you."

"When are you going back?"

"Actually, this story of yours might call for leave en route."

"What's that?"

"The one scam still permitted federal employees, we like to call it. I'm TDY now. Temporary duty, business travel. If I can get permission, I can take two days' vacation. Sixteen hours of annual leave. When I saw your tweet, I e-mailed my boss. It'll be on my own nickel, though." She didn't sound happy about that. "On the other hand, this is getting really interesting. Not that my boss would find it interesting enough to keep me here on per diem. That trick you played in Paris, though, I wouldn't have expected that from you. What's up?"

"I don't know." It was true.

"That was the Parsons grad, the designer, the wannabe SpecOps boy. And that dumbfuck attempt on your boss's truck would be him too."

"It was," said Milgrim. "I saw him."

"I mean it wasn't Gracie or Ferguson. They were still going through immigration at Heathrow. Once they got through, though, they'd be apprised of what he'd done, and what had happened. The interesting thing, then, becomes how Gracie might react to that. If he were smart, he'd let it go, fire the designer. Who's clearly worse than clueless. And it isn't that Gracie's not intelligent. He's highly intelligent. Just not smart. Did you tell Bigend?"

"Yes," said Milgrim. "I think I told him everything you wanted me to."

"Did you tell him about me?"

"I showed him your card," Milgrim said. It was on the desk now, in front of him.

"Describe his reaction."

"He didn't seem worried. But he never does. He said that he'd had some experience with U.S. federal agents."

"He might have just a little under five hundred pounds of very highly trained *Mike* on his hands soon, between the two of them. You'll need to keep me informed. Got a phone?"

"No," said Milgrim, "I left it in Paris."

"Tweet me. Or call this number."

"I'm glad about your leave."

"Not a done deal yet. Let's hope it works out. Watch out for yourself." She hung up.

Milgrim replaced the weightless plastic handset in its recess on top of the phone, causing a backlit white panel to go out.

He looked at the clock in the upper right corner of the screen. Jun was supposed to arrive in a few hours. It wouldn't yet be light out now. Wrapped in the MontBell, he went back to the foam.

55. MR. WILSON

There were few guests for breakfast.

The Italian boy and another waiter were arranging screens, to the west of the narwhale rack. She'd seen these deployed here before, for the heightened privacy of business breakfasts. The screens were made of what she'd assumed to be extremely old tapestries, faded to no particular color, a sort of variegated khaki, but now she noticed that they depicted scenes from Disney's *Snow White*. At least they didn't appear to be pornographic. She was about to take her accustomed seat, beneath the spiral tusks, when the Italian boy noticed her. "You'll be here, Miss Henry," indicating the newly screened table.

Then Bigend appeared at the head of the stairs, moving quickly, trench coat over his arm, the aura of his blue suit almost painful.

"It's Milgrim," he said, when he reached her. "Bring coffee," he ordered the Italian boy.

"Certainly, sir." He was gone.

"Has something happened to Milgrim?"

"Nothing's happened to Milgrim. Milgrim has happened to me." He tossed his trench coat over the back of his chair.

"What do you mean?"

"He tried to blind Foley, so-called, outside Bank Station. Last night."

"*Milgrim?*"

"Not that he told me about it," said Bigend, sitting down.

"Tell me what's happened." She sat opposite him.

"They came to Voytek's flat this morning. They took Bobby."

"Bobby?"

"Chombo."

The name, once heard, recalling the man. Encountered first in Los Angeles, and then, under very different circumstances, in Vancouver. "He's here, in London? Who came?"

"Primrose Hill. Or was, until this morning." Bigend glared at the Italian girl, arriving with the coffee. She poured for Hollis, then for him.

"Coffee will be fine for now, thanks," Hollis told her, hoping to give her a chance to escape.

"Of course," said the girl, and ducked smoothly behind the apparently four-hundred-year-old Disney screen.

"He was a mathematician," Hollis said. "Programmer? I'd forgotten him." Perhaps partly because Bobby, a markedly unpleasant personality in his own right, had been so deeply embedded in that first experience of Bigend being, in many ways, so bad to know. "I remember that I thought you seemed to be courting him, in Vancouver. As I was leaving."

"Extraordinary talent. Terrifically *narrow*," he said, with evident relish. "Focused, utterly."

"Asshole," suggested Hollis.

"Not an issue. I sorted his affairs, brought him here, and set him a task. A challenge truly worthy of his abilities. The first he'd had. I would have provided any sort of lifestyle, really."

"Remind me to be a bigger asshole."

"As it was," Bigend said, "because he's essentially a parasite, with an emotional need to constantly irritate the host, and because I wanted the project to remain separate from Blue Ant, I had Voytek put him up. At home. Compensating Voytek, of course."

"Voytek?"

"My alternative IT person. My hole card against Sleight. I can't be certain that Sleight didn't discover that, but he evidently did, at some point, discover where I was keeping Chombo while he worked on the project."

"What's the project?"

"A secret," said Bigend, with a slight lift of his eyebrows.

"But who took Bobby?"

"Three men. American. They told Voytek that they'd come back for him, and his wife and child, if he tried to alert anyone prior to seven this morning."

"They threatened his wife and child?"

"Voytek understands that sort of thing. Eastern European. Took them instantly at their word. Phoned me at seven twenty. I immediately phoned you. I may need you to help me with Milgrim."

"Who were they?"

"Foley, by the description. Unable to stop muttering about Milgrim. The other two, I'd assume, were Gracie, Milgrim's arms dealer, and someone else. Gracie clearly in charge, calm, businesslike. The third man had a mullet, Voytek said. I had to Google it. Foley apparently has seen the inside of an emergency ward twice this week, and holds Milgrim personally responsible. Gracie, however, assumes that Milgrim may have been following orders. Mine."

"He told Voytek that?"

"He told me."

"When?"

"On the way over here. Sleight having given him, obviously, my private mobile number."

"He sounded angry?"

"He sounded," Bigend said, "like voice-distortion software. Impossible to read affect. He told me what he requires in exchange for Bobby's safe return, and why."

"How much?"

"Milgrim."

"How much does he want?"

"He wants Milgrim. Nothing else."

"There you are," said Garreth, from the opening between the two frames. "Might have left a note."

Bigend looked up at Garreth with a peculiar childlike openness. Hollis had only seen this expression a few times before, and dreaded it. "This is Garreth," she said.

"Wilson," said Garreth, which wasn't true.

"I take it, Mr. Wilson, that you are Hollis's friend? The one recently injured in an automobile accident?"

"Not so recent," said Garreth.

"I see you're joining us," Bigend said. Then, to the Italian boy, who'd anxiously appeared: "Move the screen for Mr. Wilson. Arrange a chair for him."

"Very kind," said Garreth.

"Not at all."

"Should you even be walking?" asked Hollis, starting to rise.

As the boy slid the screen aside, Garreth stepped past it, heavily, supporting himself on the quadrupedal cane. "I took the invalid chair, then the service elevator." He put his free hand on her shoulder, squeezed. "No need to get up."

When the boy had helped him into the high-backed armchair brought from an adjacent table, he smiled at Bigend.

"This is Hubertus Bigend," said Hollis.

"A pleasure, Mr. Big End." They shook hands across the table.

"Call me Hubertus. A cup for Mr. Wilson," he said to the Italian boy.

"Garreth."

"Were you injured here in London, Garreth?"

"Dubai."

"I see."

"You'll pardon me," said Garreth, "but I couldn't help overhearing your conversation."

Bigend's eyebrows rose a fraction. "How much of it?"

"The bulk," said Garreth. "Are you considering giving them this Milgrim, then?"

Bigend looked from Garreth to Hollis, then back. "I've no way of knowing how much else you may know of my affairs, but I've invested a great deal in Milgrim's health and welfare. This comes at a very difficult time for me, as I'm unable to trust my own security staff. There's an internal struggle in the firm, and I'm loath to go to any of the many corporate security firms here. The equivalent of hiring the lousy to rid you of lice, in my experience. Milgrim, through his unfortunate actions, has endangered a project of mine, one of the utmost importance to me."

"You *are*," said Hollis, "you are! You're going to give them Milgrim!"

"I certainly am," said Bigend, "unless someone has a better suggestion. And will have done, by this time tomorrow."

"Stall," said Garreth.

"Stall?"

"I can probably put something together, but I'll need closer to forty-eight hours."

"There may be risk for me, in doing that," said Bigend.

"Not as much risk as there is in my calling the police," said Hollis. "And the *Times* and the *Guardian*. There's that man at the *Guardian* who particularly has it in for you, isn't there?"

Bigend stared at her.

"Tell them you've lost him," said Garreth, "but that you'll get him back. I'll help you with messaging."

"What are you, Mr. Wilson?"

"A hungry man. With a gammy leg."

"I recommend the full English."

56. ALWAYS IS GENIUS

Milgrim, on his side in the sleeping bag, on the medicinal-looking white foam, was caught in some frustrating loop of semi-sleep, slow and circular, in which exhaustion swung him slowly out, toward where sleep should surely have been, then overshot the mark somehow, bumping him over into a state of random anxiety that couldn't quite qualify as wakefulness, then back out again, convinced of sleep's promise . . .

This was, his therapist had told him, on hearing it described, an aftereffect of stress—excessive fear, excessive excitement—and he was there. That it was the sort of thing that a normal person could escape with the application of a single tablet of Ativan added a certain irony. But Milgrim's recovery, he'd been taught, was dependent on strict abstinence from the substance of choice. Which was not the substance of choice, his therapist maintained, but the substance of need. And Milgrim knew that he'd never been content with a single tablet of anything. It was the very *first* single tablet, he told himself, rehearsing these teachings like a rosary, as he swung back out toward the false promise of sleep, that he was required not to ingest. The others were no problem, because, if he successfully avoided the first, there were no others. Except for that first one, which, in potential at least, was always there. Bump. He hit the random anxiety, saw those few sparks thrown off Foley's car's fenders as Aldous drove it back, through that narrow space.

He tried to recall what he knew about cars, to explain those sparks. They were mostly plastic now, cars, with bits of metal inside. The surface of the body had been ground down, he supposed, to a little metal, producing sparks, and then perhaps the metal had been abraded away . . . I know that, stupid, his mind told him.

He thought he heard something. Then knew he did. His eyes sprang open in the small cave of the MontBell, the office faintly illuminated by the dance of abstract shapes on the screen of the Air.

"Shombo, always," he heard Voytek say loudly, the accent unmistakable, growing closer, resentful, "is *genius*. Shombo is genius *coder*. *Shombo*, I will tell you: Shombo codes like old people fuck."

"Milgrim," Fiona called, "hullo, where are you?"

57. SOMETHING OFF THE SHELF

The current crisis, whatever underlay it, didn't seem to have affected Bigend's appetite. They were all having the full English. Bigend was working steadily through his, Garreth doing most of the talking.

"This is a prisoner exchange," Garreth said. "One hostage for another. Your man assumes, correctly, that you're unlikely to call the police." Bigend looked pointedly at Hollis. "We can assume that he hasn't much of a network here," Garreth continued, "else he wouldn't have sent an idiot after Milgrim. Neither, at this point, do you, given the situation in your firm, and we can assume that he knows that, via your mole."

"Can one have been a mole on one's own behalf?" asked Bigend. "I would assume that everyone is that, to whatever extent."

Garreth ignored this. "Your mole will know that you aren't much inclined to hire outside security, for the reasons you stated. Likewise your man will know this. Since your man would never have signed off on such a patently ridiculous abduction plan, we can assume that Foley was the planner. Therefore, your man was either not present during the attempt or somehow out of the loop. My guess is that he was already on his way here, likely out of a sense that Foley was cocking up. Foley possibly acted when he did in order to get at Milgrim before the boss arrived."

Hollis had never heard Garreth unpack a specific situation this way, though something in his tone now reminded her of his explanations of asymmetric warfare, a topic in which he had a keen and abiding interest. She remembered him telling her how terrorism was almost exclusively about branding, but only slightly less so about the psychology of lotteries, and how this had made her think of Bigend.

"So," Garreth said, "it's likely we're dealing with an improvisational plan on their part. Your man has opted for a prisoner exchange. Those of course are eminently gameable. Though your man knows that, certainly, and is familiar with all applicable tactics, including the one I imagine I'd be most likely to employ."

"Which is?"

"Your man Milgrim. Is he obese? Extremely tall? Memorable-looking?"

"Forgettable," said Bigend. "About ten stone."

"Good." Garreth was buttering a slice of toast. "There's a surprising amount of mutual trust necessary in any prisoner exchange. Why it's gameable."

"You're not giving them Milgrim," Hollis said.

"I need to see more to hang success on, Mr. Wilson, if you'll pardon my saying so," said Bigend, forking beans onto a quarter-slice of toast.

"God's in the details, the architects said. But you have rather a bigger problem, here. Contextually."

"You refer," Bigend said, "to Hollis's unseemly readiness to shop me to the *Guardian*?"

"Gracie," Garreth said. "I imagine he's doing this because he feels you've been fucking with him, successfully. He didn't ask you for money?"

"No."

"Doesn't your mole want money?"

"I'm sure he does," Bigend said, "but I would imagine he might be in over his head with these people. I imagine he was looking for a context in which to profitably betray me, but then they found *him*. He's likely afraid of them, and likely with good reason."

"If you were to turn Milgrim over to them," said Garreth, "and get your Bobby back intact, they'd be back. You're that wealthy. This bent officer may not yet be thinking in those terms, but your mole already is."

Bigend looked uncharacteristically pensive.

"But if you do it the way I'd do it," said Garreth, "you really will have fucked with them, in a very formal and personal way. They'll come after you."

"Then why would you suggest it?"

"Because," said Hollis, "giving them Milgrim is not an option."

"The thing is," said Garreth, "you need to simultaneously fuck with them *and* neutralize them, in some seriously ongoing way."

Bigend leaned slightly forward. "And how would you do that?"

"I'm not prepared to tell you," Garreth said, "at the moment."

"You aren't proposing violence?"

"Not in the way I imagine you mean, no."

"I don't see how you could possibly mount anything very sophisticated in such a short period of time."

"It would have to be something off the shelf."

"Off the shelf?"

But Garreth had gone back to his breakfast.

"And how long have you known Mr. Wilson, Hollis?" his tone like some Jane Austen chaperone's.

"We met in Vancouver."

"Really? You had time to socialize?"

"We met one another toward the end of my stay."

"And you know him to be someone capable, in the ways he's proposing to be capable?'

"I do," said Hollis, "although I'm under an agreement with him to say no more than that."

"People who claim capabilities of that sort are most often compulsive liars. Though the most peculiar thing about that, in my experience, is that while most bars in America have alcoholics who claim to have been Navy SEALs, there are sometimes former Navy SEALs, in those same bars, who are alcoholics."

"Garreth's not a Navy SEAL, Hubertus. I don't know what I'd say he is. He's like you, that way. A one-off. If he tells you he thinks he can get Bobby back, and neutralize this threat for you, then . . ."

"Yes?"

"Then he thinks he can."

"And what would you propose I do, then," Bigend said to Garreth, "if I were to accept your help?"

"I'd need an idea of whatever tactical resources you may have, in London, if any, that remain uncompromised. I'd need an open operational budget. I'll have to hire some specialists. Expenses."

"And how much do you want yourself, Mr. Wilson?"

"I don't," said Garreth. "Not money. If I can do this to my own satisfaction, and I imagine that that would be to yours as well, you'll let Hollis go. Release her from whatever it is she's doing for you, pay her what she feels she's owed, and agree to leave her be. And if you can't agree to that, I advise you to start looking for help elsewhere."

Bigend, eyebrows raised, looked from Garreth to Hollis. "And you're agreeable to that?"

"It's an entirely new proposition to me." She poured herself some coffee, buying time to think. "Actually," she said, "I would require an additional condition."

They both stared at her.

"The Hounds designer," she said to Bigend. "You won't have her. You'll leave her absolutely alone. Quit looking. Call everyone off, permanently."

Bigend pursed his lips.

"And," said Hollis, "you'll find Meredith's shoes. And give them to her."

A silence followed, Bigend looking at his plate, the corners of his mouth turned down. "Well," he said at last, looking up at them, "none of this would have been the least attractive before seven twenty this morning, but here we are, aren't we?"

58. DOUCHE BAGGAGE

Voytek was very angry about something, probably whatever had been the cause of him receiving his mottled, yellowish, not-quite-black eye. He seemed most angry with Shombo, the sullen young man Milgrim had seen at Biroshak & Son, though Milgrim found it hard to imagine Shombo striking anyone. He'd looked to Milgrim as though just getting out of bed would have posed an unwelcome challenge.

Milgrim would have liked to be up-front with Fiona, in the passenger seat, but she'd insisted that he sit back here with Voytek, on the floor of this tiny Subaru van, an area slightly less than the footprint of a washer and dryer, and cluttered now with large, black, cartoonishly sturdy-looking plastic cases he assumed were Voytek's. Each of these had PELICAN molded on the lid, clearly a logo rather than any indicator of contents. Voytek was wearing gray sweatpants with B.U.M. EQUIPMENT screened in very large capitals across his ass, evidence of what Milgrim took to be kitchen mishaps down the front, thick gray socks, those same gray felt clogs, and a pale blue, very old, very grimy insulated jacket with that Amstrad logo on the back, its letters cracked and peeling.

The Subaru had actual drapes, gray ones, everywhere except the windshield and the front side windows. All drawn now. Which was just as well, Milgrim supposed, as it really had a great deal of glass, as well as a moonroof that was in effect the whole top of the vehicle, through which Milgrim, looking up, saw the upper windows of buildings passing. He had no idea where they were now, no idea which direction they'd taken from Tanky & Tojo, and none where they were going. To meet Bigend again, he assumed. Like urine samples but more frequent, meeting Bigend punctuated his existence.

"I did not come to this country for the terror from paramilitary," declared Voytek, hoarsely. "I did not come to this country for *mother-fucker*. But motherfucker is *waiting. Always*. Is carceral state, surveillance state. Orwell. You have read Orwell?"

Milgrim, trying for his best neutral expression, nodded, the knees of his new whipcord trousers in front of his face. He hoped this wasn't stretching them.

"Orwell's boot in face *forever*," said Voytek, with great formal bitterness.

"Why does he want you to sweep it?" asked Fiona, as if inquiring about some routine office chore, her left hand busily working the shift lever.

"Devil's workshop," said Voytek, disgusted. "He wants mine occupied. While he fattens on the blood of the proletariat." This last phrase having for Milgrim a deep nostalgic charm, so that he was moved, unthinking, to repeat it in Russian, seeing for an instant the classroom in Columbia where he'd first heard it.

"Russian," said Voytek, narrowing his eyes, the way someone might say "syphilis."

"Sorry," said Milgrim, reflexively.

Voytek fell silent, visibly seething. They were on a straight stretch now, and when Milgrim looked up, there were no buildings. A bridge, he guessed. Slowing, turning. Into buildings, lower, more ragged. The Subaru bumped over something, up, then stopped. Fiona shut off the engine and got out. Milgrim, flicking the drapes aside, glimpsed Benny's cycle yard. Benny himself approaching. Fiona opened the rear door and grabbed one of Voytek's Pelican cases.

"Caution," said Voytek, "extreme care."

"I know," Fiona said, passing the case to Benny.

Benny leaned in, looked at Voytek. "Disagreement at the local, was it?"

Voytek glared at Milgrim. "The blood," he said. "Sucking it."

"Mental cunt," observed Benny, taking another case and walking away.

Voytek scooted across the carpeted cargo area on his B.U.M. EQUIPMENT signage and climbed out, taking the two remaining cases and walking away.

Milgrim got out, his knees stiff, and glanced around. There was nobody in sight. "Seems quieter," he said.

"Tea time," said Fiona. She looked at him. "That's from the shop."

"Yes," said Milgrim.

"It's not bad on you," she said approvingly, if surprised. "You cut most of the douche baggage."

"I do?"

"You wouldn't wear one of those little leashes on your wallet," she said. "And you wouldn't wear one of his hats."

"The douche baggage?"

"The fuckery," said Fiona, closing the van's rear door. "We need your stuff," she said, walking around and opening the side door. She handed Milgrim his bag, and a Tanky & Tojo bag containing the clothes he'd been wearing before (minus the Sonny jacket) and the restuffed Mont-Bell sausage. She pulled out the retaped sleeping foam and a black garbage bag. "These are your things from the Holiday Inn."

He followed her into the littered garage.

As they were nearing the entrance to Bigend's Vegas cube, Benny emerged. Fiona handed him the keys to the van. "Carbs on the bike are sound," she told him. "Thank Saad."

"Ta," said Benny, pocketing the keys without pausing.

Milgrim followed her in. Two of Voytek's cases were on the table, open. The other two, still closed, were on the floor. He wore a pair of large black-and-silver headphones and was assembling something that looked to Milgrim like a black unstrung squash racket.

"Leave me," said Voytek flatly, not bothering to make eye contact. "I sweep."

"Let's go," Fiona said to Milgrim, putting down the foam and the black bag containing Milgrim's things from the hotel. "He can do it faster alone." Milgrim dropped the sausage beside the foam, but kept his bag. As he left the room, Milgrim saw Voytek step forward, toward one wall, raising the racket two-handed, with a sort of ecclesiastic deliberation.

"What's he doing?" he asked Fiona, who was looking down at a motorcycle whose engine lay in pieces on the littered floor.

"Sweeping for bugs."

"Has he found them before?"

"Not here. But this place is still a secret, as far as I know. They turn up at Blue Ant weekly. Bigend has a toffee box full of them. Keeps saying he'll make me a necklace."

"Who puts them there?"

"Strategic business intelligence types, I suppose. The kind of people he generally refuses to hire."

"Are they able to learn things, doing that?"

"Once," she said, and touched the broken edge of the bike's cowling with a fingertip, in a way he envied, "he sent me across town with a Taser."

"That shocks people?"

"Yes."

"He sent you to shock someone?"

"There was a LAN cable bodged into it. I pretended to be there for a job interview. When I had the chance, I plugged it, unobserved, into the first available LAN socket. Any one would do. The Taser was in my purse. Gave it a click. Just the one."

"What happened?"

"It punched out their entire system. All of it. Erased everything. Even the parts in other buildings. Then I wiped it for prints, binned it, and left."

"That was because they'd taken something?"

She shrugged. "He called it a lobotomy."

"Clean," announced Voytek glumly, carrying out two of his cases. They weren't heavy at all, Milgrim now knew, because he'd seen that they mainly contained black foam padding. Voytek set them down and returned for the other two.

"When is he coming?" asked Milgrim.

"Not expecting him," she said. "He just wants you in a safe place."

"He's not coming?"

"We're just killing time," she said, and smiled. She wasn't someone who smiled often, but when she did, he found, it seemed as though it meant something. "I'll teach you how to work the balloons. I'm getting really good."

59. THE ART OF THE THING

After a mutual exchange of various telephone numbers, both written down and entered in phones, Bigend left.

Garreth had also insisted on establishing codes, by which either could indicate that he was speaking under duress, or that he believed the conversation was being somehow surveilled. Hollis, discovering that she was actually very hungry, took advantage of this to catch up on her breakfast. Garreth began to write in his notebook, in what was either shorthand or his impossible handwriting, she'd never been sure.

"Do you really think he'd honor that agreement, if you were able to do whatever it is you intend to do?" she asked as he capped his pen.

"Initially. I imagine he'd then manage to start to see that he'd really made a different agreement, and that any subsequent misunderstanding is ours alone. But then it would become a matter of reminding him, and at the same time reminding him exactly how his little difficulty had been tidied. Quite a lot of this, and why it needs to be very good indeed, is the need to impress Bigend with the idea that he wouldn't want anything like it to ever happen to *him*. Without ever uttering anything like a threat, mind you, for which reason I would hope that you'd put your man at the *Guardian* back in the box. If he's the one I think you mean, he makes me want to believe that global warming isn't androgenic, just to spite him."

"Where's your eccentric mentor in this?"

"He'll be in the background, if he's to be involved at all, and I'm glad of it. He was happier during the previous administration in the United States. Easier to be around."

"He was?"

"Less free-floating ambiguity then. I'll need his permission to use the material we prepared for that other exploit. But Gracie seems a perfect match for his targeting mechanism, as he has a peculiar detestation for war profiteers. Who are certainly no less abundant now than they used to be, though generally a bit less flagrant. I'll also need him to hook me up with Charlie. Sweet old boy in Birmingham. Gurkha."

"Gurkha?"

"Perfect dear. Love him to bits."

"Fuck me, it's the prodigal skydiver."

Hollis swung around at Heidi's voice, and found her there, in the gap between the screens, Ajay peering around her shoulder.

"What's this?" Heidi pushed at the mahogany frame of one of the screens, causing the whole thing to wobble alarmingly. "Planning on having it off right here?"

Garreth smiled. "Hello, Heidi."

"Heard you were well and truly fucked," said Heidi. She was wearing gray sweats, under her majorette jacket. "Look about the same, to me."

"What did Milgrim do last night?" Hollis asked. "Bigend says he hurt someone."

"Milgrim? Couldn't hurt himself, if he had to. Fucker from that car was behind us. I'd known it for blocks." She raised her hand and made a concise little dart-throwing gesture. "Rhenium. Screamed like a bitch."

"A great honor," said Ajay, from behind Heidi, his eyes wide with excitement. Heidi put her arm around him, shoved him forward.

"Ajay," said Heidi. "Fastest sparring partner I've ever had. We went over to Hackney this morning and beat the living shit out of each other."

"Hello, Ajay," said Garreth, offering his hand.

"Can't believe this, really," said Ajay, pumping Garreth's hand. "Blinding, to see you're not as badly off as we'd heard. Download all your videos. Fantastic." Hollis half expected him to ask for an autograph, his waterfall bobbing with excited delight.

"What flavor, the sparring?" asked Garreth.

"Bit of everything, really," said Ajay, modestly.

"Really," said Garreth. "We should talk. As it happens, I need someone fast, in just that way."

"Well, then," said Ajay, running his hand through his waterfall. "Well, then." Like a child who'd just been told, in July, that it was actually, now, officially, absolutely, Christmas morning.

>>>

"You aren't sorry you didn't quit before the shit hit?" Heidi asked. They were back in her room, where Hollis saw that the Breast Chaser had been partially painted, though wasn't yet under construction. There was a faint smell of aerosol enamel.

Hollis shook her head.

Ajay was pacing excitedly by the window.

"Calm the fuck down," Heidi snapped at him. "Elvis isn't leaving the building. Get used to it." Garreth had asked to be taken to Number Four, in order to make some calls and use his laptop. To get him there, in the chair, they'd had to go along a hallway, to the rear of the building, and take a service elevator that Hollis had never seen before. Utterly devoid of Tesla charm, being German, nearly silent, and highly efficient, it got them to their floor quickly, but then Hollis became confused about the route to the room. The hallways were mazelike. Garreth, however, had remembered the way exactly.

"So who are these people, supposed to be fucking with us?" asked Heidi. "The dipshit with the bandage. How scary is *that*?"

"He's a clothing designer," said Hollis.

"If they aren't all pussies," said Heidi, "who is?"

"It's the man he works for," Hollis said. "A retired Special Forces major named Gracie."

"*Gracie*? What about fucking *Mabel*? You're totally making this shit up, aren't you?"

"It's his last name. And Garreth's last name, while I remember, is now 'Wilson.' That was what he told Bigend it was at breakfast. Gracie's an arms dealer. Bigend was spying on some business of his, in South Carolina. Well, Milgrim was, on his orders. In the process of that, Oliver Sleight, who you met in Vancouver but probably don't remember, Bigend's IT security specialist, defected to Gracie—"

"But you're in love, right?" Heidi interrupted.

"Yes," said Hollis, surprising herself.

"Well," said Heidi, "I'm glad *that's* sorted. The rest of this shit's just shit, right? Ajay gonna get to violate his ASBO, or what?"

There was a rap at the door.

"Who the *fuck*?" inquired Heidi, loudly.

"Garreth, luv."

"He *likes* you," said Ajay, delighted.

"He likes you too," said Heidi, "so try to keep your fucking pants on."

She opened the door, held it as Garreth powered the scooter in, then closed, locked, and chained it.

"All good," said Garreth, to Hollis. "Old chap's signed off, he's calling the solicitor about the bank, calling Charlie." He turned the chair toward Ajay. "Know this Milgrim, then?"

"No," said Ajay.

"Are Milgrim and Ajay of a similar height?"

Heidi raised her eyebrows, considered. "Close enough."

"Build?"

"Milgrim's a fucking weed."

"Bigend guessed ten stone. But Ajay's not that broad, really," said Garreth, considering him. "Wiry. Core strength. No excess muscle-mass. Wiry can *do* weed. Done any acting, Ajay?"

"At school," said Ajay, pleased. "Islington Youth Theater."

"I haven't met Milgrim either. We'll both have to. Can you do a rupert for me, then? How does a rupert walk inspection?"

Ajay straightened, thumbs aligned with the seams of his sweatpants, assumed a supercilious expression, and strolled past Heidi, taking her in with a quick and disapproving glance.

"Good," said Garreth, nodding.

"Milgrim," said Heidi to Garreth, "is your basic pasty-faced Caucasian fuck. You couldn't find a whiter guy."

"Ah," said Garreth, "but that's the art of the thing, isn't it?"

60. RAY

Milgrim, in his stocking feet and shirtsleeves, lay on the white foam, pleasantly lost in a new and deliciously seamless experience. Above him, near the room's high ceiling, illuminated by the large Italian floor lamp with its silver umbrella, the matte-black manta ray was turning slow forward somersaults, almost silently, the only sound the soft crinkling of its helium-filled foil membrane. He wasn't watching it. Instead, he was focused on the screen of the iPhone, watching the feed from the ray's camera as it rolled. He saw himself, repeatedly, stretched on the white rectangle, and Fiona, seated at the table, working on whatever she was assembling from the contents of the cartons Benny had brought in. Then, as the ray rolled, white wall, the brilliantly illuminated ceiling, then over again. It was hypnotic, and all the more so because he was causing the roll, maintaining it, executing it each time, with the same sequence of thumb movements on the phone's horizontal screen.

It swam in air, the ray. Modeled on a creature that swam in water, it propelled itself, with a slow, eerie grace, through the air.

"It must be wonderful outside," he said.

"More fun," she said, "but we aren't allowed. Once anyone knows we have them, they're useless. And they cost a fortune, even before the modifications. When we were first shopping for drones, I said go for something like this," meaning the rectangular thing she was assembling on the table. "It's faster, more maneuverable. But he said he thought we should recapitulate the history of flight, start with balloons."

"There weren't balloons with wings, were there?" Maintaining concentration on his thumb work.

"No, but people did imagine them. And this thing can only stay up for a while. Batteries."

"It doesn't look like a helicopter. It looks like a coffee table for dolls."

"Eight props, that's serious lift. And they're protected. It can bump into something and not be instant rubbish. Give ray a rest and look at this."

"How do I stop?" asked Milgrim, suddenly anxious.

"Just stop. The app will right it."

Milgrim held his breath, took his thumbs from the screen. Looked up. The ray rolled up, executed an odd little wing-tip flutter, then hung suspended, rocking slightly, its dorsal surface to the ceiling.

Milgrim got up and went to the table. Nothing had ever been quite as pleasant as this afternoon with Fiona, in Bigend's Vegas cube, though he kept surprising himself with the recognition of just how pleasant it was. There was nothing to do but play with Bigend's expensive German toys, and talk, while the toys, and learning how they worked, provided a perfect topic for conversation. Fiona was working, technically, because she had to assemble the new drone from the parts in the two cartons, but she seemed to enjoy that. It involved a set of small screwdrivers mainly, color-coded hex wrenches, and videos on a website on his Air, via the red dongle. A company in Michigan, two brothers, twins, with matching eyeglasses and chambray shirts.

It didn't look like a helicopter, though it did have those eight rotors. It was built of black foam, with a bumper of some other black material around its edge, and two rows of four holes, in which the rotors were installed. It stood on four slanted wire legs now, about six inches above the table. Its four batteries, currently charging at a wall socket, slotted into each of the corners, equalizing weight. It had a slender, streamlined black plastic fuselage underneath, housing the camera and electronics.

"No testing this indoors," she said, putting down the screwdriver. "It's together, though. I'm exhausted. Up all night. Feel like a nap?"

"A nap?"

"On your foam. It's wide enough. You sleep last night?"

"Not really."

"Let's have a nap."

Milgrim looked from one blank white wall to the next, then up at the black ray and the silver penguin. "Okay," he said.

"Turn off your laptop." She stood up while Milgrim shut the Air down. She walked over to the umbrella light and dialed it down low. "I can't sleep with these pants on," she said. "There's Kevlar."

"Right," said Milgrim.

There was a ripping of Velcro, and then the sound of a zip. A big one, by the sound of it. Something, maybe Kevlar, rustled to the floor. She stepped out of the armored pants, already barefoot, and went to the white foam, which seemed to glow faintly. "Come on," she said, "I can barely keep my eyes open."

"Okay," said Milgrim.

"You can't sleep in Tanky & Tojo," she said.

"Right," Milgrim said, and began to remove his shirt, which had far too many buttons on each sleeve. When he'd gotten it off, he hung it on the back of the chair, over his new jacket, and took off his pants.

He could see her, dimly, pulling the MontBell out of its bag. He felt like screaming, or singing, something. He walked toward the foam, then realized he was wearing his black socks from Galeries Lafayette. That seemed wrong. He stopped and removed them, almost falling over.

"Get under," Fiona said, having spread the open bag as wide as it would go. "Good thing I never use a pillow."

"Me neither," lied Milgrim, sitting down, tucking his socks quickly under the edge of the foam. He swung his legs under the Mont-Bell and lay down, very straight, beside her.

"You and that Heidi," said Fiona, "you're not a number, are you?"

"*Me*?" he said. "No!" Then lay there, eyes wide, awaiting her response, until he heard her softly snoring.

61. FACIAL RECOGNITION

They'd had a shower with H. G. Wells and Frank, Garreth's bandaged leg, tucked through something that looked like an inhumanly capacious and open-ended condom. Toweling him off, she'd seen a bit more of Frank, "Frankenstein." Much evidence of heroic surgery, so-called. As many stitches as a patchwork quilt, and indeed she suspected literally patchwork, the back of his other calf tidily scarred where they'd taken skin to graft. And within Frank, if Garreth wasn't simply taking the piss, a good bit of newfangled rattan bone. Frank's musculature was considerably reduced, though Garreth had hopes for that. Hopes generally, she'd been glad to see, and hard sensitive hands sliding all over her.

Now he lay on the Piblokto Madness bed, in Cabinet's not-velour robe, Frank encased in a slippery-looking, black, Velcro-fastened wrapper through which a machine the size and nostalgic shape of a portable typewriter case pumped extremely cold water, very quickly. Heidi had used something similar, on their final tour, to help with the wrist and hand pain drumming had started to cause her. Garreth's had arrived an hour before, by courier, a gift from the old man.

He was talking with the old man now; very much, she thought, as to a wife in a long marriage. They could convey a great deal in a very few words, and had their own slang, in-group jokes of seemingly infinite depth, a species of twin-talk. He wore a headset, cabled to his no-name black laptop, on the embroidered velour beside him, their conversation being conducted, she assumed, through one or another of the darknets they frequented. These were, she gathered, private internets, unlicensed and unpoliced, and Garreth had once remarked that, as with dark matter and the universe, the darknets were probably the bulk of the thing, were there any way to accurately measure them.

She didn't listen. Stayed in the warm, steamy bathroom, drying her hair.

When she came out, he was staring up at the round bottom of the birdcage.

"Are you still talking?"

"No." He removed the headset.

"Are you all right?"

"He's done. Folded."

"What do you mean?" She went to him.

"He had something he'd never told me about. Grailware. He's giving it to me. For this. Means it's over. Done."

"What's over?"

"The business. His mad career. If it weren't, he'd not have given me this."

"Can you tell me what it is?"

"Invisibility. A sigil."

"A sigil?"

"The sigil of forgetting."

"That thing's chilling the blood in your brain."

He smiled, though she could see the loss in him, the pain of it. "It's a very great gift. Your man will be bricking it, if he knows we have it and he doesn't."

Which meant Bigend, she knew, and shit-scared. "Then he'll want it for himself, whatever it is."

"Exactly," he said, "why he mustn't know. I'll convince him that Pep's stayed off the cameras with tradecraft."

"Pep?"

"Mad little Catalan. Perfect master car thief." He looked at his watch, its black dial austere. The men who guard the Queen, he'd once told her, were not allowed to wear shoes with rubber soles, or watches with black faces. Why? she'd asked. Juju, he'd said. "He'll be in from Frankfurt in twenty minutes."

"How are you assembling all this so quickly, yet finding the time to soap my back and whatnot? Not to complain."

"The old boy," he said. "Can't keep him from it. He's doing it. It's modular. We got that good at it. We have our bits of business, our set pieces, our people. We got really fast. Had to, as the best ones present themselves abruptly. Or did."

"Can you really be invisible? Or is it more bullshit, like your rattan bones?"

"You'll hurt Frank's feelings. Think of it as a spell of forgetting. Or not remembering in the first place. The system sees you, but immediately forgets."

"What system?"

"You've seen a few cameras in this town? Noticed them, have you?"

"You can make them forget you?"

He propped himself on his elbow, instinctively rubbed the slick, cold surface of the thing around his leg, then quickly wiped his palm on the embroidered coverlet. "The holy grail of the surveillance industry is facial recognition. Of course, they say it's not. It's already here, to a degree. Not operational. Larval. Can't read you if you're black, say, and might mistake you for me, but the hardware and software have potentials, awaiting later upgrade. Though what you need to understand, to understand forgetting, is that nobody's actually eyeballing much of what a given camera sees. They're digital, after all. Stored data sits there, stored. Not images, then, just ones and zeros. Something happens that requires official scrutiny, the ones and zeros are converted to images. But"—and he reached up to touch the edge of the bottom of the birdcage library—"say there's been a gentlemen's agreement."

"What gentlemen?"

"Your usual suspects. The industry, the government, that lucrative sector the old boy's so keen on, that might be either, or both."

"And the agreement?"

"Say you needed the SBS to rendition a dozen possible jihadis out of the basement of a mosque. Or trade unionists, should they happen to be down there, promiscuous as they are. Just say."

"Say," said Hollis.

"And didn't want it seen, ever. And shutting the cameras down wouldn't be an option, of course, as you might well pay for that, later, on BBC. So say your Special Boats boys bear the sigil of forgetting—"

"Which is?"

"Facial recognition, after all, isn't it?"

"I don't get it."

"You'll see it, soon enough. It's on its way over, courier. His last gift."

"Did he say that?"

"No," he said, sadly, "but we both knew."

62. WAKING

Milgrim woke with a leg over both of his, bent sharply at the knee, Fiona's inner thigh and calf across the front of both his thighs. She'd turned on her side, facing him, and was no longer snoring, though he could feel, he discovered, her breath on his shoulder. She was still asleep.

How long, he wondered, if he remained perfectly still, might she remain in this extraordinary position? He only knew that he was prepared to find out.

A spidery, simultaneously sinuous and scratchy guitar chord filled the high-ceilinged twilight of Bigend's Vegas cube, afloat on rainlike finger-drums. Milgrim winced. It died away. Came again.

Fiona moaned, threw her arm across his chest, snuggled closer. The chord returned, like surf, relentless. "Bugger," said Fiona, but didn't move until the scratching, writhing chord returned again. She rolled away from Milgrim, reaching for something. "Hullo?"

Milgrim imagined that the foam was a raft. Made the walls recede, horizon-deep. But it was a raft on which Fiona was taking calls.

"Wilson? Okay. Yes? Understood. Put him on." She sat cross-legged now, at the very edge of the slab. "Hullo. Yes." Silence. "I'd need to dress for it, the chartreuse vest, reflective stripes." Silence. "Kawasaki. GT550. Bit tatty for the job, but if the box is new, should do. Benny can bolt anything on. Have the manufacturer's URL? I could measure it for you, otherwise. I've already put it together. Haven't tested it." A longer silence. "Organ transplants, plasma? Autopsy bits?" Silence. "Send over enough of that precut foam from a camera shop, the throw-away-the-bits kind. I doubt vibration would do it much good at all, but Benny and I can sort that. Yes. I will. Thank you. Could you put Hubertus back on, please? Thanks." She cleared her throat. "Well," she said, "we do seem very busy, suddenly. Benny can bodge your box on, but I'll need new dampers. This drone won't travel as nicely, I don't think. Different sort of moving parts. Yes. He did. He was very clear. Bye, then."

"Hubertus?"

"And someone called Wilson. Something's up."

"What?"

"Wilson wants my bike outfitted like a medical courier, professional-looking box over the pillion, extra reflectors, safety gear. Our new drone goes in there."

"Who's Wilson?"

"No idea. Hubertus says do what he says, to the letter. When Hubertus delegates, he delegates." He felt her shrug. "Good kip, though." She yawned, stretched. "You?"

"Yes," said Milgrim, keeping it at that.

She stood, went to where she'd left her armored pants. He heard her pull them on. The zip going up. He restrained a sigh. "Coffee," she said. "I'll have Benny get some in. White?"

"White," said Milgrim, "sugar." He groped under the foam for his socks. "What was that music, on your phone?"

"I've forgotten his name. Brilliant. Saharan." She was pulling on her boots. "He heard Jimi and James Brown on the shortwave, when he was little. Carved extra frets into a guitar." She went out without turning the Italian umbrella back up. Grayish sunlight. Then she closed the door behind her.

63. CURLY STAYS, SLOW FOOD

With Garreth and Pep, the Catalan car thief, deep in electric hub motors for bicycles, she'd been glad of Inchmale's call. She barely knew what hub motors were, but Pep wanted two, for extra speed, while Garreth insisted that two were too many. If one of them were to go out, Garreth argued, the extra weight, plus the generator drag, would negate the advantage of the first one. But if there was only one, and it failed, Pep could pedal as best he could, while not expending energy on the extra weight. The clarity with which she retained this, while having no knowledge of what any of it was really about, surprised her.

Pep looked as though someone had made an apple doll out of Gérard Depardieu, soaking the apple in salted lemon juice and baking it, then leaving it in a cool, dark place to harden, hoping it wouldn't mold. He'd avoided molding, by the look of him, but had gotten much smaller. Impossible to judge his age. From certain angles, the world's most weathered teenager; from others, shockingly old. There was a dragon tattooed on the back of his right hand, bat-winged and suggestively phallic, that looked less like a tattoo than a medieval woodcut. His fingernails, which were almost perfectly square, were freshly manicured, polished to a high sheen. Garreth seemed glad to see him, but he made her uncomfortable.

Inchmale had phoned from the sitting room, where she could hear, in the background, the early phases of the evening's drinking. "Are you pregnant?" he'd asked.

"Are you mad?"

"The doorman referred to you as 'they.' I noted the sudden plurality."

"I'll be down. In the singular."

She'd left Garreth chiding Pep for having ordered something, called a Hetchins frame, for a bike that might have to be tossed in the Thames after a few hours' use. Pep's position, as she was closing the door behind her, was that it might not have to be tossed at all, and that "curly stays" were in any case a lovely thing. She saw Pep look at his fingernails, that gesture she associated with manicured men.

She found Heidi and Inchmale established beneath the narwhale tusks. Inchmale was pouring tea from one of the vintage Bunnykins services that were a Cabinet trademark.

"Good evening," he said. "We're discussing the recent shit, a variety of possible fans, your place in same, plus the possibility of your having found a viable and ongoing relationship."

"What would one of those constitute, for me, in your opinion?" she asked, taking a seat.

"Having someone to have one with, to begin with," said Inchmale, putting down the teapot. "But you know I thought he was a good chap before."

"That was what you said about Phil Spector."

"Allowance for age," said Inchmale, "misfortune. Genius. Lemon?" He proffered a wedge of cut lemon in an ornate silver squeezer.

"No lemon. What are 'curly stays'?"

"Corsetry."

"I just heard a Catalan car thief use the phrase."

"Did he speak English? Perhaps he was trying to describe a permanent wave."

"No. Part of a bicycle."

"My money's on corsetry. Do you know that Heidi's stuck a man with a Rhenish dart?"

"Rhenium," corrected Heidi.

"Rhennish is the hock, yes, and I might well ask for some, shortly. But you," he said to Hollis, "you appear to have signed on to a firm in transition."

"And on whose recommendation?"

"Am I prescient? Have you known me to be prescient?" He tried his tea. Returned his cup to the saucer. Added a second lump. "Angelina tells me that the London PR community are behaving like dogs before an earthquake, and somehow everyone knows, without knowing how, that it's about Bigend."

"There's something going on in Blue Ant," Hollis said carefully, "but I couldn't tell you exactly what. I mean, I don't *know* exactly what. But Hubertus doesn't seem to be taking it that seriously."

"Whatever that was in the City last night, he doesn't take *that* that seriously?"

"I don't think that's the same thing, exactly. But I can't talk about it."

"Of course not. That oath you swore, when you joined the agency. The ritual with Geronimo's skull. But the tonality Angelina's picking up isn't that he's in trouble, or that Blue Ant is trouble. It's that he's about to become exponentially *bigger*. PR people *know* these things."

"Bigger?"

"Whole orders of magnitude. Things are shifting, in anticipation. Things are getting ready to jump on the Bigend boat."

"Things?"

"The ones that go bump, darling. Like tectonic plates, colliding, in this city of ancient night." He sighed. Tried his tea again. Smiled.

"How's with the Bollards?"

His smile vanished. "I'm thinking of taking them to Tucson."

"Whew," said Heidi, "*lateral* fucking move."

"I'm entirely serious," said Inchmale, and sipped his tea.

"We know," said Hollis. "Have you told them?"

"I've told George. He took it remarkably well. The novelty of working with exceptional intelligence. Clammy, of course, is pissy."

"Then change his name," said Heidi, squeezing a lemon wedge above her tea with the filigreed instrument Inchmale had used before.

"What happened after you left with Milgrim last night?" Hollis asked her.

"They followed us. Probably picked up by the other car, the one that faked us into the alley. Figured out which way we were heading, got ahead of us, dropped the guy with the bandaged head, and another one. They waited for us, got behind us, followed us. Clueless. I stopped and bought some clothes, pretended we were changing our look."

"There was something open?"

"*Street* clothes. For their benefit. Then we headed for the subway. When I saw that they didn't intend for us to get on the subway . . ." She shrugged.

"Heidi—"

"In the *head*," said Heidi, tapping the roots of her bangs with a forefinger, in an inadvertent little salute. "It's *bone*. His head was probably sore already . . ."

"Milgrim's in trouble for that. They're blaming him, apparently."

"Your boyfriend's hired Ajay. What's that about?"

"Milgrim. It's complicated."

"It's got Ajay over the moon. Gave notice at his bouncing job."

"Bouncing?"

"Security at some pervy club." She looked around at the evening crowd. "Now he's gone all Secret Squirrel on me. So have you."

"Come to Tucson with us," said Inchmale to Hollis, suddenly appearing, in his way, from behind what she thought of as his exterior asshole. "Get some sun. Mexican food. You can help in the studio. George likes you. Clammy, amazingly, doesn't hate you. I don't like the weather around Bigend now. It's all on the label. You can have associate producer credit. Let Bigend reach whatever critical mass he's headed for. Be elsewhere. You can bring your boyfriend, of course."

"I can't," said Hollis, reaching across the hassock and the tray with the Bunnykins service, to give his bony knee a squeeze, "but thanks."

"Why not?"

"Garreth's trying to straighten out the trouble with Milgrim for Bigend. They have an agreement, and it involves me. I'm with Garreth now. It'll be okay."

"As a middle-aged human of reasonably sound faculties," said Inchmale, "I must inform you that it may well *not* be 'okay.'"

"I know that, Reg."

Inchmale sighed. "Come and stay with us in Hampstead."

"You're going to Tucson."

"I'm the decider," said Inchmale. "Haven't decided when to go yet. And there's the business of convincing Clammy and the others."

"Is Meredith around?"

"Yes," said Inchmale, as if not entirely pleased by the fact. "She distracts George, and is entirely concerned with her own agenda."

"I'd hate to run into anyone like *that*," said Heidi, looking at Inchmale. "I don't think I could handle it."

Hollis's iPhone rang, in the left pocket of her Hounds jacket. "Hello?"

"Are you in the bar?" Garreth asked.

"Yes. What are 'curly stays'?"

"What?"

"'Curly stays.' Pep said."

"Forks. Front and rear. On a Hetchins frame, they're recurved."

"Okay."

"Can you go out front for me and watch for a van? It says 'Slow Foods' on the side."

"'Slow Foods'?"

"Yes. Just have a look at it for me."

"For what?"

"If you think it looks right."

"What's right?"

"If it's reasonable-looking. Whether or not you'd notice it, remember it."

"I think I might remember what it says."

"I don't mind that, actually," said Garreth. "It's the plain white ones people imagine are watching them."

64. THREAT MANAGEMENT

The toilet in Bigend's cube was like the coach toilet on a plane, but nicer: Scandinavian stainless, tiny round corner sink to match, bead-blasted faucet-handles. The plumbing under the sink reminded Milgrim of aquarium tubing.

He was brushing his teeth, after shaving. Fiona was with Benny, supervising the mounting of something on her bike. Periodically, above the buzz of his toothbrush, he could hear, from the garage, the brief but enthusiastic whoop of what he assumed was a hydraulic driver of some kind.

Something was happening. He didn't know what, and didn't want to ask Fiona, else he destabilize whatever it was that had allowed her thigh and calf to find themselves across his thighs. And not be, he checked his memory again, immediately withdrawn, upon her waking. And she hadn't volunteered anything, other than that Bigend had delegated something to someone named Wilson, whose orders she now followed. She seemed quietly excited, though, and not unhappy to be. Focused.

There weren't enough towels in Bigend's toilet, though what there were were Swiss, and white, and very nice, and had probably never been used before. He finished brushing, rinsed, washed toothpaste from his mouth with cold water, and dried his face. The hydraulic driver whooped three times in rapid succession, as though recognizing one of its kind across a clearing.

He opened the bifold door, stepped out, closed it behind him. You could barely see where it was, at the edge of its white wall.

He put his toothbrush and shaving things away in his bag. Fiona had collected everything when she'd checked him out of the Holiday Inn. He tried to tidy the cube, straightening chairs around the table, spreading the sleeping bag on the foam in case Fiona felt like another nap, but it didn't seem to help. The cube wasn't very large, and now there were too many things in it. The weird-looking rectangular helicopter-drone on the table, his Air, the cartons and elaborate packing she'd removed the various segments of the drone from, his bag, her armored jacket and his tweed from Tanky & Tojo on the backs of chairs. The way this kind of space suddenly looked so much less special if you had to live in it, even for a few hours.

His eye went back to the Air. He sat down, logged on to Twitter. There was a message from Winnie: "Got my leave call me."

"No phone," he typed, then wondered how to describe where he was, what he was doing, "I think B has me on ice. Something's happening." It looked stupid, but he sent it anyway.

Refreshed twice. Then: "Get phone."

"Okay." Sent. Or tweeted, whatever it was. Still, he was glad she had leave. Was still here. He scratched his chest, stood up, put his shirt on, buttoned the front and a few of the cuff buttons on either sleeve, left it untucked, put on his new shoes. His old ones were more comfortable, but they wouldn't go with whipcord. He went to the door, tried it. Not locked. He hadn't thought it was. The driver whooped, twice.

He opened the door, stepped out, amazed to find the day gone. The filthiness of Benny's garage, under bright fluorescent light, instantly made the cube seem surgically clean. Fiona and Benny were looking at Fiona's bike, which now had a shiny white box with slightly inward-slanting sides fastened where Milgrim had sat, behind her. It looked solid, expensive, but sort of like a beer cooler. There was something on the side, in black, neatly lettered.

"Red crosses?" Fiona asked Benny.

Benny had a yellow power wrench in his hand, a red rubber hose trailing away from it. "Punters would be flagging you down for first aid. This is bog standard for hauling fresh eyeballs. Copied from one that does just that, by the look of it."

"The name and numbers?"

"You see it as received. Truck was from a prop house, Soho." He removed the cigarette tucked behind his ear, lit it. "Film and telly. That's the plan, then? You're doing telly?"

"Pornos," said Fiona. "Saad'll like that."

"Won't he just," said Benny.

Fiona, noticing Milgrim, turned. "Hullo."

"May I borrow your phone? Have to call someone."

She fished in her slouchy armored pants, came up with an iPhone, not the one Milgrim had used with the Festo ray, and passed it to him. "Hungry? We can have doner sent in."

"Dinner?"

"Doner. Kebab."

"Ready for a curry, myself," said Benny, studying the lit tip of his cigarette intently, as though it might suddenly offer curry reviews.

"I'll just make this call—" He froze.

"Yes?"

"Is this . . . a Blue Ant phone?"

"No," said Fiona. "Brand-new. So's Benny's. We've all been freshly resupplied, and the old ones taken away."

"Thanks," said Milgrim, and went back into the Vegas cube. He found Winnie's card, on which he'd added the dialing prefixes, and dialed.

She answered on the second ring. "Yes?"

"It's me," said Milgrim.

"Where are you?"

"Suth-uk. Over the river."

"Doing?"

"We had a nap."

"Did you have story time first?"

"No."

"You think something's happening? You tweeted."

The verb sounded off, the more particularly because he knew it wasn't part of a nursery theme. "Something is. I don't know what. He's hired someone called Wilson, and delegated." He was glad he'd remembered the word.

"Threat management," she said. "He's outsourcing. Shows he's taking it seriously. Have you met Wilson?"

"No."

"What's Wilson telling them to do?"

"They put a box on the back of Fiona's bike. The kind they haul eyeballs in."

There was a perfect digital silence, then: "Who's Fiona?"

"She drives. For Bigend. Motorcycles."

"Okay," said Winnie. "We'll just start again. Tasking."

"Tasking?"

"I want you to meet Wilson. I want to know about Wilson. Most importantly, the name of the firm he's working for."

"Isn't he working for Bigend?"

"He works for one of the security firms. Bigend is the client. Don't ask him. Just find out. Sneaky-ass, though. You can *do* sneaky-ass. Instinct tells me. Whose phone are you using?"

"Fiona's."

"I just e-mailed the number to someone, and they're telling me the GPS is very amusing. Unless you've taken up marathon randomized teleportation."

"It's new. She just got it from Bigend."

"That might be Wilson, the threat management consultant. Earning his keep, if that's the case. Okay. You're tasked. Go for it. Call, tweet." She was gone.

The room filled with that weird chicken-scratch sub-Hendrix chord. He rushed out the door, tripped on part of an engine, and nearly fell, but managed to thrust the phone into Fiona's hand. As he did so, he wondered whether or not it might be Winnie.

"Hullo? Yes. It's on. Very convincing. Having my dampers replaced next. They're a bit rough. You would? Certainly. I'll borrow a bike. Fast? My pleasure." She smiled. "What he was wearing yesterday?" She looked at Milgrim. "I'll tell him." She put the phone in her pants pocket.

Milgrim raised his eyebrows.

"Wilson," Fiona said. "You're required soonest, over the river. Wants to meet you. And you're to bring what you were wearing yesterday."

"Why?"

"Thinks kit from Tanky & Tojo doesn't suit you."

Milgrim winced.

"Taking the piss," she said, bumping his arm with her fist. "You're very smart. I'm borrowing a fast bike for the job while Saad does my dampers. Benny's."

"Feck," said Benny softly, a small sound but filled with resignation, as to immemorial hardship. "Don't bugger it again, can you?"

65. LEOPARD SKIN
IN MINIATURE

She stood on Cabinet's steps, looking at unexpected lights, beyond trees, in the privacy of Portman Square, Robert hovering watchfully behind her, after the tall Slow Foods van pulled away, driven by a young blonde with a cap worryingly like Foley's.

Sounds of tennis. There was a court in there. Someone had decided to play a night game. She thought the court would be too wet.

When she went back in, Inchmale and Heidi were in the lobby, Inchmale strapping himself into his Japanese Gore-Tex. "We're going to the studio to listen to some mixes. Come with us."

"Thanks, but I'm needed."

"Either offer stands, Tucson or Hampstead. You could stay with Angelina."

"I appreciate it, Reg. I do."

"Quietly stubborn," he said, then looked at Heidi. "Beats violently obstreperous." Back to her. "Consistent, anyway. Keep in touch."

"I will." She headed for the elevator. For the ferret, in its vitrine. Silently offering prayer: that Garreth's scheme, whatever it was, be as ferrety as it needed to be, or that whatever had happened to this particular ferret, to earn it its timeless somnambulistic residence here, not happen to Garreth, to Milgrim, or to anyone else she cared for.

Its teeth looked bigger, though she knew that couldn't be possible. She pressed the button, heard distant clanks from above, sounds from the Tesla machinery.

She hadn't been aware of caring for Milgrim, really, until it became apparent that Bigend would so easily feed him to Foley and company, if that meant getting Bobby Chombo back. And it wouldn't be Chombo Bigend needed, she knew, but something Chombo knew, or knew how to do. That was what bothered her, that and the fact of Milgrim having been reborn, or perhaps born, on a whim of Bigend's, simply to see whether or not it was possible. To do that, and then to trade the resulting person, possibly to trade his life, for something you wanted, no matter how badly, was wrong.

When the lift arrived, she hauled the gate aside, opened the door, stepped in. Ascended.

On her way through the corridors to Number Four, she noticed that one of the landscapes now contained *two* follies, identical, one further back, on a distant hillside. Surely it had always been there, the second folly, unnoticed. She'd give it no further thought, she decided firmly.

She knocked, in case Garreth and Pep were still deep into stays. "It's me."

"Come in," he called.

He was propped up in the Piblokto Madness bed, the black bandage of the cold-pumping machine around his leg again, the black laptop open on his stomach, headset on.

"Busy?"

"No. Just got off a call with Big End." He looked tired.

"How was that?"

"He's had the call. Gracie. They wanted Milgrim tonight."

"You aren't ready, are you?"

"No, but I knew I wouldn't be. I'd rehearsed it with him. Milgrim's done a runner, he told them, but it's fortunately now been sorted. Going to collect him. Careful not to say where, exactly, but still in the U.K. In case Gracie has a way of checking U.S. passport movement. I think it went well, but your Big End . . ." He shook his head.

"What?"

"There's something he wants. Needs. But that's not it, exactly . . . It feels to me like he's been winning, forever, and now, suddenly, there's a chance he might lose, really lose. If he can't get Chombo back, in working condition. And that makes Big End really very dangerous." He looked at her.

"What do you think he might do?"

"Anything. Literally. To get Chombo back. I've never done this before."

"Done what?"

"Exploit on behalf of a client. Concerned I've drawn the client from hell."

She sat on the edge of the bed, put her hand on the leg that was like they both had been, before Dubai.

"The old man says he's got a very peculiar smell about him now, Big End. Says it's different, recently, stronger. Can't get a handle on it."

"Reg says the same. He's been hearing it from his wife, who's in public relations here. Says it's like dogs before an earthquake. They don't know what it is, but it's him, somehow. But I'm worried about you. You look exhausted." He did, now. The lines deeper in his cheeks. "Those five neurosurgeons didn't expect you to be doing this, did they?"

He pointed at the sweating black wrap. "Frank's chilling. You should too."

"I'd say I wish I hadn't called you, but it would be a lie. But I'm worried about you. Not just Frank." She touched his face. "Sorry I left like that."

He kissed her hand. Smiled. "I was glad you did. Didn't like the way Pep was looking at you."

"Neither did I. Didn't like Pep."

"Did me a good one in the Barrio Gótico once, Pep. Saved my bacon. Didn't have to."

"Pep is good, then."

"I wouldn't go that far. But if it has wheels and locked doors, he can open it faster than the owner ever did, and close and lock it as quickly. How's my grocery van?"

"Upscale vegan. Shiny new."

"Rental through a specialist agency in Shepperton, vehicles for film and television. Slow Foods haven't taken delivery yet. Happy to let it for an art shoot, for a very handsome hourly fee."

There was something on the bedside table. Part of the fuselage of a model plane: curved, streamlined, its upper surface yellow, dotted with brown. She bent for a closer look, saw a miniature leopard print, on plastic.

"Don't touch. Stings."

"What is it?"

"Taser."

"A *Taser*?"

"Heidi's. Brought it from Los Angeles by accident, in her bag of Airfix parts. Swept it blindly up with her model-building bumf, when she was well pissed."

"TSA didn't notice it?"

"I hate to break this to you," he said, feigning grave seriousness, "but that's actually been known to happen. TSA not noticing the odd thing. *Shocking*, I know . . ."

"But where would she even get it?"

"America? But contrary to the saying, what happens in Vegas evidently doesn't always stay there. Someone in Las Vegas gave this to her husband. As a present for her, actually. Hence the leopard print. Lady's model, you see. TSA didn't spot it, Her Majesty's Customs didn't, but Ajay certainly did, this morning. She had no idea she had it. Packed it by mistake when drunk. Which is no defense, but has been known to get the odd thing handily across a border, now and again."

"What do you want with it?"

"Not sure yet. 'Follow the accident. Fear the set plan.'"

"I thought you loved plans."

"Love planning. That's different. But the right bit of improv makes the piece."

"It shocks people?"

"Capacitor inside, enough juice to knock you on your handsome. Two barbed darts, from that, on fifteen feet of fine insulated cable. Propelled by captive gas."

"Horrible."

"Prefer it to being shot, any evening at all. Not that it's nice." He leaned over, picked the thing up, sat back against the pillows. Held it up between thumb and forefinger.

"Put it down. I don't like it. I think you need to sleep."

"Milgrim's on his way. And a makeup artist hairdresser person. We're getting together with Ajay. Makeover party."

"Makeover?"

"Whiteface." He flew the Taser behind the screen of his laptop. Up again. Pause at apogee. "We don't want to leave Milgrim in Big End's hands, once this starts." He looked at her. "We want him with us, regardless of what Big End wants. I'll need something for him to do, some excuse for keeping him with us."

"Why?"

"If my scheme should fuck up, as you say in your country, and that's always a possibility, your man will very badly want to pass Milgrim to Gracie, posthaste. Very badly. Excuses for our behavior. Impossibility of getting decent help these days. But here's Milgrim, so we'll take Chombo, thank you, and sorry again for the trouble. Or if Gracie should fuck up, for that matter . . ." The Taser swept down slowly, over the keyboard, in a silent strafing run.

"Fuck up how?"

"My little op's bodged together with off-the-shelf parts. Basically I've had to build it as though Gracie's going to play nice, do the prisoner exchange, then take Milgrim off for a nice waterboarding or toe-subtraction—"

"Don't say that!"

"Sorry. But that would be playing by the rules as far as Big End is concerned. We know that nobody's getting Milgrim, but Gracie doesn't, yet. If things go according to my play, Gracie and company will have sufficient weight on them to not bother anyone. But if Gracie should decide not to play by the rules, I haven't much in the way of extra fun to throw at him." He held the Taser up again, squinted. "Wish she'd brought a few more, actually."

66. ZIP

Benny's civilian bike, Milgrim now knew, was a 2006 Yamaha FZR1000, black and red. It was lowered, Fiona said, whatever that meant, and had something called a Spondon swing arm, allowing the wheelbase to be lengthened at the drag strip. "Quick off a light," she said approvingly.

She was fully armored again, zipped and Velcro'd, the yellow helmet under her arm. Milgrim was armored too, in borrowed nylon and Kevlar, stiff and unfamiliar, over tweed and whipcord. The toes of Jun's bright brown brogues looked wrong, below the black Cordura overpants. His bag, containing his laptop and the clothing he'd worn the night before, was strapped atop the Yahama's tank, which looked as though it had been gathered to spring from between a rider's thighs. A striking image, now, with those thighs about to be Fiona's.

"Voytek is here, to fuck penguin."

They turned, at the sound of his voice. He was walking toward them through the deserted bike yard. He carried a black Pelican case in either hand, and these, Milgrim saw, unlike his screening cases, looked heavy.

"'With,'" corrected Fiona, "'fuck with.'"

"'I the pity poor immigrant.' You do not. Is Bob Dylan."

"Why are you bothering, then?" demanded Fiona. "The one in Paris was fine, and we've just gotten this one on the iPhone."

"Order of Wilson. Commissar of all fuckings with."

He brushed past them, into the Vegas cube, closing the door behind him.

"Is there another helmet?" asked Milgrim, eyeing Mrs. Benny's black one, which sat on the Yamaha's pillion seat.

"Sorry," said Fiona, "no. And I'll have to adjust the chinstrap. Had a safety lecture."

"You did?"

"Wilson." She put the black helmet on Milgrim's head, adroitly adjusted and fastened his chinstrap. The hairspray seemed even stronger now, as if Mrs. Benny had been wearing it in the meantime. He wondered if he was developing an allergy.

Fiona pulled on gauntlets, straddled the shiny Yamaha. Milgrim got on behind her. The engine came to life. She walked them off Benny's yard, and then the bike seemed to take over, a very different creature than Fiona's big gray one. A tight but intricate circuit of Southwark streets, feeling, Milgrim assumed, for possible followers, and then over Blackfriars in a surge, working the gears, the red and white railings strobing past. He immediately lost track of direction, once they were on the other side, and when she finally stopped and parked, he hadn't expected it.

He fumbled with the fastenings under his chin, got Mrs. Benny's helmet off as quickly as possible. Looking up at this unfamiliar building. "Where are we?"

She removed the yellow helmet. "Cabinet. The rear."

They were in a cobble-paved garden drive, behind a stone wall. She dismounted, Milgrim intrigued as always by the smooth flexibility this demonstrated. He got off as well, with no particular demonstration of grace, and watched as she hauled thick, snakelike anchor chains from the Yahama's panniers, to secure it.

He followed her up the tidy cobbles to a porte cochere. Pinstripes was waiting, behind a very modern glass door. He admitted them without Fiona having to buzz.

"This way, please," he said, and led them to a brushed stainless elevator door. Milgrim found that the armored oversuit made him feel strangely solid, larger. In the elevator, he felt he took up more space. Stood up straighter, holding Mrs. Benny's helmet in front of him with a certain formality.

"Follow me, please." Pinstripes leading them through one self-closing, very heavy door after another. Dark green walls, brief corridors, gloomy watercolor landscapes in ornate gilt frames. Until they reached one particular door, painted a darker green even than the walls, nearly black. A large, italic brass numeral 4, secured with two brass slot-head screws. Pinstripes used a brass knocker on the door frame: a woman's hand, holding an oblate spheroid of brass. A single respectful tap.

"Yes?" Hollis's voice.

"Robert, Miss Henry. They're here."

Milgrim heard a chain rattle. Hollis opened the door. "Hello, Milgrim, Fiona. Come in. Thank you, Robert."

"You're welcome, Miss Henry. Good night."

They stepped in, Fiona's ungauntleted hand brushing his.

Milgrim blinked. Hollis was chaining the door behind them. He'd never seen a hotel room like this, and Hollis wasn't alone in it. There was a man on the bed (the very strange bed) with short but unkempt dark hair, and he was looking at Milgrim with a seriousness, a sort of quiet focus, that almost triggered the cop-sensing mechanisms Winnie had last touched off in Seven Dials. Almost.

"You're Milgrim, then. Been hearing a lot about you. I'm Garreth. Wilson. Forgive my not getting up. Leg's buggered. Keeping it elevated." He was propped against pillows and the wall, between what Milgrim at first took to be the tusks of a mammoth, twin weathered gray church-window parentheses. An open laptop beside him. One of his black-trousered legs up on three additional pillows. Above him, suspended, the largest birdcage Milgrim had ever seen, filled, it seemed, with stacked books and fairy floodlights.

"This is Fiona, Garreth," Hollis said. "She rescued me from the City."

"Good job," said the man. "And our drone pilot as well."

Fiona smiled. "Hullo."

"I've just sent Voytek over to mod one of them."

"We saw him," Fiona said.

"He wouldn't have gotten the Taser, but he'll have it now."

"Taser?"

"Arming the balloon." He shrugged, grinned. "Had one handy."

"How much weight?"

"Seven ounces."

"I think that will affect elevation," Fiona said.

"Almost certainly. Speed as well. But the penguin's maker tells me it will still fly. Though not as high. It's silver, is it? Mylar?"

"Yes."

"I think a bit of dazzle paint's in order. Do you know what I mean?"

"I do," said Fiona, though Milgrim didn't. "But you know I'm to fly a different sort of drone?"

"I do indeed."

"The box is on the bike?"

"It is. And I should have new dampers by now."

"What are dampers?" Milgrim asked.

"Shock absorbers," Fiona said.

"Let me take your coats," Hollis said, taking Mrs. Benny's helmet, then Fiona's. "I like your jacket," she said, noticing Milgrim's tweed, when he'd shucked out of the stiff nylon coat.

"Thank you."

"Please," Hollis said, "take a seat."

There were two tall, striped armchairs, arranged to face the man on the bed. Milgrim took one, Fiona the other, and Hollis sat on the bed. Milgrim saw her take the man's hand. He remembered their morning in Paris. "You jumped off the tallest building in the world," he said.

"I did. Though unfortunately not from the very top."

"I'm glad you're okay," said Milgrim, and saw Hollis smile at him.

"Thanks," said the man, Garreth, and Milgrim saw him squeeze Hollis's hand.

Someone rapped on the door twice, lightly, not the brass lady-hand. Knuckles. "Me, innit," said a voice.

Hollis swung her feet to the floor, got up, crossed to the door, and admitted a very pretty young man and a less pretty girl. The girl carried an old-fashioned black leatherette case. They both looked Indian, to Milgrim, though he was vague about South Asians gener-ally, but the girl was a goth. Milgrim couldn't remember having seen an Indian-looking goth before, but if you were going to see one, he thought, you'd see one in London.

"My cousin Chandra," said the young man. He wore complexly distressed, very narrow black jeans, a black polo, and an oversized, ancient-looking motorcycle jacket.

"Hello, Chandra," Hollis said.

Chandra smiled shyly. She had perfectly straight black hair, enormous dark eyes, and complexly pierced ears and nose. Her lipstick was black, and she appeared to be wearing a sort of Edwardian nurse's outfit, though it too was black.

"Hello, Chandra," Hollis said. "Chandra and Ajay, Fiona and Milgrim. And Garreth, Chandra."

Ajay was looking at Milgrim. "Bit of a stretch," he said, dubiously.

"Spray you on the sides," said Chandra, to Ajay. "That fiber stuff, from a can. For covering bald spots. Have some here." Now she looked at Milgrim. "He could do with a haircut. So that's in our favor, really."

Ajay ran his hand back through his hair, military-short on the sides but a silky black mop on top. He looked worried.

"It grows back," said Garreth, from the bed. "Milgrim, would you mind taking your pants off?"

Milgrim looked to Fiona, then back to Garreth, remembering Jun in the back of Tanky & Tojo.

"The waterproofs," Garreth said. "Ajay needs to get a sense of how you move."

"Move," said Milgrim, and stood up. Then sat down again, bending to untie his shoes.

"No, no," said Fiona, getting up. "Zips for that." She knelt in front of him, undid foot-long zips on the inner seams of the armored pants. "Stand up." He did. Fiona reached up, drew the massive plastic fly-zipper down, loudly ripped Velcro, and tugged the pants to the floor. Milgrim felt himself blush, explosively.

"Come on," said Fiona, "step out of them."

67. A CRUSHED MOUSE

Ajay, looking pained but stoic, was seated on what Milgrim said was a Biedermeier vanity stool, in the bright tile cave of Number Four's vast bathroom, towels spread beneath him, while Chandra went carefully at his waterfall with a pair of scissors. Milgrim was in there with them, "moving around" as instructed, while Ajay, when he remembered to, studied him. Chandra too would periodically pause, observe Milgrim, then start clipping again. Hollis found herself waiting for dialog.

"What *is* this?" Milgrim asked, apparently noticing the shower for the first time.

"The shower," Hollis said.

"Keep moving," ordered Ajay.

Milgrim put his hands in the pockets of his peculiar new pants.

"But would you *do* that?" asked Ajay.

"Quit moving," ordered Chandra, who'd stopped clipping.

"Me?" asked Milgrim.

"Ajay," said Chandra, brushing a wet black bit of stray waterfall from her black tunic. Her black lips looked particularly dramatic, in this light.

Hollis glanced back at Fiona, who was sitting at the foot of the bed, listening intently to Garreth, asking occasional questions, taking notes in a sticker-covered Moleskine.

Garreth had just had to break off, taking a call from the man who was building Pep's electric bicycle. This had resulted in Pep losing his curly-stays frame, as it would have to be "cold-bent," to accommodate the engine hubs, something both the builder and Garreth clearly regarded as sacrilege. Garreth had opted for carbon fiber instead, but had then had to phone Pep and tell him, which had resulted in an agreement to go with dual engines.

Hollis was reminded of watching a director prep for a music video, something the Curfew had been largely able to avoid. She'd seen it later, though, via Inchmale and the various bands he'd produced, and she'd invariably found it far more interesting, more entertaining, than any final product.

In this case, she still had very little idea of what Garreth intended to shoot.

"You go out now," she heard Chandra say, "and close the door. This is smelly." She turned and saw Milgrim headed in her direction, Chandra starting to shake an aerosol can of product. "Keep your eyes closed," Chandra said to Ajay.

Milgrim closed the door behind him.

"Are you okay?" Hollis asked. "Where have you been?"

"Southwark. With Fiona." He sounded, she thought, like someone describing a spa weekend. An unaccustomed little smile.

"I'm sorry about Heidi," she said.

He winced. "Is something wrong?"

"She's fine. I meant I'm sorry that she hurt Foley, made more trouble for you."

"I'm glad," he said. "Otherwise, they would have gotten us. Gotten me, anyway." And suddenly he was weirdly and entirely present, a single entity, the sharp looker-around-corners merged seamlessly with his spacey, dissociated self. "I wouldn't have gotten to go to Southwark." For those few seconds, he was someone she hadn't met. But then he was Milgrim again. "That's a scary shower," he said.

"I like it."

"I've never seen anything decorated this way." He looked around at the contents of Number Four.

"Me neither."

"Is it all real?"

"Yes, though there are some period reproductions. There's a catalog for each room."

"May I see that?"

Her iPhone rang. "Yes?"

"Meredith. I'm in the lobby. I need to see you."

"I have guests—"

"Alone," said Meredith. "Bring a jacket. She wants to meet you."

"I—"

"Not my idea," interrupted Meredith. "Hers. When I told her what you said."

Hollis looked at Garreth, who was deep into it with Fiona.

The bathroom door opened. Ajay stood there, the sides of his head sparsely covered with some kind of synthetic nonhair, randomly directional. "Not very good, is it?"

"It's like the pubic hair of some huge, anatomically correct toy animal," said Garreth, delighted.

"It's the wrong texture, but I have another that should do," said Chandra. "And I'll do a better job of application, next time."

"I'll be down in a minute," said Hollis, to the iPhone. "Meredith," she said to Garreth. "I'm going down to see her."

"Don't leave the hotel," Garreth said, and went back to whatever he was explaining to Fiona.

Hollis opened her mouth, shut it, found Number Four's leather-bound curiosity catalog for Milgrim, then collected the Hounds jacket, her purse, and left, closing the door behind her.

Avoiding the watercolors, she made her way through the green maze, and found the lift waiting, clicking softly to itself. As it descended the black cage, she tried to make sense of what Meredith had said. The logical "she" was the Hounds designer, but if that was the case, had Meredith been lying to her, yesterday?

Passing the ferret, she emerged into the sound of the lounge, evidently in full route now, that bounced so effectively down the marble stairs. Meredith was waiting near the door, where Robert ordinarily stood, though he was nowhere in sight. She wore a translucently ancient waxed cotton jacket over the tweed Hollis remembered from yesterday, more holes than fabric, the platonic opposite of Inchmale's Japanese Gore-Tex.

"You told me you didn't know how to contact her," Hollis said. "And you certainly didn't indicate that she was in London."

"I didn't know, either one," Meredith said. "Inchmale. Clammy was giving me the gears, at the studio, because you'd promised to get him fresh kit if he helped you find her."

Hollis had forgotten about that. "I did," she said.

"Inchmale was working on one of those charts he makes, the ones around the bottom of a paper coffee cup, for each song. Is that simply more of his rubbish, or is it real?"

"Real."

"And of course he was concentrating, or pretending to. And suddenly he said, 'I know her husband.' Said he was another producer, very good, based in Chicago. He'd worked with him. Said a name."

"What name?"

Meredith looked her even more firmly in the eye. "I'd have to let her tell you that."

"What else did Reg say?"

"Nothing. Not a word. Went back to his colored felts and his paper cup. But as soon as I got my hands on a computer, I Googled the name. There he was. Image search, three pages in, there she was, with him. That was only a few hours after I saw you, here."

"That turned into quite an evening," said Hollis.

"Did you quit?"

"I didn't get a chance, but my position on quitting remains the same. Stronger, if anything. I'm right off Bigend, if you could say I was ever on him. A lot's happened."

"I've mostly been on the phone, myself. Trying to reach her, through her husband. Couldn't reach him. Threw myself on Inchmale's mercy. Had George put it to him, actually."

"And?"

"She called me. She's here. She's been here for a few weeks. East Midlands, Northampton, looking at shoe factories. Doing a boot," and suddenly Meredith was smiling, then not. "On her way back now."

Hollis was about to ask where to, but didn't.

"I can take you to her now," Meredith said. "That's what she wants."

"Why would—"

"Better she tells you. Are you coming or not? She's leaving tomorrow."

"Is it far?"

"Soho. Clammy has a car."

> > >

Which was Japanese, minute, and appeared to have been fathered by
a Citroën Deux Chevaux, its mother of less distinctive lineage but
obviously having attended design school. It had virtually no rear seat,
so Hollis was folded in sideways now, behind Meredith and Clammy,
watching a determined little rear wiper squeegee rain. Nothing could
have been less like the Hilux. A tiny retro-wagon, devoid of armor.
Everything, in traffic, was larger than they were, including motorcycles. Clammy had bought it used, through a broker in Japan, and
imported it, the only way to get one here. It was the dark glossy gray
of an old-fashioned electric fan, a shade Inchmale liked to refer to as
"a crushed mouse," which meant a gray with some red in it. She hoped
other drivers could see them. Though not if they were Foley's crew,
whom she'd started to worry about when Clammy was turning into
Oxford Street. Garreth's instruction to not leave the hotel had suddenly made a different sort of sense. She hadn't been taking all that
very seriously. She'd felt like an observer, a helper, or a woefully
unskilled nurse. But now, she realized, in this new economy of kidnapping, she herself could probably be quite valuable. If they had her,
they'd have Garreth. Though they didn't, as far as she knew, know
about Garreth. Though that depended, she imagined, on everyone in
Bigend's tiny immediate crew remaining loyal. Who was Fiona? She
knew nothing about Fiona, really. Except that she kept an eye on
Milgrim, an oddly personal one, Hollis thought. Actually, now that
Hollis thought about it, as though she fancied him.

"Is it much further?" she asked.

68. HAND-EYE

Now it was Milgrim's turn, on the Biedermeier vanity stool, the remains of Ajay's luxuriant top-curls darkly littering the spread towels. Ajay himself was in Hollis's huge scary shower, ridding himself of the aerosol product Chandra had applied to the sides of his head. Staunchly unwilling to see her cousin naked, she faced away from the shower as she used an electric clipper on Milgrim's back and sides. Milgrim, seeing Ajay naked, thought he looked like a professional dancer. He was all muscles, but none of the bulgy kind.

The idea, now that Chandra had had a good look at Milgrim, and at his hair as it had been the day before, was to give him a different cut. He found himself imagining a Milgrim wig for Ajay, something he was sure he'd never imagined before.

It was getting steamy, but he heard Ajay crank the shower down, then off. Soon he appeared beside Milgrim in a white robe with corded trim, carefully knotting its belt. The top of his head was now Chandra's initial approximation of Milgrim's previous look, though it was black, and damp. Milgrim's own indeterminately brownish hair was falling on the towels.

"I'll have to trust," Ajay said to Chandra, "that that wasn't a joke."

"For the sort of retainer your friend has me on," Chandra said, over the burr of the clipper, "you'll get no jokes at all. I'd never tried it before. Seen an instructional video. I'll do better next time. Keep your chin down." This last to Milgrim. "Really it's to cover bald spots. Up top. Going that heavy on the sides may be pushing the envelope a bit." She shut the clipper off.

"Pushing the envelope," said Ajay, "is what we're about. High speed, low drag." He toweled his head.

"Do these people know you're a perfect idiot?" asked Chandra.

"Ajay," said Garreth, through the door.

Ajay flung the towel in a corner and went out, closing the door behind him.

"He was always like that," said Chandra, Milgrim not knowing how that was supposed to have been. "It wasn't entirely the army." She gave the hair on top of his head a few brisk snips with her scissors, then removed the towel she'd draped around his neck. "Stand up. Have a look."

Milgrim stood. A different Milgrim, oddly military, perhaps younger, looked back at him from the wall of fogged mirror above the twin sinks. He'd buttoned the collar of his new shirt, to keep hair from getting inside, and this contributed to the unfamiliarity. A stranger, in an air tie. "That's good," said Milgrim. And it was. "I wouldn't have thought to do that. Thank you."

"Thank your friend on the bed," said Chandra. "Most expensive cut you'll have had. Easily."

Ajay opened the door. He was wearing Milgrim's wrinkled cotton jacket. His shoulders were slightly too wide for it, Milgrim thought. "Your shoes are a bit too long," Ajay said, "but I can put something in the toes."

"Milgrim," said Garreth, from the bed, "come and sit. Fiona here tells me you're a natural with the balloons."

"I have good hand-eye coordination," Milgrim volunteered. "They told me in Basel."

69. THE GIFTING SUITE

H ere?" She recognized the nameless denim shop in Upper James Street. Dark, faintly candlelit. A pulsing glow, almost invisible.

"They're hosting a pop-up," said Meredith.

"Won't start for an hour," said Clammy, who struck Hollis as uncharacteristically cheery. "But I'm first."

"It's a gifting suite, as far as you're concerned," Meredith told him. "Then we're even. But no questions. And no bothering Bo later. Ever. Go there again, she won't know you."

"Perfect," said Clammy, drumming a signal of pleased anticipation on the steering wheel.

"Who's Bo?"

"You've met her," said Meredith. "Come on. Out with you. They're waiting." She opened the little wagon's passenger-side door, pulled herself out and up, tipped the passenger seat forward. Hollis struggled out. "You'll have a little time before we arrive," said Meredith, and got back in. She closed the door and Clammy pulled away, rain beading on the enamel of the wagon's low roof.

The handsome graying woman opened the door as Hollis reached it, gestured her in, then closed and locked it.

"You're Bo," said Hollis. The woman nodded. "I'm Hollis."

"Yes," said the woman.

It smelled of vanilla and something else, masking jungle indigo. Candles pulsed in retail twilight, along the massive slab of polished wood that Hollis remembered from her previous visit. Aromatherapy candles, their complicated tallow poured into expensive-looking glasses with vertical sides, their wicks paper-thin slabs of wood, crackled softly as their flames pulsed. Faintly sandblasted on each glass, she saw, the Hounds logo. Between the candles were a folded pair of jeans, a folded pair of khaki pants, a folded chambray shirt, and a black ankle-boot. The boot's smooth leather caught the candlelight. She touched it with a fingertip.

"Next year," said Bo. "Also an oxford, brown, but samples not ready."

Hollis picked up the folded jeans. They were black as ink, unusually heavy. She turned them over and saw the baby-headed dog, dimly branded into a leather patch on the waistband. "They're for sale? Tonight?"

"Friends will come. When you were here, I could not help you. I hope you understand."

"I do," said Hollis, not sure that she did.

"In rear, please. Come."

Hollis followed her, ducking through a doorway partially concealed by a dark *noren* decorated with white fish. There was no white Ikea desk here, no decrease in the shop's simple elegance at all. It was a smaller space, but as cleanly uncluttered, with the same sanded, unstained floor, the same candles. A woman was seated on one of two old, paint-scarred, mismatched wooden kitchen chairs, stroking the screen of an iPhone. She looked up, smiled, stood. "Hello, Hollis. I—"

Hollis raised her hand. "Don't tell me."

The woman raised her eyebrows. Her hair was dark brown, glossy in candlelight, nicely cut, but mussed.

"Deniability," Hollis said. "I could figure it out, from what Meredith told me. Or I could just ask Reg. But if you don't tell me, and I don't do either of those things, I can continue to tell Hubertus that I don't know your name." She looked around, saw that Bo was gone. She turned back to the woman. "I'm not good at lying."

"Neither am I. Good at hiding, not at lying. Please, sit down. Would you like some wine? We have some."

Hollis took the other chair. "No, thank you."

She was wearing jeans that Hollis took to be the ones she'd seen on the table. That same absolute black. A blue shirt, rumpled and untucked. A very worn pair of black Converse sneakers, their rubber sides abraded and discolored.

"I don't understand why you'd want to see me," Hollis said. "Under the circumstances."

The woman smiled. "I was a huge fan of the Curfew, by the way, though that's not it." She sat. Glanced down at the iPhone's glowing screen, then looked at Hollis. "I think it was my sense of once having been where you are."

"Which is . . . ?"

"I worked for Bigend myself. Identical arrangement, from what Mere tells me. There was something he wanted, the missing piece of a puzzle, and he talked me into finding it for him."

"Did you?"

"I did. Though it wasn't at all what he'd imagined. Eventually he did do something, repurposing aspects of what I'd helped him learn. Something ghastly, in marketing. I used to be in marketing myself, but then I wasn't, after him."

"What did you do, in marketing?"

"I had a very peculiar and specific talent, which I didn't understand, never have understood, which now is gone. Though that hasn't been a bad thing, the gone part. It stemmed from a sort of allergy I'd had, since childhood."

"To what?"

"Advertising," the woman said. "Logos, in particular. Corporate mascot figures. I still dislike those, actually, but not much more than some people dislike clowns, or mimes. Any concentrated graphic representation of corporate identity."

"But don't you have your own now?"

The woman looked down at her iPhone, stroked the screen. "I do, yes. Forgive me for keeping this on. I'm doing something with my kids. Difficult to keep in touch, with the time difference."

"Your logo worries me, a little."

"It was drawn by the woman Bigend had sent me to find. She was a filmmaker. She died, a few years after I found her."

Hollis was watching emotion in the woman's face, a transparency that easily trumped her beauty, which was considerable. "I'm sorry."

"Her sister sent me some of her things. There was this unnerving little doodle, at the bottom of a page of notes. When we had the notes translated, they were about the legend of the Gabriel Hounds."

"I'd never heard of them."

"Neither had I. And when I began making my own things, I didn't want a brand name, a logo, anything. I'd always removed branding from my own clothes, because of that sensitivity. And I couldn't stand anything that looked as though a designer had touched it. Eventually I realized that if I felt that way about something, that meant it hadn't been that well designed. But my husband made a compelling case for there being a need to brand, if we were going to do what I was propos-ing to do. And there was her squiggle, at the bottom of that page." She looked down at the horizonal screen again, then up at Hollis. "My husband is from Chicago. We lived there, after we met, and I discov-ered the ruins of American manufacturing. I'd been dressing in its products for years, rooting them out of warehouses, thrift shops, but I'd never thought of where they'd come from."

"Your things are beautifully made."

"I saw that an American cotton shirt that had cost twenty cents in 1935 will often be better made than almost anything you can buy today. But if you re-create that shirt, and you might have to go to Japan to do that, you wind up with something that needs to retail for around three hundred dollars. I started bumping into people who remembered how to make things. And I knew that how I dressed had always attracted some attention. There were people who wanted what I wore. What I curated, Bigend would have said."

"He's curating suits that do retinal damage, these days."

"He has no taste at all, but he behaves as if he's had it removed, elective surgery. Perhaps he did. That search he sent me on somehow removed my one negotiable talent. I'd been a sort of coolhunter as well, before that had a name, but now it's difficult to find anyone who isn't. I suspect he's responsible for that, somehow. Some kind of global contagion."

"And you began to make clothing, in Chicago?"

"We were having children." She smiled, glanced down at the screen, stroked it with a fingertip. "So it wasn't as though I had much time. But my husband's work was going well. So I could afford to experiment. And I discovered I really loved doing that."

"People wanted the things you made."

"That was frightening, at first. I just wanted to explore processes, learn, be left alone. But then I remembered Hubertus, ideas of his, things he'd done. Guerrilla marketing strategies. Weird inversions of customary logic. That Japanese idea of secret brands. The deliberate construction of parallel microeconomies, where knowledge is more congruent than wealth. I'd have a brand, I decided, but it would be a secret. The branding would *be* that it was a secret. No advertising. None. No press. No shows. I'd do what I was doing, be as secretive as I could about it, and avoid the bullshit. And I was very good at being secretive about it. I'd gotten that from my father as well."

"It seems to have worked."

"Too well, possibly. It's at that point, now, where it either has to go to another level or stop. Does he know? That it's me?"

"I don't think so."

"Does he suspect?"

"If he does, he's doing a good job of pretending he doesn't. And right now he's focused on a crisis that has nothing to do with either of us."

"He must be in his element, then."

"He was. Now I'm not so sure. But I don't think he's giving Gabriel Hounds much attention."

"He'll know it's me soon enough. We're coming out. It's time. Tonight's pop-up is part of a that."

"He'll still be dangerous."

"That's exactly what I wanted to say to you. When Mere told me about you, I realized you'd already had the Bigend experience, but you were back for more, even though you struck her as a good person."

"I never planned it that way."

"Of course not. He has a kind of dire gravity. You need to get further away. I know."

"I've already taken steps."

The woman looked at her carefully. "I believe you. And good luck.

We have the pop-up starting now, and I have to help Bo, but I wanted to thank you personally. Mere told me what you did, or rather what you weren't willing to do, and of course I'm very grateful."

"I only did what I had to do. Didn't do what I couldn't do, more like it."

They both stood.

"*Totally* fucking next level," Hollis heard Clammy declare, from beyond the *noren*.

70. DAZZLE

The penguin smelled of Krylon, an aerosol enamel Fiona had used to camouflage it, so to speak. Milgrim knew more about camouflage, now, than he would ever have expected to, via Bigend's interest in military clothing. Prior to that, he had only been familiar with two kinds, the one with the Lava Lamp blobs in nature shades, that the U.S. Army had featured when he was a boy, and the creepy photorealist turkey-hunter stuff that a certain kind of extra-scary New Jersey drug dealer sometimes affected. What Fiona called "dazzle," though, was new to him. Fiona said it had been invented by a painter, a Vorticist. He'd Google it, when he had time. It had been Garreth's suggestion, and Fiona had told Milgrim that it didn't actually make a lot of sense, in their situation, though anything was better than silver Mylar. She liked Garreth having suggested it, though, because it seemed to her to be part of some performance-art aspect of what he was doing. She said she'd never seen anything quite like it, what Garreth was doing, and particularly the speed with which it was being put together.

Out in the bike yard, she'd sprayed the penguin's silver Mylar with black, random, wonky geometrics, their edges fuzzy, like graffiti. Real dazzle had sharp edges, she said, but there was no way to mask the inflated balloon. She used a piece of brown cardboard, cut in a concave curve, to mask approximately, then went back with a dull gray, to fill in the remaining silver. When that had dried a little, she'd further confused it with an equally dull beige, ghosting lines in with the cardboard mask. The result wouldn't conceal the penguin against any background at all, particularly the sky, but broke it up visually, made it difficult to read as an object. Still a penguin, though, a swimming one, and now with the Taser and the extra electronics that Voytek had taped to its tummy.

There was an arming sequence, on the iPhone now, that required a thumb and forefinger, with the other forefinger needed to fire the thing. Milgrim hadn't been entirely sure what a Taser was before, but he was getting an idea. If he accidentally fired it, here in the Vegas cube, a pair of barbed electrodes would shoot out, on two thin fifteen-foot cables, propelled by compressed gas. That was strictly once-only, the barb-shooting. If the barbs went into Bigend's spotless plasterboard wall, the penguin was anchored there, he supposed, and there was a lot of fine cable around. But if you tapped the iPhone again, in the firing circle on the screen, the wall got shocked. Which wouldn't bother the wall, but if those barbs happened to get into anybody, which was what they were actually for, that person got a shock, a big one. Not the kind that would kill you, but one that could knock you down, stun you. And there was more than one shock stored in the toy airship cabin Voytek had taped under there.

Fiona said that he wouldn't have to worry about any of that when he flew the penguin. She said it was just extra bells and whistles, something Garreth had tossed in because he'd happened to run across the Taser. That was what Voytek had indicated, grumpily, on his way out, when they'd gotten back here on the Yamaha.

But that wasn't what Garreth had told him, in Hollis's hotel room. Garreth had said that he needed Fiona to operate the other drone, the one with the little helicopters, so he needed Milgrim to operate the penguin. To keep an eye on the general area, he said. When Milgrim asked which area that was, Garreth had said that he didn't know yet, but that he was sure Milgrim would do very well. Milgrim, remembering the pleasure he'd taken in rolling the black ray, decided that simply nodding was the best course. Though the idea of anyone wanting him to operate anything was new. Other people operated things, and Milgrim observed them doing it. But, he supposed, he was really only being asked to observe something, whatever it was, through the cameras in the penguin, and it was best, as Fiona suggested, to regard the Taser as a random add-on.

It was harder to get the penguin to do anything, in the constrained space of the Vegas cube, than it had been to get the ray to do those rhythmic somersaults, but he was starting, now, to manage a repeated stationary roll. If he bumped the wall, Fiona noticed, and didn't like it, so he tried to be as careful as he could. She said that the robotics in the wings were fragile, and the penguin was helpless without them. It didn't really fly, because penguins don't, and it was a balloon; rather, it swam, through air instead of water, and once you had it going where you wanted it to, it knew how to swim by itself. He was careful to keep that overridden now. He wished they could take the thing out and really fly it, the way he'd seen her fly the other one in Paris, but she said that they couldn't, because people might see it and get excited, and because Garreth had ordered her to keep him inside.

Being kept inside with Fiona was an excellent thing, as far as Milgrim was concerned, but he was starting to recall Hollis's scary-looking shower with something other than fear. "I wish there was a shower here," he said, slowing the penguin's roll, bringing the Taser around until it was on the bottom, stopping it. There was something wonderfully satisfying about this thing, something silky about the way it worked.

"There is," said Fiona, looking up from his Air, where she sat at the table.

"There is?" Milgrim, on his back on the white foam, glanced around the blank white walls, thinking he'd missed a door.

"Benny has one rigged up. Drivers use it, sometimes. It has a geyser so old that it has a box that used to take coins. I could do with one myself."

Milgrim was simultaneously aware of the stickiness of his armpits and what even the briefest image of Fiona in a shower did to him. "You go first, then."

"You can't trust Benny's geyser," said Fiona. "Get it working, it'll go once, then stop. We should shower together."

"Together," said Milgrim, and heard the voice he only had in police custody. He coughed.

"We'll leave the light out," said Fiona, who was looking at him with an expression he couldn't identify at all. "I'm not supposed to let you out of my sight. Literally. That was what he said."

"Who?" asked Milgrim, in his own voice.

"Garreth." She was wearing her armored pants, low on her hips as she sat on one of Bigend's elegant chairs, and a tight T-shirt, white, that said RUDGE at the top of a round black emblem, the size of a dinner plate, and COVENTRY at the bottom. Between these names was a red heraldic hand, open and upright, its palm presented as if to warn anyone off the small but prominent breasts behind it.

"If it's all right with you," said Milgrim.

"I suggested it, didn't I?"

71. THE UGLY T-SHIRT

Where are you? Robert said you left with a woman."

She was leaving the denim shop with Meredith and Clammy. "Soho. I did. Meredith. On my way back now."

"Should have given you the sort of safe-word I gave your employer."

"No. It's okay."

"Better if you're not out."

"Necessary, though."

"But you're coming back now?"

"Yes. See you soon."

She looked from the phone in her hand to the faintly candlelit window. Shadows of people. Two more arriving now, to be admitted by Bo. Meredith thought she'd seen an associate editor from French *Vogue*. Clammy had ignored several other musicians, slightly older than he was, whom Hollis vaguely recognized. Otherwise, not what she thought of as a fashion crowd. Something else, though she didn't know what. But she could tell that the secret Bigend had been chasing had already been starting to emerge when he'd given her the assignment. Already Hounds wasn't a secret in the same way. He was too late. What did that mean? Was he losing his touch? Had he been too focused on his project with Chombo? Had Sleight somehow been skewing the flow of information?

Clammy's little gray wagon arrived, driven by a very Clammy-looking boy Clammy didn't bother to introduce. He popped out, handed Clammy the keys, nodded, and walked away.

"Who was that?" Hollis asked.

"Assistant," said Clammy absently, opening the door on the passenger side. He had an unmarked manila shopping bag the size of a small suitcase. "You'll have to hold this for me."

"What did you get?"

"Two of the black, two of the chino, two shirts, and the black of your jacket."

"And something for you," said Meredith, to Hollis.

"It's on top," said Clammy impatiently. "Get in."

Hollis folded herself, sideways, onto the rear bench, and accepted Clammy's bag as best she could. A potent waft of indigo.

Clammy and Meredith got in, doors closing. "It was the first thing she ever did," said Meredith, looking back. "Before she started Hounds."

Hollis found something wrapped in unbleached tissue, atop Clammy's thick, heavy pad of denim. Fumbled it out, pulling the tissue aside. Dark, smooth, heavy jersey. "What is it?"

"That's for you to work out. A seamless tube. I've seen her wear it as a stole, an evening dress of any length, several different ways as skirts. Fabric's amazing. Some ancient factory in France, this latest batch."

"Thank her, please. And thank you. Both of you."

"I'm sorted," said Clammy, turning into Oxford Street, "just don't crush my gear."

>>>

When the lift descended, answering her call, she found it occupied by a short, older, oddly broad man of indeterminately Asian aspect, his thinning gray hair brushed neatly back. He stood very upright in the middle of the cage, a bobble-topped tartan tam in his hands, and thanked her, accent crisply British, when she hauled open the cage's gate. "Good evening," he said with a nod, stepping past her, turning on his heel, and marching for Cabinet's door as he settled his tam.

Robert opened and held the door for him.

The ferret was in its vitrine.

When she reached Number Four's door, she remembered she hadn't taken her key. She rapped with her knuckles, softly. "It's me."

"Moment," she heard him say.

She heard the chain rattle. Then he opened the door, leaning on his four-legged cane, something she took to be a glossy black LP sleeve tucked under his arm.

"What's that?" she asked.

"The ugliest T-shirt in the world," he said, and kissed her cheek.

"The Bollards will be disappointed," she said, coming in and closing the door. "I thought they'd had me sleeping in that."

"So ugly that digital cameras forget they've seen it."

"Shall we have a look at it, then?"

"Not yet." He showed her the black square, which she now saw was a sort of plastic envelope, its edges welded shut. "We might contaminate it with our DNA."

"No, thank you. We might *not*."

"A single stray hair would be enough. Material like this has to be handled very carefully, given what forensics are, these days. It's nothing you want to be associated with at all, ever. In fact, there really isn't much material like this. Something of a one-off, in the field."

"Pep's going to wear it?"

"And contaminate it, no doubt, with Catalan DNA." He grinned. "But then we'll put it in a bag, seal it, and incinerate the bag. No photographs of the ugliness, though. We don't want that."

"If cameras can't see it, how could we photograph it?"

"Cameras can see it. The surveillance cameras can all see it, but then they forget they've seen it."

"Why?"

"Because their architecture tells them to forget it, and anyone who's wearing it as well. They forget the figure wearing the ugly T-shirt. Forget the head atop it, the legs below, feet, arms, hands. It compels erasure. That which the camera sees, bearing the sigil, it deletes from the recalled image. Though only if you ask it to show you the image. So there's no suspicious busy-ness to be noticed. If you ask for June 7, camera 53, it retrieves what it saw. In the act of retrieval, the sigil, and the human form bearing it, cease to be represented. By virtue of deep architecture. Gentlemen's agreement."

"Are they doing that now? Really?"

"Answering that would require a very woolly discussion of what 'they' can mean. I imagine it's literally impossible to say who's doing it. It's enough to say it's being done. In a sort of larval way, though it works quite well. We're quite far ahead, here, with this camera culture. Though we aren't a patch on Dubai. I'm still getting bits and pieces of my freeway performance, mailed in. Downside of having obsessive friends who like computers. But none of those friends, I'd gladly wager, know about the ugly T-shirt. The ugly T-shirt is *deep*. As deep as I've ever gotten, really. Deep and bad to know. After this is over, regardless of outcome, you know nothing of the ugly T-shirt."

"You're really making me want to see it."

"You will. I'm keen myself. Where did you go?"

"Back to the store that was the first place I asked anyone about Hounds." She put the designer's gift on an armchair, took her jacket off, and went to sit close beside him, her arm across his shoulders. "I met her. The designer."

"She's here?"

"Just leaving."

"Big End's been looking for something right under his nose?"

"I think there may have been some hiding in plain sight going on, but I'm sure she's enjoyed that. She's the only person I've met who's had the same job I have, so he's something of an issue for her."

"You bonded?"

"I hope I never become as aware of him as she is. I suspect that not being on his side has actually become a big part of who she is."

"Sufficiently perverse and titanic arseholes," he said, "can become religious objects. Negative saints. People who dislike them, with sufficient purity and fervor, well, they do *that*. Spend their lives lighting candles. I don't recommend it."

"I know. I've never really disliked him. Not the way some people do. He's like some peculiar force of nature. Not a safe one to be around. Like those rogue waves you told me about, when we were in New York.

I like him less now, but I imagine that's because he's vulnerable, somehow. Has he told you what it is with Chombo?"

"No idea. Otherwise, I agree with you. He's vulnerable. Gracie and Foley and Milgrim and Heidi, and you and the others, have formed a rogue wave without meaning to, and none of it could have been predicted. He has one great advantage, though."

"What's that?"

"He already believes that that's how the world is. Show him a wave, he'll try to surf it."

"I think you're like that. It worries me. I think you're doing it right now."

He touched the hair above her ear, smoothed it back. "Because you're in it."

"I know," she said, "but also because you can. Isn't that true?"

"Yes. It is. Though after this, it won't be true in the same way. That's obvious to me, and was obvious before you called me. I'd already seen it, on hospital ceilings. Same for the old man. I knew when he told me about this." He tapped the black square. "This is a big one. Probably the biggest he had. I'd no inkling about this. The potential, for one grand exploit, is fabulous. But he's given it to me to make it easier to get my girlfriend, and her freak of an employer, out of trouble."

She noticed the Blue Ant figurine on the bedside table, beside the phone. "Where's that GPS thing? I don't want to lose track of it."

He looked at his watch. "It should be headed up the Amazon by now. By boat."

"The Amazon?"

He shrugged, put his arm around her. "By courier. Slowly. If Mr. Big End is tracking it, he'll know we've played a joke. If it's someone else, they may think you're headed up the Amazon."

"Someone put it in my bag when I went to Paris."

"Staff."

"Here?"

"Of course."

"That's scary."

"But I've thought of it. And I'm always here, which simplifies things."

"Who was here, earlier?"

"Charlie."

"Graying, Asian, plaid tam?"

"Charlie."

"He's almost as wide as he's tall."

"Ghurka. Tapers toward the waist. Jewel, Charlie. How do you ever manage to do anything intimate in here, with all of these heads and things staring?"

"I have absolutely no idea. Never having tried."

"Really," he said.

72. SMITHFIELD

Milgrim made his way back from Benny's shower wearing a ragged, piebald terry robe, vertically striped in what must originally have been rust and a very lively green, and his Tanky & Tojo brogues, unlaced, over wet bare feet. Fiona followed, draped in the MontBell sleeping bag, in a pair of oversized rubber flip-flops. Milgrim hoped she wouldn't get athlete's foot. He hoped neither of them would. The concrete floor of Benny's shower had felt scarily slimy, the water scalding hot until it suddenly ran cold. Not a stall, just a length of slanted concrete floor against a wall. And had in fact been dark, which he'd actually been glad of. He didn't like thinking, now, how he must look from behind, in the bright beam of her tiny flashlight, in this robe and the brogues. There hadn't been any towels.

They picked their way through the minefield of foam cups and engine parts on the floor of Benny's workshop.

Back in the cube, Milgrim took his clothes into the micro-washroom and closed the door. Banged his elbow toweling off with the robe, which smelled faintly of gasoline. "Here's the robe," he said. "It's not that wet." He opened the door partially and held it out. She took it.

He used one of Bigend's Swiss towels for a touch-up, then struggled into his clothes. The softly scrabbling Saharan ghost of Jimi Hendrix filled the cube and the washroom. "Hullo?" he heard her say. "Yes. Just a moment." Her pale bare arm passed her iPhone in. "For you."

He took it. "Hello?"

"The tasking," said Winnie.

Milgrim, who hadn't been expecting this at all, could think of nothing to say.

"I haven't heard from you," she said.

"I did meet him."

"And?"

"I don't think he's working for one of those companies you described. I think he's Hollis's boyfriend."

"Why would he hire Hollis's boyfriend?"

"He's that way," said Milgrim, more confidently. "He prefers to hire amateurs. It's something he talks about." It still amazed Milgrim, slightly, to be telling anyone the truth, about anything. "He doesn't like"—and Milgrim strained his memory—"*strategic business intelligence types.*"

"Hiring an amateur, in his present situation, could be suicidal. Are you sure?"

"How could I be sure? Garreth doesn't feel like someone from a company, to me. Not like an amateur either. Knows what he's doing, but I don't know what that is. But I think he's sleeping with Hollis. I mean, there's only the one bed there." Which made him think of the foam, and Fiona.

"What does he look like?"

"Thirties? Brown hair."

"That's you. Try harder."

"British. And like a cop. But not. Military? But not exactly. Athletic? But he's been in an accident."

"What kind?"

"He jumped off the tallest building in the world. Then a car ran over him."

Silence. "This is why it's good we've had face time," she said.

"Hollis told me. One of his legs doesn't work very well. He has a cane. And one of those electric scooter things."

"We need more face time. Now."

Milgrim looked at the phone, seeing, superimposed on it, the government seal on her card. "When?"

"I just told you."

"I'll have to ask Fiona."

"Do that," she said, and hung up. He put the iPhone on the edge of the sink and finished dressing.

He emerged with the phone in one hand, his shoes and socks in the other.

Fiona was seated at the table, back in her armored pants and Rudge T-shirt, toweling her hair with the bathrobe. "Who was that?" she asked, lowering the bathrobe, hair sticking out in every direction.

"Winnie."

"American."

"Yes," said Milgrim. He sat down and began to put on his socks and shoes.

"I couldn't help overhearing," Fiona said.

Milgrim looked up.

"What is it that you have to ask me?"

"Hold on." Milgrim finished tying his shoes. He pulled his bag toward him, across the table, opened it, dug through it, found Winnie's card. He handed it to Fiona.

She read it. Frowned. "The Department of *Defense*?"

"Dee-sis," said Milgrim, nodding, then spelled out the acronym.

"Never heard of it."

"She says almost nobody has."

"Bigend know about this?"

"Yes. Well, not about that call. Or the previous one."

Fiona put the card down on the table, looked at him. "Are you?"

"What?"

"Dee-sis."

"Seriously?"

"Then how are you hooked up with her?"

"It's complicated."

"Have you done something? A crime?"

"Not lately. Nothing she'd be interested in. Much. She's after Gracie."

"Who's that?"

"He has Shombo. Gracie was watching Bigend. Thought he was a competitor. In a way, he is. So she started watching me. Now I need to meet with her."

"'Chombo,'" she corrected, "not 'Shombo.' Where?"

"I think we decide. Not here."

"That's for sure."

"Do you have to tell Hubertus?" he asked.

She put the tip of her index finger on Winnie's card, moved it slightly, like a little Ouija board, divining something. "My relationship with Bigend isn't strictly business," she said. "My mother worked for him when I was a kid."

Milgrim nodded, but really just because it seemed to fit.

"Is she going to try to stop whatever it is that Garreth is doing for Bigend?"

"She wants to fuck Gracie over," said Milgrim, "any way she can. She's hoping Bigend will do it for her, because she can't do it herself."

Fiona tilted her head. "You sounded like a different person just then. Different kind of person."

"She might explain it that way herself," he said. "But if it were just a matter of my going out and meeting her, I'd do it, and tell Bigend when I could."

"Okay," said Fiona. "I've got the keys to the Yamaha. Call her. I'll need to explain where she's meeting us."

"Where is she meeting us?"

"Smithfield."

>>>

This time, removing the hairspray helmet, which he was starting to accept as an inherent and not entirely unfair cost of riding with Fiona—and almost, possibly, to enjoy—Milgrim found himself beneath a sort of deep, glassy, probably plastic awning, slung horizontally from above, running the seeming length of a very long building, apparently the only one on this very long block, ornate to American eyes but probably leanly functional to its Victorian builders. Sections of brick alternated with narrower sections of gray cement. A pair of obvious couriers sat their bikes, the big Hondas Fiona called maggots, about twenty feet away, smoking cigarettes and drinking from tall cans.

"Stay on the bike," Fiona said, removing her own helmet. "We may have to leave quickly. If we do, get the helmet on and hold on."

Milgrim lowered the helmet to his side.

Opposite the Market was what looked to him like fairly generic London, some thoroughfare curving past, relatively light traffic, and currently none whatever on this lane immediately adjacent the Market, but now he heard an engine approaching. He and Fiona turned in unison. One of those anonymous, usually Japanese two-door sedans that seemed to Milgrim to comprise the bulk of London traffic. It didn't slow when it passed them, but Milgrim saw the driver's glance.

Then it did slow, after passing the two couriers, pulling in several car-lengths beyond them. The couriers looked at it, looked at one another, set their tall cans down, put on their helmets, started their engines, and rode away. Then the car's passenger-side door opened and Winnie emerged, wearing a beige raincoat over a black pantsuit. She closed the door and walked toward them. It was the first time Milgrim had seen her out of a South Carolina souvenir sweatshirt, and she wasn't carrying a bag full of toys. Instead, she had a businesslike black leather purse, matching shoes. Milgrim watched her shoes click past the two cans.

"Special Agent Whitaker," she said to Fiona, when she reached them.

"Right," said Fiona.

The driver emerged from the car. An older man, he wore what Milgrim supposed might be called a fedora, a raincoat roughly the color of Winnie's, dark slacks, large brown shoes. He closed the car door and stood, looking back at them.

"Milgrim and I will talk in the car," Winnie said. "He'll be behind the wheel. My driver will wait at a distance, where you can see him. Fair enough?"

Fiona nodded.

"Come on, then," Winnie said to Milgrim.

He got off the bike, feeling clumsy in the armored nylon oversuit, put the hairspray helmet on the seat. She walked him to the car. Past

the cans, which Milgrim saw had contained some sort of boldly la-
beled cider, the London couriers apparently being health-minded in
spite of smoking. "Your friend doesn't have any trouble making her
terms known," Winnie said.

"I heard. But she has orders not to let me out of her sight. And she
did agree to bring me here, on very short notice."

She opened the driver's-side door for him.

Milgrim, who hadn't driven a car for a decade or more, got in
behind the wheel. The car smelled of air-freshener, and had a large
St. Christopher medal affixed to the dash. Winnie walked quickly
around the back, opened the door, got into the passenger seat, closed
the door.

"Nice suit," Milgrim said as she crossed her legs.

"It's perverse of me."

"It is?"

"Navy or charcoal being the norm. Fed shows up wearing a wedding dress, it'll be described as a black suit. A black suit and she
shoved her badge in your face. She was wearing charcoal gray from
Brooks Brothers, the credentials were presented slowly, respectfully,
at midtorso level. But then it's a black suit, and she shoved the badge
in their face. Know what's weird about that?"

"No," said Milgrim.

"You don't present the credentials, you don't get that. That's why
cards are so much better. The badge is like something out of a
role-playing game, some seal of elder doom. When your job's building
relationships and establishing rapport, the credentials are murder."

Milgrim considered her. "*That's* your job?"

"You're here, aren't you?"

He thought about it. "I see what you mean. Who's that man?" he
asked, to change the subject.

"I'm renting his spare bedroom. Really, the suit's for him. If
he's going to drive me around, I figure I can look like his idea of a
professional."

The man had strolled a little farther, stopped, and now stood with
hands in raincoat pockets, staring out in what Milgrim thought might
be the direction of the City. Milgrim twisted in his seat, saw Fiona

watching them, astride the Yamaha, her helmet-hair a tousled dandelion.

"What's going on?" she asked.

"Gracie and Foley have kidnapped someone who works for Bigend—"

"'Kidnapped'? That has a very specific meaning, for me. That's a crime. Kidnapped who?"

"Shombo. Chombo, I mean. He works for Bigend. They went to the home of the man Chombo was staying with, hit the man, threatened him, his wife and child as well, and took Chombo away."

"You didn't tell me?"

"I haven't had time," said Milgrim, which in a way was true. "And I've had to infer a lot of it."

"What's Chombo?"

"He seems to be some kind of researcher, on a project of Bigend's. Bigend wants him back."

"Ransom demand?"

"Me."

"You what?"

"I'm the ransom. Fiona told me. She figured it out when Garreth was tasking her."

"Go on."

"They're giving them someone else instead. Ajay. They're making him look as much like me as they can. I think he was a soldier. Or something."

Winnie whistled. She shook her head. "Shit," she said.

"I'm sorry," he said.

"What does Garreth want Fiona to do? Do you know that?"

"Fly a video drone. When they do it."

"Do what?"

"I don't know. Get Chombo back."

Winnie frowned at him, drummed the fingers of one hand on a pant-suited knee, looked away, then quickly back. "Thank God for leave en route."

"I'm sorry I didn't tell you sooner."

"Garreth," she said.

"Garreth?"

"You're arranging for me to speak with him. Soonest. Tonight."

Milgrim looked at the St. Christopher. "I can try. But . . ."

"But what?"

"Don't bring *him*." Indicating the retired Scotland Yard detective, but keeping his hands below the level of the dashboard.

"By phone. And not my phone, either. He'll have a number that's a throwaway. Get me that."

"Why do you want to talk with him? He'll ask me."

"He's building something. He's building it for Gracie. I don't want to know what it is. At all. The kidnapping angle puts things in a different light."

"Why?"

"Makes me think Gracie is indulging himself, over here. Kind of midlife adventure. Kidnapping. Sort of like a red convertible, for a certain kind of guy. Businessman, in his position, can't afford it. At all. But they don't actually teach you business, in the schools. He doesn't know that, though."

"What should I tell Garreth?"

"Tell him it won't take long. He won't have to tell me anything, admit to anything, provide any information. It won't be recorded. He can use voice-distortion software, which he will anyway, unless he really is an amateur, in which case you're all liable to wind up with Mike all over you, real soon now, and there's nothing I'll be able to do about it. Tell him I have an Easter egg for him. And what I'll give him isn't mine, in any way. Nothing to do with me."

"Why should he believe you?"

"Context. If he's any good, he'll be able to find out who I am, and see where I'm coming from. But what he won't get, from that, is that I've got a hard-on for Gracie. That's up to you. You've got to convey that. That it's just personal that way." She smiled, in a way that Milgrim didn't like. "Maybe it's my midlife adventure."

"Okay," said Milgrim, not feeling in any way that it was.

"Tell me something, though."

"What?"

"If you're what they want in exchange for Bigend's guy, why are you being driven around by a girl, on the back of a bike? Why aren't you locked down, watched over, massively surveilled?"

"Because Bigend has almost nobody he can trust right now."

"Shit's *deep*," she said, with what he took to be a kind of satisfaction. "Out now. You've got your orders. Go."

Milgrim got out. Seeing the man in the raincoat approaching, he left the door open. He turned and walked back, past the two cider cans, lonely sentinels of Smithfield, as Fiona started her engine.

73. THE PATCHWORK
BOYFRIEND

In the dark, Garreth asleep beside her, the round and looming bottom of the birdcage barely visible in the faint glow of the power telltales on his laptop and various phones; tiny bright points in red and green, a constellation of potential trouble.

She'd finally and truly met Frank, which had taken less getting used to than she would have imagined, though at first she'd cried a little.

Frank had been stabilized in Singapore, then variously reconstructed, in a surgical odyssey funded by the old man. Frank had seen arcane facilities in the United States, ghost wings of otherwise workaday military hospitals. In one of these, shattered bone had been replaced with custom segments of calcified rattan, fastened in place with ceramic screws whose main ingredient was the primary constituent of natural bone. The result, so far, was Frank, a patchwork thing, more stitches than skin. A taut and shining mosaic, reminding her of expensively mended china.

He'd initially voted to have it off, he'd told her, knowing quite a bit about the current state of prosthetics, a field being rapidly driven by America's wars, with their massive improvements in rates of wound survival. But the surgeons the old man had gotten him to were chancers, he said, and he'd found himself infected by their eagerness to see what they could do, out at the very edge of the possible. This had caused her to weep again, and he'd held her, and made jokes, until it passed. And he'd been curious, too, about the officially nonexistent levels of expertise and technology he'd correctly assumed to be involved. Something demanding the temporary severing of certain nerves had been the least pleasant part of it, he'd said, and the recent procedures in Germany had been to reconnect those, so that he could now feel, increasingly, what Frank was feeling. Which, while not pleasant by any means, was far superior to previous disconnection, and absolutely essential in terms of getting back to walking.

He made the dressings progressively smaller, each time he changed them. The rest of Frank was that aerial Kansas patchwork of found-object dermis, reassuringly leg-shaped if a bit withered from the nonuse.

Most animals, he'd told her, apparently seriously, preferred bilaterally symmetrical mates, to the extent that it formed a sort of biota-wide bottom line, and that he'd understand if she felt that way. She'd told him that the bottom line as far as she was concerned was men who didn't sound like utter fucking idiots, and had kissed him. After which, more kissing, much else, laughter, some tears, more laughter.

Now she lay in the minute glow of LEDs, and willed silence, absence of messaging, an empty in-box, this peace, here in the Piblokto Madness bed, which now no longer seemed that, to her, the arch of the right whale's jawbone even bespeaking something matrimonial, if she thought about it, which she was still unwilling generally to do.

But okay right now. Okay so far. His breathing beside her.

Beneath her pillow, the iPhone began to vibrate. She slid her hand under, cupped it, considered the option of skipping the call. But these were not times for skipped calls.

"Hello?" she whispered.

"What's wrong?" It was Milgrim.

"Garreth's sleeping."

"Sorry," whispered Milgrim.

"What is it?'

"It's complicated. Someone needs to speak with Garreth."

"Who?"

"Please don't get the wrong idea," whispered Milgrim, "but she's a U.S. federal agent."

"That's as wrong an idea as I've heard in a while," said Hollis, forgetting to whisper.

"What is?" asked Garreth.

"It's Milgrim."

"Give him to me."

She covered the phone, realizing she had no idea where its microphone might be, or if covering it would help. "He wants you talk to a U.S. agent."

"Ah," he said, "the odd bits emerge now. The localized high-pressure zone of weird begins to manifest. Always does. Give me the phone."

"I'm scared."

"Makes perfect sense." He reached over, squeezed her arm reassuringly. "Phone, please."

She handed him the phone.

"Milgrim," he said. "Been networking, have we? Slow down. Does she have a name?"

And she heard a pen on paper as he wrote in the dark, something he was very good at.

"Does she? Really? She put it that way herself?" She felt him prop himself on the pillows. When he opened the laptop, its light was light of some weird and other moon. A lucky one, she hoped. She heard him begin to type, with one hand, while he asked Milgrim questions, brief ones, and listened to longer answers.

74. MAP, TERRITORY

The heels of Milgrim's Tanky & Tojo brogues, as he sat astride the high, raked pillion of Benny's Yamaha, didn't quite touch the cobbles of this tiny square. Something about the angle of his feet recalled some childhood line-drawing from *Don Quixote*, though whether those feet had been the knight's or Sancho Panza's, he didn't know. Fiona sat, saddled lower, in front of him, boots firm on the pavement, holding them upright. He held her iPhone behind her back, seeing exactly where they were now, on the bright little window, via the application she'd shown him earlier: amid these narrow lanes, his eye backtracking to Farringdon, the straight run to the bridge, river, Southwark, Vegas cube. Comprehending the route for the first time.

He'd phoned Winnie from this courtyard, reading off the number Garreth had given him. He'd written it on the back of her card, which was becoming a softer object, its sharp corners blunted. She'd repeated it back to him, made him check it. "Good work," she'd said. "Stand by in case I can't reach him."

But that had been eight minutes ago, so he assumed she was on the phone with Garreth.

Fiona's yellow helmet turned. "Finished?" she asked, muffled by the visor.

He looked down at the screen, the glowing map. Saw it as a window into the city's underlying fabric, as though he held something from which a rectangular chip of London's surface had been pried, revealing a substrate of bright code. But really, wasn't the opposite true, the city the code that underlay the map? There was an expres-

sion about that, but he'd never understood it, and now couldn't remember how it went. The territory wasn't the map?

"Done," he said passing her the bright chip. She turned it off,
pocketed it, while he put on Mrs. Benny's helmet and fastened the
chinstrap, scarcely noticing the hairspray.

He put his feet on the pegs as she rolled forward, and curled in
closer to her armored back, watching day-bright vignettes of headlit
wall-texture as she wheeled them around, the Yahama's engine
sounding as though it were anxious for the bridge.

What would Winnie and Garreth be talking about? he wondered
as Fiona drove out of the courtyard and down the lane to Farringdon
Road.

75. DOWN THE DARKNETS

Watching Garreth as he listened to his headset, she wondered what the American agent was saying.

She'd watched him free a phone she hadn't seen before, from a vacuum-sealed plastic bag, then install a card selected from a black nylon wallet containing a few dozen more, like the duplicates folder in a very dull stamp collection. He'd connected the new phone to a power unit, and then, with another cable, to something black, and smaller. When the new phone rang, the tone was a variant on Old Phone, her own most frequent choice.

Now he listened, occasionally nodding slightly, eyes on the screen of his laptop, forefinger poking, as if of its own accord, at keys and mouse patch. He was down his darknets again, she knew, communicating with the old man, or unspecified third parties. There seemed to be no advertising on Garreth's darknets, and relatively little color, though she supposed that was because he tended mainly to read documents.

Now a color photograph of a woman appeared, Chinese, thirtyish, her hair center-parted, expressionless, in the style of a biometric passport photograph. Garreth leaned forward slightly, as if for a better look, and wrote something in his notebook. "That wouldn't actually be of much help," he said. "I have better numbers than that myself." He fell silent again, listening, opening screens on his desktop, making notes. "No. I have that. I don't think you can really do much for me. Which is a pity, considering your willingness. What I could really use would be something heavier. Massive, really. And the goods will be there. Worth massive's time, amply. Massive'll come along, I imagine. But massive immediately would be the business." He listened again. "Yes. Certainly. Do. Good night." He touched the keyboard, the photograph vanishing. He looked at Hollis. "That was well queer."

"That was her, the photograph?"

"Probably."

"What did she want?"

"She was offering something. Didn't really have what I'd most like, but may be able to get it."

"You won't tell me?"

"Only because you'd be less safe knowing at this point." He stroked her hair back from her face, on one side. "Do you know what you'd take with you, if you were going away forever? No more than you can carry at a brisk run."

"Forever?"

"Probably not. But best to assume you wouldn't come back here."

"Not the author's copies," indicating the boxes.

"No. But seriously. Pack."

"I'm not going anywhere without you."

"That's the plan. But pack now, please."

"Is this too big?" indicating her roll-aboard.

"Perfect, but keep it light."

"Is it about something she told you?"

"No," he said, "it's because I doubt we have much more time. Pack."

She set the empty roll-aboard on the nearest armchair, unzipped it, and began to select things from the drawers in the wardrobe. She added the Hounds designer's jersey tube. Went into the bathroom, gathering things from the counter.

"How's Frank?" she asked, emerging.

"Complaining, but he has to get used to it."

She noticed the Blue Ant figurine on the bedside table. Picked it up. You're in, she thought, surprising herself, and carried it, with bottles and tubes of product, to the roll-aboard. "Won't you need some sort of follow-up for neural surgery?"

"Woman in Harley Street," he said, "as soon as I can."

"How soon is that?"

"When this is over." A phone began to ring. Yet another variant on Old Phone. Not hers. He took a phone from his pocket, looked at it. After the third ring he answered. "Yes? From now? Venue? No? Crucial." He thumbed a key.

"Who?"

"Big End."

"What?"

"We're on. Ninety minutes."

"What's crucial?"

"We don't know where. Venue matters. We need exterior, need privacy. But so do they. You ready?"

"As I'll ever be."

"Get a pullover. Back of the van's unheated." He'd brought out a second phone. "Message all," he said, tapping a few tiny keys. The phone beeped.

She glanced around Number Four. The insect-parts wallpaper, the shelves with their busts and heads. Would she see this again? "Are you taking the scooter?"

"No further than the door," he said, rising from the bed with the aid of his cane. "It's Frank's turn." He winced.

She'd just pulled a sweater on. "Are you all right?"

"Actually," he said, "I am. Be a dear and get the ugly T-shirt from the bedside hutch. And the other package, the smaller one."

"What's that?"

"Almost nothing. And a world of woe, for someone. Quick. There's a vegan van waiting for us."

"What the fuck is up?" demanded Heidi, from the other side of Number Four's door.

Hollis opened the door.

Heidi stood, glaring, majorette jacket open over Israeli army bra. "Ajay just got a text, hauled ass down the hall, said he had to see his cousin." She saw Garreth. "Was that you?"

"Yes," said Garreth, "but you're coming with us."

"Whatever the fuck this is," Heidi said, "I'm coming with—"

"Us," interrupted Garreth, "but *not* if you make us late. And put a shirt on. Trainers, not boots. In case there's running."

Heidi opened her mouth, closed it.

"Time to go," said Hollis, zipping her bag shut.

"Not without the party favors," said Garreth.

76. GONE-AWAY GIRL

Milgrim stood, feeling lost, remembering the sound of Fiona's Kawasaki fading to nothing at all.

She'd gotten a message from Garreth and was gone, leaving her chicken and bacon sandwich uneaten on the table in the Vegas cube, but not before she'd snapped a short length of transparent nylon line to tiny eyebolts, front and rear, on the paint-dazzled penguin. He'd helped her steer it through the door, and she'd anchored it, atop Benny's huge red tool kit, by placing a hammer on the fishing line. Then she'd quickly returned to the cube, where she'd given him the penguin's iPhone. "That little van I brought you here in," she said, "will be here shortly. Wait in the yard, with the penguin. It'll fit in the back."

"Where are you going?"

"Don't know." Zipping up her jacket.

"Am I going to the same place?"

"Depends on Garreth," she'd said, and for a moment he'd imagined she might be about to kiss him, maybe just on the cheek, but she hadn't. "Take care of yourself," she said.

"You too."

Then she was out the door, and gone.

He'd carefully rewrapped her sandwich, tucking it into one of the huge side pockets of the nylon jacket, which he'd kept on. He'd give it to her if he saw her later. Then he noticed Mrs. Benny's black helmet on the table, and took it to mean he wouldn't be riding with Fiona tonight. He picked it up and sniffed the interior, hoping for hairspray, but couldn't find it now.

He put his bag, with the Air, over his shoulder, dialed the Italian umbrella down, and went out, closing the door behind him. If there was a way to lock it, he didn't know it.

He went to Benny's toolbox, freed the penguin, and walked out into the yard, the line through his left fist, which he held upright, as though he were holding a subway strap.

"Going out?" asked Benny. He held one of the fiberglass cowlings.

Milgrim had had no idea that he was there. How late did Benny work? Or was he another cog, now, in Garreth's plan? "They're picking me up," said Milgrim.

"Have a good one, then," said Benny, seemingly paying no attention to the penguin. "I'll lock up."

Then the little Japanese minivan with the curtains and the moon-roof pulled up, the driver's-side window powering down. A Japanese mini-driver, looking about fifteen, in a crisp white shirt. "I'll help you put that in the back," he said, with a British accent. He cut the engine and got out.

"Where are we going?"

"Haven't been told yet, but we're in a bit of a hurry."

77. GREEN SCREEN

The broken wheel on her roll-aboard woke, like some ominous precision measuring device, as she pulled it along the corridor to the rear lobby. She'd gone to say goodbye to the ferret, though she doubted she'd ever be able to explain that to anyone. Garreth might understand, who had his own odd ways with fear. She saw the empty scooter-chair, abandoned beside the glass slab door, where Robert now stood.

"Congratulations, Miss Henry," he said, inexplicably and rather tenderly, as he opened and held the door for her. Unwilling, after more definitely having noted a multiplication of identical follies in the watercolors upstairs, plus her moment just now with the ferret, to risk further liminality, she thanked him, smiling, and clicked swiftly on, out beneath a porte cochere she supposed had been built for actual coaches, and on toward the back of the tall Slow Foods van, drawn up near it. Tall, the van, a big one, and newly painted a rich aubergine, lettered and trimmed in a dull bronze, as if the Queen herself were vegan, if vegan was what Slow Food was about, and fond of Aubrey Beardsley.

"Hello," said the driver, brunette under her Foleyesque cap, and prettily Norwegian. Both a professional truck driver and an actress. Hollis knew all this because she'd overheard Garreth hiring her, via some third party, and hadn't realized until now that this was what that had been about. "There are two zippered panels, inside these doors," the driver said, indicating the back of the truck. "I'll open the first for you, then close it, then you'll open and close the second. It's to make sure no light escapes. Clear?" The girl smiled, and Hollis found herself smiling back. Aside from driving, Hollis knew, she was there to engage the authorities, should there be any trouble with where they were parked later. Now the girl opened one of the van's rear doors, revealing a taut wall of black canvas, like something in a conjuring trick, and climbed three very sturdy-looking folding aluminum steps, where she raised a tall vertical zip. "Give me your bag." Hollis passed it up. The driver put it through the slit, climbed down. Hollis went up the steps, through the slit, the zip's plastic teeth odd against her wrist, then turned and pulled the zipper most of the way down. The girl pulled it the rest of the way, leaving Hollis in absolute darkness.

Behind her, the other zip went up, admitting startlingly bright light. She turned and saw Garreth, and behind him Pep, wearing what she instantly knew must be the ugly T-shirt.

"I didn't think it would literally be that ugly," she said, stepping through the second zip.

It was. Pep, in black cyclist's pants, wore the largest, ugliest T-shirt she'd ever seen, in a thin, cheap-looking cotton the color of ostomy devices, that same imaginary Caucasian flesh-tone. There were huge features screened across it in dull black halftone, asymmetrical eyes at breast height, a grim mouth at crotch-level. Later she'd be unable to say exactly what had been so ugly about it, except that it was somehow beyond punk, beyond art, and fundamentally, somehow, an affront. Diagonals at the edges continued around the sides, and across the short, loose sleeves. Pep leered at her, or perhaps only looked at her, and pulled the strap of a dark green messenger bag over his head, tucking what she recognized as Garreth's other party favor into it.

"Don't forget to take that bag off," Garreth said. He was seated in a black workstation chair that appeared to have been taped to the shiny aubergine floor. "Queer the visuals, otherwise."

Pep leered, or perhaps smiled, in reply, then stepped past her, through the open zip in the second scrim of black canvas. She saw the same hideous features repeated on the back of the shirt. He bent, picked up her bag, deposited it inside, then ran the zipper down, vanishing. She heard the other zipper being opened, then closed, then the sound of the door being closed.

She turned to Garreth, but saw that he was mounting his black laptop in a sort of clasp that extended from a framework of black plastic pipe. The pipe, like a geometric model of a rectangular solid, almost filled the interior of the van. Like Garreth's chair, it was held in place with that nonreflective black tape that kept film sets together. There were things mounted on the framework: two plasma screens, one above the other, cables, boxes and bits the cables plugged into, and several very stylish-looking LED lamps.

"Where we going?" asked Heidi, sounding oddly subdued, seated on the floor at the front, her back against another centrally zippered sheet of black canvas.

"Should know shortly," Garreth said as he finished locking his computer in place, so that it sat before him on an invisible desk.

"Where's Ajay gone?"

"Wherever we're going," Garreth said, "but with Charlie."

It all smelled of pipe cement, new electronics, lighting.

"Sit down beside Heidi," Garreth said as Hollis heard the driver's door slam shut. "There's foam."

Hollis did.

"Crazy," said Heidi, eyes wide, looking from Hollis to the rig that surrounded them. "Claustrophobia."

"What about it?" Hollis asked.

"I've got it," said Heidi.

The driver started the engine. The van was moving away from Cabinet.

Deal, said Hollis, silently, to the ferret, though she hadn't really been aware of making one.

"I've never heard you say anything about claustrophobia," Hollis said.

"Fujiwara says it was being married to fuckstick. Why I went to him in the first place. I thought it was just wanting to beat the living fuck out of somebody, y'know?"

"You don't think it was?"

"When he got me calmed down, building models, I could see that it was not wanting to feel trapped."

"Did you finish your Breast Chaser?" Thinking it might help, to keep her talking.

"Not enough detail," Heidi said, sadly.

"Have an ETA?" Garreth asked someone. He was conversing in clipped but genial near-code, with some unknown number of people, his headset plugged into a switchbox attached to an octopus galaxy of phones.

"How 'bout us?" said Heidi. "Do we?"

"Hush. He has to concentrate."

"Understand what he's doing?"

"No, but it's complicated."

"Ajay's cousin got him up in whiteface. Filled the notch in his nose with putty. Dyed his hair shit-brown and sprayed stuff on the sides."

"They want him to be mistaken for Milgrim."

"I *got* that. Why?"

"Someone's kidnapped Bigend's star researcher. They're demanding Milgrim in exchange for him."

"Why would they?"

"Actually," Hollis said, "it seems to be because you stuck the man who was following you with that dart, though Milgrim had already fucked him up himself."

Heidi, her large white hands locked tightly across her knees, black nails chipped, regarded Hollis from just above them with utmost seriousness. "Are you shitting me?"

"No," said Hollis.

"What are they, pussies?"

Hollis, framing her response, saw that Heidi was struggling not to laugh. She dug her swiftly in the ribs with a knuckle.

"Win," announced Garreth, his hand extended to mute all phones. "The Scrubs. The model worked. Optimal venue. Unless there's wind."

"What model?" Hollis asked.

"Someone at the University of Colorado ran one for us. Scrubs was best for us. Excuse me." He took his hand off the box and began to type. The van slowed, honked, changed lanes, stopped briefly, turned.

"Scrubs, dear," he said to someone else. "Need you in the air. Don't run lights, don't speed, get there."

"What's happening?" Heidi asked quietly.

"I think they've agreed on where they'll do the exchange," Hollis said. "I think we like it."

"They're getting one ugly-ass version of Bollywood boyfriend." Heidi shrugged.

"I thought you were trying not to go there."

"Trying," agreed Heidi.

"Do you feel better?"

"Yeah," said Heidi, and reached under the majorette jacket to rub her ribs, "but it'll come back, if I can't get out of this fucking truck."

"Somewhere to go now," Hollis said.

"Not yet," Garreth said to someone, "but she's airborne." Then he said something in a language Hollis didn't recognize at all, and fell silent.

"What language was that?" she asked, as the van made another turn.

"Catalan," he said.

"Didn't know you spoke it."

"I can only say very rude things about his mother." He sat up straighter. "Pardon." He fell silent again. "Fully operative," he said, finally. "Optimal so far." He was quiet again. "I appreciate that, but no. You'll have to keep them back. Well out of the area. I have a lot on the ground. Too many moving parts to have anyone of yours in the mix. Not negotiable, no." She saw his hand come down on the switchbox. "Bugger."

"What?"

"Bastard's got a private ambulance on the prowl, so he says. Specialists sitting up late in Harley Street, in case Chombo should be damaged."

"I hadn't thought of that."

"I had. We've medical backup ourselves. Big End's ambulance won't just have medics in it. Snatch squad for Milgrim, that would be."

"Does he know where it is?"

"They call him first."

"How bad is that?"

"No telling," he said. He took his hand off the box, and immediately smiled. "Darling," he said. "Brilliant. Above it? Give me the fix. Four? Moving away from it? Pull back, drop. Approach about two feet off the ground, car between you. Need the number, make, model. Then make sure no one's inside it. But no IR, in case it flares off the glass and they see it."

"Infrared," said Heidi.

The uppermost of the two screens mounted on black pipe came on, a washed-out oscilloscope green. He dialed the lighting down.

Hollis and Heidi edged forward on the foam, peering up at the screen. Image from a moving camera, abstract, unreadable. Then Hollis saw a big British license plate, as if recorded by some robot on the bottom of the sea.

"Good girl," Garreth said. "Now raise it a bit and give us a look inside. Then follow them. The one with the parcel: that's Gracie. Get on him and stay on him." He touched the box again, turned. "We don't like a parcel," he said to Fiona, then back to the green screen.

78. EL LISSITZKY

C are for mineral water," asked the driver, "or fruit? The basket's right there."

Milgrim, seated on the floor behind the passenger seat, noticed the small basket for the first time. He'd been watching the penguin joggle against the moonroof, and wondering what would happen if the Taser went off. "Is there a croissant?" he asked, leaning toward the basket.

"Sorry, no. Apple, banana. Prawn crackers."

"Thank you," said Milgrim, and pocketed a banana. He wanted to ask what the driver thought they were doing, actually, out in the night with a dazzle-painted robotic penguin, filled with helium, but he didn't. He suspected that the driver had no idea; that he was someone who drove, who drove and rather specifically had no idea, and was pleasant, unobtrusive, an extremely good driver, someone who knew the city very well. So Milgrim opted to ask nothing at all. Wherever they were going was where Garreth wanted them, and perhaps Fiona would be there too.

The penguin rolled slightly as they executed a roundabout. Milgrim sensed the scrupulousness of the boy's driving; he'd be doing nothing at all in violation, probably driving a steady two kilometers below the speed limit. Milgrim had seen people, sometimes quite unlikely people, drive this way on their way to drug deals. Transactional, he thought of it. Really the whole evening felt extremely transactional, though he'd never been offered mineral water or fruit, doing that.

The boy wore one of those headsets designed to look as much as possible, it seemed to Milgrim, like a pinball flipper had been pounded into his ear, the flipper part being the microphone. He periodically spoke softly to this, though mainly to answer yes or no, or to repeat the names of streets Milgrim promptly forgot. Milgrim gathered, though, that the boy now knew where they were going.

And suddenly, no prior announcement, it seemed that they were there.

"Where are we?" asked Milgrim.

"Wormwood Scrubs."

"The *prison*?"

"*Little* Wormwood Scrubs," said the driver. "You'll cross the road, straight in from here, keep going straight, into the grass. He said to tell you she's under a sheet of camouflage and may be difficult to see."

"Fiona?"

"He didn't say," the boy said primly, as though unwilling to be further involved. He got out, closed the door, walked quickly around to the rear, and opened that door.

Milgrim kept the penguin low, away from the moonroof, as he edged crabwise back to the open rear door. There was something inherently cheerful about the buoyancy of a balloon, he thought. It must have been a wonderful day when they first discovered buoyant gases. He wondered what they'd put them in. Varnished silk, he guessed, for some reason picturing the courtyard at the Salon du Vintage.

The boy held the balloon for him as he climbed out, his shirt eerily white in the light from the nearest streetlight. Milgrim became aware of the presence of a large empty space, an utter anomaly in London. Opposite side of the road. Empty and dark.

"A park?" he asked.

"Not exactly," said the boy. "Go straight across." He pointed. "Keep going. You'll find her." He handed the balloon's tether, the loop of nylon fishing line, to Milgrim.

"Thank you," said Milgrim. "Thanks for the banana."

"You're welcome."

Milgrim crossed the road, hearing the van start behind him, drive away. He kept walking. Through grass, across a paved walk, into more grass. Such a peculiar, slightly ragged emptiness, the grass uneven.

None of the landscaping, the deep architecture, the classical bones, of this city's parks. Waste ground. The grass was wet, though if it had been raining earlier, he hadn't noticed. Dew, perhaps. He felt it through his socks, though Tanky & Tojo's brogues were better for this than pavement, the black lugs digging in. Walking shoes. He imagined walking somewhere with Fiona, somewhere as wide as this but less spooky. He wondered if she liked that. Did motorcycle people like walking? Had he ever liked walking? He stopped and looked up at London's luminous, faintly purple sky, all the lights of Europe's largest city caught, held there, obscuring all but a few stars. He looked back, across the wide, well-lit road, to an ordinary, orderly jumble of housing he didn't culturally understand, houses or flats or condos, and then back to the oddness of these Scrubs. It felt as though you could score here. He couldn't imagine that a city this size wouldn't conduct drug traffic in a place like this.

Then he heard a low whistle. "Here," Fiona called softly, "get under."

He found her huddled under a thin tarp, in one of the more esoteric new camouflage patterns Bigend was interested in. He couldn't remember which one, but now he saw how well it worked.

"Not with the penguin! Get your controller. Hurry." She sat cross-legged, spoke quietly, her own iPhone glowing green on her lap. She pulled the balloon down, unclipped its tether at either end, and released it. It rose slowly, burdened with the Taser. Milgrim took the penguin's iPhone from his pocket, squatted beside her, and she drew the fabric around them both, leaving heads and hands exposed. "Get on it," she said. "Fly. Take it up, away from the road. I can't talk now, work of my own." He saw she wore one of the earplug headsets. "You're looking for a tall man. He was wearing a raincoat, overcoat. No hat. Short hair, probably gray. He has a parcel, something wrapped in paper, a few feet long."

"Where?"

"Lost him. Tap the green circle if you want night vision, but it's no help on the penguin unless you're right up on something."

Milgrim turned on his iPhone, saw a blank glowing screen, then realized that the penguin's camera was seeing empty sky. It was so much nicer, he instantly realized, when you didn't have to worry about bumping the wall or ceiling of the cube. He swam higher, strangely free.

"Is this guy wearing a hockey jersey with a face painted on it?" She showed him her screen. Looking down on a figure in a huge pullover of some kind, the back presenting a grotesque and enormous face.

"Looks Constructivist," he said. "El Lissitzky? He's breaking into that car?" The man stood close to a black sedan, his back to the camera on Fiona's helicopter.

"Locking it. Already broke in, now he's locking it." Her fingers moved and the image blurred, her drone, compared to the air penguin, moving with startling speed.

"Where are you going?" Meaning the drone.

"Have to check the other three. Then I have to set it down, save batteries. Been in the air since I got here. Are you looking for the man with the parcel?"

"Yes," said Milgrim, and sent the penguin swimming down, into the relative darkness of the Scrubs. "Who are the other three?"

"One's Chombo. Then the one from that car, that tried to block you in, in the City."

Foley.

"The other one's a footballer, with metal hair."

"Metal hair?"

"More like a mullet. Big lad."

79. DUNGEON MASTER

Hollis stood behind him, trying to pretend she was watching someone play a game, something tedious and self-importantly arcane, on multiple screens. Something that didn't matter, was of no great importance, on which nothing depended.

A game with undergraduate production values. No music, no sound effects. Garreth the dungeon master, defining the quests, setting tasks, issuing gold and sigils of invisibility.

Better to look at it that way, but she couldn't make it stick. She leaned back, against aubergine-coated automotive steel, the coolness of it, and watched the video feed from Fiona's drone.

Whatever Fiona was flying felt hummingbird-swift, capable of brilliantly sudden pause and sustained hover, but also of elevator-like ascents and descents. All in the pale green monochrome of night vision. Her cameras were better than Milgrim's, expensively optimized. Hollis, with no idea what it might look like, imagined it a huge dragonfly, its body the size of a baguette, the pulsing wings iridescent.

It had hovered, watching four men emerge from a black sedan. A Mercedes hire-car, Garreth had said, having somehow checked plate numbers.

Two of the men were tall, broad-shouldered, and efficient-looking. Another, shorter, almost certainly Foley, limped. The fourth, whose posture she now recalled from Los Angeles and Vancouver, a perpetual petulant slump, was Bobby Chombo, Bigend's pet mathematician. That same annoying haircut, half of his thin face lost behind an unwashed diagonal curtain. There he'd been, below Fiona's dragonfly, as if in a pale green steel engraving, wrapped in what looked like a robe or dressing gown. Neurasthenic, she remembered Inchmale delighting in calling him. He'd said that neurasthenia was coming back, and that Bobby was ahead of the curve, an early adapter.

Garreth took it for granted that one of the taller men, the one in the dark raincoat, carrying a rectangular package, was Gracie. This based, Hollis gathered, on the other's having some kind of archaic rocker hair, hair that reminded her of one of Jimmy's junkie friends, a drummer from Detroit.

When the four of them, Foley seeming to be leading Chombo, had moved on, away from the car, Garreth had had Fiona dip down to read the car's plate number, and peek through the window, in case they'd left someone to watch it, a complication that Hollis gathered would have required some other and more unpleasant skill on Pep's part. The car had been empty, and Fiona, aloft again, had found them easily, still moving, but the one Garreth thought was Gracie was gone, missing, and still was, his package with him. Fiona had been unable to look for him then, because Garreth had needed her back at the car, so that he could vet Pep's arrival and subsequent burglary, which had taken all of forty-six seconds, passenger-side door, complete with lockup.

Pep, following instructions, hadn't been wearing the messenger bag, and Hollis assumed he'd deposited the other party favor, whatever it might be, in the car, that being evidently the plan. And then he was gone, his dual-engined electric bicycle, utterly silent, capable of an easy sixty miles per hour, never having intersected with the focal cones of any of the cameras showing on the screen of Garreth's laptop. Had it, Garreth said, the resulting image of a riderless bicycle might have negated the whole exercise.

The camera-map, on Garreth's laptop, was grayscale, the cones of camera-vision red, each one fading to pink as it spread from its apex. Occasionally, one of them would move as an actual given camera motored on its axis. She had no idea where this particular display was being darknetted from, and she was glad that she didn't.

The screen that offered Milgrim's video feed, she thought, seemed entirely out of step with the operation, and perhaps for that reason she found herself going back to it, though it wasn't very interesting. With Gracie still unaccounted for, she felt Garreth's nerves. He could have used someone who knew what they were doing, she guessed, on another drone like Fiona's.

Whatever Milgrim was flying, it seemed leisurely, almost comical, though capable of invigorating bursts of sustained forward motion. Having been instructed, via Fiona, to make a circuit of the area, looking for Gracie, he had, though Garreth had complained that he was too high. Now he was cruising, she saw, above vegetation scrubby enough to warrant the name, Garreth apparently having forgotten about him. But nothing had been expected of Milgrim and his drone, she knew. He'd been given the job to keep him out of Bigend's hands.

The sound of a very long zipper being stealthily undone. She glanced to the right and saw Heidi touch her upraised forefinger to her lips.

"Our two," Garreth said to the headset, "are starting for point now. Put it down about twenty meters west of point. We'll have to run with the batteries you have." That would be Fiona.

As he spoke, Heidi slipped through the fly and slowly lowered the zipper, closing it behind her.

Point, Hollis knew, would be the GPS coordinates that Gracie had specified as the site of the exchange.

On Fiona's screen, the perspective suddenly dropped to knee-height, then raced forward over darkly blurred grass, as if from the viewpoint of a hyperkinetic child.

Milgrim, she saw, had reached the end of the scrub, and was turning slowly around for more.

I hope she just had to pee, thought Hollis, glancing back at the long plastic zipper.

80. FIGURES IN A LANDSCAPE

L ook," said Fiona, "it's you."

Garreth had ordered her aloft again. Now she showed Milgrim her iPhone, the camo tarp rustling around them.

"That's Ajay?" Two figures on the little screen, from a high angle, steel-engraved in washed-out green. One of them shuffling, dejected, head down, shoulders too wide for Milgrim's jacket. The other man was short, broad, something round and flat on his head. Ajay's hands were together, crossed, just above crotch-level, in what looked like a gesture of modesty. Handcuffed.

Fiona swung down, hovered, catching them as they passed, into and out of frame. Milgrim thought Ajay was doing a good job of conveying abject surrender, but otherwise he didn't see the resemblance. Chandra seemed to have done a better job with the spray-on hair this time.

The other man, Milgrim thought, looked as if someone had subjected the Dalai Lama to the gravity of a planet with greater mass than Earth's. Short, extremely sturdy, age-indeterminate, he wore a sort of beret, level across his forehead, with a pom-pom on top.

As the subjects left her frame, Fiona's thumbs moved, whirling the point of view back up, reminding Milgrim to check his own iPhone, where he found his penguin looking at grass and low bushes.

When he glanced back, Fiona had found three more figures, approaching on the Scrubs.

One was Chombo, still furled in his tissue-thin coat, and looking much more convincingly unhappy than Ajay's Milgrim. To Chombo's left came Foley, limping visibly, wearing darker pants than the ones that had elicited his nickname. He still had his cap, though, and the short dark jacket he'd worn in Paris. On Chombo's right, Milgrim saw, to his horror, was the man from Edge City Family Restaurant, Winnie's other Mike, the one with the mullet and the knife in his Toters.

"He wants you over here," Fiona said, meaning where her drone was, "looking for the one I lost. Move."

Milgrim sank his concentration into the bright little rectangle, penguin-space, his thumbs tapping. He rolled, corrected for it, swam higher in the air.

Fiona's drone's night vision was so much better than the penguin's. The penguin's suffered from a kind of infrared myopia; the darker it was, the closer he had to get, and the brighter he had to make the penguin's infrared LEDs. Which were none too bright to begin with, according to Fiona. The grass below presented in a sort of cheesy pointillism, monochrome, faintly green, stripped of detail. Though if anyone were there, he thought, he'd see them.

And then he found Chombo, and Foley, and the man from Edge City Family Restaurant, still walking.

He had the penguin on auto-swim. He took over, stilled the wings, and let momentum carry him out in the gentle arc provided by his adjustment of the tail, something he was already better at.

Over something in the grass.

A hole? A large rock? He tried to slow himself, using the wings in reverse, but this caused him to roll, catching a blank screen of light-pollution. He righted himself. Nothing below. He began to swim down, using the wings on manual.

A man sat on the grass, cross-legged, something rectangular on his lap. A dark coat, short pale hair. Then gone, the penguin, in spite of Milgrim's best efforts, having overshot, glided on.

Fiona had told him, twice, how lucky they were to have no breeze tonight, all calm in the Thames Valley, yet he couldn't steer the penguin well enough to see a man somewhere immediately below him. He took a deep breath, lifted his thumbs from the screen. Let things settle. Let the penguin become a simple balloon, up in the windless air. Then start again.

"Twenty feet off site," he heard Fiona say, very quietly, "and closing."

81. ON SITE

saw him," Hollis said, not quite believing it herself. "I think Milgrim saw him too, but then he was gone."

"I know," said Garreth, "but we're go now."

Fiona's drone hovered as Ajay and the man called Charlie reached
the other three, who now stood waiting. Charlie put his hand on
Ajay's arm, stopping him. Ajay stood with his head lowered.

Now Foley led Chombo forward. Chombo squirmed, looking in
every direction, and Hollis saw the black O of his mouth. Foley jabbed
his hand into Chombo's ribs.

Garreth touched the switchbox. "Hit him," he said.

She saw Ajay blur, or teleport, across the space separating him
from Foley. Whatever befell Foley, on Ajay's arrival, was equally, invisibly fast, with Ajay seeming to have spun and grabbed Chombo before
Foley had hit the grass.

Now Charlie, the short, fridge-shaped man with the plaid tam,
was between those two and the man with the mullet.

She never saw the man's knife, only the way he held his hand, as
he closed with Charlie, and then she saw him fall, though Charlie
seemed only to have stepped back. The man rolled, sprang up, almost
as quickly as Ajay had pounced on Foley, lunged again, fell.

"Charlie tried to teach me that, once," said Garreth, "but I couldn't
bring myself to be sufficiently superstitious."

By now the man was on the ground again, without Charlie ever
having seemed to touch him.

"Why does he keep falling?"

"Some kind of Ghurka feedback loop. But your Foley's not getting up. Hope Ajay didn't overdo it."

Hollis glanced up, saw Milgrim's screen. The gray-haired man. A rifle— *"He has a gun—"*

"Fiona," he said, "shooter. Under the penguin. Now."

82. LONDON EYE

Thumbing the wings to rotate, slowly, just briefly enough, in opposite directions, had brought the penguin around, but had presented Milgrim with the iconic silhouette of a *Ruchnoy Pulemyot
Kalashnikova*, for which he'd instantly lost all English.

It lay across Gracie's legs, metal shoulder-stock unfolded, as Gracie
attached the curved magazine, a humble unit about which Milgrim, in
his period of government employment, had known an absurd amount.
The Russian for terminologies for every piece of machinery used to
produce them: stampers and spot-welders and so many more. He'd
noticed them ever since, on television screens, those magazines: ubiquitous objects in the world's harsher places, never auguring good.

"Fuck," from Fiona, beside him, just the least little plosive.
Then: "On it."

Gracie pulled something back, on the side of the rifle, released it,
sat up and forward, bringing his knees up, settling the orthopedic-
looking stock against his shoulder.

The penguin paddling down, it seemed, of its own accord, as
Gracie leaned his cheek in. Barrel moving, slightly—

Jerking, as something dark and rectangular shot beneath it.
Fiona's drone.

Gracie looked up. Through the penguin, directly at Milgrim. Who
must have done that awkward thing, though he could never remember it, the configuration she'd shown him in the cube.

Something smashed Gracie down, and sideways, out of his snip-
er's posture, an idiot giant's invisible hand, the penguin jerking si-

multaneously, image blurring. Milgrim never saw the wires at all, those fifteen feet of them, but he supposed they were very thin.

Gracie rolled on his back, convulsed as Milgrim fired the Taser again. "Galvanism," the word recalled from high school biology. Gracie grabbed invisible strings. Milgrim tapped the screen again. Gracie jerked again, held on.

"Stop!" Fiona said. "Garreth says!"

"Why?"

"*Stop!*"

Milgrim raised both thumbs, obedient now, terrified that he'd done something irrevocable.

Gracie sat up, clawing at his neck, then gave the invisible string a vicious yank, blurring the image again.

And then the penguin was rising, slowly, away from him. Milgrim's thumbs went to the wings. Nothing happened. He tried the tail, tried auto-swim. Nothing. Still rising. He saw Gracie stagger to his feet, sway, then run, out of frame, as the penguin, freed of its unaccustomed ballast of Taser, ascended of its own accord into the calm predawn air of the Thames Valley.

He thought he glimpsed the wheel of the London Eye, just as Fiona thrust her own iPhone in front of his.

83. PLEASE GO

What was that?" she asked.

"Milgrim," he said, shaking his head, "Tasered Gracie. It's a good thing I'm retiring. Milgrim just saved our bacon."

"*Milgrim* had the Taser?"

"On his balloon. Hello? Darling?" To the headset now. "Get us over the car, please. And hurry, you're running on fumes."

"Who was Gracie trying to shoot?"

"Chombo first, I imagine. Do Big End the most harm that way. Either when he saw that we weren't dealing in good faith, or because he'd planned to all along. Initially, I thought he might just play it straight, local rules, get Milgrim, make his point. Hoping he wouldn't go the full American on us, in London, in a public place, dead of night. Mad, really. But Milgrim's secret agent thinks it's a midlife crisis. If he'd fired, the area would be knee-deep in police in another minute, and entirely the wrong kind. Which would actually put him where we want him, though then they'd likely have us too."

"He's an arms dealer. Didn't you think he might have a gun?"

"Arms dealers are businessmen. Mild old gents, some of them. I knew there was cowboy potential"—he shrugged—"but hadn't much way to cover it. Just a bodged-up little exploit." He grinned. "But Milgrim jolted him, sufficient that he left without the gun. Imagine he wants space between it and himself now." He raised a hand, head tilting, listening. "You didn't. You *did. Bugger.*"

"What?"

"Ajay's sprained his ankle. In a sandbox. Chombo's run away." He drew a deep breath, blew it slowly out. "You're not seeing my machinations at their genius best, are you?"

Something slammed against the back of the truck. "Stay the fuck still!" commanded Heidi, her voice muffled but fully audible through the steel door and two canvas scrims.

Garreth looked back at Hollis. "She's *outside*," he said.

"I know. I didn't want to interrupt you. Hoped she was just going for a pee."

The long zip went up then, and Bobby Chombo was almost simultaneously injected through the fly, his face slick with tears. He fell on the aubergine floor, sobbing. Heidi's head appeared near the top of the fly. "He's the one, right?"

"I've never told you how *very* beautiful I find you, have I, Heidi?" said Garreth.

"Pissed his pants," said Heidi.

"In good company, believe me," said Garreth, shaking his head.

"Where's Ajay?" Heidi asked, frowning.

"About to get a Ghurka-ride. Piggyback. He's been wanting to get to know Charlie better." He turned back to his screens.

Milgrim's, Hollis saw, was blank, or rather, dimly Turneresque, faintest pink behind steel gray, the greenish hue gone now. But Fiona's was very busy. Figures climbing into the black car.

"Go," said Garreth to the car on the screen, with a little chivying gesture. "*Please* go."

The car drove out of frame.

"I'm going to have to ask you all to step outside for a moment," Garreth said.

"Why?" asked Heidi's disembodied head.

"Because I need to do something very dirty," he said, producing a phone like the one he'd used to take the American agent's call, "and because I don't want him"—with a nod in Chombo's direction—"weeping in the background. Gives the wrong impression."

Hollis knelt beside Chombo. "Bobby? Hollis Henry. We met in Los Angeles. Do you remember?"

Chombo flinched, his eyes screwed shut.

She sang the opening line of "Hard to Be One," probably for the first time in a decade. Then sang it again, getting it right, or in any case closer.

He fell silent, shuddered, opened his eyes. "Do you happen to have anything like a fucking cigarette?" he asked Hollis.

"I'm sorry," she said "I—"

"I do," said Heidi. "Outside."

"I'm not going anywhere with you."

"I'll go with you," said Hollis.

"You can have the pack," said Heidi, spreading the black fly with her white, black-nailed hands.

Chombo was already on his feet, tugging his thin knit coat around him. He glared at Hollis, then stepped gingerly through the zip-toothed vertical gap.

She followed him.

84. NEW ONE

Fiona's drone's batteries had died, and it dropped like a stone, almost as soon as Foley and the others had left in the black car. Milgrim had helped her fold the tarp, which was now stuffed into one of the side pockets of his riding jacket, and then had been the one to find the drone, though he'd done so by stepping on it, cracking a rotor housing. She hadn't seemed to care, tucking it under her arm like an empty drinks tray and quickly leading him to where she'd left her Kawasaki. "We'll FedEx it back to Iowa and they'll rebuild it," she'd said, he'd guessed to stop him apologizing.

Now Milgrim held it as she dug in the eyeball-carrier Benny had mounted over the pillion seat. He shook it gingerly. Heard something rattle.

"Here," she said, producing a very shiny black helmet, sealed in plastic. She ripped the plastic, pulled it off, took the drone, and handed him the helmet. She put the drone in the carrier, snapped it shut. "You were getting tired of Mrs. Benny's."

Milgrim was unable to resist turning it over, raising it, sniffing the interior. It smelled of new plastic, nothing else. "Thanks," he said. He looked at the Kawasaki. "Where can I sit?"

"I'll be on your lap, basically." She reached out, took the strap of his bag, lifted it over his head so that it was on the other shoulder, diagonal across his chest, then kissed him, hard but briefly, on the mouth. "Get on the bike," she said. "He wants us away from here."

"Okay," said Milgrim, breathily, out of hyperventilation and joy, as he put on his new helmet.

85. TO GET A HANDLE ON IT

ornwall's okay," said Heidi, on Hollis's iPhone. "Haven't found a place to spread Mom 'n' Jimmy yet, but it's a good excuse for driving."

"How's Ajay's ankle?" Hollis was watching Garreth, on his back on the bed, exercising Frank with a bright yellow rubber bungee. They had the windows open, admitting occasional breezes and the sound of afternoon traffic. It was a larger room than the one she'd had the week before, a double, but it had the same blood-red walls and faux Chinese nonideograms.

"Fine," said Heidi, "but he's still using that trick cane your boyfriend gave him. It's a miracle he's washed his hands."

"Has he gotten over the rest of it?"

Ajay had been embarrassed over losing Chombo, and frustrated that he hadn't gotten a chance to go up against the man with the mullet. Hollis herself, he'd said, could have taken Foley, who'd looked like he belonged in hospital to begin with. And Milgrim, to cap things for Ajay, had taken down Gracie, who'd turned up with not just a gun but an assault rifle. On the upside, Ajay seemed to have bonded with Charlie, and on his return from Cornwall intended to try to learn to make skilled opponents repeatedly fall down, seemingly without touching them. Garreth, Hollis gathered, doubted much would come of this, but didn't tell Ajay.

"It isn't like he's got that long an attention span," said Heidi. "Where's Milgrim?"

"Iceland," Hollis said, "or on his way. With Hubertus, and the Dottirs. He phoned this morning. I couldn't understand whether he was on a plane or a boat. He said it was a plane, but that it had hardly any wings, and barely flew."

"You happy?"

"Apparently," said Hollis, watching Frank, now free of dressings, flex repeatedly against mild Parisian sunlight. "Weirdly. Today."

"Take care of yourself," said Heidi. "Gotta go. Ajay's back."

"You too. Bye."

Milgrim and Heidi, Garreth said, had each saved his bacon on the Scrubs. Milgrim by zapping Gracie, who'd brought the gun that Garreth had hoped he wouldn't; and Heidi, as she treated herself to a claustrophobia-reducing jog, by spotting Chombo, headed in the direction of Islington, and bringing him back, against his will, to the van.

Hollis remembered standing outside the van, with Bobby demanding time for a second cigarette, the pretty Norwegian driver demanding they be quiet now and get back inside. Pep had come scooting up then, on his eerily silent bike, running without lights, to hand Hollis a tattered Waitrose bag, leer at her, then whip away. When she'd renegotiated the black canvas flies, she'd found Garreth slumped in his chair, his screens blank. "Are you okay?" she'd asked, giving his shoulders a squeeze.

"Always a bit of a letdown," he'd said, but then had perked up a few minutes later, the van under way. Someone on his headphone. "How many?" he'd asked. Then smiled. "Eleven unmarked vehicles," he'd said to her, a moment later, quietly. "Body armor, Austrian automatic weapons, a few in hazmat suits. Heavy mob."

She'd been about to ask what he meant, but he'd silenced her with a look and another smile. She'd handed him the Waitrose bag then. When he opened it, she'd glimpsed one huge horrid eye of the world's ugliest T-shirt.

"What was that about a plane without wings?" he asked now, lowering Frank, the sequence completed.

"Milgrim's on board something Bigend's built, or restored. He said it was Russian."

"Ekranoplan," said Garreth. "A ground-effect vehicle. He's mad."

"He's had Hermès do the interior, Milgrim says."

"Dead posh, too."

"What kind of police came, for Foley and the others?"

"A very heavy mob. Aren't on the books. Old man knows a bit about them, says less than he knows."

"You called them when you sent us outside?"

"Dropped the dime, yes. Milgrim's American agent called me again when I was waiting for you in the van, behind Cabinet. Gave me a number and a code word. She hadn't had them when she'd called before. Offered me numbers I already had. I asked her for something massive. She came through too. Massively. I used them, gave the make, color, and registration number. Bang."

"Why did she do that?"

"Because she's a bad-ass, according to Milgrim." He smiled. "And, I'd guess, because it couldn't be traced back to her, her agency, her government."

"Where would she have gotten it?"

"No idea. Phoned a friend in Washington? But then, I never cease to be amazed at how the oddest things float about."

"And they arrested Gracie and the others?"

He sat up, doubled the yellow bungee in front of his chest, and slowly pulled his fists apart. "A special kind of detention."

"Nothing in the news."

"Nothing," he agreed, still stretching.

"Pep put something in their car. Then locked it up again."

"Yes." The bungee at full extension now, quivering.

"The other party favor."

He relaxed, the yellow elastic drawing his fists together. "Yes."

"What was in it?"

"Molecules. The sort you don't want a bomb-sniffer to find. They were sampled from a particular batch of Semtex that the IRA were heavily invested in. Plastic explosive. Distinctive chemical signature. Still a few tons of it out there, as far as anyone knows. And the card from a digital camera. Photographs of mosques, all over Britain. The dates on the images were a few months old, but not over sell-by, as suggestive evidence goes."

"And when you said you were using something 'off the shelf,' that was it?"

"Yes."

"Who was it originally for?"

"Not important now. No need to know. When I jumped off the Burj, silly tit, I blew the window of opportunity on that one. But then I had a girlfriend in trouble. Vinegar and brown paper."

"Vinegar?"

"Improvised fix. Whatever's handiest."

"I'm not complaining. But what about Gracie? Won't he tell them about us?"

"The beauty of that," he said, putting his hand on her hip, "is that he doesn't know about us. Well, you a bit, possibly, through Sleight, but Sleight's without a governor now, with Gracie a secret guest of Her Majesty. Sleight's busy getting himself well away from all of it, I'd imagine. And it's looking better than that, actually, according to the old man."

"How better?"

"American government seems not to like Gracie. They're turning up all sorts of things on their end. He's getting major interagency attention, so the old boy hears. I imagine ours will eventually decide he's been the victim of a practical joke, but then he'll have genuine problems back home. Huge ones, I hope. I'm more worried about your Big End in the long run, myself."

"Why?"

"Something's happening there. Too big to get a handle on. But the old man says that that's it exactly: Big End, somehow, is now too big to get a handle on. Which may be what they mean when they say something's too big to fail."

"He's found Meredith's last season of shoes. Tacoma. Bought them, given them to her. Via some weird new entity of his that targets and assists creatives."

"I'd watch the 'targets,' myself."

"And he's paid me. My accountant phoned this morning. I'm worried about that."

"Why?"

"Hubertus paid me exactly the amount I received for my share of licensing a Curfew song to a Chinese car company. That's a lot of money."

"Not a problem."

"Easy for you to say. I don't want to be in his debt."

"You aren't. If it hadn't been for you, he might not have gotten Chombo back, because I wouldn't have turned up. And if he had gotten him back, swapping Milgrim, he'd have eventually had to deal with Sleight and Gracie, down the road. I wasn't just putting the wind up him with that. He knows that. You're being rewarded for your crucial role in getting him wherever he's now gotten."

"On his way to Iceland, that would be."

"Let him go. How are you at kitchens?"

"Cooking? Minimal skills."

"Designing them. I have a flat in Berlin. East side, new building, old was entirely asbestos so they knocked it down. One very big room and a bathroom. No kitchen, just the stumps of pipes and ganglia sticking up from the floor, more or less in the middle. We'd need to fill that in, if we were going to live there."

"You want to live in Berlin?"

"Provisionally, yes. But only if you do."

She looked at him. "When I was leaving Cabinet," she said, "following you out to the Slow Foods van, Robert congratulated me. I didn't ask him what for, just said thanks. He'd been odd since you turned up. Do you know what that was about?"

"Ah. Yes. When I first struck up a conversation with him, when I was waiting for you, I told him that I was there to ask you to marry me."

She stared at him. "And you were lying."

"Not at all. Moment never presented itself. I assume he thinks we're engaged."

"Do you?"

"Your call, traditionally," he said, putting down the bungee.

86. DOILIES

Fiona was getting her hair cut.

Milgrim stayed in the cabin, finishing Hollis's book, then digging deeper into the archival subbasement of Cabinet's website, where he might learn, for instance, that the watercolors in the hallways leading to Hollis's room were early twentieth-century, by the expatriate American eccentric Doran Lumley. Cabinet owned thirty of these, and rotated them regularly.

He looked up at the decor of the cabin, remembering Hollis's room at Cabinet, how much he'd liked it. Designers from Hermès had based these cabins on ones in transatlantic prewar German airships, though nobody was making much of a point of that. Frosted aluminum, laminated bamboo, moss-green suede, and ostrich in one very peculiar shade of orange. The three windows were round, portholes really, and through them, if he looked, an empty sea, gone bronze with the setting sun.

The ekranoplan reminded Milgrim of the *Spruce Goose*, which he'd toured in Long Beach as a high school student, but with its wings largely amputated. Weird Soviet hybrids, the ekranoplans; they flew, at tremendous speeds, about fifteen feet above the water, incapable of greater altitude. They had been designed to haul a hundred tons of troops or cargo, very quickly, over the Black or Baltic Sea. This one, an A-90 Orlyonok, had, like all the others, been built in the Volga Shipyard, at Nizhni Novgorod. Milgrim already knew more about them than he cared to, as he was supposed to be translating a four-inch stack of technical and historical documents for Bigend. With Fiona here, he hadn't made much progress.

He'd tried working in the smallest of the four lounges, on the top deck, directly behind the flight deck (if that was the term, in something that arguably voyaged, rather than flew). There was scarcely anyone there, usually, and he could take the papers and his laptop. But the wifi was excellent onboard, and he'd found himself Googling things there, eating croissants, drinking coffee. That was where he'd discovered Cabinet's site.

"That's Cabinet, isn't it?" the Italian girl had asked, topping up his coffee. "Have you stayed there?"

"No," Milgrim had said, "but I've been there."

"I used to work there," she'd said, smiling, and walked back toward the galley, looking very smart in her Jun Marukawa tunic and skirt. Fiona said that Bigend, with the Hermès ekranoplan, had gone totally Bond villain, and that the crew uniforms were the icing on the cake. Still, Milgrim had thought, no denying the girl looked good in her Marukawa.

But when he'd finally settled down to translate what was really quite dreadful prose, Bigend had emerged from the flight deck, the Klein Blue suit freshly pressed.

He'd taken a seat opposite Milgrim, at the small round table, the suit contrasting painfully with the orange leather upholstery. He'd proceeded, with no preface whatever, as was his way, to tell Milgrim a great deal about the history of the rifle Gracie had left on Little Wormwood Scrubs. It had, Milgrim had already known, been found, just after dawn, by a dog walker, who'd promptly phoned the police. Stranger things, Milgrim now knew, had been found on the Scrubs, including unexploded munitions, and not that long ago.

He'd learned then that the police who'd responded to the dog walker had been ordinary police, so that the rifle's serial numbers had been, however briefly, in ordinary police computers. Shortly to evaporate, under the attention of spookier entities, but long enough for Bigend, however he might have done it, to acquire them. He now knew, somehow, that the rifle, Chinese-made, had been captured in

Afghanistan two years before, and dutifully logged. After that, a blank, until Gracie had turned up with it, folded, in a cardboard carton. It bothered Bigend, the rifle. It was his theory (or "narrative," Milgrim's therapist in Basel might have said) that Gracie had gotten the gun from some opposite number in the British military, after it had been secretly deleted from stores and smuggled back to England. But Bigend's concern now was just how opposite a number this theoretical person might have been. Might Gracie have had a British partner, someone with similar inclinations? Someone who hadn't been rolled up by whatever supercops Garreth had called down?

Milgrim hadn't thought so. "I think it was about the gun," he'd said.

"How do you mean, 'about the gun'?"

"Things happen around guns. This happened because a gun was there. You've told me that you can't understand why Gracie brought the gun. That it doesn't fit with your sense of who he is. That it was stupid. Over-the-top. Gratuitous. Bad business."

"Exactly."

"He did it because someone he knew here had the gun. The gun was captured by British troops. Someone smuggled it back here. That's not arms dealing. That's an illegal souvenir. But Gracie *saw* the gun. And then he *had* the gun. And then things happened, because the gun was there. But whoever he *got* the gun from wants *nothing* at all to do with any of this. Ever."

Bigend had stared at him. "Remarkable," he'd said, finally, "how you do that."

"It's thinking like a criminal," Milgrim said.

"Once again, I'm in your debt."

In Winnie's, Milgrim thought then, though Bigend didn't know it. When he'd tweeted her, after learning more from Hollis, he'd asked, "How did you do that?" Her tweet in reply, the last he'd gotten from her, though he still checked for them, periodically, had simply said, "Doilies."

"It's the order flow, isn't it?" Milgrim had had no intent to ask this at all. Hadn't been thinking of it. Yet it had emerged. His therapist had told him that ideas, in human relations, had lives of their own. Were in a sense autonomous.

"Of course."

"That's what Chombo was doing. Finding the order flow."

"He found it a week before they kidnapped him, but his work, to that point, would have been useless. Without him, I mean."

"And the market, the whole thing, it's no longer real? Because you know the future?"

"It's a very *tiny* slice of the future. The merest paring. Minutes."

"How many?"

Bigend had glanced around the empty lounge. "Seventeen, presently."

"Is that enough?"

"Seven would have been entirely adequate. Seven *seconds*, in most cases."

>>>

Fiona's dress was a seamless tube, lustrous black jersey. She was wearing it with the top rolled down, forming a sort of band across her breasts, her shoulders bare. A gift from her mother, she said, who'd gotten it from an associate editor at French *Vogue*. Milgrim knew almost nothing about her mother, other than that she'd once been involved with Bigend, but he'd always found the idea of girlfriends having parents intimidating.

He wore his freshly dry-cleaned tweed jacket and whipcord trousers, but with a Hackett shirt, no extraneous cuff-buttons.

Cocktails were being served in the ballroom, so-called, which ordinarily was the main dining room. The walls were decorated with quasi-Constructivist murals of ekranoplans, looking, as Milgrim thought they somewhat actually did, like the Pan American Airways Flying Clippers of the 1940s, but with truncated wings and that strange canard that supported the jet engines. As he and Fiona descended the spiral stairway, he saw Aldous and the other driver towering elegantly above the assembled passengers, many of whom Milgrim hadn't seen before, as he and Fiona had been spending most of their time in the cabin. There was Rausch, too, his black suit rumpled, his matte hair reminding Milgrim of the stuff Chandra had used on Ajay, though with a different style of application.

As they reached the deck, Aldous arrived at the bottom of the stairs. "Hello," said Milgrim, not having seen Aldous since that night in the City. "Thanks for getting us out of that. Hope it wasn't too hard on you, after."

"Bigend's silk," said Aldous, with an elegant shrug, which Milgrim knew meant lawyer. "And the courier," he said to Fiona, winking.

"Hullo, Aldous." She smiled, then turned away to greet someone Milgrim didn't know.

"I've been wondering," said Milgrim, lowering his voice, glancing across the ballroom at the polished head of the other driver, "about the testing. It's been a while."

"What testing?"

"Urinalysis," said Milgrim.

"I think they discontinue that. Gone from the call sheets. But everything's changing, now."

"At Blue Ant?"

Aldous nodded. "New broom," he said, gravely, then nodded to his own earpiece, and slipped silently away.

"We found your mouthwash," said Rausch. "In New York. Sending it to your cabin." He looked unhappy with Milgrim, but then he always did.

"Aldous says that things are changing at Blue Ant. 'New broom,' he said."

Rausch's shoulders rose. "Everyone who matters," he said, "who's made the cut, is on this plane."

"It's not a plane," said Milgrim.

"Whatever it is," said Rausch, irritably.

"Do you know when we reach Iceland?"

"Tomorrow morning. A lot of this has just been cruising, breaking the thing in."

"I'm almost out of medication."

"That's all been placebos for the past three months. I suppose the vitamins and supplements were real." Rausch watched him carefully, savoring his reaction.

"Why tell me now?"

"Bigend told everyone to afford you full human status. And I quote. Excuse me." He scooted away into the crowd.

Milgrim slid his hand inside his jacket, to touch the almost-empty bubble-pack. No more tiny purple notations of date and time. "But I *like* a placebo," he said to himself, and then there was a burst of applause.

The Dottirs and their unpleasant-looking father were descending the spiral, down the thick steps of frosted glass. Milgrim knew, via Fiona, that their album had just gone something. Ermine-haired and glittering, they stepped down, on either side of their glum Dottirs-father. Who Fiona said now owned, in partnership with Bigend, though in some arcane and largely undetectable way, a great deal of Iceland. Most of it, really. It had been Bigend, she said, who'd sold those young Icelandic fiscal cowboys on the idea of internet banking in the first place. "He put them up to it," she'd said, in the cabin, in Milgrim's arms. "He knew exactly what would happen. Out of their heads on E, most of them, which helped."

A toast was being poured. He hurried to find Fiona and his glass of Perrier.

As he took her hand, Pamela Mainwaring walked quickly past, headed in Bigend's direction.

"Hi, Mum," said Fiona.

Pamela smiled, nodded, made the briefest possible eye contact with Milgrim, and continued on.

87. THE OTHER SIDE

Clockwise, this dream: eighteenth-century marble, winding, worn stone unevenly waxy, tones of smoker's phlegm caught in its depths, profiles of each step set with careful segments of something lifeless as plaster, patching old accidents. Like the scribed, transected, stapled sections of a beloved limb, returned from voyaging: surgery, disaster, a climb up stairs taller still than these. Westernmost, the spiral. Above the lobby, the stripes of Robert's shirt, the Turk's head atop the stapler, above the subtly rude equine monkey-business in the desk's carved thicket, she climbs.

To this floor unvisited, unknown, carpet flowered, faded, antediluvian, beneath incandescent bulbs, an archaic controlled combusion of filaments. Walls hung with madly varied landscapes, unpeopled, each haunted, however dimly, by the spectral finger of the Burj Khalifa.

And at the far end of a vast, perhaps endless room, in a pool of warm light, a figure, seated, in a suit of Klein Blue. As it turns, pale fur, muzzle rouged, the wooden painted teeth—

She wakes beside Garreth's slow breathing, in their darkened room, the sheets against her skin.

THANKS:

My wife, Deborah, and daughter, Claire, were on-site first readers and sensitive critics, as ever.

Susan Allison, to whom this book is dedicated, and who has been my editor in one sense or another since the start of my career, of course was excellent with this one.

As indeed was Martha Millard, my literary agent since I first required one.

Jack Womack and Paul McAuley read pages almost daily, with Paul keeping very particular track of London. Louis Lapprend was enlisted as Milgrim arrived in Paris, to similar ends.

Cory Doctorow provided Sleight with Milgrim's problematic Neo.

Johan Kugelberg very kindly put me up in the club on which Cabinet is loosely based, and which is very nearly as peculiar.

Sean Crawford kept Winnie honest.

Larry Lunn gave me the order flow, when asked for a macguffin of ultimate scale. I don't know anyone else who could have.

Clive Wilson very kindly offered boots-on-the-ground Melbourne geography and vegan bacon.

Douglas Coupland introduced me to the concept of the Vegas cube by showing me, years ago, the one he'd built to write in.

Bruce Sterling, having been emailed exactly the wrong question about CCTV, graciously extruded the concept of the ugly T-shirt in one of his characteristic, demonically focused bursts of seemingly effortless imagination.

Michaela Sachenbacher and Errolson Hugh introduced me to the architecture of a "secret" brand, and the passion behind it.

Everything I know about being a fashion model in the 21st Century I learned from Jenna Sauers' wonderful *Jezebel* memoir, "I Am The Anonymous Model." Meredith's modeling career is based on it. Available with a quick Google.

Likewise available is Mark Gardiner's very informative "Artful Dodgers," from the February 2009 issue of *Motorcyclist*, where I learned everything I know about London motorcycle couriers.

Meredith's line of shoes was modeled after the brand Callous, launched by Thomas Fenning and Tomoaki Kobayashi in 2003, and which I gather met a somewhat similar fate.

Thank you all.

—Vancouver, June 2010

PATTERN RECOGNITION∙ SPOOK COUNTRY∙ ZERO HISTORY

ABOUT WILLIAM GIBSON

William Gibson lives in Vancouver, British Columbia, with his wife. He is the author of *Neuromancer*, *Count Zero*, *Mona Lisa Overdrive*, *Burning Chrome*, *Virtual Light*, *Idoru*, *All Tomorrow's Parties*, *Pattern Recognition*, *Spook Country*, and *Zero History*. Visit the author's website at www.williamgibsonbooks.com.

DISCUSSION QUESTIONS

1. "Secrets are the very root of cool." The major players in this series exist solely to expose or protect undisclosed information. Compare Hobbs Baranov's "old-boy networks," Hubertus Bigend's "viral agency," and the old man's covert operatives. How do these groups measure up to Cayce Pollard's Gabriel Hounds company, Stella Volkov's Film Footage family, and Dorotea Benedetti's international associates? Which of these characters have access to the most heavily guarded intel? While Bigend "wishes [his agency] could operate as a black hole, an absence," are any of these groups actually untouchable? Why or why not?

2. Milgrim has an addiction to antianxiety drugs. Cayce Pollard has an unusual aversion to logos. Bobby Chombo cannot sleep in the same space twice. Where do think these allergies, addictions, and obsessive behaviors come from? What do these conditions say about each individual? What other unusual personality disorders appear throughout these stories? How do these traits define these characters?

3. "They broke laws, but they weren't crooks." Examine how certain characters are driven by a sense of patriotism. Does this devotion to

their own country blind them from making decisions on a multinational level? Explain. Give examples of when patriotism usurps a character's perception of morality.

4. Gibson's characters derive power from knowledge, technology, and money. Which character stands to lose the most power if one of these elements is taken away? How would such an event change that individual's drive for success?

5. Several characters are introduced or exposed gradually as double agents. Analyze these two-faced individuals and identify the motivation for their actions. Do they all shift from ally to adversary in each story? If so, do any of them ever see the error of their ways and redeem themselves?

6. How are government agencies portrayed in these stories? Which characters are directly influenced by the private sector? How have these agencies changed through the eyes of these characters in a post–Cold War and post-9/11 world?

7. Whether it's the loss of a loved one, a sister's devotion, or a mother and daughter's bond, family plays an important role in all three of these stories. Evaluate the positive and negative influences familial relationships have on Cayce, Stella, Fiona, and others.

8. A general feeling of mistrust is interwoven into almost every character's life. In what ways do Cayce, Hollis, and others exhibit this sentiment? Are they justified in their thinking? Why? Which character(s) allows their suspicions to sway their actions? Which character(s) prevents paranoia from influencing their decisions?

9. How do mobile phone technology, social media, and wifi impact the level of security in the lives of Gibson's characters? Which character would be the easiest to monitor regardless of location? Which character is immune to all three forms of "tracking"?

10. We're introduced to several villains or opposing forces throughout this series. Which character or group of characters do you feel is the most ruthless in accomplishing their goal and why?

For the full readers guide, go to www.penguin.com/guides.